Rivers of Belief

Rivers of Belief

RICHARD CRAIG ANDERSON

Dedication

THIS ONE IS FOR NATHANAEL

Acknowledgment

FIRST and foremost I want to thank L.B. Hart of National City fame for the generosity of his spirit, the inspiration he provided and the contributions he makes toward a better society. In a world of class acts, he sets the standard.

Next I want to express my heartfelt gratitude to Jean Jenkins of San Diego's famed Writer's Haven Writers. J.J., you're a wonderful woman and you mentored me through this book with great skill and care.

The venerable editor C.J. "Jerry" Hannah helped shape the overall story, while the great Toni Michael proofread the final manuscript with her usual brilliance.

I want to thank all who read early drafts and offered their opinions, comments and not a few suggestions to have a beer and lighten up. Mike Furnari, Jon Heist, Cliff Hawrey and Gregg Rinta—thank you for your unsparing critiques.

Finally I want to thank the members of Writer's Haven Writers for their support and friendship since 1987, and of course Michael DuFour—my brother since 1989. I am so lucky to have known everyone here.

Prologue

THAT first night he killed the engine and slid low in his seat. When the light blue Trans Am approached, he grabbed the binoculars and watched intently as she parked along the dark street. The girl emerged slowly, placed the strap of a Prada handbag over her shoulder, and walked confidently toward the door of the Ocean City vacation home. She was unutterably beautiful: tall and slender, with tanned legs that glistened below fashionably skimpy black shorts, and when she tossed her head with a practiced motion, the ends of her waist-length black hair whisked regally across her lower back.

A smile threatened his somber features as he whispered, "Oh yeah—top drawer goods for the top of my list." After ten minutes he slipped quietly from the car, and by keeping to the shadows he got past a cluster of olive-green trashcans that shielded a pathway to the rear yard. He found his way easily, aided by dim light that shone through flimsy curtains drawn across the patio doors. Then he paused. When he felt satisfied that she was alone he went unhurriedly to the door and tested it. The door slid silently; it wasn't even locked.

He stepped inside, listened carefully, and determined her location by homing-in on her joyous singing. He said softly, "Fucking aye. Right down that hallway." He found her in the master bedroom sorting through a closet. But when she stiffened unexpectedly, he sprang forward and got his arm around her neck. Her hands flew up to meet his arm but it was already too late. He tightened his elbow and disrupted the oxygen flow. Only two seconds passed before she slumped unconscious to the floor.

He tied the girl's hands with a purple bungee cord, turned her onto her back, and roughly tore her shorts and panties away. Then he took her without mercy, and when he was done only a few seconds later he slapped the girl hard across her face with the back of his hand. Blood blossomed across her delicate face as the small veins in her nose burst open. He looked around, smiled, and disappeared into the dark shadows.

She woke up half an hour later. Her violation was so complete that she couldn't bring herself to report the crime. Nobody else would know until later, *after* the increasing number of attacks shook the region from its slumber. But I knew. I knew everything after it was all over; got it straight from the suspect in fact—and it surprised the hell out of me when I found out who it was.

CHAPTER 1

I turned my cruiser onto Seaweed Lane in Ocean City's north end and drew to a stop beneath the sheltering shade of a mature elm tree—anything to escape the murderous late-afternoon sun. Then I reached into my shirt pocket and retrieved the small note and read it again: *Michael, did you know that no matter where you are in London, you're never more than thirty feet from a rat?* Levi Hart's bold cursive handwriting dominated the crisp white paper that I'd found taped to my briefcase earlier, another in his series of enigmatic offerings, gleaned from who-knew-where. I put it away, knowing he'd elaborate upon it later. I smiled for a split sec, then wondered what I'd do at end-of-shift when three sharp tones broke the silence. I turned up the volume on the portable police radio as a report of an auto accident went out over the air.

"Communications to seventy-three-oh-nine, for a 10-51 P.I., Coastal Highway and 120th Street. Rescue units have been dispatched."

I grabbed the mike attached to my left shoulder and said, "Seventy-three-oh-nine's en route." Then I hit the overhead lights, toggled the siren and stomped down on the accelerator.

The scene was less than a mile away and I screeched to a halt about a minute later. A dark blue '66 Buick—a real dinosaur—had rear-ended a tractor-trailer. The Buick was smashed like an accordion and white steam from its ruptured radiator hissed into the crisp blue sky. A wall of heat and humidity hit like a tsunami as I leapt from my cruiser. The stench of spilled anti-freeze and burned rubber was everywhere. I pulled a small trauma kit from my trunk and hustled toward the beach-goers gathered around the Buick. My shoes slapped hard against the pavement, creating an eerie contrast to the diminishing moan of the radiator.

"Police," I announced. "Move aside." The crowd parted, revealing a young woman pinned behind the steering wheel. The impact had driven the hood through the windshield, and the leading edge had nearly cleaved her head from her body. Her eyes bulged from their sockets, and bright red blood oozed from severed arteries. I checked her vitals and shook my head; probably died instantly.

Then I heard the crying.

I sprinted to the other side and found a young kid trapped in the rear seat. He couldn't have been more than five. The Buick was folded securely around him, but a big chunk of the drive shaft had torn through the floorboards and jammed itself against his gut. He was twisted around so that he faced the rear. Painful as it must have been, it spared him from the bloody scene in the driver's compartment.

I keyed my mike and told the dispatcher, "I've got an *F* and a serious *P.I.* Start the helicopter." Jesus H—a fatality and a serious personal injury. A burst of siren followed by the screech of brakes announced the arrival of another cruiser. "Take care of traffic," I shouted to the assisting officer, and then I got busy with the boy.

He wasn't bleeding and there were no marks on him, but he was done for. Like a railroad worker pinned between two train couplings, everything's okay while the body remains pinched together. The victim talks and they may even say they feel fine. Then the couplings are pulled apart and they do a nosedive over that bottomless cliff.

What's taking the paramedics so long?

The boy wailed as I moved into his field of vision, but there seemed no way to get next to him. I thought I was tall enough and lanky enough to squeeze in and help him, but I found that it was all I could do just to brush his outstretched fingers with mine. I pushed further anyway, and grimaced as a shard of glass ripped into my knee. We finally interlocked our fingers, and as tears flowed down his cheeks he called out, "Mommy, mommy! Where's my mommy?"

I knew abandonment, and sweat streamed down my face as I looked into his eyes and said softly, "Your mommy hasn't left you. She's in the front seat but she can't talk right now. So you know what? I'm gonna stay here with you."

He stopped his terrified wailing, hitched and snuffled a couple of times, and then he grew quiet and watched me with a sense of awareness beyond his years. As his eyes held mine in an unwavering gaze he asked in a tiny voice, "Am I going to die?"

I didn't want to tell him what I suspected, but was damned if I'd lie—that would have been more obscene than the carnage that had torn his world apart. So I looked at him and said evenly, "I'm right here, you're not alone, and I'm not going to leave you."

The sun was jackhammering the car, turning it into an oven. My clothes clung to me and I had to struggle to breathe normally. But of course that was nothing compared to his pain. "What's your name?" I finally thought to ask.

"Matthew," he replied in a strained voice.

I said simply, "Hi, Matthew. My name is Michael. I'm going to take care of you. Is that okay with you?"

Sirens and air horns filled the air as I tried to comfort him. "Hold on, Matthew," I said. "For God's sake, hold on." Quietly, for his ears alone, I even sang parts of Simon and Garfunkel's *Bridge Over Troubled Water.*

He watched me in silence the entire time, his face both composed and solemn. All at once he said in a weak voice, "I'm … afraid."

I squeezed his hand and whispered, "Of course you are. Even big boys would be scared, but you know what? You're a brave boy—braver than most grown men. Did you know that?"

"No," he said. "Really?" Then his voice trailed into nothingness as a Diesel roar and the chuff of air brakes announced the fire department's arrival. A minute later the *whump whump whump* of the state police medevac helicopter drowned everything as it circled overhead.

The helicopter seemed to agitate him and he abruptly cried out, "Where's my mommy?" Then his voice got noticeably weaker. A minute later his eyes rolled wildly and he blurted, "I'll be a good boy! Yes I will! Mommy will come back if I'm good. She *will*." Then his voice faded as he proclaimed a final time, "Yes she will."

"I'm sure of it," I whispered.

Although it seemed an eternity, no more than three or four minutes passed before his eyelids began to flutter. Finally they closed. His head fell to one side and his body went limp. But I couldn't let go. I couldn't. I held his hand even as the firefighters worked around me to free him. I held his hand and felt the warmth as it deserted him, first from his fingers, then from his palm, and finally from his arm. I held his hand until the firefighters got him out and took him away.

His mommy never came back.

Mine never did, either. Not after my old man nearly beat her to death that night.

───────────────

Levi Hart shuffled drowsily toward the kitchen table the next morning, naked but for his green plaid boxers. He was five foot eight, slender and angular, with heavy auburn hair brushed straight back. He had a lean face, a shy grin, and knowing eyes.

Women loved him.

He plopped down into the chair opposite me and asked, "Michael, did you know that no matter where you are in London, you're never more than thirty feet from a rat?" He leaned back, lazily hooked a thumb in the waistband of his boxers and added, "Got that from a Mike Leigh film the other night. *'Naked'*. Dark, dark flick, ya know? Not what I was expecting. Still in the VCR if you wanna watch it."

I put down my fork, pushed my breakfast plate away and adjusted my terry-cloth bathrobe. "Sounds like one of those angst-ridden flicks, bro. Yeah, definitely not you."

He shrugged as he lifted his legs and settled his feet on the chair next to mine. "It was edgy, alright." His large blue eyes narrowed as he studied my plate, then deep lines erupted across his forehead. "Oysters? *Raw* oysters? Isn't it a bit early in the day?"

I snickered. "Around here they're pronounced *arsters*." Then I said kiddingly, "When're you gonna get it through that cosmopolitan head of yours that this is a provincial town?"

Levi wagged his eyebrows and said, "So I'm from Seattle. Sue me."

The air conditioner kicked in and stirred the air. I wrinkled my nose; Levi smelled earthier than usual. "Jennifer didn't stay last night?"

"Big case this morning; depositions to file. Wanted to be rested." He yawned, then flicked his eyes toward my exposed knee. "Say, what's with the bandage?"

"Ripped it last night. The fatal."

He nodded and said quietly, "Yeah, heard about the kid." He looked somberly at me and said, "Guess you'll talk about it when ..."

"When I'm ready, *mi amigo.*"

Levi offered a half-smile as he got up and squeezed my shoulder. "When you're ready." He stifled a yawn. "Almost forgot. This girl I know wants to meet you and I promised to give her number to my 'blond friend with the big, brown beautiful eyes and pretty skin.' Her words pal, not mine." He rapped his knuckles against my upper arm. "I'll give it to you later." He yawned again. "Think I'll go stand in the shower."

I said robustly, "Good idea."

As he ambled down the hallway he looked over his shoulder, smiled and flipped me the bird. Then his smile vanished as he walked on while asking, "Seen Natasha?"

I said to his retreating back, "Didn't come home last night."

No, she hadn't. She'd been staying out more often lately and it wasn't like her, just as fixating on rats wasn't like Levi; he'd been places, done stuff, and he could make his laughter understood throughout the world. But while I believed Levi's shared revelation about rats, I focused instead on life's virtues. It was a quest for virtues that compelled me to pin on a badge when I turned twenty-three. Where had those four years gone?

Levi was a year younger and he also wore a badge, and 1994 marked two anniversaries—our fourth year working the streets of Ocean City, Maryland, and the third year with our free-spirited housemate, Natasha Panova. She was a seldom seen waitress who sought only the freedom to explore, while Levi demanded a life to be lived on his own terms. As for me, I wanted only two things—to be accepted for myself rather than for certain physical traits—and to go after the bad guys, especially those who victimized others. Beyond that I'm no hero, doing my best to be playful while not taking myself too seriously. But I took my job seriously. So did Levi, and he and Natasha and I worked to sort the positives from the sordid, whether it was making sense of the death of a child, standing by your best friend no matter what—or pursuing a serial rapist.

Roll call would begin at three o'clock so I put on a T and baggy shorts, slipped my feet into a pair of flip-flops, and gathered my uniform and brief-case. We lived in a country club community known locally as 'The Pines,' and we shared our rented house with George, a Chesapeake Bay retriever gone white around the muzzle. It was far from being a traditional household, but it was ours and we thought of ourselves as a family. Just thinking of them—even of George—pushed a bit of yesterday's hell further away.

I walked out of the house at two. It was a light blue clapboard rancher with white trim, furnished collectively with an assortment of whatever we could bring to the table. So what if the Early American sofa didn't match the SCAN dining room set? Three beds, two baths, an eat-in kitchen and a living room met our requirements. The kitchen door opened onto a screened-in redwood deck, ringed by tall shrubs for privacy and equipped with salvaged patio furniture and a grill. The deck led to a gravel driveway large enough to accommodate three cars.

I climbed into my candy-apple red, '67 Mustang Fastback and turned the key. The eight cylinders of the 289 cubic inch engine coughed to life, and a cloud of blue exhaust belched from the dual pipes flanking the vanity license plate: *MB*—my initials. I stepped on the clutch, shifted to first, and nudged the accelerator. The humidity hit and my T instantly clung to me. I turned on the air, drove over the short, gated bridge that marked The Pines, and turned east on Maryland Route 90. The Mustang's pipes roared as the speedometer touched sixty-five. I turned on a local country western station and settled back as Chris Isaak crooned about a *Wicked Game*.

A few minutes later I crossed the long, low-slung St. Martin's River Bridge and approached the estuary at the Isle of Wight. I let off the gas, pulled over, and coasted to a stop. I prized this place. It remained for me a sanctuary where I could unwind, wax poetic, and take refuge from certain realities that tormented my soul. I'd studied books on tidelands, and I spent a lot of time watching what went on in this tiny universe.

The small promontory of land sits midway between the free-flowing St. Martin's River and the more sluggish Assawoman Bay. Ocean City lay just beyond. The estuary's water is the color of mud, its salt-streaked basin home to countless crabs and bottom feeders. The bay meets the land head-on here, buffered only by a flimsy barrier of gray-green salt grass. The grasses filter the muddy water through innumerable turnstiles until they blend with the salt marsh. Here the black, primordial ooze swallows tiny worms, mollusks and fishes into the recesses of its trackless expanse, shielding them from time-honored predators. Terns wade with patient expectation through the mire, poachers of all they find, while other unseen animals prowl and gorge themselves on the fruits of this paludal ecosystem.

Tiny anemones and hulking horseshoe crabs lurk beneath the surface of the brackish water, amid dead leaves and rotting roots and the waste products of countless creatures. The whole separates into the parts, and here was the part that caught my attention the most: the odor, an aroma as sweet as any nectar ripened by golden sunlight, and so exclusive you must know precisely where to seek it out. Someone must guide you, because on your own you are helpless in sorting the pungent scents from their cousins. It was a place to go, a place to cope with all the stuff that goes on when your world turns crazy. It could be a safe place, like a closet.

When you come from a hard life—when you're trash, and you know it—the struggle kicks in: fight or flight. Sometimes it *is* possible to climb and learn and acquire a new life, one with new tastes—*cultured* tastes. With effort, a kid forced to hide in closets can get past all that. He can learn proper grammar from a dedicated teacher and practice with a loyal friend. Sometimes I tried too hard; sometimes I came on too strong as I tried to pry my way into a better world. But I tried, and whenever my world turned crazy—whenever I needed a vantage point from which to note the sludge at my feet, to filter it and compare it to the clear skies above—when I needed such a place, I found solace in this estuary. A person could dream in a place like this, dream of a better life—a life after poverty and abuse. I lingered a few more minutes and then I left the Isle of Wight. I drove on, mentally switched off this lyrical leaning on life, and crossed the Assawoman's long and narrow bridge into Ocean City.

Ocean City, Maryland was a quirky place, a resort town slathered atop a narrow barrier island along the Atlantic. I liked this town, especially the tourists who flocked to the shore each summer. Here it was June already, and I just kept on finding virtues instead of rats. I rolled down the window to let the salt-tinged air sweep through the car as I weaved my way through the early afternoon traffic. I drove past the honky-tonk bars that defined the older section of town, and sighed contentedly when I glanced westward: the Assawoman Bay was still there.

Summers reign supreme in Ocean City. Summers bring heat and heat beckons tourists and tourists convey cash. The locals sense replenishment and open their shells like so many bi-valves to accommodate them. They accept all tourists with one exception: the June Bugs, those high school grads with too little money and too much attitude. The Bugs have descended upon Ocean City for decades, and over time an adversarial relationship developed between them and the police. In a town with few homicides or rapes, they were what united us; they were our necessary enemy. Yeah, sure—and there we were, safeguarding freedom and democracy. Likely as not, confrontations turned into scenes of men yelling, dogs barking and mothers pulling their children from the streets.

I didn't look for enemies, although they exist despite best intentions. I'd grown up in rural California, where enemies were isolated by distance. But so were friends. It was different here. People knew one another. Funeral processions seemed frequent, and they often stretched for a mile or more. I hadn't noticed how rare funeral processions were in California until I moved here. In the final analysis, Ocean City gave me a place to anchor myself. I could go without shoes during the summer, kick back on a beach with a book, and read and learn and grow. Best of all, I knew that I had at least two friends in my life whom I could always count on. Well, there was George, too.

I pulled into the police parking lot and went to the locker room. Levi entered five minutes later, indifferently attired and barefooted. I said, "Some day you'll cut yourself to ribbons going 'round like that."

He shrugged. "It's happened often enough."

"At least wear flip-flops."

"You know how I am." Then he looked at me and grinned.

I knew. Levi was a true bare footer. "I've always gone barefoot," he once told me. "When I was a kid I'd run 'round all day. My ma washed my feet for me before I went to bed. It felt good. Made me sleep better."

Levi's mom might have helped him as a kid, but as an adult, Nature Boy sometimes neglected his hygiene. He could get ripe when off-duty, yet scrupulous with a bar of soap when required. His approach toward clothes was equally carefree; Levi typically grabbed whatever was at hand, and damned if he didn't carry it off. Once during college we embarked on a spring-break trip. He jumped in the car clad only in faded blue sweat pants and said, "Let's go." We drove straight through the night. When a Denny's hostess turned him away for being shirtless and shoeless, he shrugged and returned to the car and upended his travel bag. It contained one pair of jeans, two pairs of shorts, a toilet kit and some tunes. No shoes, no shirts, not even any underwear. He got no service at *that* Denny's—not until he rifled through *my* bag.

Truth is I envied him his spontaneity, even while acknowledging that it eluded me completely. And yet I always offered this brief coda: "Good for you, my friend." I guessed my deficiency stemmed from childhood; never knowing what might happen from day to day I had the art of S.A. *nailed.* But while Situational Awareness might've sensitized my fight-or-flight instincts—S.A. will serve me well if I ever find myself face to face with a rhino on the African veldt—it was anathema to naturalness.

"You're a piece of work," I concluded, and then I got back to the process of getting dressed for work. Levi simply arched an eyebrow as he took his highly polished shoes from his locker. Our uniforms consisted of white shirts, French blue trousers adorned with broad black stripes along the outer seams, and Stetson headgear that everyone carried but seldom wore. After we hitched our gun belts we reported to roll call for the three-to-eleven shift, where Sergeant Burke informed us of an assault on a young woman the night before. I hit the streets by four, headed toward 145th Street near the northernmost town limits, and began a lookout for anything suspicious in my patrol sector. As I drove past countless Bugs wandering aimlessly along the city streets I thought, 'Yeah, 1994. This could be the summer that matters.'

I handled a few calls and then took my dinner break. Around nine I parked beneath a streetlight near the deserted Calvin B. Taylor Bank and settled back against the seat. I had reports to write.

*   *   *

He ducked behind the neglected poinsettia that concealed the unlit rear yard from passersby. Even if he was seen he wasn't concerned; he had his cover story and he *knew* he blended in. After a quick look around he slid open the patio door and stepped inside. The nineteen year-old-girl was unusually pretty, clad only in black panties and a white sleeveless T. She had her head in the fridge and her back to the door as he crept silently toward her. He covered the remaining few feet softly and methodically, and then he triumphantly slid his arm around her neck. He slapped his other hand across her mouth and tightened his bicep against her carotid before she could react; a tweak of his bicep and she went limp. He eased her to the floor and bound her wrists behind her back with a purple bungee cord. Panting heavily, he tore away her panties and viciously spread her legs apart. "Cunt!" he said to the unconscious girl. "Fuck you, *cunt!*" Then he raped her. He finished quickly, left her sprawled on the floor with her blond hair dank and disheveled, and crept out the way he entered. The fashion model remembered little, but as the lawyers say, it's all there in the details.

*   *   *

I'd just signed my name to a report and I had the pen poised above another when three sharp tones stopped me. This time it was a fight call.

"Communications to seventy-two-oh-four, respond to a ten-ten, Rudy's Tavern, Coastal and 78th. All units Code Three."

Levi acknowledged with a clear edge of excitement. *"Seventy-two-oh-four's en route."*

Fistfights at Ragnar Rudy's Uptown Tavern could be nasty business. Levi would need help, and because we worked solo, he needed it now. Three patrol units and Sergeant Billy Burke answered the call.

I called out, too. "Seventy-three-oh-nine's en route." I slammed the transmission into drive, hit the lights and siren, and went south at about Mach 1.

"Seventy-two-oh-four is 10-23," Levi announced as he got on-scene.

I keyed my mike. "Seventy-three-oh-nine … ETA thirty."

I stood on the brakes half a minute later and the cruiser shuddered as I jammed the front tires against a curb. Mercury-vapor streetlights cast an unearthly glow over a large crowd gathered in the street, while the red and blue lights of my cruiser danced crazily against their faces.

Levi stood poised between two belligerent factions of June Bugs. An alarming number of them loomed over his short frame. Levi stared ahead through narrowed lids, his mouth set firmly. I pulled my baton from the front seat and dashed forward.

Levi said matter-of-factly to a beefy six-footer in front of him, "You've got two choices. Walk away now, or I'll arrest you for disturbing the peace,"

The Bug wore a ripped tank top and frayed jeans. Two of his buddies swayed drunkenly in support. "Fuck off, or you're next," the Bug shouted.

Levi bounced slightly on the balls of his feet. "Feeling froggy, huh? Better start hopping, then."

A siren shattered the air behind me as another officer forced his cruiser through the traffic. I was almost at Levi's side when the Bug made a fist. Levi said firmly, "That's it. You're under arrest. Turn around and put your hands behind your back. Do it now."

Instead of obeying, the Bug stabbed his right forefinger toward Levi's chest. Bad move. Levi's right hand shot forward in a flash. He grabbed the Bug's hand and bent it backward in a wristlock. Levi neatly spun him around as the Bug yelled, "Mother *fuck*."

Another Bug lunged forward. I jabbed my baton toward his midsection, angled it upward at the last second, and trapped his raised arm.

Two more Bugs leapt toward Levi.

One held a beer bottle.

That's when Levi went wildcat.

He pushed his pinioned Bug to the ground and faced the bottle-bearing Bug. A bottle justified lethal force; a broken bottle could guarantee it. Levi showed no fear. The guy rushed. Levi dodged. The Bug groped empty space; Levi's left arm uncoiled. He struck the Bug's neck; hit it with the knife-edge of his hand. Perfect brachial stun. The Bug's legs folded; he collapsed in a heap.

Levi spun around, hands clenched, prepared for further attack.

Now I had a problem. I knew Levi could be hard and quick and dangerous, but I had a prisoner. Do I hold him, or help Levi? My dilemma was solved as a blur of blue and white rushed past me. Jarl Jackson, a.k.a. *seventy-two twenty*, arrived as another Bug went for Levi's throat.

Levi pounced forward with teeth bared. "Haaah!" he roared, and then he went to work on this latest Bug's torso. The guy outweighed him by at least seventy pounds, but Levi worked him like a side of meat. Levi's arms moved furiously as his fists crashed into him. "Back away!" Levi shouted. But the Bug wouldn't quit, so Levi pounded him again. Chest. Ribs. Gut. His fists landed everywhere. "Get back," Levi shouted at him. "Get back! *Now!*"

I felt a mixture of fear and excitement. If more Bugs jumped in we'd be hard pressed to knock them back, yet I couldn't help but admire Levi as he battled away. The crowd surged forward, but I couldn't tell whether it was to join the fray or to get a better view, so I tightened my grip on my prisoner and pushed him toward Levi and Jarl. Tires screeched behind me. "*Seventy-fifteen to communications*," Sergeant Burke yelled over the radio, "*On-scene and signal thirteen! Signal thirteen!*"

Officer needs help.

Levi whirled left and right and the crowd drew back. Jarl drew his baton and raised it. Several Bugs scurried away. Then Levi grabbed his adversary in an arm-lock and took him to the pavement. His left hand flashed to his gun belt in a blur. It came up bearing a set of cuffs. He slapped them on the Bug's wrists with a satisfying ratchet of metal-on-metal. Then Levi leaped to his feet and stared down the crowd. Sergeant Burke pushed people away. "Clear the street!" he roared. "Clear this fuckin' street!"

I'm six inches taller than Levi, my prisoner shorter than his, and I had gotten so amped-up that just the slightest torque of my baton beneath the kid's wrist hiked him to his toes. I cuffed him with my free hand and quick-marched him toward my cruiser. "You okay, Hoss?" I yelled to Levi.

"I'm alright, bro." His heavy umber hair was ruffled, and his chest heaved as he labored for breath, but he was untouched.

A hail of sirens sliced the air as other units rushed to our aid. Signal thirteen's were big stuff. An officer needed help; our brothers and sisters were in trouble.

Burke keyed his mike. "Seventy-fifteen to Communications. Slow 'em down. We got it under control." Three alert tones broke the squelch as the dispatcher told responding units to stand down.

Levi's face was sweat-streaked as he marched his prisoner toward his cruiser. The mixed crowd of locals and tourists parted respectfully. He put his prisoner in the rear seat and slammed the door shut as a girl yelled, "Hi, Levi." He turned and scanned the crowd. So did I. She was beautiful. Her legs were brown and slim, her skirt short. She waved and he acknowledged her with a bright smile, but he had no time to chat. Levi moved forward gracefully, his strength flowing from well-muscled shoulders, down his torso and to his waist in a classic swimmer's build. He wore his uniform well and he was effortlessly rakish.

"Where's my Bug with the bottle?" he asked.

"I got him," Jarl said. Jarl Jackson was tall and solid without an ounce of excess fat. He had swarthy skin and jet-black hair, and he held a loose-limbed Bug in his clutches. "Been keepin' him nice and fresh for ya."

Levi nodded curtly and said, "Thanks." Then he looked at the Bug and declared, "You, my friend, are under arrest for assault with a deadly weapon." He took the prisoner from Jarl and pointed to the six-footer who had jabbed a finger at his chest earlier. "This one goes too." The Bug didn't protest when Jarl grabbed him roughly.

"I'll get your cuffs back to ya," Levi promised. He was leading the dazed Bug toward his cruiser when the prisoner transport wagon pulled to a stop in front of Rudy's. Levi swung the other way and guided his detainee to the wagon.

I met him at the back of the wagon. We called it 'Battlestar Gallactica' for its dazzling array of emergency lights. It spent each night shunting arrestees from various venues to the lock-up. This fight call had certainly shaken me from my earlier funk. I swiped a hand across my forehead and shifted my weight. "Hey, Donkey Breath. How're you doing? Got hot, didn't it?"

"Hot as it gets, but what the hell," Levi said as he flashed a grin. "Up you go," he said to his prisoner. "Be sure not to hit your head on the top." He turned to me with a shrewd look and said *sotto voce*, "Yeah, right. Hit your goddamn head and drop dead." Then he looked at me with strangely lit eyes. "Can you believe these jerks? Glad you were here. Knew you would be. Mister Golden-Gloves," he kidded. "Always there when I need you—long, lean and lanky, and furious with the footwork."

I jabbed at him playfully. "That's me," I boasted. Then I paused and studied him. "And you were in there *mi amigo*, kicking ass and taking names. You *are* okay, aren't you?"

He put a hand to his mouth as if to stifle a yawn and asked, "Ibba da?"

I reacted to his unintelligible jabber before I could catch myself. "Huh?"

Levi beamed. "Gotcha!"

"Bastard," I swore beneath my breath. He'd gotten me fair and square in the game we played. It began life as a private joke wherein we did our best to trip each other up during unguarded moments with, *ibba da*—nonsense words of his invention. The objective was to stand mute whenever it was uttered. Seeking clarification of the blather relegated the loser to crash and burn status.

He reached out and tapped my elbow with the backs of his fingers. "I'm fine. Like you said—kicked some ass. Now I've gotta get their damn names." Levi suddenly shifted gears as he looked directly at me and said quietly, "Let me know when you feel like talking about the dead kid." He seemed to understand more than he was letting on.

"Sure," I finally said.

Levi's face appeared grim as he inclined his head. "We'll talk later," he said, and then his eyes shifted past me as another female voice called out. "Levi! Hey, Levi."

I turned and searched the soft blur of faces in the thinning crowd. A tall, radiant redhead waved tentatively from the corner of 78th and Coastal.

"Janet," he announced. "E.R. nurse at Ocean General. She's seen you around." He elbowed my ribs and said from the side of his mouth, "Wants me to introduce you."

I regarded her carefully but shook my head. "She's a looker, but the last thing I need is a caregiver. Besides, she's not my type. We'd go together like gin and marshmallows."

"As I well know, my friend. But a promise is a promise, so come here." He pressed his hand in the small of my back and pushed me forward.

I resisted. "Another time. We've got work to do."

"Damn job," Levi muttered, but then he chuckled. "What's this world coming to when a man can't meet someone so sweet?"

Yeah. Jesus. So what if she wasn't my type? I truly loved women. I savored their companionship and I loved their laughter and their blushes when I flirted. I enjoyed their presence, their touch, and of course their skin against mine.

But when I turned to search the crowd she was gone. Then my eyes settled on another woman—mid-thirties, ash blonde, her breasts high and full. She seemed sure of her power to please, and she stood poised and indifferent to the crowd as she stared at me. I tapped Levi's forearm. "Where do I know her from?"

Levi screwed his eyes tight as he studied her. "Looks familiar," he murmured, "but I can't place her. Gorgeous, whoever she is."

I held her eyes until she turned away and got swallowed by the sea-swell of anonymous spectators.

Sergeant Burke helped move our prisoners into the Battlestar. Bandy-legged and red-haired, with cold eyes incapable of seeing below his bulging gut, Billy Burke had worked Ocean City's streets for more than two decades. I constantly ribbed him about his name ever since being told that the actress *Billie* Burke played the Good Witch of the North in *The Wizard of Oz*.

I said, "Hey, Sarge. Got these Munchkins under control yet?"

He ignored me and asked, "What started it?"

I shrugged. "Who knows? Probably fighting over a girl."

"Yeah," Jarl chimed in as the offshore breeze blew a tattered scrap of newspaper past our legs. "Probably. But who cares? So long as we're okay." He pushed a prisoner toward the wagon and snapped, "Spread 'em, asshole." He kicked the guy's legs apart and held his cuffed hands with a cruel grip as he searched him. When he was finished he moved him toward the wagon's yawning back doors and hefted him in.

Jarl was a local, a political animal who had lived all his life in Ocean City, leaving him privy to inside information. This fact conveyed to him a degree of status. He turned to me. "You did good ... got yourself a Bug." He held out his hand.

"Thanks," I began as I accepted the handshake. "Truth is, I was about to toss him aside 'til you charged in like a freakin' locomotive."

We were still shaking hands when Jarl's dark eyes seemed to go far away. "Hey, you doin' anything after work?"

I let go his hand. "Why?"

"Let's you an' me have a couple of beers. Linda and the kids are visiting her mom up in Jersey. I could use some company. Why don't you stop by my place for a cold one. You can stay over if you drink too much. Plenty of room," he quickly added.

My gaze instinctively swept the parking lot and then I nodded toward the Battlestar. "Thanks, but I'm gonna have paperwork up the ass. How about a rain check?"

Jarl smiled handsomely. "For you, *anytime*."

"If Levi didn't have so much paperwork you could've asked him."

"That's okay," Jarl said through half-lidded eyes. "Look, I'll catch you another time." He moved as if to walk off but then stopped. "Levi still having that party? You know if I'm invited? I can score a keg, you know."

"It's still on," I assured him, "and I'm sure you're invited. You know how forgetful he is. Just show up. If you need an invite then I'm giving you one."

"Thanks," he said, visibly relieved. Jarl walked off and disappeared around the far side of the Battlestar just as a bright flash of light erupted a few feet to my left. I instinctively went for my pistol as I jerked my head to see what it was. It was only Demmings. He was standing next to his cruiser as he flashed another photo of the scene. Guy must've gotten another new camera.

Levi walked over, his hair damp and heavy from perspiration and ocean mist. His triangular face was calm, his eyes solemn. "Damn, I've got three prisoners to process." He worried a loose pebble beneath the sole of his shoe. "I promised Jennifer I'd stay with her tonight. She's gonna think I'm avoiding her."

"Why? She knows the score."

"You think?"

"I'm sure of it. Besides, you're both seeing others. She has no lock on you."

He brightened. "Yeah, guess you're right. No sense getting my bowels in an uproar. Comes with the territory." He was about to close the Battlestar when a male voice sang out. "Levi! Over here!"

We turned as one. He was young and sloe-eyed, smartly dressed and slightly effeminate. He stood alone, the green neon sign of *Ragnar Rudy's Uptown Tavern* backlighting him. "Where've you been, Levi? Why haven't you called?" He stared woodenly as he waited for a reply.

"Who's your homo friend?" Billy Burke demanded as he strode up. He looked the guy up and down and declared, "Little cocksucker!" He fished a cigarette from his shirt pocket, jammed it between his lips, lit it with a careless flick of his Zippo and disappeared in a huff of nervous energy.

Levi's face flushed a deep red. "Fuck if I know." He slammed the Battlestar's door shut, twisted the lock viciously, then hurried off. I looked at the guy again. He stood with set jaw set as his gaze followed Levi's retreating back in some strange, nether-worldly way.

Jarl stepped next to me and looked him over. "Humph. Bit light in the loafers. Wonder how much AIDS *that* little bastard's spread—fucking faggot!" He charged off hard on Burke's heels, his arms oddly animated.

I stared at the guy and shrugged. I didn't see any problem and Levi knew where I stood on gay issues. I only wondered at Levi's reaction as I distractedly banged my palm twice on the Battlestar's side panel. As it moved away I automatically gave my cruiser the once-over, and damned if something didn't catch my eye. I crossed the short expanse of debris-strewn parking lot and found an astonishingly beautiful rose stuck beneath a wiper blade. "Huh," I whispered. Maybe that nurse put it there. Levi might know.

I sprinted forward and caught up with him as he was opening the door to his cruiser. He looked as if somebody had sucker-punched him. His shoulders sagged and he appeared distracted; his damp hair was disheveled and Levi's blue eyes would not meet mine. He looked back toward the now-faceless crowd as he eased himself inside.

To cheer him up I mumbled, "Ibba da?"

Levi glanced over his shoulder in the direction of Rudy's green neon sign as he got behind the steering wheel. His leather gun belt creaked as he grunted and said, "Did you know that no matter where you are in London, you're never more than thirty feet from a rat?" He slammed the door shut, dropped the cruiser in gear and drove off.

Just then my radio crackled as a cover unit was sent to take a report of a rape that had just occurred. I watched Levi drive off, not sure what he meant about the rats.

Another burst of light lit the scene.

Burke growled, "Jesus, Demmings. Enough with the camera already."

CHAPTER 2

DETAILS of the rape had yet to be disseminated when I went off-duty at 3:00am, and that irked me. I'd swept my sector earlier in response to the first assault report, and now someone—possibly the same attacker—had gotten bolder, and I had a big issue with rapists. It went beyond professionalism—I held a personal grudge. I knew how it felt to be violated; to have your spirit ripped apart. But there was nothing further to do, so I turned in my reports, changed, and drove home.

I parked next to Natasha's car, and getting out I could hear it click and groan as it cooled from recent use. Levi's usual spot was vacant because he was still working on his arrest documents. I'd given him a hand with his other reports, but only he could complete the charging documents. Now that I was home, the last few hours caught up with me. The fight at Ragnar's I could handle, but the images of Matthew would take some work.

I went inside, kicked off my flip-flops and put some ice cream that I'd picked up for Natasha in the freezer. I went to see if she was awake and found her bedroom door closed. I smiled while wondering if she'd changed her hair to another day-glo color. George lay curled protectively at the base of her door, kicking his legs as he dreamed of retrieving ducks from the Chesapeake. He stirred at my approach. Good old boy. No truer sentinel lived, not in this house. When I nudged him with my big toe he looked up, wagged his tail half-heartedly and haltingly got to his feet. I smiled, reached down and scratched his ear. So much for our dear Centurion. "How're you doing old buddy?" He wagged his tail and followed me to my room, where I stripped down to my boxer shorts.

George trailed me to the kitchen and nudged me impatiently until I got him a treat, when a sudden vigor infused him as he snatched it from my finger-tips. Then I got a treat for myself. I went to the liquor cabinet and grabbed the bottle of Johnny Walker Green Label—the one we kept for special occasions. I'd picked up two liters during a recent trip to the British Isles. The fifteen year-old single malt Green was markedly better than the Black—though not quite up to the level of the Gold Label—and nowhere close to the Blue, which none of us could afford even on our best days. But the Green still worked for those memorable moments in life—and I decided that this was one of those events. I got one of Natasha's Salviati crystal tumblers, added a large ice cube, and splashed two—okay, make it three fingers of the Scotch over it. When I shook the crystal glass slightly, the liquor sloshed around a bit and the ice tinkled as it began to melt and release the flavors. Then I padded slowly into the paneled living room, where I put Harry Connick, Jr. on the CD player and set the volume low to keep from disturbing Natasha. As the tender strains of *Little Clown* spooled up, I plopped down on the couch. A dog-eared copy of *Catch-22* lay on the coffee table, its spine broken from years of abuse. I'd only ever leafed through it—when my self-improvement mode caught hold, when it seemed that catching-up with the fifties and sixties was necessary before moving toward contemporary literature. But I wasn't in the mood for literature; Yossarian's exasperations would be too vexing, and I wanted only to veg.

George came over and rested his head on my leg. As I petted him absently I whispered, "Ah George. You don't know how good you've got it." His tail moved back and forth and he pushed his head harder against my leg. I held the tumbler to my nose, sniffed its mellow fragrance, and tossed back a healthy gulp. Jesus, but it tasted so damned good as it flowed down my gullet. I could taste the honey, the sweet spices and oak. Its warmth and cedar smokiness went to work instantly, gently easing those images of Matthew from my mind. But images did persevere, and all at once I looked into George's accepting eyes and said, "Life sucks."

"Yeah? How come?"

Natasha, just shy of thirty and tall, slender and elegant, shuffled across the carpeted floor into the room. Her hand went to her mouth as she yawned, and then her long tapering fingers rubbed delicately at her high Slavic cheekbones. She *had* dyed her hair, a fluorescent orange this time. One of her breasts protruded slightly from beneath her pink bathrobe. She glanced down at it and absently closed the robe. "Hiyah, Michael. How's my best bud doin' tonight?"

"Fine, I guess."

Natasha leaned over and pecked my cheek, then sat beside me and tucked her rather delicate feet beneath her. She traced her fingers along the partially open fly of my boxers and said, "I like you in these. They the ones I bought you?"

I nodded. "Just after we began dating, remember?"

"Oh, yes. Blues an' reds are good colors for you, an' you look so sexy when they're a bit baggy—not like those others you wore." She plucked at the fly and then snuggled closer, resting her head against my bare chest. I put my arm around her as she shifted gears. "So tell me, darling—why does life suck?"

"Ah, you know me. One of those hard days." I offered her a sip of the Scotch.

She wrinkled her nose and pushed it away with her lovely hand. "Ugh. No thanks. Just polished off two glasses of Chardonnay. Scotch won't do for me now."

I said in a serious tone, "Hey, be careful around town. There've been a couple of rapes."

She patted my leg and said, "I've got you and Levi to protect me. And George."

I snickered. "Doubt old George would be much help."

"Maybe," she said absently. She touched the gauze pad on my knee. "What's this?"

"Nothing." I drank a bit more, and as the warmth moved through me I asked, "So how're you doing? Love the hair, by the way."

She smiled prettily as Harry belted out *Sunny Side of the Street*. "You're such a dear. I'm doing fine, thank you for asking. Oh, didn't get a chance to tell you, but what a party the other night! You and Levi should've come, my two princes, there to protect me—although from what I don't know." She rolled her eyes and broke into a grin as she gave my thigh a little squeeze. "Then again, you two would have gotten in the way of a little fun. So—what's new and exciting in your life?"

I scratched George's ear absently. "Picked up some ice cream for you. It's in the fridge. Your favorite. Pistachio."

She smiled radiantly. "You're such a dear. Hope you got something for yourself. Ate the last of your Ben & Jerry's the other night."

I snorted. "No shit. What, you think I was shopping for you?" I suppressed a smile and added, "Hell, girl—I picked up that pistachio as an afterthought."

She laughed and plucked again at my fly. "I've got your afterthought."

I yawned and said, "What do you say we catch a movie? *Schindler's List* is playing at the Gold Coast."

"That's right. You said you wanted to see it. Love to. When?"

"Don't know. Couple days, maybe." Topic change again—casual segue as I took another sip of the good stuff and nonchalantly said, "Met someone the other day."

Natasha sat up and said with huge eyes, "Michael Brennan! You must like her if you're …" She shook my leg vigorously. "Is she local? Do I know her?"

"Name's Sarah. New girl at the Taylor Bank."

She elbowed my ribs. "So come on! Is it serious?"

Harry Connick merged into his jazzy *Vocation* as I replied, "Ah come on, Nat. It's nothing."

"Like hell it isn't. Three years I've lived with you guys. Two things I've noticed. One," she began as she held up a finger, "there is a constant line of women trooping in and out of Levi's bedroom …"

"Ha!" I jostled her playfully and said, "I see *you* in that line often enough."

She play-slapped me and said, "Often enough?"

"Come on. I hear you an' Levi humping all the time."

Natasha demanded with mock indignation, "What's wrong with that?"

I chuckled lazily. "Nothing. You guys have always been best friends. Why shouldn't you be intimate? Besides, you knew him before you knew me."

She laughed throatily. "Remember the time you walked in on us?"

"Haven't looked at the stove the same way since." Then I quipped in a robust drawl, "Noticed it didn't slow ya'll down none, neither."

"Hmm, yeah. Never skipped a beat, did we?"

"Not a one. Yeah, you two were good for each other." Then I added without thinking, "You sure picked the best when you asked him to be the father."

Her eyelids fluttered. "Jeez, why'd I think I needed to be a mommy?" She smiled fleetingly. "But oh, that lovely look on his face when I asked him to give me a baby, no strings attached. I needed sperm; I wanted his—simple as that." She smiled mischievously. "Was fun, too—especially that standing on the head part."

"Oh, you did that?"

She nodded and smiled briefly. "Just as you suggested. Yeah—the little stud held me up by the ankles each time. God knows we both wanted it so much …"

I said gently, "You came back swinging, though."

The CD beeped as another song ended. "Yeah. Jeez." She sighed. "Sixteen weeks. Sixteen weeks until …"

"Stop blaming yourself. You caught the flu. It wasn't your fault."

Natasha nudged my hand and whispered, "I don't blame myself. Not really. But God, she would've been so beautiful." Then in a stronger voice she said, "I got over it. *We* got over it. Oh, Michael—you were so good for both of us." A pause, and then, "Levi worships you for being there."

"He was devastated. Think he took it harder than you."

She said softly, "I so loved knowing that I had a baby growing inside of me."

"Nat?"

She looked up at me. "Yes?"

As another tune began I cleared my throat and said, "I know he'd still love to give you his child, and if you want, then …"

Natasha smiled deliciously, her languor abruptly gone. "Then I'd love to have yours, too. One with Levi, one with you." She hugged me hard and said, "Hey, think I will have a sip of that Scotch." She picked up the tumbler and had a swig, then she looked pensive until finally she said, "He really wants to try again?"

I looked directly at her. "Yes, and you'll be ovulating in another day or so."

She smiled delightedly. "Oh, Michael … you're still tuned into me! Yeah. I will be." She appeared deep in thought. "I've still got that fund set aside, and sperm *can* live for a couple of days after sex. Maybe I'll jump his bones next time I see him."

"Yeah, maybe you should," I heard myself say.

Natasha nodded slowly, then brightened and said forcefully, "We're getting off the topic—*you're* getting me off the topic. Where was I? Oh, I remember." She held up a finger again. "One—they're lining up for Levi." Then she held two fingers an inch from my face on the fat chance I'd miss them. "Two. Said line does not exist for you. Now then," she continued as she curled her legs beneath her again. "That means you are either gay, which I know you're not," and here she poked me in the ribs, "or you're being a gentleman by doing what all girls love best, by spending your nights in *their* beds and loving them very well—and I know you're lovin' lots a ladies, sweetheart, 'cause this town just ain't big enough for no secrets." A fleeting darkness crossed Natasha's divine face as she pushed back to scrutinize me. "Have you found that irresistible someone? *Have* you?"

I took another gulp of Scotch. "Hell, I just met her." I looked at her upturned head and found her watching me with a solemn look, so I brushed my lips against her forehead and whispered, "Come on Nat. Don't get green, okay? She's just someone I met." I looked at her and added defensively, "I know a dozen guys that would give their left nut just to be seen with you, and—and I don't get jealous when you're with Levi. Hell, Jen knows he's boinking you, an' she's okay with it."

Natasha looked away, a wistful expression on her face. "That's because she's pressuring him to knock her up, and doesn't wanna drive him away."

"I didn't know." I grunted. "She might even prevail—she's got great negotiating skills."

Her body sagged against mine. "Most attorneys do." She said nothing more for one or two minutes. Finally she murmured, "Where were we? You got me off-track again. Oh. The three of us are friends, Michael. We don't get jealous. We love one another." She looked at me with unwavering eyes and added, "I love Levi. I loved carrying his child. That doesn't mean I'm *in* love with him. I just think he's adorable." She dropped her eyes and fidgeted with my gauze pad. Then she said, "You're such a sweetheart, but I worry about you." Her mouth moved wordlessly as she groped for the right thing to say. "You're such an easy guy to love, but you don't know that, do you?" Natasha moved slightly and looked at me. "You've never really felt loved, have you?"

"I've felt loved," I countered, and I took another sip of the good stuff to prove it.

She looked questioningly into my eyes. "Really? By whom?"

I knew by whom. So did she. Maybe she just needed to hear me say it. Instead, I asked a little testily, "Just what is it you want?"

"What do I want? I want to take risks. I want to win at life. Most of all I want to be loved ... don't you?"

I stared at the ice cube as it melted from the power of the alcohol and said, "I held a little boy's hand while he died yesterday. There was nothing anyone could do for him. So that's it. He died. Dead. He's gone."

Natasha stared at me for a long time, and in that silent moment George got up and waddled away. "Michael," she finally said. "That's terrible. Tell me all about it."

I gave her the Reader's Digest version. A sanitized summary, gory details removed, thank you very much.

She pushed herself upright and all of a sudden she had my head between her hands like warming loaves of bread. She kissed my face several times— softly, pleasantly … lovingly—as I slowly caressed her hair. "There," she said when she finished. "That's for being 'Michael,' the sweetest man I've ever met; always caring more about others than he does about himself." Then she eased her head back against my chest and a moment passed in silence. Finally she exhaled and said, "That was a wonderful thing you did for that boy. You gave him spirituality during the most frightening moment of his life."

"I did my best," I mumbled, wondering at her grammatical shift as Connick's moody *On Green Dolphin Street* played.

"I don't doubt that. Sometimes all we can do is *be* someone's friend, as you were for that frightened little boy. Sometimes that's enough." She looked up at me again. "But why am I not surprised?" She tapped a delicate forefinger against my sternum and said, "You've such a wonderful heart in there."

I nuzzled her ear with my lips and whispered, "Thanks. I feel better already. You always go right to the core, don't you?"

She turned and studied me. Finally she said, "Remember when you let it slip that the Peace Corps dropped you when you couldn't get a handle on Spanish?"

"Okay, yeah—I remember. It was on our second date, right?"

Natasha cuddled closer and said, "Telling me was an afterthought—not meant to impress. But it told me that you looked beyond yourself, that there was much more beyond the surface. I liked that about you."

I smiled at the memory and said, "Yeah, and I loved how you could talk about almost everything." I grazed the top of her head with my lips.

Natasha gave me a little squeeze. "We've always been such good friends, you and I—even through the hard times." She moved her face close to mine, and her brown eyes softened as she asked, "Wasn't Levi quoting Oscar Wilde the other night?"

I stroked her cheek with my fingertips and nodded. "'We are *all* in the gutter, but some of us are looking at the stars.'"

She nodded vigorously. "Yes. That's it. Describes the three of us perfectly, don't you think?"

I smiled. Whether it was the liquor that had loosened me up, or Natasha, or both, I felt less anxious than before. "Here's another. 'It's important to know the difference between tragedy and burned potatoes.'"

"Hah!" Natasha pinched me playfully and said triumphantly, "Thought I didn't know that one, didn't you? Anton …"

"Chekov," I finished for her.

She grazed my cheek with the back of her cool hand and then she got up. Her fine silky eyebrows rose a trifle as she tugged me to my feet. As winsome sounds of Harry Connick's *Little Waltz* played, I put down the unfinished Green Label for the truly spiritual stuff as she took my hand, led me to her bedroom and closed the door. We undressed, got between the sheets, and held each other. We said nothing and did nothing other than lie next to one another. We had often pushed sex aside in favor of being together this way—our 'skin-on-skin' time. But as I settled into this level of intimacy that we so thoroughly enjoyed, I still thought of Matthew. Natasha was right; he had felt little pain, and I'd made sure he wasn't left alone. I felt grateful to her for that—for helping restore my peace of mind along with *my* dignity.

The Dream jerked me from sleep.

A fight! It's another fight. The door. The glass door … it's breaking! I can hear it. Now he's screaming at her! I can almost see his face, twisted and red like those beets I hate so much. Those words. He's using those words again, but I don't understand them. "Get away from me, you whore." What's that mean?

I grab my doggy. He's my best friend, even if he's not a real doggy. There's so much yelling. I slip out of bed and pad past my door. I'm in the hallway. My sister Mary's door is open. I don't want her to see me in my underpants, so I run past her door. I run toward the fight. They're in the living room. Everything's a mess! They don't see me, but I see them. Her housecoat is so worn out; I wish I could get her a new one. And him. His undershirt is ripped, and now … now he's making a fist. He's pulling his arm back. He's going to hit her!

"Daddy?" I whisper. I whisper because I'm afraid he might hit me, like last time. He turns. His eyes are hard and glassy. "You little sonuvabitch! Whaddya want, ya cocksucker? Get back in bed where you belong!"

I stick my chest out and yell back, crazy to do so, crazier if I don't. "No! You leave Mommy alone!"

He stares at me. His upper lip curls and I can see his teeth. They're ugly teeth. I hate them. They're rotten from those cigarettes he smokes all the time. "Do as I say, ya little bastard!"

I won't move, even though I'm shaking harder than I can remember, even more than a week ago when he hit me for no reason, no reason at all.

Uh oh. I think he's really, really mad now. He's making a fist. He's coming at me! Mommy's trying to hold him back. "Run, Michael! For God's sake, run!"

I run. If she tells me to do something I do it. Daddy's yelling at me. Why? I don't know. It's not my fault.

"Ya little sonuvabitch," he screams, and this time I hear Mary crying in her bed as I run past; I'm running hard as I can for my room. It's safer there; it's safe. It's okay, and it'll be better. I'll hide. I'll hide in the closet. That's always best.

He's still yelling. "Ya goddamn little sonuvabitch, I wish ya'd never been born!"

All I have to do is hide. All I have to do is be a good boy. Then he'll like me. Yes he will!

I woke up with a moan. Natasha stirred and I pushed the dream aside and smiled at her orange hair. Then I brushed my fingertips along her smooth and very pale skin, and buried my nose against her ear until the still-familiar scent consumed me. I whispered, "I love your smell."

Natasha's naked body moved against mine in her slumber. Her breasts were warm against my chest, her nipples large and delicate. I pressed against her, smelled her, felt gratitude for her friendship—but then I thought about The Dream. Maybe it helped explain why I always looked out for others. I got up and went to my own bed.

I stretched out naked atop my unmade mattress, dozed off and dreamed.

He's coming into my room. He's sitting on my bed. I freeze; I know what'll happen next, but maybe this time he won't. No! Please, no! He's going to do it ... he's sliding his hand beneath the sheet. He moves until his fingertips touch between my legs.

"Damn, boy—you ain't old enough to get no hair, but damned if you ain't got more hangin' than most men."

I squirm and try to pull away. Finally I cry—just a little whimper.

He jumps to his feet. "Whaddya cryin' for? You're a loser, ya know that? A goddamned loser. What good are you? Damn you, boy—I wish you'd never been born!"

It's too much. I clap my hands over my ears. I don't wanna hear this. Not again.

"Oh, whas' a matter? Poor little Mike gonna cry? Go ahead. Cry. Yeah, thas' right. Cry,
ya little faggot."

He's wobbling now, about to fall down. I hope he does. I hope he breaks his neck. Then
maybe I can run away, like Mary. I should have gone with her. After Mom died I should
have run away, too.

"No son of mine's gonna cry like a girl. You're almost nine, boy. When ya gonna grow up?
Be a man, fer Christ's sake!"

I'm trembling with rage now. I hate him and I hate the way he calls me 'Mike'! I open my
mouth and roar, "My name is Michael*!" Then I cry; so much pain.*

The pain—and now there's moaning. Where am I? My mouth is dry, the
mattress is damp and I'm exhausted. Finally I remember as someone stirs in
Levi's adjacent room. A girl laughs softly. Now she moans. It's Jennifer. I was
right. She understood. She came here to be with Levi. Now they're having
sex.

I rolled over with a groan. God, I'm so freaking tired. I didn't *want* to take
care of my mom. Didn't want to, but knew I had no choice. The cancer had
already taken hold. There was nobody else to help. But I'm getting tired of
looking out for others. I want to look out for myself for a change. Maybe I
should see someone. A doctor. No, not a doctor, but a … well, I can't see a
shrink. They're for people with real problems. Besides, it wouldn't look good.
I'm so tired.

As the sun slipped past the window a beam found its way past the shade
and stabbed my eye with great malice. I didn't need a clock to know it must be
past ten.

Damn.

I dragged myself out of bed, pulled on a pair of gym shorts and walked
into the hallway. Natasha's door stood open. I peeked inside and found it empty.
Where had she gone? George was asleep in front of Levi's room. When I
reached down and scratched behind his ear he got up and went in search of his
water bowl. I rapped my knuckles against Levi's door and turned the knob.

Oh.

I'd forgotten about Jennifer. She's uncommonly beautiful, blond and blue,
draped across Levi and fast asleep. Her head is on his chest and her lips are
parted so that she snores delicately. Levi's also out; crashed and burned. One
foot protrudes from beneath a flimsy sheet and dangles over the edge of his

futon. The knuckles of his left hand graze the carpet. A bottle of Jameson's sits atop the nightstand, its contents half gone. Two glasses, one on its side, lay on the floor next to an empty condom wrapper. My copy of Saul Bellow's *Humboldt's Gift* is propped against the nightstand. I make a mental note to remind Levi to return it when he's done. The window A/C whines steadily from one wall, while a computer and printer sit silently on a small table against another; Levi's gotten interested in a burgeoning field—information technology. He keeps his room cluttered enough to be happy, yet clean enough to be healthy—unlike the disaster area that passes for mine. I clear my throat.

His eyes snapped open. "Michael," he began, then he paused as he summoned a cavernous yawn. Levi covered his mouth with one hand and pulled the sheet with the other a bit to shield his girl. Then his body went rigid as he stretched, cat-like. His toes splayed outward, then returned to their natural position when he relaxed. Jennifer stirred and pushed herself up from Levi's chest. One of her boobs showed. The sheet fell back and exposed her rear. She tugged at it absently, her modesty undisturbed.

"Hello, Michael," she said dreamily before settling her head on his chest.

Levi asked, "What's up, Horse Breath?" His tanned face was composed yet stark against the pure white pillowcase. Another yawn. "What time is it?"

"A bit after ten. Sorry," I said as I leaned against the doorjamb. "Should've knocked louder."

He rubbed his eyes. "Hell, don't sweat it. Jen doesn't mind, do you?" he smiled as he traced a finger along the curve of her spine.

"Not a bit," she answered from somewhere far away.

He stretched lazily again. "What time did you get in?"

"Around three. You?"

"Late," he replied through fluttering eyelids. "Five."

I shifted from one foot to the other. "So who was that guy last night? You never did say."

He turned his head slightly and regarded me in silence until he said, "Nobody. Let it go." Levi smoothed the sheet covering Jennifer's rear end. "How about you? Ever hook-up with Janet?"

I dropped my voice. "No. Go back to sleep, bro. I'll catch ya later."

He replied through closed eyes. "Okay, just a few more Zs. What've you got planned?"

"Gonna go for a work out." I added, "Might stop by headquarters—see about that rape from last night. Hear anything before you left?"

"No. Not a thing," he replied from someplace far away.

I waited until his breathing eased into a rhythmic slumber, and gently closed the door.

I grabbed my gym bag and headed for Johnny's Fitness Center. A yellow VW with its top down rushed past me a mile from town, the two guys in front dangling their arms and legs over the sides, while two girls in back waved with uproarious abandon. I smiled at their zest for life as I slowed and got in the left-turn lane. Seconds later I turned north onto Coastal Highway, goosed the accelerator, and glided serenely the few remaining blocks to 63rd Street. Business must've taken an upswing for Johnny, judging from the number of cars that packed the front lot. I spotted an empty space in the back lot and parked there. I didn't mind the walk, and careless drivers were less apt to dent my 'stang there.

Johnny's Fitness Center. I worshipped here regularly. It had become my temple, my tabernacle, and my church. My workouts had become a religion for me—what I had in place of a religion, when body, mind and soul came together. Johnny owned the gym that bore his name. He'd trained professional wrestlers from Oregon to Florida before scraping together enough dough to open a gym of his own. I found him behind the counter, leaning forward with both hands planted on the polished counter top as he talked to a new member. Johnny had a ruined potato sack of a face, stood six four, and always wore a Cleveland Indians ball cap centered on his bald scalp. His huge arms were neatly rippled and marked by gnarled veins. Johnny was a class act. He supported his community and cut a deal for cops, offering us half price on annual memberships. I respected the hell out of him.

I waved and shouted, "Hey, Johnny! How're they hanging," and then stopped in mid-sentence as a girl sauntered past. Her bleached-blonde hair put me off a bit, but her long legs were a definite turn-on.

Johnny regarded me with eyes screwed almost shut and asked in his thick brogue, "What're ya planning on doing with that one, lad? Ya gonna arrest her or ask her out on a date or what? Maybe a little of both, hey? A good-looking lad like you, perhaps ya plan on sweepin' her off her feet, first. Is that it? Will you ask her out, only to trick her an' slip the old handcuffs on her? Will ya yank her over to that *hoosegow* you call a home? Are ya plannin' on coopin' her up in a cage? Is that the plan? Confine her to some bullpen of a barracoon? Or perhaps you'll remand her to the custody of one a yer mates after yer good and done with her. Well? Is that yer game now, boy?"

I shrugged with feigned indifference. "Nah. Been there, done that. It's all so boring. Time for something truly insidious. Dinner, maybe. And dancing. Maybe a moonlit walk along the beach."

Johnny's eyes softened. "Ah now, go on with ya. I've known ya long enough to understand you've a kind heart and a direct manner. Ya don't put up a façade, and I like that quality in a man." Then he stepped back, looking suddenly small beneath the naked steel girders that towered above him. "And besides, you're a good Christian lad in a good Christian town—leastwise it's Christian with respect to those of us what lives here the year 'round." He turned slightly and handed a locker key to another member. "Not like these twits and wastrels and queers what come here for holiday, spreading their diseases and whatnot," he said with a slight nod at the departing member's back. Johnny closed his eyes, made the Sign of the Cross and murmured, "Bless me sainted wife. May she always rest in peace, secure from this madness."

I said nothing. Tales of his long-dead wife loomed large in these parts.

He planted his hands on the counter and asked with clear-eyes, "So how's that fine motor car of yours running?"

"Great, thanks."

He gazed at the ceiling. "Aye, beautiful piece of work, that. I like how you treat it so. Shows respect for God's fine resources." Then Johnny regarded me carefully. "The morning telly told of a young lass, raped the evening past."

It was just like Johnny to probe for the inside word. I shook my head and told him truthfully, "You know as much as I."

He nodded and said staunchly, "Well, there'll likely never be stopping rapes from taking place. Just so long as the tourists still come, that's what matters."

His remark surprised me, but before I could challenge him he switched topics completely. "Aye. And what of your roomie? That Levi? What's he up to these days? I hear he's gotten yet another offer of employment."

"He's just busy being Levi. Kicked some ass at a fight last night. Made three arrests, and ..."

"Heard it on the scanner on me way home. Tried me best to avoid the traffic, but there's the luck—Ragnar's *is* along the way."

"Yeah, guess it is. But umm, no—I haven't heard about any new job offers, unless you're talking about the one from Customs."

"That'd be the one," Johnny confirmed with a sweep of his hand to his ball cap. He took it off, caressed his rubbery scalp, replaced the lid and stared at me. "What's he want, anyway? This town's not good enough for him?"

"It's not that," I said, wondering why Johnny felt hostile toward him. "Levi's talented. He's gifted—has his master's degree. Hell, he's been getting job offers ever since I've known him. Women and Federal agencies ... they all want a piece of him."

"Aye, if you say so." He examined a membership card thrust at him by an older guy in a crimson tank top and blue nylon shorts. Johnny mumbled his assent and passed the card back. Then he regarded me with patient eyes. "I hear talk Levi's throwing another of his parties. Guess the whole lot of ya will be boozin' an' whorin' an' vomitin' all over the place, hey?"

I shrugged, smiled and said, "If we're lucky!" and got the hell out of there before he could respond. He acted gruff toward sex in general, so I figured to play it safe.

I dumped my stuff in a locker, slammed the door and spun the combination, and then touched the St. Michael's medal that hung from my neck. Levi had given it to me one Christmas. We hadn't planned on exchanging gifts, but somewhere around nine on Christmas Eve he impulsively slipped it from his neck and fastened it around mine.

"There," he had said, admiring it as he took a step back. "St. Michael, patron saint and protector of police. It's yours now." He paused and his eyes dropped momentarily, until he looked at me and said, "This has been in my family a long time. Don't treat it lightly. It's a line that's not to be crossed. Are we clear on this?"

I assured him that I respected its significance. Now I held it between thumb and forefinger before turning to leave the locker room, conscious of how seldom it had been off my neck.

I love women. Their slight builds, soft skin and smooth faces never fail to quicken my pulse. My God, she was beautiful.

She stood nonchalantly near the free weights and I pegged her for mid-thirties. She had on black tights and her hips were to die for. Her limbs were long, her stomach flat; her eyes were quite green and her oval face, dark and rather delicate, was framed not by night but by shining black hair.

She was also with a guy.

I caught his eye and nodded. Ed Bell returned the nod. I liked him. His fellow firefighters also liked him, although some were frankly envious of this extremely handsome man. He stood next to her with a protective hand on her elbow and called out, "Michael. Come meet Anna."

Anna was a looker, and I damn well right would come and meet her. Her body glistened beneath a thin veil of perspiration, and her green eyes dilated with a sudden sensuality as she offered her hand, palm down. "Hello! My name is Anna." She smiled, and those green eyes flashed.

"Hi, Anna. Michael Brennan." I took her hand, held it briefly, and let it go. Her fingers brushed mine as she drew her arm away. She had a kittenish sex quality that I loved, and I'd have made a play for her at any other time, but she was with Ed.

"Are you a firefighter?"

Ed coughed and said, "No, babe. He's a cop, a *good* cop."

Anna gently bit her lower lip with dazzling white teeth as she suppressed a smile. Then she said, "I'm overwhelmed. I've never known my brother to speak highly of any cop." She looked at Ed and patted his back, and her eyes were full of mischief as she added, "He was such a *naughty* little boy growing up."

Hmm. Her brother. That changed things. "You're very beautiful," I told her.

Her eyes sparked again, and this time she looked at me with more interest. "Why thank you, Mike. I'm flattered."

"It's *Michael*," I gently corrected. "Not Mike. Michael."

She pulled slightly away from Ed and stepped toward me. "What a handsome name to go with such a handsome man." She smiled a North Star smile and asked, "Is your hair naturally blonde?"

"Tow-head from birth." I gazed appreciatively at her full lips. "You're here visiting?"

She moved further from Ed and rested her cool fingertips on my forearm. "I come down for a few days every other week or so. I have a condo."

I nodded thoughtfully. "I'm impressed. Very few single people own condos."

She arched an eyebrow. "Who said I'm single?"

I laughed. "Fishing expedition. But fair's fair. You got me."

A tiny smile tugged the corners of her mouth. "What're you working today?"

"Chest," I replied with a direct look.

She nodded gravely. "What are the chances of that? So am I." She moved still further from Ed. He glanced sideways at her and a message must have passed between them, because he put a hand on her shoulder and let it linger. Then he patted it affectionately and gave me a look that said, *be good to my sister*. He walked off toward the shoulder press as Anna gave me a coy look and said, "I am, by the way. Single. Divorce came through last week. You're also single," she added with certainty, "though I doubt you have the least difficulty finding a date whenever you want one." She stopped abruptly and paused to scrutinize me as a brief, indulgent smile appeared.

Yeah. I liked that kind of directness in a woman. I looked at Anna with renewed interest, automatically putting my arm out to shield her as two guys passed by on their way to the bench press. I chuckled softly. "You're perceptive."

"And not averse to fishing expeditions of my own."

"Ouch! Got me again." I grinned and nudged her toward the free weights. "What do you do?"

"Reporter," she replied dryly.

Now I offered a full-throated laugh. "That explains a lot."

"Travel editor actually—for *The Washington Post*," she added with a hint of pride.

"Travel editor, huh? I love to travel. Bet you've had some great adventures. I'd like to hear about them. We can compare notes."

Anna showed white teeth. "I show you mine, you show me yours?"

"Hey," I began with a direct look. "I'm not a bonehead, if that's what you're after. Look, I like you. That quickly," I said with a snap of my fingers. "I know what I like—and I'd like to take you to dinner."

She stepped closer to me, "Yes. I would love to have dinner with you, Michael Brennan. I can see that you've a very kind heart." She studied me and said finally, "You must have had wonderful parents."

I shook my head. "Wish that was true. My mom did her best but she's been dead a long time. My father's in prison and I don't know where my sister is."

Her eyebrows knitted together. "I'm sorry." She regarded me from the corners of her eyes. "But your sister? You don't know where she is? You're a cop. Do you mean to say you can't trace her?"

"I did find her. Years ago. Called her up. We spoke. She's married. Lives far away."

Anna nodded. "And doesn't care to be found again."

I said quietly, "No."

We stood in awkward silence until I broke the spell with a smile. Then we chatted it up, settled on dinner the day after tomorrow, and then I impulsively invited her to Levi's party the next evening. Turning to her I asked, "Anna, have you ever had one of those friends you can never think about without smiling?"

She regarded me curiously and said, "No, I am sorry to say that I have not."

"Then wait until you meet my buddy Levi. We're like brothers. I know you'll like him, and he'll like you."

Her full lips pulled upward into a grin. "That *is* interesting," she said in a fine, warm voice. She reached out and put her cool fingers against my cheek. "That's so sweet of you, to want to introduce me to your friend."

"What friend?" Levi asked as he turned the corner from the lobby. He smiled the instant his eyes found Anna, and his smile broadened as his eyes moved back and forth from her to me. "My God you're beautiful! Michael, what are you waiting for? Why haven't you introduced us?"

I put a proud, protective arm around her shoulders. "Anna Bell, Levi Hart. Levi, this is Anna."

Anna held out her hand. "It's Anna Stewart actually, and I am very pleased to meet you, Levi. You must be quite remarkable to be Michael's friend."

Levi gently took her hand and offered a shy grin. "He's the remarkable one. Only ..."

"Yes?"

A bemused look crossed his face. "Please tell me you haven't agreed to go to dinner with him."

Anna leaned toward Levi and stage-whispered, "Oh? And why not?"

His face lit up. "Stand your ground, girl! Don't let him take you to some cheesy restaurant. Make him cook for you!"

She glanced over her shoulder at me while asking Levi, "What's he holding back on?"

"Only that he can cook. He's quite the gourmet."

Anna stared at me with renewed interest. "Really? I *love* good food. But I should warn you—I've been to some of the world's finest restaurants. I'll hold you to a very high standard."

Levi laughed and his eyes turned bright as he said, "Ahh, you won't be disappointed. Michael's a stud in the kitchen and a chef in bed."

She blushed deeply and her eyelids fluttered as she dropped her gaze to the floor. But then she beamed as she said to Levi, "Hmm, he sounds as though he'll be an exciting man to get to know."

I smiled inwardly at Levi's mischief. Turning to him, I coughed into my fist and said, "Ibba da?"

His head jerked around and his mouth fell open. "Wha …?"

I pounced. "Gotcha!"

He fought to maintain his composure. Finally he caved, grinned, extended his middle finger and walked away.

We worked out for an hour. Levi, always the friend, gave us our space by excusing himself and going to the far side of the gym to work his abs. Ed Bell watched discreetly as I helped Anna with her routine, and then she spotted me while I showed off with some strenuous lifts. Afterwards we separated and hit the communal showers. Levi chatted amiably about Anna, pausing only to give a cop's once-over to a guy in his early twenties as he entered the shower room.

As we dried off a few minutes later he ran a hand through his heavy damp hair and smiled when I touched the St. Michael's around my neck. He wrapped his towel around his waist and said, "You really like her. I can tell. I've never seen you like this before." Levi put his foot on a bench, rested his forearm on his knee, and leaned forward. Then he looked directly at me and added, "I'm happy for you. I worry about you sometimes, ya know? You are my best friend, so naturally I want the best for you." He flicked his eyes in the direction of the ladies locker room. "I think you've got something with that one out there." He chuckled. "So much for that Janet chick I wanted to set you up with." He wagged his eyebrows and stepped away to get dressed.

I said, "Yeah, I have a good feeling about her."

Levi was halfway into his jeans when he gestured broadly. "Say, why don't we do a double? *Les Miz* is playing in D.C. We'll drive there with Jen, hook-up with Anna, and see the play. What do you think?"

I nodded thoughtfully. "Hmm. Maybe." Then I frowned as something occurred to me. "Umm, I don't know. Natasha wanted to see it, so …"

He grinned impishly. "You freaking kill me. When will you ever admit it?"

"Admit what?" I countered innocently. Then I pulled on T-shirt and shorts, stepped into flip-flops, threw my wet stuff into my bag and zipped it shut. Then to change the subject of Natasha I said matter-of-factly—if not obliquely, "Yeah, I really do like her." All at once I said, "I told Nat last night that you still wanna give her a baby." Then I stared through him and added in a near-whisper, "She's ready, amigo."

"Yeah?" He suddenly got quiet and stared at the lockers.

We left it there and walked to the lobby where we found Anna waiting. Her bright teeth accented her high cheekbones as she called out, "There you are." She had on a modest white blouse, dark pajama-like pants that reached to her ankles, and delicate black sandals. She appeared stunning in her simplicity.

Levi tactfully stepped to one side so she and I could talk, and I'd just walked past him when I heard him say very tenderly, "Hello there. What's your name?"

I turned and discovered a little girl standing directly in front of him. I guessed she was about three, with sun-bleached hair and unblinking brown eyes that stared without shame at Levi.

He crouched down to one knee, opened his arms wide and said in a soft voice, "Come here, little one. It's okay. There's nothing to be afraid of."

She stepped into his arms without the slightest hesitation, wrapped her arms around his neck, and pressed her cheek against his. Levi held her with sublime tenderness as he closed his eyes and gently rocked her back and forth. She eased away after a few seconds and held Levi's expressive blue eyes with hers, before turning and walking into an adjacent office where a woman's voice exclaimed, "Where did you run off to?"

Levi stood and found us watching him. "Oh, kids take to me. I don't know. Guess it's the way I was raised."

"His folks are really something," I piped in.

"Yeah," he said. "Free-spirits."

"Explains his aversion to soap, clothes, and shoes," I quipped.

"Fuck you," he said to me. To her he said, "The house was always full of friends. Always someone to take care of me." He beamed at some pleasant vision. "Always got my needs met, you know? Someone to hold me, someone to change my diapers before I could cry. Gosh, my feet never touched the ground." He chuckled deep in his throat and then blurted, "I have such *great* folks."

I felt a twinge at my own childhood even as I threw my arm around his shoulders.

"That's my buddy. Kids and animals just love him."

She leaned against me and whispered into my ear. "He's a darling. Tremendous sex appeal, too. Any girl would be lucky to have him."

A bellowing voice twenty feet away reminded me of my manners. "Michael me lad, ya gonna introduce this fine lass or what?"

We moved toward the reception counter. "Anna Stewart, Johnny," I began.

His eyes narrowed as he looked directly at her. "Young Michael's a fine man, as fine as you please."

Anna nodded. "Yes, I think so. I've even accepted a dinner invitation from him."

"That's so? Magnificent." He paused and arched an eyebrow. "I take it you're in town for an extended stay, then?"

"Off and on. I have a condo."

Johnny nodded. "Oh? Grand. On the beach, is it?"

"Yes. Around 145th Street," she said vaguely.

"Aye, good place, that." He looked away as a customer approached. "Cheers, then. Nice to have made your acquaintance. You make sure young Michael here treats you right," he commanded, and then he attended to business.

Just then the main door burst open and Jarl Jackson sauntered in. He seemed to brighten when he saw me. "Hey, Michael—howzit goin'?" He walked past Levi without greeting him and stopped in front of Anna. "Who're you?"

I made a quick introduction. Jarl nodded automatically, then turned to me and said, "Guess you heard about the rape."

I frowned. "Of course. It went out over the air last night."

Jarl puffed his chest and said, "Not that one. There's been another."

"*No*," Levi and I chorused. This was genuine news. Rapes were rarities in Ocean City. That only exacerbated them when they did occur, because rapes

tend to be even more vicious when committed in nameless, faceless resorts—
the, *anonymity inherent in large resort towns incites increased levels of violence*—police
science theory. "What happened?" I asked.

Jarl shrugged, rudely ignored Anna and Levi, and said to me, "North end
again. Suspect got in through a patio door. Caught some young chickee by
surprise an' choked her out. She came to 'bout the time he was done pokin' her.
She don't remember much. Didn't see him. Can't describe him."

Levi groaned and said in a flat voice, "Jesus. Poor girl. Hope she's okay."

"Aye, what a terrible thing," Johnny said from behind his counter.

I drove a fist into my palm. "Why do people do that shit?"

Jarl snorted and said, "Life's a booger. Well," he added as he transferred
his gym bag from one hand to the other, "we'll just have to catch his ass, won't
we?"

Levi rolled his eyes as Ed Bell walked past us on his way to the locker
room. I looked him in the eye, nodded slightly to let him know that I would
honor his sister, and he nodded in response. A few moments later we said our
goodbyes and parted, Levi to go wherever, and Anna to her north end beachside condo.

I ambled across the parking lot and shook my head at Jarl's news of this
second rape. I'd planned on dropping by headquarters and nosing around a
bit, but now that I'd gotten 'the word' from Jarl, I reconsidered. Police theories
aside, one constant ran true in most agencies: there is always at least one cop
with access to backroom dealings. Jarl filled that role in this department. If he
didn't know about it, likely it hadn't happened. I figured I'd just wait until roll
call and see if there were any new developments.

I got my car keys out but stopped short when I reached the Mustang.
Someone had stuck a note to the driver's window. As I grabbed the small,
plain piece of white paper I wondered if Levi or maybe an old girl friend had
put it there. The typed text appeared too perfect to be from a typewriter so it
must have been generated by a word processor. It read, *Think you are man enough
to catch me?* My first thought, admittedly narcissistic: maybe Nurse Janet was
having some fun. But the clincher came as I read on. *I can get more girls than you.
Don't believe me? Look at the one I got last night.*

A chill ran down my spine as I realized that a rapist had just thrown down
the gauntlet.

CHAPTER 3

WHOEVER wrote the note would have taken measures to avoid leaving latent prints—but then criminals get stupid all the time. If good fortune had blessed us, then any of the excellent crime lab techs might discover a partial. I drove directly to headquarters to see Lieutenant Joe Santoro. He wasn't in, but one of his investigators looked up from her desk when I held the paper aloft and said, "Found this on my car not ten minutes ago. Could have something to do with last night's rape."

Katie Dixon put down her pen and took off her glasses. Her eyes moved back and forth as she scanned the copy. "Why *your* car?"

"Dunno. Could be a case of mistaken identity; I've seen two similar Mustangs in town."

She studied the paper again and said, "I'll turn it over to Joe." Then she put her glasses back on and said dismissively, "Thanks. We'll get back to you."

"Wait one sec. Why not call Joe? Let's do something with it now."

She stared back as if she'd found an insect in her food. "He'll be in later. Don't you work tonight? If he thinks it's important he'll send for you. Personally, I think someone's neurons are firing out of synch. This note is nothing but babble." She looked back down at her paperwork.

I thanked her and left for home.

Natasha's car sat in the driveway next to Levi's, and when I walked inside I found a trail of clothing that began with her blouse atop the living room couch, and ended with his boxers at the base of her closed bedroom door. Their sex sounds and the creaking of bedsprings carried throughout, and I surprised myself when I sighed involuntarily. Suddenly I had to get out of the house. I grabbed George's leash and took him for a walk, all the while mulling over the note and the rapist. They were still going at it when I returned, so I got some things for work, said a silent prayer for their success and left. I hoped they were doing the right thing—and I wondered if she'd still want mine.

Levi clamped his hand on my shoulder just as I reached the door to roll call. His stern look said everything. "Jesus, Michael. I'm your friend. Somewhere it says I'm supposed to be there for you."

"Huh?"

"The kid, Numb Nuts. Come on, it's been on the news."

I looked at him wordlessly until I finally said, "The media know that you and Natasha are making a baby?"

He peered incredulously at me and then shook his head. "No! Channel Six interviewed a bystander at that fatal. Guy heard you talking to the kid. It's big-time; slice of life an' all that. You did a helluva good job. Hey," he said as he held up a hand, "I know it comes naturally to you, but I'm still impressed."

"Thanks," I replied as we entered roll call. Most of our shift had already taken their seats, and various cliques were engaged in disjointed discussions. Jarl Jackson held court with some newbies near the back, while others cops worked on reports from the previous evening. Whoever described police work as glamorous never had to deal with the stultifying reams of paperwork that follow even the most mundane arrest. Billy Burke stood at his lectern, looking bored as the troops rolled in.

Officer Quenton Jones—a.k.a. Hacksaw Jones—swept a pile of reports to one side and bounded to his feet. "Saw the news, bro. Man, I'm damned proud of ya. Wouldn't want that job. No sir! I got soul like all brothers got soul, but not enough for that kinda act." He pumped my hand and continued, "My boy's same age as that kid. Don't know if I coulda handled any a *that*. Damn!" He blew out his cheeks, looked me up and down with renewed interest, and nodded slowly as he returned to his seat.

"Thanks, Hack." But I suddenly felt embarrassed by the attention, so I walked off and took my usual seat next to Levi. He grinned and shook his head.

Burke moved to the center of the room with the blinding speed of a slug on lithium. His perpetually wrinkled uniform needed cleaning, and his gut preceded him as he knuckled his thinning red hair. "Alright, faggots. Gimme yer eyes an' ears front 'n center." He waved a bulletin for everyone to see. "Had a couple a reported rapes last night. First one's a no-brainer; girlfriend/

boyfriend dispute. She's taken everything back. Doesn't know it yet, but she's gonna get charged with making a false report.

"The *real* rape happened sometime 'round that knockdown, drag-out at Rudy's. Victim got herself raped when a suspect as-yet-unknown got inside her condo. That was up on 142nd, by the way." He surveyed the faces before resuming. "Crept up on her from behind. Choked her out. Victim never knew what hit her." He paused as he read from the report. "Suspect bound her wrists with a bungee cord—a purple bungee cord."

Someone quipped, "A bungee fetish?"

Burke shrugged. "Anything's possible." He put down the paper and looked at us. "That's all we've got for now. You north end cars be sure an' keep an eye out."

I wondered why Lt. Santoro hadn't called for me yet. Then I leaned toward Levi to whisper, "Jesus. 'Got herself raped?' King of the Keystone Kops, that's Burke."

Levi nodded. "Real charmer. What can you expect from someone who smells like King Kong? And what's with that 'faggots' bit?"

I shrugged. "Like you said—a charmer."

Burke seemed not to notice us as he drew a long breath. "We got a long fuckin' night ahead of us, and this," he said as he picked up a news clipping, "is gonna make it longer. Anyone read today's rag? No?" He put on a pair of tiny reading glasses and stared at the clipping. "Listen to this shit. 'Ocean City officials welcomed the economic bonanza provided by the three hundred and fifty thousand vacationers who made Ocean City their destination of choice last weekend. When asked to explain how they were able to determine the number of tourists, Barney Hobart, Director of Waste Management for Ocean City, explained. Hobart told *The Atlantic Herald* that he measured the increase in solid waste flowing through the city sewage tanks, then calculated the number of tourists as a percentage of raw sewage.'"

Burke folded the paper and looked past his glasses at us as he glared. "Now isn't that fucking wonderful. Just when we need them waste-wad tourists on our side, that cocksucking Hobart tells every one a them sons-a-bitches they're pieces of shit." He angrily threw the paper to the floor. "Way to go, dickhead!"

Jarl leaned forward in his seat. "Yeah Billy, but what the fuck? In your heart of hearts, you know he's right."

Burke laughed wickedly as some others joined in. "Hell, I know that. All tourists are turds. That's not the point. Point is, I wanted something to throw in that dickhead's face come next council meeting, but this is all I've got?"

I shook my head at how easily I'd grown to accept the east coast mentality that supported this work environment. I wasn't big on political correctness, but Jesus—Burke would have been shown the door if he'd conducted such foul-mouthed roll calls on the west coast.

Burke rubbed his hands together. "Fun's over. Let's get started." He began with the ritualistic roll call. "Alston!"

Ray Alston answered with the equally ritualistic, "Yo."

Burke made a small tic mark on a notepad atop his desk. "Brennan."

"I'm here."

"Well, well, well. Mister Brennan. Got yourself in the news today, did ya?"

I scowled. "So I'm told."

Burke feigned mock surprise. "So you're told? Fuck me to death, Brennan. Were you there or weren't you? Do you need to be told what you did?"

"Yeah, something like that."

Levi elbowed me and whispered. "Don't take his shit."

"*Something like that,*" Burke mocked. "Christ, don't fuckin' cave on me. What'd you do, sing to the kid?"

"Yeah, something like that."

He snorted and nodded slowly. "Figures. You pretty boys always got songs in your hearts. Guys like you give me headaches."

"Whatever," I began. "We all get headaches." Yeah, those of us who have heads. I leaned forward and said loudly, "Wanna hear the song I wrote in honor of your selection as hippo of the year? Hey, don't you have some Munchkins to chase down?"

Burke glared and opened his mouth.

Levi beat him to it. He cleared his throat and said, "Songs always work for me." Then he stared defiantly at Burke.

"Another pretty boy with something to add."

I whispered, "You're not a pretty boy."

He grunted. "I hope not! Chiseled good looks, yes. Hell, Jarl's the pretty one."

"Hey," Burke prodded, "you guys live together, right? Scrub each other's backs, too?" His eyes narrowed. "Or maybe Hart's too busy with his little friend. You know the one … the free-roamin' spirit that showed up last night askin' for you. What's up with that? Can't find a girl? You not been getting lucky these days?"

Levi's mouth curved into an indulgent smile. "I don't get lucky. I get laid."

Burke opened his trap but then closed it, too taken aback by the legitimacy behind Levi's response; even Burke respected a true swordsman. He let it drop without so much as a rebuke, since all of us in the room accepted Levi's declaration as the indisputable fact that it was.

Burke buried his nose in his roll call list, but then he wasn't about to let it go after all. "You got anything else to add, Mister Hart?"

Levi straightened up as a smile flickered across his lean face. "Yeah, I do have something to add. The riddle of time is baffling because no one knows whether it flows past men, or whether men pass through it. For example, if you fire a rifle, does that mean that firing it is what the future was?"

Laughter rippled through the room as Burke looked up from his list. He studied Levi closely. "You tell me, smart-ass." Then he went back to his list and made a small mark.

"Be glad to," Levi said as his face turned hard. "Time *is* relevant. For example, it's time you kept your adolescent insults to yourself." He got to his feet and said loudly, "Being a supervisor doesn't give you the right to insult me or anyone else. Under normal circumstances I'd have this out with you in private, but you made your insinuations in public. I'm not questioning your authority—but don't do it again." He sat down to a sudden—and brief—round of applause.

Burke acted as if nothing had happened, but we all knew better. Although Levi had him dead to rights, Burke would get even. Burke's face flushed red as a vein stood out from his forehead. An uncomfortable silence passed until Burke continued taking roll. "Demmings!" he yelled.

"Right here, Sarge." Demmings was a tall, gaunt man with thinning brown hair and freckled skin. He'd come on the job with Burke, blasted two marriages apart, and was on his third. He had no children and he habitually spoke ill of his current wife.

Then it hit me. I nudged Levi and whispered, "Last night. Woman at the fight. One who gave me the eye. Remember?"

He studied Demmings through half-lidded eyes. "Yeah," he said beneath his breath. "His old lady."

"Right. Thought she looked familiar. Wonder what …?"

All at once Burke demanded, "What's in the bag, Demmings?" Burke looked like he'd bitten into a cherry apple as he stared at a gray nylon bag at Demmings' feet.

Demmings shifted in his chair and mumbled, "Nothing, Sarge."

"Nothing? Hell, gotta be something. Wouldn't happen to be a camera, would it?"

The room burst into raucous laughter while Demmings busily examined his fingernails. "It's a seat cushion. You know, for after you chew my ass."

Burke nodded and made a tic on his sheet. "Just be sure it ain't a camera." He put down his pen and stared directly at Demmings. "Got it?"

"Got it."

Burke fumed and said, "You're cover car tonight. Make sure an' do some sweeps through the north end. Help the sector cars on that rape thing." Then he pointed a fat finger at Levi. "By the way, Hart. Word has it the F.B.I.'s processing your application for special agent." He beamed like an egg-sucking dog. "That's so special, Hart. I do hope you get the job. Sincerely, 'cause I'll be the first to show you the door."

Levi yawned and said, "You really need more filler in your diet."

Burke frowned, picked up his pen and bellowed, "Franko!"

A dozen officers gathered around Levi when roll call broke. I half-listened as he turned the conversation toward tomorrow's planned party. Jarl appeared at my side. "Me and some others are goin' water skiing tomorrow. Wanna come?"

"Hmm, maybe." I *could* use a break in the routine, and I *might* even talk Anna into going. But something else motivated me: the rape. I already had that personal stake, and now there was the note—and we weren't getting feedback from Investigations. On the other hand, Jarl usually got the inside word on hot cases, and that made him my new best friend; I might even pull off some insider trading in exchange for a favor down the road.

"Come on," he insisted. "We can toss back some beers an' talk a little shop."

"Talk?" He'd just sealed the deal. "Sure. When and where?"

"My place. Noon. Boat's gassed an' ready to go." He paused and added, "Linda and the kids are still at her mom's. Won't be back for another three weeks. You can shower up afterward—even run 'round in the buff if ya want. Won't be nobody to see ya but me."

"What do I need to bring? Food? Beer?"

Jarl smiled and tapped my shoulder. "Just bring your bod."

"Can I invite someone?"

His eyes narrowed. "Who?"

"Girl I met today."

A shadow crossed his face. "Yeah, I guess. Bring her along."

"Thanks. What about Levi?"

He clammed up as something worked behind his dark eyes. "Nope. Won't be enough room." With that he turned his back and sauntered off.

It rained heavily until six. And during that time I answered calls, took a meal break, and prowled the north end. At seven I took an M.D.O.P. report— malicious destruction of property—from the tenant of a summer rental in the Caines Woods neighborhood. Someone—kids, probably—had dumped the malodorous contents of a trashcan all over his car. The owner indignantly pointed out a quarter inch-long scratch in the center of the roof. I know cops who would've been rolling their eyes, muttering 'whatever' under their breath. Tough. They knew the job was dangerous when they took it, and if the bad guys didn't get you, the paperwork surely would.

By nine the streets were unusually empty. I swept through the sector once more, then found a phone booth and called Anna. She seemed tired. When I asked if she felt up to some water skiing she politely declined. She had work to do, she explained, but she did accept the invitation to Levi's party. "Seven o'clock," I told her. "Assateague Island pavilion. I'll pick you up." She gave me her address.

After hanging up I parked in a vacant lot to play catch-up with the reports. I had the first one almost knocked when the crackling roar of a Harley split the night air. I looked up just as it cruised past. For some reason the driver looked in my direction, and when he did he appeared startled. He twisted the throttle and leaned into it, and as the engine growled he popped a wheelie and roared off at high speed.

"No way," I said. I tossed my report book aside, dropped the car in gear and took off in pursuit, hitting the overheads and calling out the high-speed chase. "Seventy-three-oh-nine with a 10-80. Southbound Coastal from 139th. Black and silver Harley. Driver's a white male adult; forties; no helmet. Speed in excess of seventy." The road was wet and slick as a duck's ass. Fortunately, traffic was sparse. I pushed the cruiser to eighty in the forty-mile zone.

"Headquarters to all units. 10-80. Southbound Coastal from 139th Street... ."

The dispatcher's voice faded as I focused on the Harley. Blue lights lit my rear-view as others joined the pursuit. More blue lights danced far ahead as units set up a roadblock. I was considering ending the chase—at these speeds it wasn't worth it—when the dispatcher came back on.

"All units, be advised, armed robbery just occurred, Ritchie's Mini Mart at 146th Street ... suspect's a white male adult, armed with a handgun. Last seen southbound Coastal Highway on a black and silver motorcycle."

Jesus—this was the guy! The Harley pulled away.

I kept it at eighty.

The Harley jigged to the right, then to the left.

I pressed on.

The bike's rear tire began to fishtail, giving me the opening I needed. I stomped down on the gas and keyed the mike. "Seventy-two-oh-four's passing 98th in excess of eighty. Suspect still in sight."

The driver kicked it and sped up.

"Fucker!" I screamed.

All at once a blaze of lights erupted from 77th Street as the Battlestar Gallactica lunged across the highway and shuddered to a stop, effectively blocking the road.

The Harley slowed, then slowed some more.

"Got you now," I yelled, and stomped on the gas.

The driver feinted to the left, then executed a hard right onto the 79th Street sidewalk. I spun my wheel furiously, but the cruiser swerved drunkenly on the wet pavement. Hitting the brake was out of the question, so I mashed the gas to the floorboard, instead. The cruiser straightened smartly. I turned onto 79th and closed the distance. But he was on the sidewalk, and I was on the street. I looked quickly. A six-foot high chain-link fence ran parallel to the sidewalk on his right.

Maybe.

I drew next to him; I spun my wheel to the right; the cruiser hit the curb with a bang; I was sure I'd blown a tire, but I made it onto the sidewalk. Then I shot forward, crossed in front of the Harley, and cut off his escape. I leapt out, drew my pistol and raced toward him as he tried desperately to push himself backwards.

I leveled my pistol at him. "Hands in the air! Do it now!"

He looked right at me—but remained motionless.

"Hands in the air," I yelled.

He glared defiantly. I stepped forward, aimed straight for his nose and growled, "Get your hands up and get 'em up now."

His arms went slowly up as Jarl screeched to a halt. Jarl dashed forward, got behind the suspect, and roughly wrenched his arms behind his back and cuffed him.

I was pumped on adrenaline and breathing heavily as I holstered my pistol. I frisked him thoroughly and found a nickel-plated .32 revolver with faux pearl handgrips stuck in his waistband. Checking further, I located a switchblade in his right boot. Both items confirmed his punk-status in my eyes. The Battlestar took him away and some of the troops stood around and chatted until the excitement died. After they drifted away I impounded his 'machine' and finally smiled. I'd made a good arrest and it was a beautiful thing. When Johnny cruised past and waved I felt even better; it's always nice when local citizens see their police at work. I had to hand it to Johnny—he sure did have a way of staying on top of things.

An inverse rule of police work kicked in: the bigger the crime, the faster the booking process. I wrote my reports in less than an hour. Armed robbery is a felony, so the investigators would handle the legwork. I merely dashed off a supplemental to capture my actions in the arrest, and cited the driver for fleeing and eluding, reckless driving and speeding. Then I hit the streets with an hour remaining. Sure, the arrest gave me a warm and fuzzy, but I still wanted that rapist. I keyed the mike: "Seventy-three-on-nine's 10-8."

Levi's voice crackled right away. *"Seventy-three-oh-nine, meet me at Jolly Roger."*

I turned south on Coastal and headed toward the Jolly Roger Amusement Park on 28th Street, a favored meeting place by virtue of its deserted rear lot. I arrived five minutes later and pulled alongside Levi.

"Good job on that robbery suspect," he said by way of greeting.

"Thanks. Broke the night up." We chuckled at the understatement.

Levi slumped low in his seat and blew air from his cheeks. "I'm beat. Glad this is our Friday. I need some time off. Party's coming at the right time."

I settled back. "Roger that. Can't wait to get home tonight. I can use some booze and a snooze. By the way, I've been invited to go skiing tomorrow."

Levi's eyebrows knotted together. "Don't tell me. Jarl Jackson."

"Yeah. Why, is that a problem?"

"Not really, unless you care to count his unbridled hatred of me."

I looked at him with interest. "I've never asked, but what is it between you two?"

He shrugged. "Ahh, who knows? Maybe he's jealous. You know, married guy wanting the freedom of single guys. Remember that guy from college? Played water polo with us?"

"Barney," I said. "Hated his wife and he was pissed 'cause you swam like a fish."

Levi nodded. "That's the one. Same deal." He squinted. "Let's just say that I make an effort to be civil when I'm around Jarl, otherwise I keep him at arm's length." Levi looked sidelong at me and fidgeted with his turn signal. Then he said, "Michael, I didn't get a chance to tell you this earlier." He paused and chewed his lower lip before continuing. "I really admire you."

"Yeah? Why's that?""

"The way you are around people; you know, like with that kid."

"Aw, come on. I did what anybody would've done."

He faced me directly. Then in a voice filled with conviction he said, "Bullshit. You don't have to be modest. Not with me. Hell, I saw the news. I heard what went on inside that car." Levi reached across the gulf that separated our cruisers and tapped his finger against my forearm. "Jarl couldn't have handled it in a million years."

I snorted. "Probably not. Never did trust those closet commando types."

Levi sneered. "For sure that asshole Burke wouldn't have made the effort. He'd have called for a wrecker, then stood back and wound his watch."

"Burke. He needs help, that one. Maybe a book on how-to-grow-the-fuck-up would set him straight."

Levi chuckled and stared through his windshield. "Trouble is, he's one of those who thinks you find *Mein Kampf* in the self-help section. He's definitely the type of guy they make guns for."

I turned serious for a moment. "I don't blame you for setting him straight tonight, but aren't you afraid he'll try an' screw you out of a Fed job?"

His face got that hard look again. "He won't. That'd upset his plan."

"And that is?"

"To see me out of here."

I nodded. "Yeah. Probably. Damn. I sure don't wanna see you leave, but I don't blame you. This is a dead-end place for someone with your energy. Hey," I said as something occurred to me, "ever see Burke's place? What a hole. I mean, Shad Landing. What kind of name is that?"

Levi laughed and said, "Yeah, I've seen it. Nothing but a swamp. What the hell is a shad, anyway?"

"A fish. Bottom feeder, I think. Goes upriver to spawn."

"That's Burke, all right ... a freakin' bottom feeder. Living near the swamps must've done something to him, 'cause he's one *bain dramaged* son of a bitch."

"Agreed. That sum-bitch is crazy, and has papers to prove it."

He looked away. "Crazy or not, he'd better not mess with me."

I nodded. "Wouldn't be a wise thing to do."

"I'm like Israel. I might be small, but I'm nuclear capable."

I burst out in laughter. "You've got that right, *mi amigo*. You are one tough stud, and I'm proud to have you as my best friend."

He toyed with the switch on his spotlight and said quietly, "Michael? I love you like you were my brother. Especially now, after what I saw on the news today." He regarded me with a handsome mask of a face as he waited for me to say something.

I rubbed the end of my nose and stared straight ahead. I didn't know what to say. His naked honesty disturbed me; Hollywood vs. certain realities aside, Levi showed no fear in a world where guys would rather eat dirt than tell another guy—even their best friend—how they felt, so I stared at him and said nothing for a while. Finally I asked, "What makes me any different than before?"

He looked at me evenly and said, "Because now I see your heart. I've always known that about you, but I needed to see it. Now I feel safe around you."

"Safe? What do you mean?" I narrowed my eyes at him. "You trying to tell me something? Are you in trouble?"

Levi took his time answering. Then he said quietly, "Maybe all it means is that now, whenever I see you, I see a hero."

I sat still, unsure how to respond or whether I even should. "Thanks," I finally said. "I'm not sure why, but that's probably the greatest compliment I've ever gotten. I gotta tell you, I don't know what to say."

Levi studied me for a long time before replying. "You don't have to say anything. I understand you a lot more than you think. It's okay. Only ..."

"Only?"

He looked at me with a face that was compassionate, troubled, and still. "Only, if I was ever in trouble, you—you'd stay with me the way you did that kid ... wouldn't you?"

Levi seemed lost, enveloped by a sense of desperation that I knew so well, yet one that I'd never seen in him. I sorted through our adventures: I enlisted in the Army at seventeen, did three years, got out and went to college on a G.I. loan. That's when we met. He and I got an apartment with two others, and Levi tutored me the whole way through. I graduated with a low "A" compared to his 4.0, but it marked a turning point for me. Then he coached me through the police academy. I should have followed-through and gone after my master's, as he had—but I hadn't. We grew to be best friends, and when he gave me his St. Michael's that Christmas Eve, our friendship was permanently bonded. As ocean mist rolled past our cruisers I turned and said, "You're my bro, Levi—I'll always be there for you."

He nodded. "Like when Nat lost the baby. Yeah. Thanks."

I drew a deep breath. "Anytime."

"Umm, bro? Thanks for cluing me in on Nat. I know you still have a thing for her. And you know I wanna give her my child in the worst way. Anyway, thanks."

I said glibly, "She *wants* your child, and why shouldn't my best friends make each other happy? Now let's talk some shop," I said before he could reply. "Found something on my car today. Tell me what you think." I described the note and my subsequent conversation with Detective Katie Smith. We tossed it back and forth but neither of us could make much sense of it. Levi tended to agree that it sounded like a nut case, but the cop in him forced him to yield to the possibility that it could be the rapist, taunting me for some bizarre reason. I finally said, "I'm gonna nab that cockroach."

Levi looked at me, his face at an oblique angle and darkened by shadow. Quietly he said, "Not if I get him first."

"Yeah?" I asked with real interest. "What's *your* beef with him?"

He stared at me solemnly for several long seconds until finally he whispered, "Maybe I know someone who was raped. Okay?"

We ran into each other in the parking lot after end-of-shift, a time when half the guys—myself included—changed from police duds into more casual stuff. I gave him a once-over; he had on a good shirt, expensive trousers and—most unusual for him—shoes. I glanced down at my standard T, shorts and flip-flops and said, "Damn! What're you dressed-up for?"

Levi flicked his eyes toward the north end of town, shifted from one foot to the other and licked his lips before saying. "Nat's goin' out with some girlfriends tonight. It's someone's birthday an' she wants to indulge in a few glasses of wine before she's pregnant." He fidgeted and said, "We started trying today and she'll be ovulating for sure by tomorrow, so tonight will be her last chance to drink." He looked away. "She's staying overnight so she won't have to drive. Umm, I'm heading out to do some partying of my own."

I snorted. "I can see that, Toejam. Where?"

He didn't smile when he replied, "Just out. Clubs are still open and—and now I feel like getting my ashes hauled."

"Don't you wanna save it for Nat?"

"I've got plenty to spare. Hey," he said irritably, "I wanna get laid tonight. That okay with you?"

I put up my hands in mock self-defense. "Sure, sure. That's cool." I scuffed my flip-flop against the rough pavement and said, "Why not see Jen?"

He pursed his lips and said, "She wants a child. She'll raise it on her own, but that's not the problem. I don't wanna have a kid with her." He grimaced. "I told her Nat and I are trying again. Jen's cool with it, but now she wants one more than ever.'"

"Certainly sounds determined."

He grunted. "I don't feel like hassling with her. Not tonight."

I shrugged. "Sounds reasonable. So where're you going? Any place special?"

Levi looked away and said, "Why do you ask?"

"Jesus, I don't know! Just making conversation. What's with the hostility?"

He stared at me, said nothing else, then started toward his car.

"Hey," I called out. When he stopped and looked over his shoulder at me I lowered my voice and said, "Ibba da?"

He stood mute and cracked a smile to signify victory, but then his face turned solemn again. With that he walked away and drove off in his black Firebird.

As he disappeared around the corner I pondered my next move. Maybe he had the best idea—go out and meet someone nice. A fleeting thought—I'd give Anna a call. Or maybe I'd hit one of my local hangouts, see what was up. Or, just go home and watch a movie. I had *Mister Roberts* sitting atop the VCR. I loved the great interaction between William Powell and Henry Fonda aboard the U.S.S Reluctant, and there was nothing finer than watching old Hank as he tossed Jimmy Cagney's stinking palm tree overboard. But none of those would do. Something was eating at me, and on a whim I jumped in my car and drove toward Coastal Highway. The night's action had gotten me psyched. First there was that high-speed chase in pursuit of an armed robber, with all the attendant possibilities of going to guns with him. And then of course there was the note and the hunt for a rapist. It all amounted to a testament of why I pinned on a badge each day—it was exciting work, and there was the real possibility of catching bad ass hombres. Roaming the side streets and poking around would be a healthy way to unwind—and I might even spot that shit head rapist before he hurt someone else.

I turned north, and a few minutes later the Club Montage popped into view on the east side of Coastal. It was a singles bar with plenty of action, and some movement in a dark corner of the parking lot caught my eye. I slowed down and was surprised to find Levi talking to someone beneath the shadows—and damned if it wasn't the guy that had called out to him at Rudy's. They seemed locked in deep conversation.

Whatever. I got off the main drag and cruised the dark neighborhoods. I'd lost track of time when a dark blue Nova drifted slowly through an unlit intersection. I knew that car. I got behind it and flashed my headlights. The driver pulled to the curb and we got out and met between the cars.

A slight smile tugged at Quenton 'Hacksaw' Jones' lips, his teeth bright against his coffee-colored skin. "Out lookin' too, I see."

"Of course."

"An' we'll find him, sure as the hands on a clock go 'round."

I smiled. I'd always liked him; he could find laughter when others saw only dark spots. "Think we're the only ones who care?"

He shrugged. "Saw Demmings drive by a while back. 'Course, he mighta just been on his way home. Never did know him to care 'bout nothin' but himself."

I nodded. We had our portable radios and promised to call if either of us spotted anything unusual. We'd get this bastard. Maybe not tonight, or even the next, but as Hack put it, catching him was only a matter of time. We chatted a few more minutes and then went in separate directions.

I cruised the back streets until nearly two and thought about Hack. He had a way about him, an indefinable something that I'd labeled *Quenton Cool*. When our friendship developed I altered his name to 'Hacksaw' Jones—Hack, for short. The appellation suited him: he worked part time as a locksmith.

*　　*　　*

He watched silently as she left the Club Montage. She was blonde, tall and lithe, and a pleasant looking guy accompanied her. He waited in his dark car beneath the shadowed overhang of the gas station across the street, studying them as the boyfriend led her to a car. She got in and started the engine and waited until the guy climbed into his car. Then she drove off and the boyfriend followed.

So did he.

She parked in front of a small stucco house in the north end and he drifted past as the boyfriend parked behind her. Then he pulled over half a block away and watched in his mirror as the boyfriend walked her to the door. They talked until she pushed her arms gently against his chest. After he stepped away she opened the door and went in alone. The rejected suitor lingered momentarily, then got in his car and drove off.

He waited ten more minutes before getting out of his car, and by sticking to the shadows he approached the house unseen. He watched with an animal patience until he felt satisfied. Then he crept around to the postage-stamp rear yard and went to the patio door. He got it open without a sound.

She was alone and already asleep on the couch, snoring from a drink-induced weariness. He crept slowly; time was his ally. Finally he leapt forward, clamped a hand over her eyes and wrapped an arm around her neck. Then he rendered her unconscious in the time it took her body to start with a jump. He blindfolded her and tied her hands behind her back with a purple bungee cord.

He raped this girl from behind, his hand clamped against the back of her neck as she began moaning. As she regained consciousness he jammed her head hard against the carpeted floor. When she began to cry he crashed both fists against her face. He dared not say anything, for fear she might recognize his voice on the nearly impossible chance that he'd be taken in as a suspect. But hitting her? Better that way; better to let her know who the boss was; better that she should learn not to cry or whimper or plead for mercy.

When she didn't 'get it' after the first blows caved-in her left cheek bone, he pummeled her breasts with his fists, powerful hammer blows designed to leave her bruised and incapable of having another man interested in her for a long time. Let's see her turn away suitors *now*.

After her whimpers died away he flipped her onto her back and tried to rape her again, but he remained flaccid. That pissed him off. A surge of anger flashed through him, so he kicked her viciously in her buttocks. Then he left the same way he got in.

CHAPTER 4

THE next morning I found George curled in front of Levi's open door, and one glance inside revealed that his bed hadn't been slept in. Natasha's room was also empty, her bed neatly made. I leaned against her doorframe and wondered where she and I might be headed—and whether it might already be too late.

I had breakfast, called Anna, fed George and let him outside. While I waited for him I wondered about the rapes. I was off the next two days—two days when I could be hunting the rapist. But experience taught me that foundations are laid in the strangest ways; links fall into place—links leading to resolutions too abstract to see from close perspectives. Jarl might inadvertently provide a connection, one born of an innocuous ski party. It was time to head to Jarl's.

George scratched at the door and I let him inside on my way out. As I reached my car a horn honked and Levi turned into the driveway. He climbed out of his black Firebird and greeted me with a smile and a casual wave, wearing only a pair of green and yellow flowered shorts that hung loosely from his hips, a thin shell necklace that gleamed against his tanned neck, and a braided black cord around his right ankle.

"Nice look," I began as he ambled toward me, "for a sixteen year-old." I gave him another once-over and said, "Your foot's bleeding. What happened?"

He looked down at his dusty bare feet and shrugged. "Dunno. Must've stepped on something."

"You're a mess." Then I thought of something. "Where're the clothes you had on last night?"

He yawned and said tiredly. "Left 'em someplace. Can't remember where."

"Wait a minute. What about your badge, your I.D.?"

He chuckled deep in his throat. "Just messin' with you. Stuff's in my car. Went for a swim."

As I climbed into my Mustang I asked, "So where'd you end up?"

"Rehoboth."

"All the way up there?"

He stepped forward and stood next to my half-open door. "Yeah. Went to Club Montage first but there wasn't any action. Then I felt like dancing. So I went to Rehoboth."

A burst of humid air rustled through the trees as I asked, "Gay or straight?"

"Started out straight, ended up gay."

I nodded in complete understanding. While our childhoods might have been polar opposites, we'd been exposed to these realities: great dancing can be found in gay clubs, and the clubs are frequented by beautiful straight women in search of good looking guys who can dress *and* dance, but make no sexual advances. The irony is that the women often did sleep with their dance partners, in the flawed belief that even gay men were incapable of resisting their beauty. But those dance partners aren't necessarily gay; plenty of straight studs frequent the clubs and let the girls think what they want. I discovered this reality by virtue of the gay and lesbian friends I'd had while growing up on the streets, friends who unfailingly respected the fact that I was straight, while I championed their right to live life on their terms. My gay friends kept me company in straight clubs, and I ventured into gay and lesbian venues without a second thought. Girls assumed I was gay and asked to dance, and after a night of great sex they believed they'd transformed me into a confirmed hetero. Manipulative? Maybe, but all parties came away satisfied, so where was the harm? Levi followed my lead long ago, and Rehoboth Beach, Delaware, boasts an active gay nightlife. "What's her name?" I asked.

Levi wrinkled his brow. "Her name?"

"Yeah, Toecheese. Last night. You usually hook-up with someone."

His eyes drifted away. "I don't know." He laughed. "Guess I forgot already."

I glanced at the congealed blood on his foot. "Shoes. Girls. Pretty interchangeable, is that what you're trying to say?"

He smiled disarmingly. "Bare feet, bare naked girls. Yeah, I see your point."

"Your only point is between your legs, Butt Wipe. Seriously, was it anyone I know? Come on. Break loose with some details."

Levi shook his head doggedly as another breeze pushed a large cloud over-head. "Not this time, pal."

I grabbed his elbow. "Hey, wait a sec. What's with the secrets?"

A shadow fell across his face as he pulled away and began walking toward the house. "Not this time, Michael." But then he stopped and turned. "Hey, you don't think I'm shallow, do you? I mean, fuck ... not after all these years?" He briefly studied the ground between us and said, "Sure, I like my fun. Who doesn't? But there's more to me than that, and you know it." Then he added crossly, "At least Nat sees that side of me."

"Hey, come on. I ..."

Levi looked around impatiently, "Where the hell is she, anyway? I only rushed home because she's dropping an egg an' wants me to ..." He stared at the ground for a few seconds and said, "I need some shut-eye. She knows the way to my bed."

I said in a sudden, harsh voice, "God forbid you should do her any favors."

He stared at me and blurted, "Fuck you. It's my kid she wants, not ..." He looked away and kicked at the loose gravel.

"You scrawny fuck! I'll knock you into next week!" He mumbled some-thing in response, and as he turned and stormed inside I said, "You son of a bitch! I don't know what crawled up your ass, but you'd better get it disen-gaged!" Grumbling, I started the car and drove slowly away. "Where the hell does he get off? Ah, fuck it!"

*   *   *

"Son of a bitch," he muttered as he went to the toilet to urinate. All at once he thought of that bitch he'd done last night and how he punished her; how it felt to land those blows. He was startled from the image when his stream splashed against the toilet tank. He adjusted and sighed. "Maybe I'll smack another bitch tonight!"

*   *   *

Jarl's four-bed, three-bath waterfront home sat on Assawoman Bay, slightly upstream from its convergence with Sinepuxent Bay. Two vehicles were parked next to Jarl's red Ford Ranger—a white Chevy Impala and Roy Townsend's black Ram pick-up. Jarl stepped from the front door and bounded down the steps as I locked the 'stang. "You made it! Was startin' to worry." He looked expectantly at me. "Thought you were bringing a date."

"Other plans. She'll be at tonight's party."

He flashed white teeth and somehow seemed relieved that I'd arrived solo. We stood in awkward silence until I asked, "Who else is going?"

"Couple a others. Come on," he said as he turned toward the steps. "Get changed and we'll get going." He took me to a second floor bedroom and lingered as I took off my shirt. When he finally left, I changed into black and white surfer jams, grabbed my shades and found my way to the back yard, where the air was still, the heat, stifling.

"There's our pretty boy," Jarl called out. He looked me over and said, "Good thing Linda's away. She'd have her hands all over you."

I nodded and smiled at Roy Townsend, a surly, overweight paramedic. Then I looked at the thirty-something blonde at his side and did a double take: it was Demmings' wife. She stared expectantly at me with a smile that seemed applied with a fence brush.

I walked over and said, "Hi. We've never been introduced. Michael Brennan. Pleased to meet you."

She played her fingers against Roy's thigh and said, "Hello, Michael. I'm Donna, and I'm *very* pleased to meet you."

I picked up bad vibes from the get-go. "How come?"

She tilted her head back and laughed. "Come now. There're no secrets in this town. I've heard a lot about you." Then she shifted gears. "Nice thing what you did for that kid the other day … I think you'd make a great daddy."

The conversation needed to end and I felt grateful when Jarl clapped his hands together. "It's hotter 'n hell, so let's get going. Here." He reached inside a dockside cooler and got a frosty bottle of Bass Ale. "Might as well toss one down."

I popped the cap and took a long pull. Then I asked, "Hey, what do you hear about that latest rape? Come on, you always get the inside word."

He looked at me and shrugged. "Fuck work; we're here to have fun." Then Jarl turned his back and worked to get the boat ready. The old Glastron had a souped-up Volvo inboard/outboard, scarlet seats, and a metallic purple paint job. I've never been one to peer inside the gift horse's mouth, but the boat stuck out like Pee Wee Herman in a biker bar. Jarl finally announced, "Time to get it on."

He turned the ignition and the engine caught with a puff of blue exhaust. It chugged uncertainly as he nursed the throttle, then settled into a dull rumble. Jarl juiced the gas and we moved slowly until we cleared the dock. Then he fire-walled the throttle and we surged ahead, leaving a broad rooster tail to define our wake. The sun sparkled on the water and warmed my shoulders, and the steady thrum of the engine's vibrations felt good against my feet. As I leaned forward for balance I had a strong sense of being alive. The wind swept my hair, the bay smelled pungent and all seemed well with my world.

Donna smiled at me as she made her way to the front. She leaned intimately against Jarl and whispered in his ear, and then Jarl looked over his shoulder at me and smiled. Donna patted his backside and then sat next to Roy, and it was from this vantage point that she stared at me with a shopper's appraising eye.

Jarl chopped the throttle and the boat slowed ponderously until it finally stopped. Jarl heaved the ski line overboard. "Who's first?" Roy jumped in without a word and swam to the end of the line. He got the skis on, gave the thumbs-up, and Jarl slammed the throttle forward. Roy wavered, teetered precariously, but finally got his balance. We dragged him up and down the Assawoman while he braced, grimaced, and fought the skis. After only ten minutes he drew a finger across his neck and dropped the line.

Jarl maneuvered toward him with one hand on the wheel, the other wrapped around a beer. He stared at Roy. "You ski the way old people fuck, you know that?"

Roy peered up from the usual detritus of the muddy bay and spit a stream of water at him. "Guilty as charged. So shut the fuck up an' gimme a brewski."

Donna went next. She rose expertly from the sluggish water and dazzled us with her smile as she leaned back. The line drew taut and turned her arms into slender shafts of bronze. Tiny, feminine ripples of muscle showed beneath her skin as her hair trailed behind, shedding sparkling droplets of water. Cop's wife or not, she was a looker. Donna pushed down on her right ski and zoomed to the left, the skis slapping the ripples as she worked the line's inertia into a half-circle, until finally she drew abreast of us. The instant her line grew slack she stepped down hard on her left ski and zipped off in the opposite direction. "Great," she shouted. "Love it."

After a while Donna signaled that she'd had her fill. She released the line and sank majestically into the bay. "Wonderful," she proclaimed as we came alongside. "Best fun I've had all day." She swam to the boarding ladder and I went to help her. She handed up her skis and climbed aboard, giving me an eye-full of cleavage. She caught me staring and suppressed a smile.

I handed her a towel. "You're a terrific skier."

"Thanks. I'll bet you're a terrific player … I mean, skier, yourself." Donna laughed un-self consciously as she toweled herself.

We skied for two hours. I took a turn in the water, then Jarl. Roy made another desultory attempt at skiing. After Donna plunged in for a cooling swim, Jarl looked meaningfully at her and Roy and announced, "That's enough. Let's go home and see what we can get into." He took us back at full throttle, the wind stinging our faces as the Glastron protested every wave.

Donna struggled to keep her balance as she came to my side and put her mouth to my ear. I could feel her warm breath as she said, "You have beautiful eyes. Lovely skin, too." As I turned, her hand brushed the front of my jams. She whisked me again, stared defiantly into my eyes and purred, "Bare chest, bare legs—soon to be bare bottom?"

I said evenly, "I see you use sex as an icebreaker."

She brushed me a third time. "What was that? Don't think I quite got it."

After a heartbeat I replied, "Oh, I think you got it for sure that time."

Donna smiled sweetly. Roy stood less than a yard away, and if he saw anything he didn't seem to care. But I did. I didn't play around with married women and I especially didn't screw with a brother cop's wife. I started to back away when she brushed my crotch yet again. This time she let her hand linger. A surge of adrenaline coursed through my body and struck deep into my knees as she got quite a handful—and then she abruptly pulled it away. It usually happened that way. God knows why; it shouldn't be the size or functionality of my penis that mattered, only its friendliness—but I sensed no friendship here.

I said glibly, "Not enough there for you? Gosh, and I'm so into sharing."

Her mouth fell open. "*Enough*? I …"

"It's like this. You're married to a cop and I have a girlfriend. I don't think with the head of my cock, and I'm not interested in your vagina. Are we done now?"

She squinted and said, "My, aren't we full of ourselves?" Then she looked beyond me and whispered, "I wouldn't worry about my husband." A flash of misery crossed her features. "He stopped taking an interest in me long ago."

I nodded somberly and said, "That's unfortunate, but ..."

Donna put a finger to my mouth. "But nothing. Don't worry. You've made your point. I envy your girlfriend. She's a lucky girl. Just be sure and call if things don't work out, so I can fuck your socks off." She smiled with a kittenish quality that would have been a turn-on any other time and added, "One more thing. Tell me you'll think of me whenever you touch yourself." Her laughter filled the boat as she sat next to Roy. He put a hand on her thigh and showed white teeth as he smiled at me.

Jarl docked ten minutes later and I wasted little time getting out of the boat. Jarl's house had three baths. Roy disappeared upstairs and commandeered the first, while Donna took the second for herself. I was content to just get my clothes and split, but Jarl pointed me toward the master bedroom and said, "Use ours. I don't mind waiting."

I hesitated and then said, "Yeah, why not?" I jumped in the shower and finished five minutes later, thinking I'd make a quick exit. I had the towel to my eyes when the door burst open. A rush of cold air sliced through the steam as I thought, *Christ, don't let it be Donna.*

Jarl entered instead, closing the door behind him. "Whoa," he exclaimed as his eyes dropped to my crotch. "Jesus, Michael! You're hung like a fucking *horse.* Must be more'n twelve fucking inches." He appraised me again. "Damn! More like fourteen!"

"Hmm. Yeah. Probably."

His eyes were still riveted to my waist. "How come you never got circumcised?"

"Christ, Jarl." I wondered if he could comprehend poverty so all-encompassing that my folks couldn't afford to have me cut. Now he'd struck a raw nerve. The day had already turned sour; I didn't need to be reminded that I was trailer-trash on top of everything else. Finally I said, "Would you give a dime's worth of damn if I asked, what the fuck's it matter?"

Jarl held his hands up and said, "Calm down. I ain't seen that many anteaters. I'm curious, that's all." He licked his lips and whistled softly. "Man, that thang's something. How many times a week do ya dip that wick?"

"I don't know," I replied as I wrapped the towel around me. "Three, four times. What the hell do you care?" I cinched the towel tighter, combed my fingers through my damp hair and hoped he'd get off the topic.

He pouted. "No need to get pissed." Then he stepped closer and lowered his voice. "Hey, you're cool, aren't you?"

"I like to think so. Why?"

Jarl looked around conspiratorially. "Linda an' the kids are gone, see? They won't be back for another week."

"I know. So?"

He lowered his voice another notch and smiled. "Donna's gonna pull the train. You'll do her first, I'll take sloppy seconds and Roy gets thirds."

I shook my head. "Not interested."

He frowned. "Why the fuck not? Don't tell me you've never done no tag-team action. Come on. Good lookin' guy like you?"

"Been asked, but it's never interested me. Besides, I don't mess with wives." I gave him a direct look. "She's a brother officer's wife, Jarl. I'm surprised at you."

He folded his hands together and stood like a solemn prelate "She wants you to do her, so stow the sermon 'bout married broads an' go fuck her brains out."

This was turning stupid. "No. Thanks for asking, but I'm outta here." I made a move toward the door, but Jarl edged to the right and blocked the way. Something clicked inside me as I said in a low voice, "Move, Jarl."

"You don't understand," he whined while moving aside. "She won't do me an' Roy unless you fuck her first. Goddamn it, do it for us at least."

Now I knew why Jarl had insisted on my coming along, and it pissed me off that he'd snookered me in as a set-up. I let the towel fall away, pulled the wet jams back on and shouldered my way into the bedroom.

Jarl frowned. "Christ, what're you doing? Come on. Take 'em off. Fuck, man—she's already undressed. She's in the hallway with Roy."

I looked at the ceiling and said, "This is too bizarre. I'm out of here." I went to the door and yanked it open, and sure enough they both stood naked on the other side.

Donna opened her mouth but I brushed past them and took the stairs two at a time. My hands shook from anger as I swung the door open and stepped into the humidity and sunshine and birdsong, noticing for the first time how deathly silent the house had been.

I banged my car into gear and drove off, still so pissed that I'd gone two miles before I realized that I'd left my clothes behind. "Screw it," I said aloud, and pushed harder on the accelerator. Let Jarl and Donna fight over them.

*   *   *

He knew he had a way with the ladies and that he could have one whenever he wanted. But where was the fun in that? Then the urge struck him hard the instant he thought about *her*. He'd loved her the moment he met her but she never returned the feeling. It had hurt him; it had pissed him off. He would have to hunt down the next one.

*   *   *

I turned onto 142nd Street at precisely seven o'clock and parked in front of Anna's brown, two-story ocean-side condo. She greeted me at the door. She had on a jade-green blouse open at the neck to highlight her dark skin, and black slacks that embraced her long legs to just below her knees. The sides of her slender, unblemished calves touched mine as she leaned forward and kissed my cheek. Her shiny black hair smelled wonderful. She stepped back and took in my partially buttoned shirt, loose shorts and Diadora running shoes, and said despairingly, "Dressed for the beach, I see."

We left immediately. The car magnified her odors, and everything about her smelled pleasant. Her aroma was of citrus, like a freshly cut pear. I shifted gears at a light and weaved elegantly through the traffic, the pleasure of Anna next to me making the time pass unnoticed as we set off for Assateague.

Assateague Island; it's as long as its name and twice as narrow. It's a barrier island that lies due south of Ocean City, home to great expanses of unblemished beaches and the legendary wild ponies of Assateague and Chincoteague. The State of Maryland transformed the northern point into a rustic park, and a large pavilion loomed majestically along the leeward side of the dunes—close to the ocean, far from campers. The pavilion offered restrooms, electricity and solitude—the perfect venue for a cop party.

We pulled to a stop. There was barbecue in the air, and a boom box belted out some vintage Billy Joel. Levi detached himself from a knot of revelers to greet us. He wore a white polo shirt with a flipped-up collar outside of olive drab fatigues, and the legs were rolled up to just above his typically bare feet. He raised his eyebrows at me, and when I nodded to signify closure of the morning's tiff he beamed and went to Anna's door. "So good to see you again! Glad you could make it." He embraced her, draped an arm around her and walked her toward the party. "Can't wait to introduce you to Jen."

Jennifer waved to us from the small crowd, and I double-clutched when I saw someone step from behind her. I wasn't disturbed, just surprised.

"Oh," Levi said cheerfully as we approached them. "And this is Natasha."

Natasha's shapeless black dress reached below her knees. Its fringes brushed the tops of her Doc Martens, and the ensemble offset her orange hair perfectly. I could only admire her wry attempt to blend in with the beach-casual crowd. She glanced at Levi, and they exchanged a private smile as she touched splayed fingers beneath her navel. Then she bravely stuck out her hand to Anna and said, "Hi ya," in a nasal twang.

Was Natasha being rude, down-home, or had I made her uncomfortable by being seen with another woman? I pushed them together and excused myself—it was time to duck and cover so I went in pursuit of some beers. Levi had filled a large galvanized tub with ice, and an assortment of blue, green, brown and clear beer bottles sparkled beneath the pavilion's incandescent lights. I plunged my hands in and grabbed five bottles.

"Thanks," Anna said as I handed her an ice cold Bass. She put it to her forehead and sighed. I handed the other Bass to Levi, gave a Corona to Jennifer and presented a Rhino Chaser to Natasha, since she loved micro-brews. I took the other Rhino Chaser for myself, because I liked the taste. Natasha and Anna seemed to hit it off, and Jennifer had fallen right in with them.

Levi took me aside. Barbecue smoke wafted past as he tapped my arm and said, "Sorry for being a total asshole today. I've got stuff on my mind. Sorry, bro."

"Impotence would get anyone uptight," I said with a straight face. Before he could respond I said hurriedly, "It's okay. Nat told me you can't get it up anymore, but don't sweat it—your secret's safe with me."

He grinned. "Kiss my ass, Brennan." Then he looked sideways at me. "Let's not turn this into a Kodak moment, but I am sorry."

I acknowledged him and we rejoined the girls. Anna touched my arm and said she was going to the ladies room. As she walked off Jennifer mumbled something to Natasha, and she replied, "I just don't think she's good enough for him. If you ask me, she's a snooty dame who would pretend to order a Pina Colada, when what she really wants is a penis erectus." Jennifer burst into laughter, and as they moved away I frowned and shook my head. The day had been turning south since morning; how much worse could it get?

Anna returned as more guests arrived. By nine there were fifty people in clusters of three to six each. At one point Natasha leaned toward Jennifer and whispered something. Then she placed her palm to her abdomen and flicked her eyes toward Levi. Both girls laughed conspiratorially. A moment later Natasha struck up a conversation with another cop while Levi, Jennifer, Anna and I stood in a loose knot and chatted with the guests. Some of the cops discussed the merits of the investigators assigned to the rapes, but the topics were generally light.

A tall cadaverous woman in her fifties stepped next to Levi. Grace Martin worked in Records, smoked like a fiend, and flitted about when rushed. She smiled at Anna, placed a hand on her hip, and leaned toward Levi. "I probably shouldn't tell you this, but I'm so damned mad, so here it is." She looked over her shoulder. "I was in Communications yesterday and who do you suppose was there?"

Levi shook his head. "I don't know."

She pointed a finger at his chest. "That Priscilla woman, that's who! And I don't have to tell you how *she* is, or do I?" Levi was shaking his head when Natasha joined us. Grace pulled a Benson & Hedges Menthol Light from a crumpled green pack and lit it. "Captain Leaks was also there." She arched her eyebrows knowingly as she exhaled a steady stream of blue smoke.

Anna looked at me quizzically. I put my lips against her ear. "Tell you later."

Grace touched Levi's forearm with a long, nicotine-stained index finger. "*Well*. Captain Leaks was praising you for locking up those Bugs the other night. Said you're a good man with your fists."

"Thanks for the scoop. Never hurts to know what the captain thinks."

She tapped his forearm again. "No. I haven't finished." Grace lowered her voice. "That so-and-so Priscilla turns right around and says to him, she says, 'What'd you expect? Levi's like all them damn Jew Boys. Ain't good for nothing, but they know how to fight.' And what do you suppose Leaks did?"

She folded her arms across her chest, then leaned back and surveyed us as cigarette smoke swirled around her head.

Levi put his hand on Jennifer's neck and caressed it with the tips of his long fingers. "I haven't the faintest."

"Well. Leaks stood right there in front of God and all His witnesses and laughed. He just laughed. What do you think of that?"

"I think it sucks," he said reasonably, while glancing at Natasha. "It's terribly rude, but what can you do? Opinionated people are everywhere."

Grace raised an eyebrow. "Well. You're taking this rather calmly."

Levi shrugged. "Why shouldn't I?"

She reared back. "Why *shouldn't* you? *You're* Jewish, yet you ask *me?*"

"I'm not Jewish."

Her mouth fell open. "But you are."

"Nope," he said while shaking his head slowly. "Not at all."

Grace got busy with her cigarette. "Oh, come now—with *your* name? *Levi Harf?* I know something of the Bible, and *Levi* is definitely of Hebrew origin."

He laughed. "I get that all the time. Nah, it's just my name. But I'll wear a yarmulke if it'll make people feel better."

Jennifer smiled wickedly, slid her fingers down his belly to his fly and tapped it with a long, sharp fingernail. "Levi? Jewish? Sure did miss a vital birth ritual." To the onlookers she said, "There's a Briss amiss. Knife, anyone?"

A single woman in the crowd smiled and nodded knowingly. "But he has such a lovely foreskin. Exquisite cock. *Beautiful* balls. Why desecrate perfection?"

Grace's cigarette dangled from her lip as she threw her hands up into the air. "More than I needed to know, but there it is."

When another said, "Cut or uncut, I'd fuck him in a heartbeat," Natasha burst into laughter, while Jennifer smugly wagged her finger. "Stand in line, girls."

Levi shrugged. "I'll wear that yarmulke, but I draw the line at getting trimmed."

Grace smiled laconically. "Do you really own a yarmulke?"

"Never go to temple without it," he replied poker-faced.

Grace was about to respond when Natasha approached and said in a low voice, "I'm Jewish—Russian Jewish. If Priscilla has a problem with that, I'll show her how us Jew Girls can fight."

Anna tugged my sleeve and said in a monotone, "I moved from L.A. to D.C. twelve years ago, and I'm still astounded by the mentality on this side of our nation."

"Guess I've gotten jaded. I barely notice it anymore."

She looked thoughtfully at me. "You're an officer of the law. Aren't you supposed to guard against prejudice?"

I took her arm and led her away. "Someone once said that 'laws are the crystallized prejudices of the community.' Does that mean that in order to do my job in its purest sense, I have to safeguard unfair laws that victimize others?"

Natasha walked off and our conversation had taken a turn on the road to nowhere, so I nudged Anna toward the eats. We found the buffet table and she plucked a slender piece of celery from a veggie platter. "The whole East Coast, West Coast thing gets to me," she said as she stared into the darkness. "I mean, try selling an idea to East Coast friends and you're met with a hundred reasons why it won't work. Offer that idea to West Coast friends, and they provide a hundred suggestions to *make* it work." She indicated Grace Martin with a bob of her head. "Perfect example. It's 1994. This behavior should have gone the way of mirrored sunglasses." She slowly shook her head and quipped, "'What we've got here is, failure to communicate.'"

This was supposed to be a party. I spotted Hacksaw Jones, and taking Anna's hand, I walked her over to introduce them. I asked him, "Did you come solo?"

His eyes flashed. "Nope. Brought my new girl. See that one over there?" He pointed toward a slender black girl.

"Hack, she's gorgeous!"

"Reminds me of my ex, an' that ain't exactly a bad thing."

"So where's this girlfriend of *yours*?" The voice startled me—it wasn't a voice I'd expected to hear.

I spun around. "Jarl. Didn't think you'd show tonight." I caught Hack's eye and flashed a message. He nodded and moved away.

Jarl chuckled. "You mean you was *hoping* I wouldn't show. Am I right?"

"Yeah, well …"

Jarl seemed to take it in stride. "Hey, I don't blame you. I had way too many beers. I get stupid when I'm drunk. Anyway, I'm sorry." He held out his hand.

"It's history," I said as we shook.

He winked. "An' it stays between us, right?"

"I haven't told anyone, if that's what's worrying you."

"Good," he said as he nervously patted his stomach.

I turned to Anna, "Remember Jarl Jackson? From the gym?"

Anna turned to greet him, but Jarl ignored her and picked up something from the ground. "I believe you forgot this," he said to me. It was my gym bag.

I glanced inside and found my shirt and shorts carefully folded atop my flip-flops.

He reached over and buddy-slapped my shoulder. "Not like you to forget stuff," he scolded good-naturedly. "An' speakin' of stuff, I'm gonna grab some food."

"Wait." I brushed my hand through my hair and said, "Jarl, do you know why New Jersey's called The Garden State?"

He frowned. "No. Why?"

"Because they couldn't fit 'Toxic Polluted Wasteland' on the license plates."

"Hey, I *like* Jersey. I go to Atlantic City all the time."

I knew that. "Oh, then you know what I mean."

His eyebrows drew together. "You've lost me." He finally walked away.

Anna and I moved around and talked and ate and drank. I caught sight of Natasha a few times, and got the distinct impression that she was avoiding eye contact. I suddenly wondered what job I'd have in twenty years, where I would be, and with whom. I looked from Natasha to Anna—and back again to Natasha.

Just then Natasha's eyes did meet mine. She held them for a second before looking away. I felt a stone in my chest. *She's my friend! Jesus, why did I let her go?* I half-turned to Anna and found her studying me carefully. When I looked again, Natasha was walking toward a knot of single cops. My heart sank a bit but I sucked it up—Anna was my date and she deserved my total attention.

Levi sidled up to us around ten with a dripping burger in one hand and a beer in the other. He wagged his eyebrows at Anna as a blob of ketchup oozed from the bun and landed on his white polo shirt.

Anna said, "Doesn't being reduced to sexually explicit dimensions trouble you?"

He regarded the stain with amusement and replied, "You mean my explicit penis? Why should it? Sex is a wholesome function; it's Nature's gift. Nature gave me a penis and I like to use it." He shrugged. "Bottom line? Natasha and Jen care about me, so that's all I ..." He stopped abruptly as Jarl appeared. "Hey, Jarl. What's up?"

Jarl's thick brows worked up and down as he peered unsteadily at Levi. He'd had more than a few. "Hey, come here a minute."

"Sure thing."

"No. Closer," Jarl insisted. He tugged Levi's shirtsleeve and rested a hand on his shoulder.

I was about to move on until the voyeur in me said, *no*.

Jarl leaned unsteadily against Levi and said something in an undertone.

Levi's eyes got wide and he tugged violently away from Jarl. His face was crimson as he marched past me while muttering, "Goddamn sonuvabitch!"

I looked at Jarl and found his face hidden in shadow. I started after Levi when Jennifer intercepted me.

"Michael. There's an ambulance here. They asked for you. Seems urgent."

"Ambulance? Wonder what ...?" I quick-marched to the parking lot, where an Ocean City ambulance chugged rhythmically in the dark. Anna's brother Ed Bell was at the wheel and he said, "Listen, thought you should know. Just took a patient from the North End to Ocean General. Looks like you guys have another rape on your hands."

"Whaaat?"

"Young girl. Gorgeous. Motherfucker tied her up and beat the shit out of her. Happened sometime last night, early morning. She's been out of it until now. Lieutenant Santoro's with her. He ... told me where I could find you."

Assateague was a good deal out of the way to drive to inform me of a crime that wasn't assigned to me. I said, "Joe's a good investigator. Umm, I appreciate you letting me know but I'm curious. Why?"

Ed's partner discreetly looked away before Ed replied, "Because I know you, Michael. I meant what I said the other day at Johnny's. You *are* a good cop. You also work the North End. Anyway, well ..."

"Say no more," I reassured him. "I'll keep an eye on her condo."

Ed paused and then said, "Thanks. I owe you big time." He put the ambulance in gear and drove off before I could tell him that I didn't keep books on such favors.

A fresh breeze promising rain by midnight blew in as I rejoined Anna and Levi. Natasha showed up, and then Jennifer stepped from the ladies room, her eyes bright, her cheeks flush. She went to Levi and gave him a sudden, passionate kiss. I put on some Madonna and several couples went to the pavilion floor and began dancing. Levi turned to Jennifer, said, "Come on, babe," and led her through a mixed lot of awkward men whose partners obviously wanted more. But Levi could dance; he could be a playful pup one moment, inventive the next and sassy in between, and Jennifer matched his elegant moves skillfully. Levi's fluid motions evidently pleased the other women, because they began to smile with pure pleasure as they watched.

"He's very good," Anna observed. "Quite charming to watch."

"Yeah," Natasha piped-in. "He's got the gift." I stared at her, surprised to see her mouth set in a tight line, her hands clasped tight as she avoided eye contact.

Anna nodded. "I find his confidence intriguing. Also, I couldn't help but notice that several women have been giving him the eye this evening. At first I couldn't understand his attractiveness. To some women, yes. But to so many? Now I see it."

Natasha said, "Oh, it's always been obvious to me. Devastating charm. Effortless, subdued, lethal." Then she glanced at me and said in a low voice, "Go on, Michael. Show everyone how it's done."

I held out my hand to Anna and guided her past a small knot of dancers. Sure, Levi could dance—but not as well as I. As we merged into the music's beat I moved with a grace born of total self-control. I had that kid-from-the-wrong-side-of-the-tracks rhythm that couldn't be ignored, and as we danced Anna looked full into my eyes and impulsively kissed my cheek. I couldn't help but be aware that most of the women and even some of the guys watched with varying degrees of admiration. As I urged Anna on her dancing became sexier. Others whispered and pointed. We soon found ourselves next to Levi and Jennifer. Levi smiled at us while Jen stared at him with obvious desire.

We danced through three more numbers before calling it quits, all of us covered in perspiration. Levi leaned toward Jennifer with a casual air of companionship and whispered in her ear. She giggled as they joined us at the pavilion's edge, near the largest dune.

Grace Martin walked up, snuffing one cigarette as she lit another. "Michael, you dance divinely. So do you, Levi."

"Thanks," I said. "Comes with practice. Ya see, Levi and I danced at some clubs for a couple of years. You know, to help with college expenses."

She looked quizzically at me. "Clubs? I don't quite understand."

Levi explained. "He means, ladies clubs. We did the male strip club circuit."

Jennifer gasped. "Oh my God!"

Levi whirled around. "Jen! What is it?"

She pointed at the large dune behind us and said, "Look!" A huge moon had risen, and as it ascended, its orb settled precariously atop the dune.

Then Levi's body turned rigid. "Jesus!" he rasped, and he stared wide-eyed, as someone appeared as if by magic on the dune's ridge. He was well dressed and intent upon Levi; he was the guy from Rudy's.

Levi's neck turned crimson. "What the hell is *he* doing here?" Then he swore through clenched teeth, "Goddamn *rat*."

The visitor trudged down the dune as Levi's hands clenched and unclenched. He finally stopped, and confronted Levi. "You said we'd get together tonight."

Levi's face flushed red. As the self-appointed savior of all who faced adversity, I stepped forward and got in the visitor's face. "Who the hell do you think you are?"

He replied evenly, "I'm Dan. I'm Levi's friend. Hasn't he told you about me? I'm his friend? His Rehoboth *Beach* friend?" When that failed to elicit a response he narrowed his eyes and said, "Hey, haven't you people figured it out? I'm Levi's lover!"

Jarl's sudden laughter ripped the air apart, while other guests coughed nervously or stared into their drinks. Several guests shuffled away; Jennifer's eyes grew wide, but she held her own and stared at Levi for an explanation.

The ketchup stain stood stark against Levi's white shirt as he held his arms open beseechingly, his mouth working silently as the party broke apart. Guests vanished, some quietly, others in a burst of amusement as they glanced over their shoulders at Levi. Jarl laughed the loudest and stuck around the longest, until finally even he drifted off toward the dark parking lot. Only three other cops and their wives or girlfriends remained to watch as Dan slowly ascended the dune and disappeared over the ridge. I went directly to Levi and squeezed his shoulder. "It's okay. I'm with you, buddy. It's okay."

Levi said nothing at first. Finally he coughed and said, "He's a friend. That's all." Then he examined the sand until he looked up and asked, "So we're okay?"

Jennifer kissed him and announced, "You're okay and I can vouch to all that you are exceedingly straight." She met all the faces and said, "Let's clean up, hey?"

Natasha embraced Levi and said something, and then she and Anna pitched in to help. He said nothing as we cleaned up, while the earlier breeze brought the first traces of clouds, casting a pall over everything. The remaining guests finally split, and when Natasha headed toward her car, Anna and I went to Jennifer and Levi. "Come on, *mi amigo*. Let's go home and relax."

Levi shook his head doggedly. "Thanks, but I'm all right. Hey, I've got Jen."

Jennifer molded her body to his and said, "Damn right you've got me," and with a sly smile she whispered, "And tonight you're gonna get me pregnant."

"But I …"

Her face glowed as she slid a finger beneath his untucked shirt and hooked it through a belt loop. "Think about it. Nobody will think you're queer once you've knocked up Nat *and* me. They'll see that we're pregnant, and we'll tell 'em by whom."

He stared into the distance and slowly nodded.

She kissed his cheek. "You see it, don't you?"

"Yeah, but …" Levi scuffed his foot through the sand. "I don't know."

Jennifer gave his fatigues a little tug. "I want to grow heavy with child! *Your* child! I want this town to see that you're a straight arrow!"

He nodded again, his eyes still far away, but then he worried the end of his nose. "That's no reason to have children. We should talk this over some more."

Jennifer backed away and said curtly, "Talk, hell." Then she indicated

Natasha's retreating back with a flip of her head. "You nailed her twice today. Good enough for Nat, good enough for Jen. You're giving me a baby, Stud."

I made a sign that Anna and I should go but Levi said, "No. It's okay." To Jennifer he said softly, "Let's discuss it later. There's so much to deal with right now."

"*Deal* with?" She put her hands on her hips but abruptly showed a charming smile. "You've got such good genes," she said, and reaching out she undid the top button of his fatigues. "Come on. Let's make a baby."

He said plaintively, "Jen! This isn't the best time. Can't we wait 'til tomorrow?"

She stamped her foot. "No! I just checked my temperature *and* I've got mucous! I'm ready and I won't let this chance slip away! Damn you—we have to start tonight!" Jennifer rolled her eyes and said, "What's the big deal? Jesus, I just want a kid!"

"I know," he whispered. Then to my surprise he said, "Okay. Here's the plan. We go home, we see what happens; maybe let Nature run its course."

Jennifer's eyes lit up, and as she kissed his face all over I coughed lightly. "Levi? You're my bro. You can be gay or straight. You can have a dozen kids or none at all. I'll always be your buddy."

He nodded but he was embarrassed, and we weren't doing him any favors by hanging around. While Anna said something to Levi, I stepped away and looked around. Jennifer appeared at my side and chirped happily, "Don't worry. Nat's fine." She smiled. "She went home, Michael. Alone." Jennifer was no dummy. I wished her luck, found Anna, and we left. We'd spend some quiet moments, and then I'd go home in case Levi needed to talk.

As we drove down a dark road she said, "Tell me about Levi fathering babies."

"Long story. Call it, 'women living the myth of a self-determined life.'"

"He's impregnating Jen *and* Nat, have I got that right?" When I nodded she put her hand on my thigh. "So Natasha is one of *Levi's* girls? Because for a while there I thought ..."

"Another long story." I glanced at her. "Nat's her own woman. She sees whomever she wants, does whatever she wants. The same goes for Jennifer. Right now they both want a child with Levi."

Anna caressed my thigh and announced, "Then he can't be gay."

I braked hard as a car darted in front of us and said, "Anything's possible. He'll tell me if he thinks I need to know. Look, he's my bro and that's that."

Anna removed her hand and regarded me in silence. "I admire your loyalty. But something else is eating at you, and has been ever since the paramedics stopped by. What is it?"

I glanced outside my window before asking, "We off the record here?"

She gave me an oblique look. "We're off the record."

"A girl was raped the other day. That's already been reported. Then there was another attack. You were at the gym when Jarl mentioned it." I paused, down shifted for traffic, and continued. "Another girl was attacked today or possibly last night. Nobody's sure. That's more rapes in two days than are reported in a year."

"Jesus! There could be a serial rapist running loose. This will be big news!"

"He—or she—can't be classified as a serial rapist until three victims have been attacked, each in separate locales. There must be intervening days, and there has to be a link." I didn't add that serial or not, I would pursue him, her, or them with equal vigor.

The first drops of rain began to fall as Anna unlocked her door. I said, "I feel lucky to have you as my friend." When she swung the door open I said, "I want to see you again. Tomorrow. Okay?"

Anna moved into my arms, and neither of us talked as she rested her head against my shoulder. Levi's problems—even the rapes—took a sudden back seat. "Come inside, Michael," she finally said, and she pulled me through the door.

We let our clothes fall to the floor as we undressed each other in the dark. We held one another and kissed one another, and I was thrilled to see her open delight when I looked up and found the power of her gaze focused on my eyes. I touched her face, her shoulders and her breasts, completely taken by her textures and her warmth. Then I guided her to the bed and eased her down while outside the skies erupted with thunder and a cascade of rain.

But here we were safe. Anna touched my cheek with the very tips of her cool fingers, and then moved them to my lips. I kissed them one by one. She smiled, brushed her lips against my ear and slid her hand along my chest and down my belly.

I buried my nose in her hair and breathed deeply, and a groan of pleasure rattled my throat. We touched one another, tasted one another and gloried in one another, until that moment when the whisper of her breath graced my cheek and I claimed her naked body. The earth went away, and she went with me to that place of rapture until we were utterly consumed. Afterward we lay in silence and trembled from wondrous sensations.

We slept and woke and loved again.

CHAPTER 5

A rare and intimate smile, beautiful in its brightness greeted me. "Good morning, Michael."

We lay on our sides facing one another; ours legs and arms entwined. The air conditioner kicked in and a gust of her scent swept over me. It was an odor of zest—of lemons and oranges and pears, combined with sweat. The distant sound of a siren intruded and momentarily overwhelmed the roar of the air conditioner. There were also the roaring echoes of a party left in tatters by a strange visitor from another planet. But for now it all existed in another world. "It *is* a good morning," I affirmed as I stretched well-rested muscles. I felt as though I'd awakened from an anesthesia; I luxuriated in the sense of satiated sleep. My mouth tasted filmy, of texture and of her. That was fine, too.

Anna slid her hand to my buttocks and patted them. The sun broke into her eyes when I moved my knee between her bare legs. She moved atop me. We made love again. Afterward she pecked my cheek with her wonderful lips and announced, "I love the way you make love." She patted my buttocks again and regarded me thoughtfully. "I'm not promiscuous. I hope you understand that."

"I didn't think you were." I shrugged. "Sex is healthy. It's an act of friendship."

She stroked my flanks, deep in thought. After a pause she said, "I enjoy your companionship. You're shy without being shy, because when it's all said you've got total confidence in yourself." Then she touched my cheek and looked at me. "Don't take this the wrong way," she began hesitantly, "but with your looks, your attitude, you could shine up like a brand new penny." I started to say something but she put her fingers to my lips. "What I mean," she said in a rush, "is that I'd like to take you shopping. Buy you some clothes, some jewelry."

That stopped me. The kid with the deprived childhood took over. "Something wrong with what I wear?"

She double-clutched and said quickly, "Heck, you'd look good in a potato sack. I only meant that perhaps you'd like to explore. There's absolutely nothing wrong with the beach look you've adopted. I just thought ..."

"It's okay," I said as I caressed her cheek. "Hey," I began tenderly, "I appreciate your offer. It's *also* an act of friendship. Let's do it! I've got a three-day break coming up soon. You can take me shopping then."

We lay together a while longer. I finally left her arms, showered and dressed, and as Anna walked me to the door she whispered something about calling D.C. and settling in for a day of editing. I suspected there might be more; that she might try to persuade the *Post* to go national with news of the attacks. I could already see the headlines: "Resort Rapist Runs Rampant." I wouldn't blame her; she had her job to do, I had mine. We made a dinner date for that evening. Before leaving I held her arms tightly in my hands and said, "Be careful, Anna." I didn't want to disclose the severity of last night's rape, or her brother's request. "Keep your doors locked and the curtains closed."

"You worry too much. And I like them open," she said as I turned to go.

The humidity from last night's storm smacked me with a one-two punch as I stepped through her door. So far this morning I had shied away from any thought of last night's party, but now I wondered how Levi was doing. Under ordinary circumstances I'd have felt guilty for deserting him. But he'd had Jennifer, so I felt absolution for my sin.

When I reached the parking lot I saw that something wasn't right. "What the hell?" I trotted toward my car. A red rose like the one on my cruiser was pinned beneath the wiper blade, its petals already wilted by the scorching sun.

I guess I should have felt flattered, but I didn't relish being stalked. *Donna?* Could be. She was at the fight and she knew my Mustang after Jarl's ski party. I scanned the streets; nothing. I tossed the rose to the ground and drove off, slightly pissed that someone had an advantage over me, just as some turd had victimized those girls.

*   *   *

He felt exhausted, but tilted his head back anyway and inhaled deeply; he sniffed the air and wondered at the excitement he felt when he did so—he got off on odors, even if it was his own. But the odor he savored most was that of fear; primal fear that coursed through his victims with a shudder, only to exude through their pores in the form of cold sweat—a fear that he could only begin to realize after he moved to the next level, that level where he let them regain consciousness before he fucked them. A thrill ran through him until it ended in his testicles as he thought about the next girl on his list. "Yeah—I felt this fucking *thrill*, 'cause I was the top fucking dog in this doggy-ass town!"

*   *   *

I turned south on Coastal and decided to hit the gym. A good workout would help me sort through the mysteries behind the rapes, the roses, and now Levi. I walked inside and found Johnny stationed as usual at the reception desk. He took a soiled towel from a customer and scrutinized me as I covered the distance from the front door in three easy strides.

"I hear Levi's a fag."

My jaw dropped. "*Excuse* me?"

Johnny tossed the towel into a large bin behind the counter. "That's what I hear." He grabbed a fresh one and placed it on the counter in front of me.

I swept it to one side and said, "What the *hell* are you talking about?"

His eyes screwed up protectively. "Don't get all pissy with me, laddie. I'm only telling you what's goin' 'round."

"Well what *did* you hear, and from whom?"

Johnny leaned his arms atop the counter. "Whas' his name—new kid on the force. Pete, I think it is." He brushed absent-mindedly at the air. "Aye. Claimed honorifics as an attendee at the party you lads hosted the evening past. Said something about some queer what come there looking for Levi."

Pete had recently joined our shift. Too much talk, not enough walk. "Just what'd Numb Nuts tell you?"

He folded his arms across his chest and leaned back against a display case filled with colorfully labeled nutritional supplements. "He told me that a rather distraught queer demanded an audience with Mister Levi."

"Damn," I whispered.

Johnny leaned forward. "Aye, and quite the embarrassed look Levi had on his face, or so I'm told."

I said hotly, "Well, forget it. Some guy has an attraction for him. So what? He's got a 'D' ticket for the 'E' ride. What's that prove?"

He pointed his finger like a pistol. "It proves he's got some explaining to do, that's what it proves. Young Levi has his work cut out for him, that he does."

I regarded this man whom I'd always respected, pointed a finger back at him and mentally cocked it. "He's got nothing to explain. Not to me, not to you, not to anyone. And," I added as I turned on my heel to leave, "don't ever call Levi a fag again!"

Johnny's Fitness Center isn't exactly an obscure filling station. If rumors concerning Levi had gotten this far, there was no telling what else might be brewing. I had to get home.

I was roaring across the Isle of Wight minutes later. The estuary loomed in a broad expanse on either side of the islet, and all of a sudden I wanted to get out and transit the estuary on foot, to smell the fertile mud flats and savor the peaceful solitude of its sluggish waters. The tide had gone out and I could spot crawling things even as I drove past. Life was so much simpler for them. They might be forced to deal with predators, but abusive fathers, gossip and raw hatred remained great unknowns for them.

Levi's car was in the driveway when I pulled in and so was Natasha's, but I didn't see Jennifer's. I *did* find Levi's clothes on the porch, piled next to the chaise lounge. A gust of wind blew an empty beer bottle into my path. I moved quickly to the screen door and it emitted a squeal as I pulled it open.

A feminine voice called out tiredly, "There you are, Michael. And how are you this fine morning?" Natasha met me in the kitchen. Overnight she had dyed her fluorescent orange hair a soft shade of lavender. Her eyes revealed dark circles. She had on a ball cap from a long-ago trip to Cancún, a white, long tailed men's shirt with thin blue stripes over who-knew-what underneath, and a black braided cord on her slender ankle. I grimaced when I recognized the cord as the one Levi had worn the day before.

She caught my eye and pointed at it proudly. "Levi put it there yesterday. *Instructed* me to wear it. Sweet of him, actually. I took this shirt from his closet." She held it out from the sides and spun around. "What do you think?"

"I like it!" But my stomach was turning drum-tight at the thought of her wearing his things. At the same time a part of me felt guilty for going home with Anna last night, but why? Natasha slept with other men when she wasn't bedding down with Levi, and I certainly saw plenty of women. Natasha knew this, even condoned it in a fashion. So why did I feel a pang—and why did I feel grateful that she'd come home, instead of spending the night elsewhere?

George waddled over and sniffed my hands, realized I had no treats to offer, and went away.

"I missed you last night," she began. "I shoved off when I saw how absorbed you were with your new main squeeze."

"Please, Natasha. I'm not in the mood. And don't call Anna my squeeze."

She tossed her head and put her arms around me. "Well o-kay, Kiddo. She's beyond 'main squeeze.' I'm happy for you." She rested her head against my chest and whispered, "Levi took a big hit last night."

"Yeah," I whispered, "and it's not just country-club talk anymore."

Natasha reared back and scrutinized my face. "Damn! *That* didn't take long. But why am I surprised? This can be such a *hateful* town." She made a face. "Why do I even waste my time here?"

"You tell me. You're the most logical person I know; you could live anywhere."

She hesitated, pursed her luscious lips and whispered, "Maybe what I want is to be close to you."

I hugged her. "Babe," I said into her ear.

Natasha pushed slightly away. "Sorry. I am jealous of Anna. I shouldn't be and I feel even worse, because you're not jealous of all the bumpin' an' grindin' I'm doing with Levi."

"That's different and you know it. It's quality repro sex and anyhow you and he have always been lovers, except for when you and I were …"

She brushed non-existent lint from my shirtfront and spoke slowly, feeling her way. "Oh, Michael. I feel so awful. I shouldn't have acted so distantly last night."

I caressed her face and guided her cheek to mine. "Hey, I didn't know you'd be there. Come on, I'd never rub your face in my business."

Natasha laughed nervously. "It's okay," she murmured. "I didn't take it personally." She pulled her head away and looked at me. "Well, not too personally," she added with a brave smile.

"Thanks," I said softly. "You're such a sweetheart."

Natasha laid her head against my shoulder and sighed. "I was … once."

"Yes, you were my sweetheart." We held each other and said nothing while I pondered how to let her know that Anna did not pose a threat—not yet, anyway.

"Why did it have to end?" she whispered.

I stroked her cheek with the backs of my fingers. "I believe you accused me of being emotionally unavailable. Afraid to show my feelings, you said—as if that isn't par for most males on this planet."

"Guilty as charged," she murmured.

"And I didn't want you hanging out with some of the people you work with."

She nodded in deep thought. "*That* pissed me off."

"Not to mention the time I accused you of being evasive with me."

She wrapped her long arms around my back and hugged me close to her slender body. "Ah, yes. That was in Hawaii I believe, when you and I enjoyed such a wonderful time together, until you …"

"Inquired too deeply into your past." I kissed her forehead. "We're still friends, though. How do we make that happen?"

"It works because you're kind enough to let me live my life …"

"While you so graciously let me live mine …"

Her eyes were focused on something distant as she murmured, "Without me throwing a jealous fit whenever I hear about you and some new …"

Time to change the topic; I looked into her eyes and renewed an old game of ours. It was exponentially more sophisticated than the *ibba da* ritual that Levi and I played, a game more suited to her brilliant—or perhaps brilliantly camouflaged—intellect. "So," I began with our invariable opening gambit, "*does* God exist?"

She giggled into my chest and said, "Logically speaking, no. That's because there's nothing more complex than an Almighty Creator. However, physicists will argue that the beginning of the universe was heralded by irreducible minimums. Now then, theories with foundations built upon simple premises are awarded greater credibility than those with complex, statistically improbable ones …"

I squeezed her lightly and said, "Quit showing off." Then I looked around. "By the way, didn't Jen come home with Levi?"

"She did, but …" She stopped and whispered, "Let's discuss this outside."

I urged her to the privacy of the porch. The air was warm and torpid as we took chairs and sat with our backs to the door. A cricket sang beneath the rough boards as Natasha kicked idly at an empty beer bottle near her feet. She said, "I was about to turn in when they came home. Jen's bursting at the seams; can't wait to get him into bed. They sit out here instead while Levi puts away one beer after another." Natasha shifted in her seat as a bead of sweat trickled from her forehead to her eyes. "Finally he has one too many. Jen sees her opening, does a full court press." She flicked her eyes at the chaise lounge. "Gets him on his back, strips him and mounts him." Natasha grunted. "The little stud might be semi-conscious, but he has an erection!" She grimaced. "Jen's about to take him bareback when he comes to his senses. He stops her—says he wants to be sober if he dives into daddyhood. They have words." Natasha kicked the bottle away, revealing a glimpse of plum-colored panties beneath the long shirttails. "Jen gets pissed, digs her nails into his foreskin, and threatens to fix it so he'll pass for Jewish. Then she calls him a fag and storms off."

"That's terrible!" Then I frowned. "Wait. You saw all this?"

Natasha looked as if she'd bitten into a lemon. "Of course not. I went to bed soon as they got home; he crawled in with me after she left, covered in sweat; trembling; miserable." She looked away distractedly and added, "He told me what happened, took me in his arms and held on for dear life until the shaking stopped." Natasha made a tepee out of her hands, rested her fingertips against her lips and whispered, "Jen pulled into the driveway a bit later; he went out there buck-assed to see what she wanted."

"Good thing we've got all those bushes." I snorted. "Not that he cares."

She nodded. "Doubt he was even aware. Anyway, Jen apologized. She wanted sex. He declined and she accepted it graciously." Natasha smirked. "Then he came back inside and *we* made love." She made a brief fist. "Levi didn't want to—not at first. He was overwhelmed by everything, but I worked my magic on him." Natasha offered a wan smile. "If I wasn't pregnant yesterday I am now. Or will be—Levi will see to that."

I reached over and squeezed her hand. "Having second thoughts?"

She seemed surprised. "Gosh, no. I want this child more than ever." Her eyes blazed and she raised her voice. "And I better not see *Jen* carrying his baby before *I'm* pregnant, that's for goddamn sure." She settled deeper into her chair, licked her full red lips and smiled deliciously. "Tell you what, she missed out on a good fucking! Of course by then he had this absolutely … *raunchy* B.O. so God, the pheromones! I had the mother of all O's, Michael!"

I said harshly, "I don't wanna hear any more of this."

Natasha looked mournfully at me. "No. I suspect not." A sudden shiver coursed through her, and then she asked in a near-whisper, "Michael? You'll still give me a child after I have Levi's?"

"Love to," I declared.

Natasha nodded slowly, then switched gears abruptly and asked, "So. This Dan character—what's going on there?"

I shifted uncomfortably in my chair, took a deep breath and said matter-of-factly, "He materialized at a fight call one evening. Next night I spotted him jawing with Levi at Club Montage." A sudden breeze caught the bottle and rolled it back toward Natasha.

She arched her beautiful eyebrows, tapped the bottle daintily with her foot and sent it spinning. "Hmm. That's interesting. Levi ever say anything before last night?"

"No, not a word about …"

"About what," a clotted, gravel voice demanded.

We turned our heads as one and looked over our shoulders.

"About what," Levi repeated.

The screen door squealed as he stepped naked onto the porch, his heavy umber hair disheveled, a two-day growth on his face. He looked like death warmed over, reeked of booze and B.O., and he smelled of both women as he asked wearily, "And today's topic is?"

Natasha picked up the missed beat. "I was asking about Dan."

"You've been talking about me, is that it?"

She met his eyes calmly. "Naturally."

Levi nodded, put his head against Natasha's and held her in his arms as he whispered in her ear. Then he drew back and watched her with an intent gaze.

Natasha smiled, placed her hand on his forearm and replied gently, "And I adore you, my darling Levi."

He kissed her, settled a hand on her belly and caressed it lovingly with his long fingers as they exchanged a glance. Then he drew his hand away, walked untroubled to his clothes and fished his wrinkled fatigues from the pile. He pulled them on absently, leaving the legs unraveled; the ends frayed and exhausted. He plopped into a chair next to Natasha, settled his blue eyes on her and cracked a smile. "Damn! What a way to end a party!" He shook his head in silent wonder.

I said awkwardly, "Um, the shit about Dan is all over town. What're you gonna tell the guys?"

He shrugged with great indifference. "Nothing. What's the point? Besides, what I do is none of their business."

I replied with a flat, "You're right." I looked down at my hands, then raised my head and stared at him. "Levi."

His eyes settled on mine. His lips barely moved as he said, "Go ahead."

I hunched forward and put my palms together. "Remember what I told you last night. You're my best friend. Nothing will ever change how I feel about you."

Natasha said, "You're my prince and always will be."

His body sagged and he looked away. After a bit he said, "I was afraid you guys would …" Then he slouched low in his chair and spread his feet wide on the deck. An uncomfortable silence passed before Levi drew a deep breath. "Guys? I'm gay." He shook his head in wonderment. "Wow! First time I said it aloud." Then he looked from me to Natasha, and finally into the distance. "I almost came out to you a few months ago but I panicked. I was afraid you'd be pissed that I'd said nothing after all this time." He grimaced and said, "No, that's not it. I just wasn't ready to face reality. Maybe I *needed* to be outted— maybe I needed a kick in the ass before I stepped into the light." He paused and then said to his feet, "I let you guys down."

Nat asked, "Did you think either of us could ever feel differently about you?"

"Levi," I began soothingly. "You're my brother … *our* brother. What you do, who you sleep with—that's your business and I'm on your side."

Natasha leaned toward him and said lovingly, "I only want happiness for you. Nothing has changed. It's all love between us."

He held up a hand. "I need to talk." Then he sat up, cleared his throat and looked us both in the eye. "I'm not totally gay," he began, feeling his way as his clotted voice cleared. "I'm not straight. I'm somewhere in between—a four or maybe even a five on the Kinsey Scale. It's not something people have a choice in."

"We know," Natasha replied.

"It's not as if I woke up one day and said, 'wow, I like guys.'" He stopped and groped for something and blurted, "I got tired of holding back. I want to be *me*."

Natasha patted his arm. "It's okay, Levi. You don't owe any explanations."

He continued as if he hadn't heard, which I suspect he hadn't. "Life's a huge buffet table for me. I'll take a little of this," he began, moving his hands as if prodding delectable treats with a fork, "and a little of that. But whoa," he said, holding up a hand as if stopping traffic, "no thanks … don't care for any of this." He grew more animated. "I see what I like and I pursue it. How can that be evil?" He looked at us with the eyes of a five-year-old and shrugged. "I'm all appetite. I devour. I see a guy and a girl walking down the street and I think … hmm, she's cute. But if the guy's my type then I think, wow! Nice!" He paused and whispered, "I do love women, an' I like female friendships. But I also love men." Then he looked at us once more with child-like eyes. "Is that so bad?"

Natasha replied in a tranquil voice. "No, Levi. It's not."

"Hey, bro. You're my best friend in the world."

He lowered his eyes. "Thanks, Michael." Then to Natasha he said, "Hey, I've gotta say this. I've always practiced safe sex with the others. And hell, you already know that I get tested routinely for *all* STDs." He scowled. "Jen's been tested, of course. I wouldn't consider making a kid otherwise. So everything's fine. Okay?"

She smiled but she also seemed relieved. "I've always trusted you to do the right thing, my love."

I fidgeted and asked, "So what's with this Dan guy?"

Levi sighed. "Met him a few months ago. In Rehoboth. *Numbers*."

"Know the place," I said.

He lit up with a genuine, full-of-sun smile. "Yeah. You would. Anyway, we danced, went to his place afterward, and I rocked his world for him. What's left to say?" He paused and scuffed his bare feet against the rough wooden deck. "He wanted a relationship but I didn't." A strange, nervous unease took hold of Levi. "But I did keep social contact. He and his sister are fashion models. They lived in the north end for a bit. Now *he* lives in Rehoboth Beach. She's still in the north end." Levi stared into space before continuing. "He's been popping up everywhere, stalking me."

I bolted upright. "Yeah! Like this morning." I looked from one to the other. "You know I don't kiss and tell, but I did spend the night at Anna's."

Natasha and Levi ceremoniously applauded me.

"No, wait," I said in exasperation. "Someone's stalking me, too." I told them about the two roses—the one on my cruiser and the other at Anna's.

Levi stirred suddenly. "*Jesus*. Someone left *me* a rose. Found it on my Firebird, night of the fight." He sat deep in thought. "It was late, remember? I was in a hurry to get home because Jennifer called to say she was coming over. I went to my car and there it was." He swatted at a bloated fly near his head and grimaced. "I figured Jen left it." He looked questioningly at me. "Think it could've been Dan—or Donna?"

Nat turned to me with a puzzled look. "Donna?"

Levi explained. "Married to a guy on our shift. Turned up at that fight; had the hots for Michael."

"It could be her," I said. Then I told them everything about Jarl's ski party.

Levi leaned forward, planted both feet on the deck, and rested his elbows on his knees as he stared straight ahead. "She's looking more and more like a chief suspect." He frowned. "But that still doesn't explain the rose on *my* car."

"While we're on the topic of the strange and unusual …" Then I told them about Ed Bell's report of another rape. "Let's nab this guy," I concluded.

Levi slowly nodded. "Yes, while I can."

Nat and I looked at him in surprise.

"I'd planned on making the announcement last night. Got a letter from Customs yesterday. They made an offer." He looked down at the floor and fidgeted. "I could be gone soon."

"That's wonderful news," Natasha said. "I'm so excited for you!"

I said sadly, "Don't know what I'll do without you." Then with more cheer I got up and pounded him on the back, "Good for you, though! Well done, amigo!"

"Thanks." Then he looked at Natasha. "What about the baby?"

She laughed. "All the more reason to knock me up before you leave. Come on," she scolded, "we've discussed this possibility. You'll visit. You'll love him or her."

Levi nodded while stifling a yawn. "I need some more shut-eye."

"Wait." Natasha got up and kissed him, saying, "I love you very, very much, my dearest Levi. Nothing has changed between us. Nothing."

He pulled her close and held onto her as a serene look transformed his face. When he let go he gave me a shy half-smile, then he grabbed the rest of his clothes and turned toward his room. I caught Natasha's eye, pointed at Levi's retreating back and followed him. He was already stepping out of his fatigues when I knocked and entered his room. He seemed suddenly bashful as he hitched them back up and looked at me.

To break the tension I said, "Christ, do you need a freakin' shower! I mean, damn—you are fucking ripe!" Then I tossed the guy-stuff aside and said, "Come here, bro." I took him in my arms and kissed the top of his head. "Levi," I said as I stepped back, "you coached me through college an' kept me strong in the academy. Most of all, you've shown me how to feel again." I paused. "I'll always love you for that. For that and—well, just because you're Levi." I looked right at him and added, "Bro. I don't care what your darkest secrets are; I'm in. I'm with you. Okay?"

He made a show of studying the floor. This man whose naked honesty once disturbed me was too shy to respond. Then he reached out to me as he had with the little girl at the gym. Levi seemed in control, affectionate in the way that only truly masculine men are able to be. He hugged me and said a simple, "Thanks." Then he pushed away, cracked a smile and said, "Better stop. Wouldn't do to get a woody just now."

I covered my mouth and asked, "Woody da?"

He said nothing, scored points for winning the round, then pushed me out and closed the door.

Natasha was seated on the couch with the TV tuned to *The Weather Channel.* When I sat next to her she asked quietly, "Did you ever suspect?"

I turned down the volume. "No. Not ever."

"You're not upset that he never said anything before?"

I shrugged. "Nope."

She bit down gently on her lower lip. "He thinks he's let me down. I can tell."

I took her hand in mine. "Well of course it's different. You guys have a history as lovers." Then, "I'm betting there are some things you two need to discuss privately."

"Yeah," she whispered. Natasha studied the TV. "Maybe now is the best time. He has to know nothing's changed between us."

"Hey ... Nat?"

She faced me squarely. "Yes?"

I groped for the words. "Nat, I ... I mean, you and me, I ..."

Natasha grabbed both my hands in hers. "Yes, Michael. What is it? *Tell* me."

My tongue felt thick. Finally I croaked, "Nat, I need you ..."

Her pupils dilated, her cheeks flushed red. "Yes, dear Michael. What do you need? Just *say* it!"

My mouth opened and closed of its own accord, but then I turned away. "Nat, I need you to tell me again. About wanting my child, too."

Natasha's nostrils flared, and for a second I thought she might hit me. "Michael Brennan, I'll want your child when you let me know that you need something more. But if all you have to offer is some limp-dick excuse for commitment, then I'm sorry. No, I won't guarantee a thing."

I swallowed hard and looked fully into her eyes. "Please? Please, Nat? Tell me that you'll still want my child? Please?"

A long minute passed until she looked down and whispered, "I want ... I *will* want your child, Michael." Then she looked back up at me. "Okay?"

I squeezed her hand and brought it to my lips and kissed her fingers and whispered, "Thanks, Nat." Then I flicked my eyes toward the bedrooms and said without looking at her, "Better hurry. He looked like he was going down for the count."

She touched her cool fingers to my cheek, then got up and went down the hallway. I heard his door open and then close again. After a while I heard her shriek with laughter, followed by some unintelligible response from him. The next few minutes passed quietly until the door opened and her footsteps echoed down the hall. She curled next to me as if nothing had transpired between us, Levi's black cord still stark against her white ankle. I sighed and wrapped my arm around her shoulder.

"He's finally sleeping. I'm so glad I went to him. You were right—he had so much more to say." She touched my arm as her voice turned soft. "Jen's rejection apparently hurt him a lot more than he let on. Something else. He was *so* relieved when you hugged him. It made all the difference."

"It's a guy thing," I quipped. "The zenith of male bonding and intimacy."

"Think how fortunate the three of us are to share the intimacies that we do."

I said matter-of-factly, "He gave you that baby—there's intimacy for you."

"Yes," she whispered. "But I never gave him what he's always wanted in return."

"Yeah. I know."

Natasha's voice caught when she asked, "Do you think he understands why I love you, and not him?"

Levi yawned noisily two hours later. I left Natasha and knocked at his door. Green shades were drawn against the windows, and the A/C hummed in its unceasing tempo. Levi was sprawled as usual atop the futon, his legs and arms poking from beneath the sheet. "Move over," I said. After he edged to one side I plopped down next to him and rested my back against the wall. Then I elbowed his ribs and declared, "Time for some pillow talk. Look, nothing's changed between us, okay?"

He cleared his throat. "What we talked about earlier … 'bout love and all that stuff." He paused. "I hope you realize that I've never been *in* love with you. I've always just loved you …"

"As a brother. Sure. I know. See? We even finish each other's …"

"Sentences." He grunted. "But you understand the difference, right?"

"Of course. Anyway, I've never felt threatened around gay people."

His eyes appeared solemn and his lips were compressed as he slowly nodded. "I never, and I mean never *ever* had any desires for you. Never peeked at you in the locker room or any of that crap; it's important that I know you understand this."

"I never questioned the purity of your feelings for me. Not ever."

Levi whispered, "That's good." Then he stared off at something beyond my perception. "It's just that I've never had a friend like you."

I turned my head and looked at him questioningly.

"That's right. Despite the perfect childhood you seem to think I had …"

"I'd have traded mine for yours *any* day."

He paused. "Okay. I deserved that. It's this way. I never had a friend whose loyalty I could count on. I'm … inspired when you take care of others."

The irony didn't escape me. I envied Levi for the stability he'd enjoyed growing up. Now he drew strength from his interpretation of compassion and loyalty—qualities I regarded as nothing less than basic friendship.

"I should have come to you last week, Michael—after Dan threatened to out me if I didn't give in. After I told him to fuck off."

"Didn't you think he was serious?"

Levi grunted. "I *knew* he was. It was only a question of time. Then I ran into him at Club Montage the other night. He threw down the gauntlet. I told him where to shove it. His reaction was simple—Assateague."

"You did the right thing."

"Sure as shit wasn't gonna give in to extortion."

"You've had a lot on your mind. No wonder you've been such a moody prick."

He burst into laughter. "I have been, haven't I? Hey, I'm sorry, bro." Then he turned serious again. "Can't believe I was such a dickhead to you yesterday."

"Nat wants a kid with each of us. You're just first," I said neutrally.

He seemed relieved. Then he said, "You heard about me and Jen last night?"

"Of course."

He lapsed into silence, and as the air conditioner whined he crossed and uncrossed his ankles until large creases erupted across his forehead. "I never told you this, but in high school I got careless one night. She was my best friend, Michael. After she went away I never saw her again. I heard rumors that she'd had a little boy, but I've never known for sure."

I nodded and said reassuringly, "You were a kid. Don't beat yourself up."

After a few seconds he cleared his throat. "It's just that it means something to me—having children. Michael? I *do* care about Jen. I just didn't want to get her pregnant. But now something in me wants to!" He blew air from his cheeks and said, "If people are going to categorize me then they should get it right— that 'gay Levi' loves *women* as well."

I made a show of wrinkling my nose. "You *smell* from two women."

"Pretty much, yeah." He fidgeted with the sheet and said, "If Jen had waited until I sobered up we *might've* fucked for effect. But then she went and ..."

I punched his arm. "Stop right there! I do see her side. From where I stood last night you implied that you would."

He wet his lips and said, "That's why I'm gonna ask if she still wants a child." Then he set his jaw and shook his head fiercely. "No. It'd be for all the wrong reasons. Jen's still my friend despite what she did, but I don't wanna make a baby with her! I don't love her!" He glanced at me and said, "But I do love Nat. God, when I'm with Nat I'm on top of the world!"

Natasha said as she walked into the room, "That's comforting to hear." She walked to the far side of the futon and lifted the sheet away. "What a surprise—Levi's commando. 'I am shocked, shocked to learn that there is gambling going on in this establishment.'" Then she tossed her head and sent her hair flying. "Slide over."

Levi hesitated as he traced his finger along the leather cord on her ankle. "I like seeing you wearing my stuff; gonna *love* seeing you carrying my baby. What am I saying? *Babies*. Let's have two, or three or four!" Then he wrapped his long fingers around her ankle until finally he sighed and made room for her.

Natasha glanced at me but said nothing as she slid beneath the sheet. Her hands disappeared and there was a brief commotion until they reappeared clutching her panties. She flung them to the floor and quipped, "When in Rome." Then she kissed Levi tenderly before settling her head atop his chest. "Feels so good being with the two men I love." All at once she sniffed. "Ugh! Time you showered."

"Maybe later."

She looked pointedly at the ceiling. "Why do I even bother? Levi Hart's never been one to stand close to a bar of soap—not if he didn't have to."

"No," he agreed amicably, "But I'm still *your* friend and Michael's, despite an absence of soap, of shoes ..."

"Of sense!" Natasha and I chorused.

Levi grinned and said whimsically, "Of sense! You guys stick by me no matter what." He punched my shoulder, put his arm around Natasha and exhaled contentedly. After a minute he whispered, "Thanks, guys."

Natasha bussed his cheek. "What, you expected something less? After all, *you* love *me*, and I'm as kooky as they come!"

"Ah, come on," I said. "Don't sell yourself short. You're *weird*."

We made small talk for an hour, each of us acknowledging in our own way this level of intimacy and friendship that defined our non-traditional household. I could ask for little else at that moment. But the moment passed as all do, and I had to get ready for my dinner date. As I got up I asked, "What've you guys got planned?"

Natasha rested her hand atop Levi's belly. "Think I'll put the stud through his paces. My temperature's still prime, and gay or straight, he has to earn his keep." Then she gave him a stern look. "But take a shower first, okay?"

Levi crowed lustily as he moved beneath the sheet and wrapped an arm around her waist. He wagged his eyebrows and stage whispered, "Showers? *Showers?* We don't need no stinkin' showers," and then he slowly pressed his hips against hers.

Natasha moaned. "Okaaay. Erections supersede showers." She shifted invitingly and tugged him closer until she let out a gasp. Then she ran her fingers through his thick hair and laughed deep in her throat. "You nut-case, you're impossible."

Levi smiled disarmingly, wiggled his hips, and undid the top button of her blouse.

I rolled my eyes, closed the door, and went to my room to get ready. The wall reduced their antics to a low rumble as I riffed through closets and opened dresser drawers. Minutes later Natasha burst into clear laughter, followed by Levi's easy chuckle. I smiled at their playfulness, and shook my head at their mischief. But when panting broke a protracted silence and merged into a rhythmic *creak creak creak* of the futon, I had to stop and stare out the window for several seconds as something clutched at my chest. I sought refuge in the shower, then shaved and got dressed.

I dressed to suit both Anna's tastes and mine: tan, tailor-made double-breasted suit and a pure white shirt. I chose a bold black and gold tie but eschewed the classic knot, putting an alternative spin on the silk that said, *this is Michael*, by purposely reversing the dimple below the knot to make it full and robust. I slipped my feet into a pair of black Bally lace-ups, and finished the look with a pocket square that peeked discretely from my breast pocket.

"You're put together very well," Anna said when I picked her up. We began our private evening with dinner at *Zabor's On The Bay*, Ocean City's singular fine-dining establishment. The main dining room was richly paneled and a crystal chandelier cast soft sparkles of light. The tables were covered by snowy white tablecloths and carefully set with superior silverware. A house photographer politely interrupted us during our drinks and asked if we'd like to capture our Ocean City memory. When we nodded he snapped a photo and brought it for our inspection later on. Anna and I showed our pleasure in the photo not only in our closeness, but also in our cheerful smiles.

The waiter reappeared. When I ordered steak Anna regarded me with a curious expression. "Michael, I know this restaurant. Their seafood is heavenly."

I clasped my hands atop the table. "Seafood's for rich people."

She took the hint and we merged into small talk, instead. After dinner was served, Anna gave me her life story and offered to support me in high style if only I would come live with her. She asked one or two desultory questions about the rape, but otherwise she seemed uninterested. She never inquired after Natasha, said nothing about last night's disastrous party, nor did she ask about Levi. And what would I have told her if she had asked—that he'd revealed his sexual orientation? Or that when last seen, he and Natasha were lying naked in bed?

*   *   *

He lay naked atop his bed; bitter at the turns his life had taken, livid that he still had no child to call his own, until he thought about how good that last fuck had been. He smiled at the image, relished the fact that he'd done her so well. He finally got up to take a shower. As he stood beneath the steaming water he looked down and considered shaving his pubic hair, since it could be evidence. "But what the hell—I knew you boys would never suspect *me*, so why bother?" Besides, he *wanted* to leave something behind; he wanted to show just who was fucking whose girlfriends. When he finished he decided to slip away and fuck the other girl. After a short drive he blended with the heavy Ocean City traffic, and not finding her car he silently cruised one street after another. Discouraged at last, he stopped at a convenience store and picked up a little something to bring home. He would find her another time, and when he did …

*   *   *

After the main course we had a cheese soufflé, an aperitif apiece, and then we topped the meal with a fine coffee. Then I took her dancing. She appeared to enjoy herself, and when she finally cried uncle we went to her condo. Anna excused herself and slipped into her room, only to reappear moments later in a luxurious dark blue robe. I took off my coat and tie and draped them on the back of a chair, then slipped my shoes and socks off. She put on a Leonard Cohen CD while I prepared drinks, and then we went to the balcony. A lamp inside cast our shadows in long slanted patterns against the damp sand, and beyond where the light could reach, the waves lifted to the stars. The waves found their way to the shore beneath a low, seductive murmur, while sea-smoke enveloped us.

Leonard Cohen's raspy voice broke the spell as he launched into his assertive, *I'm Your Man*. As I laughed inwardly at the absurdity I asked, "Where are we headed?"

She chose her words carefully. "I think we're on to something grand. I want you to come live with me—I insist on it. Why? Because it would be a serious start to something more."

"I do have a job," I said humorously. "I do have a career."

Anna waved her hand dismissively. "A career as a cop? Come now. You don't need it." She smiled indulgently. "I make more than enough to support us both. I'll dress you and we'll take fabulous vacations. First-class all the way! Hong Kong. Bruges. Rio. The Maldives! Now what do you say?"

"I say that I love my job. I mean, Christ—how could I contribute toward our relationship without it?"

Anna smiled and gulped the last of her drink. As the melted ice tinkled against the crystal glass she replied drunkenly, "By keeping me happy in bed. That will be your uppermost contribution."

I nodded and filed *that* under 'Bad Moves,' and then I cursed myself for letting Natasha slip away. As I stared at the now-dismal sea, an image of Natasha locked in Levi's embrace flashed unbidden from the deepest recesses of my cerebral cortex. Then I stood and took Anna inside. We made love, slept, and made love again beneath the photo of our dinner at Zabor's.

I left at sun-up the next morning. Anna would stay one more evening before returning to Washington. I had to work the evening cover shift and wouldn't get off until three in the morning. I suggested we get together. I had something to tell her.

"I'll prepare a nice meal for when you arrive," she said as I turned to go.

I recalled an old joke, the one that suggests that the best plan is no plan at all, because that way nothing can go wrong. We had made a plan.

CHAPTER 6

AN array of satellite antennae reached skyward from the half dozen news vans sprawled in front of police headquarters. At least three reporters craned their necks to see if I might be newsworthy as I glided past them on the way to the employee lot. Levi pulled to a stop in his Firebird thirty seconds later. "Showtime," I said.

He nodded thoughtfully. "A single rape wasn't worth their time. Now it's a feeding frenzy. What's worse, being raped or being raked over the coals by news freaks?"

We hit the locker room and got changed. Levi appeared understandably haggard but he managed a tired smile as we walked into roll call. The room turned silent as we took seats at the back of the room. Levi sat with his back ramrod straight and his eyes roamed from cop to cop while I watched each in turn, wishing I could read their minds.

Sgt Billy Burke entered in his usual huff, his eyes showing huge expanses of white as he surveyed the room. He placed both hairy hands on the paunch over his gun belt and stared at us before announcing, "Lieutenant Santoro has something to pass along before we get started."

Lt. Giuseppe "Joe" Santoro walked in. Second generation Italian, early fifties, salt and pepper. Joe was handsome, still in good shape, and he deigned to wear the open-collar shirts and khaki trousers sported by his investigators; instead he wore tailored suits and hand-tooled leather shoes. I liked him. He was my sergeant when I came on the job and he personally broke me in. Joe Santoro taught me that you could never be a successful cop unless the invisible people were visible to you. He meant the store clerks and the trash collectors, the dispossessed, the destitute—all who mattered, all with a story to tell. I understood; I'd been among the invisible.

The chief made a wise decision when he assigned the newly promoted Lieutenant Santoro to the top slot in investigations, instead of a pro forma admin job. There was something else of interest about Joe, a little tidbit that only a few were privy to—a shrewd stock market investor, he was worth a couple mil.

He began in a clear voice. "You guys are coming off your two-day break so here's what we know about the rapes." He cleared his throat. "Both victims are in their early twenties. They both live in the north end. Victim number one resides at One Forty-Second and Seaweed Lane; victim number two at One Thirty-Ninth and Bayside. Both have female roomies. Coincidentally—or not—they are surpassingly beautiful." He looked around the room. "I mean, they are gorgeous." Joe paused as he consulted a notepad. "In each case the suspect entered through closed patio doors and choked his victims unconscious. He tied their hands with purple bungee cords and blindfolded them. Both girls were penetrated vaginally, but no semen's been found …"

"'Cause he's using rubbers," a bored voice from the back intoned.

"Right," Joe said. "Probably wasn't a sex toy because we found pubic hairs, so your conclusion is well-founded." He held up an 8x10 glossy. "This is the bungee cord used on the first victim. The attacker amped it up a notch and roughed up the second victim." He moved the photo back and forth until he seemed satisfied that everyone had seen it. "Both attacks took place around ten o'clock. That's all we know. Neither girl remembers a thing between the times they were rendered unconscious until they came to. The victims do not know one another, nor do they have any idea who might have attacked them. We have no witnesses, no suspects and no idea what motivates this guy." He stopped abruptly, consulted his notes and asked, "Any questions?"

When there were none, a voice from the front said indignantly, "Christ, wait 'til the press gets hold of their names—and they *will*. Always someone willing to sell their soul to them rat bastards."

"Yeah," Demmings moaned. "As if that crap about sewage disposal wasn't bad enough. There go our raises."

"Fucking assholes," another interjected.

Joe cleared his voice. "We're going to saturate the north end with plain-clothes units. I'd like you guys to cruise up north too, because he'll *expect* us to step up our activities. Show the flag. Be proactive, but stay out from underfoot of my guys. Okay?"

The furor over the rapes died as suddenly as it had flared. Burke thanked

Joe for his briefing. Joe left, and Burke surveyed the room impassively. Then he seemed to study Levi carefully.

"Fall in for inspection," he ordered in a strangely neutral voice.

A shuffle of chairs, jangling keys and scuffing shoes filled the room as we formed three clumsy rows of eight. Levi stood front row center. I walked over and stood next to him.

Burke trooped the line at a fast pace. "Get those trousers pressed," he murmured to Demmings. "Suck in that gut," he admonished another.

When he drew abreast of me his face tightened as if he'd bitten into something sour. "Where's your nightstick, Brennan?"

Hmm. Checked up your ass lately? "In my briefcase," I said.

He smelled of too much sweat and hair grease. "In my briefcase, *Sergeant*." He looked me over from head to toe. "How come it's not on your gun belt?"

Fuck this. I dropped my eyes to his. "If I can't talk it out I duke it out. If I can't duke it out, I slap leather and shoot it out." Blood roared in my ears as Burke leaned closer, looked me in the eye, then nodded as he moved to Levi.

"*Mister* Hart," he began with unconcealed glee. "What're those you're wearing?"

"Don't you mean, *Officer* Hart?" Levi responded in a loud, clear voice.

Burke's smile filled my peripheral vision as he stared at Levi's feet. "Those are low-quarters you're wearing," he announced in a flat tone. "Why're you wearing low-quarters?"

"Low-quarter boots are authorized for swing shift," he said firmly.

Burke's tone took on a high note of sarcasm. "Well, that's true. They are. I won't argue you there, *Mister* Hart. But you should be wearing loafers, shouldn't you?"

Asshole. I knew what Burke had in mind. I'm sure Levi did, too.

"No," Levi replied stubbornly. "I should not."

Burke put both hands on his hips and leaned into him. "I say you should. I say cops who're light in the loafers should goddamn well wear loafers. That's what I think."

I would have felt stunned had I heard this remark in any other place in America. I kept forgetting that this was the East Coast, and that this town in particular struggled endlessly with its dual fears of change and growth.

Levi said calmly, "You're obviously under the mistaken impression that I give a fuck about what you think."

Burke looked as though Levi had slapped him. He recoiled and said, "You'd damned well *better* care, 'cause I don't allow no fruits on my shift. You got that, Mister?"

The room closed in. Microseconds ticked past. I sensed rather than saw Levi's head move as he stared at Burke and said in a flat, inflectionless voice. "Watch yourself, Burke. Do *not* fuck with me."

Burke reared back in mock consternation. "Don't *fuck* with you? Why the fuck not? Hell, you're supposed to be the big cock hound 'round here, but I never … and I mean never, ever realized until now just how close to the cock you get."

Levi snorted. "Yeah? And I hear you just had an exhausting night of sex. That means you'll have to use your other hand if you have sex tonight."

Hacksaw Jones chuckled.

"Why you insubordinate little fuck," Burke snarled. "I should …"

"You should *what?*" Levi snapped. He leaned into Burke. "If you *ever* say anything like that again I will sue your ass 'till a fly won't land on it." His voice dropped an octave as he wrapped it in steel. "Do not fuck with me, *Burke.*"

Burke's body went rigid and he clenched his fists as he lit into Levi with a shriek no one there could forget. "You little cocksucker! You can't talk to me that way! You hear me, you cocksucking sonuvabitch!"

I jumped between them and yelled, "Back the fuck off, Burke! You don't talk to my friend like that. You got a beef, meet me outside! You don't wanna meet me, then get fucked. Either way, back off and back off *now!*"

"You're suspended," Burke roared. "Both of you. Give me your guns and badges!"

Levi shot back in his best good-old-boy voice. "Well suck-a-tash. Looks like the ole Sarge is turnin' into a drama queen. Lands sake, I'm jist a quiverin' in my boots."

"They're right, Sarge," Hack broke in. "You're dead wrong to talk to any of us like that. I ain't gonna stand for it, neither." Hack paused but then continued in a softer voice—standard police tactic for defusing heated situations. "You're gonna get yourself jammed up. Can't say shit like that no more. Nope. Not these days."

"Who the fuck asked *you?*" Burke screeched.

Hack jutted his jaw forward. "I'm *tellin'* you. They is always two sides to every story. Even if there ain't in this case, it's none a your business and you can't be sayin' none a this shit. You get yourself sued, sayin' this sorta stuff."

Jarl jumped in. "They got nothin' on you, Sarge. They're bein' insubordinate. You got 'em by the short hairs." He paused. "Hart, anyway."

I turned toward Jarl and sneered. "Ass-kisser!"

Levi nudged my arm with his elbow and said with killing casualness. "You want our badges and guns? They're yours. I *want* you to take them. Come on, Burke. Let's get it done. Then I'm going straight to the Chief. I'll hit you with a hostile work environment charge so fast, you won't know whether to shit or go blind. After I bury you in EEO paperwork, I'll file against you in court for slander."

"Homo," an anonymous voice from the rear whispered.

Levi whirled around, his jaw firm, his muscles tight. "You! The punk who just called me a homo. And you, Jarl. You call yourselves officers?" He looked around with a look of disbelief, rage and frustration. "You fall all over yourselves to be my friends. You beg to come to my parties. Then you hear something and you don't even have the common fucking decency to ask what it's all about. Have any of you asked to hear my side? Did you even fucking think to act like cops, and check out the story?" He surveyed the ranks, and in a voice tinged with acid he said with deliberate slowness, "You're not police officers. You're no better than June Bugs. And you," he began as he whipped around and faced Burke, "are going to pay for this." Then Levi turned and plowed through the double doors and into the sterile corridor outside.

I ripped into Burke. "We've got a town to protect, and you waste time with this horse shit? Fuck this, and fuck *you*," I said. I turned on my heel and hurried after Levi.

"Levi. Wait."

"Like hell," he said as he darted down the hallway.

I sprinted forward and got a restraining hand on his shoulder just as he reached the elevator to the executive offices. "Levi, you're wasting your time. This chief won't do anything."

He drove his fist into his palm and said, "I won't leave him any choice."

I grabbed his elbow and yanked him away from the elevator. "You know what? Sometimes you're too ballsy for your own good. Listen to me! The Chief won't get involved. He's all about himself."

Levi blew air from his cheeks and waited until two secretaries got in the elevator before saying, "You're probably right. Goddamn it, you are right. He does nothing for the troops as it is. He'll cover for Burke if I push. The Chief's a genius at keeping his skirts clean; gotta give him that. Jesus, now that I think about it, there's not much we *can* do, is there?" Levi appeared vulnerable for the first time ever.

"Civil suit," I said decisively. "It's the best route. There were twenty people in that room. They all heard Burke."

Levi stared at the closed elevator doors until he said, "That's what I'll do. I'll sue his ass. Shit." He put both hands on his hips and chewed at his lower lip. "Burke *is* a smart dog—I'll give him that." He looked away toward some distant horizon beyond the solid walls of the police headquarters and said, "But I'll get him." Then Levi grabbed my arm and moved until his face was inches from mine. His eyes were large and fierce with pain. "Michael, you'll stick by me, won't you? No matter what?"

I pulled him close, not caring if anyone was watching, and hugged him. "It's okay, Levi. It's okay. You're not alone. I'm right here."

He huffed angrily a minute later. "Dumb fucks. No indignation whatsoever about this rapist. All they're worried about is who I keep company with." He shook his head in wonderment.

"You're very brave, Levi. I'm proud of you." I figured he'd punch in sick for the night. Go home. Take things easy. A lesser man would have. I know I'd have taken that route. But Levi didn't. He marched back in, got the keys to his cruiser, and told Burke where to find him if he had anything more to say. Burke refused to meet Levi's eye and acted as if neither he nor I existed. We played out the charade in unspoken yet mutual agreement, and while I stayed behind to finish my paperwork, Levi hit the streets with his head held high.

I proofread my reports, plopped them into Burke's in-basket, and called the house to give Natasha a heads-up concerning Levi. She didn't answer and I felt a stone in my chest. Her absences alarmed me now. I hung up, sick at heart that I'd pushed her away those many months ago, upset at the possibility that she'd given up on me, and sicker still when I considered Anna's expectation that I be her sex toy.

Natasha had always loved me for myself, not for how I might accessorize or satisfy her—though of course we'd always enjoyed the sex. But we'd always been such good *friends*. She could sleep with Levi and I could feel happy for her *and* for him. I grabbed the keys to my cruiser and reaffirmed my decision to end things with Anna tonight. Tomorrow? Tomorrow I'd expound on some deep thoughts with Natasha over a Scotch or two. Or three. Johnny Walker; the Green Label.

Hacksaw radioed around nine and asked for a meet. I keyed the mike. "Name it."

"*Make it twenty six-eleven.*"

"Ten-four." I turned south on Coastal and drove toward the 26th Street 7-11. We used their parking lot for quick confabs but don't ask me why. The lot was too small and not even convenient—as convenience stores go. Maybe force of habit played a role, or maybe we liked to hear ourselves say 'twenty six-eleven' in our secret cop talk.

We pulled abreast of each other five minutes later. The news of the rapes was having its effect—there were far fewer tourists than usual, although enough hardy souls still streamed up and down the sidewalks, their clothes plastered against them by the sweltering night air. Some drifted past our cars to chance a quick peek inside, while others feigned indifference and bumped along as if we didn't exist.

"Howzit goin'?" Hacksaw asked.

I settled into my seat and let out a long breath. "It's obviously not." I turned the A/C up a notch and waited.

He got to the point. "Man, I sure do 'mire you for standin' up to Burke the way you did. Levi's a lucky sumbitch to have you for a buddy." He ran his tongue across his lips and continued in a softer voice, "I missed the brouhaha at the party. Me an' my girl hit the road 'fore the shit hit the fan. Got to tell you though," he paused as he wiped a broad hand across his coffee-colored forehead, "I wish I'd a been there."

"Why?"

He grabbed his steering wheel abruptly with both hands and edged closer with some sort of electrified excitement. "'Cause I wouldn't a left, that's why not." He looked at me with large clear eyes that seemed alive with something profound growing inside them. "Levi didn't deserve none a that. The boys shoulda stayed an' heard him out. 'Specially the brothers. Hell," he said as he gripped the wheel tighter. "Ain't nothing worse than havin' people look at you like you was dog meat, know what I mean?"

I nodded. I knew exactly what he meant.

Hacksaw jumped in his seat, eager to finish what he needed to say. "It's like, people don't wanna hear good things 'bout a person, ya know?" He fought for the right words, the correct meaning. They finally came in a rush. "Jesus Christ, Michael. People only wanna see the bad stuff, so they can feel better 'bout themselves. That's why they all walked out without givin' him a chance, an' that's why they climbin' all over him tonight, cause he's got style an' they don't. An' they hate him for it. That's what I think," he said, and then he settled back against his seat with great force.

I'd just opened my mouth to say something when Hack blurted, "You know this, but I'll say it regardless—I've got a bachelor's degree, the same as you. I'm quite capable of utilizing proper grammar. But this is my home, and I fall back on learned behavior. I've acquired correct attributes, but I … well, this *is* my home. So I revert to old habits in my effort to establish a comfort zone. My point? A majority of those whom we associate with are intimidated— '*timidated*," he said with a tired smile—"by knowledge. That is why they pursue vendettas against those who are singular."

Hacksaw made the best sense of it all. I smiled at him with genuine affection and said, "Yeah, you've got 'em pegged, all right." I made a vague gesture in the direction of police headquarters. "They're jealous and miserable and pissed at the world."

Hack stared through the windshield and slouched further against the seat. After a bit he said, "Michael, you can bed down a thousand girls and eat a thousand pussies, an' nobody ever calls you a pussy eater. But suck one dick, and you're a cocksucker for life." He wiped his hand across his forehead again and looked at me with liquid eyes. "I ain't got no issue with gay folk, an' it don't make no difference to me at all what Levi is or isn't. Gay or straight, it just don't matter. He's a good cop and he's a friend, and that's all I gotta say about that."

I nodded. "Levi knows he can be anything he wants around me." I glanced sideways at Hack. "Hell, you know my background."

Hacksaw looked at me with great compassion. "Yeah, and I 'spose I'm 'bout the only one 'round here what does." He paused. "How come you dumped on me that night?"

I couldn't help but smile at the memory. It happened a year ago. Natasha and I had ended our committed relationship. I'd put away a few too many at a local cop hangout. Hack was there, he drove me home, and he listened attentively as I described a childhood on the streets, encountering—and often befriending—the full gamut of unconventional lifestyles. "Well, you know. You were there for me."

He nodded.

I sighed. "Sure. I've had gay friends. What do I care what gives people happiness? Look, there's stuff I do with a woman to get *my* pulse going. No doubt you get turned-on some other way. Levi's my friend. I would never turn my back on him."

He arched his eyebrows and said, "You got that right. We all in this together. You. Me. Levi. We're brothers. Got it?"

"Got it," I said.

Hacksaw shifted around and faced me squarely. "Still an' all, we gotta be careful. That redneck Burke's an idiot—we all know that. But he's no dummy, an' that makes him a dangerous idiot."

I nodded rapidly. "Gotta admit, he's the man I'd follow if I was trapped in a minefield."

Hack said, "Now this is just 'tween you, me an' the wall, but a couple of the guys got to talkin' to Burke after you an' Levi left. They convinced him to settle down, but only 'cause they figger you an' Levi got something on him … you know, for what he said durin' roll call."

I nodded. "They're right. We do."

He stared with an unwavering gaze. "Maybe you do, an' maybe you don't."

I sat up straight. "What is it you're not telling me?"

"All I'm sayin' is, you know how some a them boys are. They'd sell their souls for a promotion—you get my drift?"

"I get your drift. You're saying not to count on them to stand up for me and Levi."

Hack nodded. "Not if push comes to shove." He dropped his eyes and said, "Another thing. I wouldn't put it past Burke an' Jarl to set you an' Levi up."

"We can handle ourselves!"

"I know you can, but …"

"Jesus! Why are they wasting time on us? We've got a friggin' rapist running loose!"

"It's 'cause they don't know how to do real police work. Leastways, they ain't got no motivation for it. So they turn on you guys, instead. They're bullies." He rubbed his jaw thoughtfully and added, "Well, not all of 'em. But the dickheads? They got this need to pick on somebody. Thing is, they ain't got the *cojones* to go after a real threat, so they gone and turned on you an' Levi. You guys are their necessary enemy."

I stepped on the brake and shifted into drive. "Thanks for the talk. I'll tell Levi how you feel about him. I know he'll appreciate it. By the way, how's the locksmith business these days?"

A few minutes later I was working my way north through sluggish traffic. Angry motorists slammed fists against horns, shouted epithets through open windows and flipped the bird in reaction to a variety of slights and offenses. A kid in a rust-bucket Chevy cut me off at 45th Street. Maybe he did it on purpose, maybe not. I grabbed the mike. "Seventy-three-oh-nine with traffic. White Chevelle. Maryland registration, three Victor Edward George seven two three. Make it Coastal and 48th."

"Communications to Seventy-three-oh-nine, ten four."

I toggled my overheads and the driver made a right on 48th Street, but then he drifted halfway up the block before stopping, an act of stupidity or defiance that never failed to piss me off. I angled my cruiser behind him and lit the car's interior with my spotlight. Then I grabbed my flashlight and summons book and leapt out, reaching the driver before he could fasten his seatbelt.

I flashed my light through the car in a perfunctory search for weapons. There were three passengers, all Bugs. I stood just behind the driver's door and got right to business. "Good evening. I'm Officer Brennan of the Ocean City Police Department. I stopped you for making an unsafe lane change and I'm going to issue a citation. I need your license and registration card."

Even seated, the driver appeared tall. He had on a reversed ball cap, black T and brown shorts. A ring pierced his left ear. "Unsafe lane change?" he asked, hamming it up for his friends. "I didn't make no unsafe lane change." Then he monkey-grinned me and said, "You got the wrong car ... *Officer.*"

"I appreciate that," I said neutrally, "but I stopped *you* and I need your license and registration."

"But …"

"But nothing." I pinned him with a stare. "Let me explain something to you. I have a job to do and I've stopped you for committing a traffic violation. I've treated you with respect and I've asked for your license and registration." A middle-aged couple on the sidewalk appeared in the corner of my eye as they stopped to watch, but I stayed on track with the violator. "I intend to write you a citation. I do not intend to debate its merits with you, not here, not now. That's for a court of law. I'm going to request your license and registration one more time. If you don't give them to me I'm going to place you under arrest. Now, I'd like to think that we can take care of this so you and your friends can get on with whatever you've got planned for this evening. For the last time, give me your license and registration."

It was a long speech, but it worked. The rear seat passenger jabbed the driver's shoulder and said, "Come on, so we can get out of here."

The driver handed me his license and registration card. I took the documents, stepped to the fender of my cruiser, and wrote him a coupon redeemable for forty bucks in the local court of law. As I finished dotting the i's and crossing the t's, Levi's cruiser drifted ghost-like up the street with its lights off and came to a silent stop behind me. I gave him the barest nod to signify that I'd seen him.

I tucked my flashlight under my left armpit to keep my gun hand free and returned to the driver. I held the ticket book in my left hand and said, "This citation charges you with an unsafe lane change."

"Yeah, yeah, yeah. Fuck you and your unsafe lanes. Just give me the fucking ticket."

I continued unfazed. "You can pay the fine of forty dollars prior to the date at the bottom of the citation, or you can appear in court. If you choose to appear, follow the directions on the back of your copy and …"

"You bet your ass I'll take this to court! And I'm gonna make *you* show up on your fuckin' day off!"

That worked for me. My court dates were prescheduled for normal working days. "That's your right. However, you must sign this citation. By signing you are not admitting guilt. You're only promising to pay the fine or appear in court." I held out the ticket book for him to sign.

He turned his face away. "I'm not signing anything … prick."

The couple on the sidewalk hurried off as Levi opened his door with a soft squeak. I closed the book and leaned forward. "I appreciate that, but you have no choice. You are required by law to sign the citation. I'm going to offer you one more opportunity to sign. If you refuse to sign I'm going to place you under arrest." I held the book out to him.

Before the driver could say or do anything, the Bug seated next to him chimed in. "Fuck him, Davey. You don't gotta sign nothin'. Don't do it."

The driver looked from his buddy to me, and back again.

Levi stepped cat-like to the car's right rear fender and stood silent vigil.

The driver thought it through and caved, but to save face he said, "The only reason I'm signing is because I got some pussy waiting for me. Some real pussy," he snickered. "Not a pussy like you."

"That's fine," I said as I tore off his copy and handed it to him.

"Hey," he said as he threw the unread citation into the back seat. "You forget something?"

"Nope. Not a thing," I said while handing him his license.

He held out his hand and fluttered his eyes at me. "My registration, you pussy."

"I'm not finished," I said in a monotone. Then I pointed to the passenger seated beside him. "You. Do you have a driver's license?"

The Bug held a forefinger to his chest and pantomimed my question. "Yeah. You."

"Whatever for ... *Officer*?"

I cut his eyes with mine and said in an even but unmistakable command voice, "I asked you a question. Answer me. *Now*. Do you have a license?"

"Yeah," he snarled. "I got a fucking license. What's it to you?"

"A moment ago you told the driver not to sign the citation. You can't do that. It's illegal to tell the operator of a motor vehicle to break the law. I'm going to write *you* a citation, and I want your license."

"Fucking bullshit! I don't believe this fucking shit." He tore at his rear pocket and produced a wallet. He found his license but then he flipped it at me. It struck my gun belt squarely in the buckle.

I caught Levi's eye. He stepped back into the shadows as I quick-marched to the passenger door. The Bug stared at me with hate-filled eyes as I yanked it open. "You're under arrest," I informed him. "Step out of the car."

"Under arrest for *what*," he wailed.

"Assault and battery. You threw your license at me. Now get out of the car."

"I don't fucking *believe* this bullshit," he screamed, but he got out anyway, slamming the door and puffing his chest. "Fucking pussy," he taunted.

"Turn around," I ordered with a deadpan face. "Put your hands behind you back. Do it now."

"Pussy," he muttered, even as he complied.

I slapped the cuffs around his wrists before he could change his mind. It works best that way. Forget the Hollywood stuff. Get 'em out, get 'em cuffed, then let 'em hoot and holler all they want. I frisked him from head to toe, front and back. He was hard-muscled and could have put up a good fight.

The driver poked his head through his window and said, "I hope you're satisfied. You just better fuckin' hope I don't catch you off-duty somewhere."

Stupid jerk. Didn't know when to let it go. I nodded at Levi and he stepped forward and took hold of my prisoner. The guy's eyes bulged as he asked, "Where'd you fucking come from?"

"Howdy, pardner," Levi twanged. "Jist passing by."

I went to the driver and held the registration close to his face. "Sir, I just noticed that you have a broken tail light." Then I made a show of examining his car. "Your left rear tire has got a bit too much tread wear. Not only that, but your side mirror's broken." I offered my best vaudevillian sigh. "I'm afraid I have no choice but to declare this an unsafe vehicle. Now then," I said with sudden iron, "do you want to call *your* wrecker, or shall I call *mine*, because you're not driving this car. Your call."

"Fuck you," he muttered.

"Very well, sir. I'll make that call for you. Your car is hereby impounded." I radioed dispatch and summoned the nearest reliable tow service. The driver would now have to wait until the impound lot opened the next day, and pay an enormous fee to have it released. His troubles wouldn't end there. He'd have to repair all the items I checked off on the Safety Equipment Repair Order and then have his car inspected. In all, his threat would cost him about six or seven hundred dollars, not to mention the time he would waste in reconciling the myriad administrative issues.

I seldom resorted to that tactic but it taught some people a better lesson than placing them under arrest. Had I chosen arrest he would have gained status as someone who got locked up for threatening a cop with physical violence. By taking away his wheels, I taught him never to mess with the police again—not unless he had a lot of spare time and money to spend.

Forty bucks, man. Forty bucks, and these nimrods would have been on their way to brag or drink or whatever. Now their wheels were gone and their friend stood humbled before them in a set of my handcuffs. Even if they had the money to pay his bail—which I doubted—he'd still have to appear before the judge for a bond-review hearing, and that wouldn't take place until ten o'clock the next morning. Either way, they had screwed themselves into a bad night instead of turning a hot night into a good screw—assuming they even had girlfriends.

I took my prisoner from a very somber Levi. "Always glad to see you as my back-up."

He said quietly, "Not a problem. Go take your prisoner and book him. I'll store the car for you."

"Thanks," I said, grateful to be free of that paperwork. "Hey. You okay?"

He yawned. "Yeah, I'm fine. Just tired. Go on. Get out of here."

I held the Bug firmly with one hand. "You sure? Got anything planned after you get off?"

"No. Think I'll go home. Crash and burn time, ya know?"

"I have to work until three—why not ride with me a bit?"

"Yeah. Sure. That'd be fine. Thanks, Michael."

I left Levi to deal with the car and turned into an alley to get back to 50th Street when I discovered Demmings' cruiser parked in some shadows. I wondered what he was doing because he'd been assigned to the northern sector. Even more puzzling: since he apparently *was* here, why hadn't he backed me up on the traffic stop?

I let it go and drove to headquarters, where I turned my prisoner over to the booking officer. Then I found an unused cubicle in the report-writing room, signed-on to the computer and got to work. Twenty minutes later I finished the Statement of Charges that would introduce my nemesis to the convoluted world of the criminal justice system. I spent another ten minutes typing the formal language for the criminal investigation report that would accompany the charging document. I was almost done when Demmings walked in and greeted me. "What's up?" I asked perfunctorily. I wasn't sure which side he'd taken in the earlier battle with Burke.

He broke into a grin and fished around in his shirt pocket. He produced some photographs and asked with a boyish glee, "What do you think?"

I knew what they were but asked anyway. "What've you got?"

He had a strange gleam in his eyes as he handed them over. "See for yourself."

The photos showed a young couple atop a bed, too consumed in sexual intercourse to know that Demmings was standing on the other side of their window and clicking away with a camera. The photos showed it all: foreplay, coupling, and climax.

Demmings' breathing picked up. "Jesus, they were really gettin' it on."

I edged my chair away and said, "I guess."

He eyed me suspiciously. "Don't you think she's hot looking?"

"She's a great looking girl but her privacy was invaded. I don't want any part of it."

"Well aren't we the snob," he said as he took the photos back. "Maybe you've been hanging around your boy Levi too much." He held one of the photos aloft. "Is that why she doesn't do anything for you?"

"No, Demmings! I am not a snob, and leave *Officer* Hart out of this." On impulse I added, "Besides, I know how it feels to be spied upon."

That piqued his interest. "Yeah? Someone been taking pictures of you and some chickee? Where are they? I wanna see 'em."

I shook my head. "You're something else."

He grinned crazily, apparently not sure how to take my response. Then he stood around and fidgeted for another half-minute before taking the hint and leaving. Our encounter held one small virtue—at least he hadn't tried to show me pictures of his wife, Mrs. Donna Demmings.

When I finally finished and checked the wall-mounted clock it was ten o'clock, and I still had five hours to go. I hit the streets and started north, wondering why so many of my colleagues got so wound up over sexual issues, yet didn't feel motivated to nail a rapist.

Levi radioed me when he got off at eleven. I drove past a news van that was still staked-out in front of headquarters and picked him up. I told him what Hacksaw said earlier and that seemed to buoy his spirits. Then we set out to prowl some of the darker streets. He had changed into a dark blue aloha shirt, baggy shorts, and of course he had no shoes. We devised a plan: he would roam the streets on foot while I prowled a larger geographical area in my car. He nodded his consent, tucked his pistol inside his waistband and shoved his portable radio into a back pocket, letting his shirt conceal both. I drove off leaving him in my rear-view mirror. Anyone seeing him walking barefoot along the streets would immediately write him off as a tourist. Only another cop would know that he wasn't.

*   *   *

He had no doubt that he would get away with this one, too. The media coverage had become a challenge to his potential to succeed, and he *would* succeed, because he'd been outsmarting them all. "You losers were looking everywhere when ya shoulda been looking for me right here."

Two days had passed since he'd raped that last one, although he preferred to think that he'd nailed her. He'd roughed her up because she'd asked for it—just thinking about the way she rejected her suitor riled him. Now he would teach a few more lessons, because despite the quality of those last few fucks—despite that great orgasm he'd recently had—he just flat-out needed his fix.

He'd done his homework on this one and he *knew* she'd be alone. He stole silently to the low sand dune along the dark side of the building, confident that his presence would go unchallenged. After all, didn't he belong? When he reached the patio door behind the dune he noticed how much sand he'd picked up. He made a mental note not to be so careless next time, and pulled on surgical gloves. After a last look around he checked the door and discovered that it wasn't locked. Stupid fucking bitch! He'd teach her—and he wouldn't be as gentle as he'd been with the others.

He slipped past the door and drifted across the carpet like the panther he knew himself to be. She was busy at the stove, stirring a light broth in a medium-sized cauldron. Fresh greens lay on the counter next to a bottle of pinot noir. The woman, stunning in her beauty, seemed totally absorbed in her activity. He felt bolstered by his cover story—he knew she'd accept his presence if she turned before he pounced. His smile dissolved beneath his tightly pressed lips as he watched her suddenly put down the wooden spoon and pick up a knife. Then he flicked his eyes toward the greens, and when she began chopping he understood.

No! She's stiffened. Maybe she heard him after all. He covered the remaining distance in three quick strides and got his arm around her neck before she could turn. But he wasn't quick enough! She rammed her elbow into his gut before she passed out.

"Whore!" he said as the pain knifed through him. He purposely let go of her limp body and she hit the floor with a thud. His anger overrode the pain as he bound her hands with the bungee cord and gagged her with a foul-smelling dishrag. Then he grabbed a pure white linen napkin from the nearby dinner table, and after he wrapped it around her eyes he took her from behind. *I will be in charge of you. I'm the dominant one.*

He raped her hard, fast and furiously. When he finished twenty seconds later he went to a nearby closet and searched inside. He found what he wanted, and wincing from the pain in his abdomen, he shoved the broom handle as far into her vagina as it would go. "Like a dog marking its turf—you fucking *whore!*" He was about to spit on her but caught himself at the last instant. Instead he zipped himself up—leaving the condom on to prevent evidentiary leakage—peeled off the gloves, stuffed them in his trouser pocket, and left the way he had come in.

*   *   *

"I'm just west of the cinema," Levi radioed at two o'clock.

I'd just finished a drive-by of Anna's. I keyed my mike twice and swung toward 145th Street to pick him up. As he got in I raised an eyebrow. "My, don't we smell more pungent than usual." He couldn't help but be sweaty and smelly after a two-hour walk in the sluggish night air—but I did wonder why he smelled of recent sex. I inclined my head toward his bare feet and said, "Jesus, where'd you pick up all that sand and shit?"

His shoulders jerked and then he glanced down and said, "Just tramping around." Then he shrugged very causally and added, "I decided to check some of the condos—you know, from beachside."

I nodded. "See anything?"

"Nothing." He laughed nervously. "I felt like Chief Brody, chumming for a great white that ain't about to bite."

I uttered a harsh laugh. "Long as you didn't come off as Quint ... or the Dreyfuss character. Matt Hooper?"

Levi cracked a smile. "Yeah. Hooper." He glanced outside his window and mimicked Dreyfuss: "'Well, this is not a boat accident!'"

"And this is no shark we're dealing with. Wonder how long it'll take before more tourists react?"

Levi seemed deep in thought. Finally he said, "Yeah, forget about thinking it's safe to go back in the water. They'll avoid this town like the plague."

"That they will. *Humph*, and Burke was afraid the 'people are sewage' article would scare away tourist dollars. Just wait."

Levi sighed. "Yeah. Trouble is, it's still not enough to get some of these guys off their dead asses."

All at once I asked, "So what's in it for you? Why are you so involved?"

"Good question," he replied, glancing sideways at me. He said nothing for a few seconds and then he said, "Let's just say that I don't like rapists any more than you do. I don't like seeing others being made the victim." He paused for just a heartbeat and added, "Be it man, woman ..." and now he looked straight at me and said, "or child."

I let the clock run out until just before the buzzer sounded, when without looking at him I asked in a whisper, "Why do you say that?"

He looked at me at an oblique angle and said, "I'm a cop. I can deduce. Let's just say that I see things and let it go at that."

I opened my mouth to thank him but couldn't speak.

Levi tapped my shoulder and said, "We shared that college pad for almost four years." He held me with an unwavering gaze and said kindly, "Sometimes you talked in your sleep. Loudly."

I couldn't let it go. Not now. Turning to him I asked, "Is that why you're doing this—spending your own time—for me?"

Levi slowly nodded. "For you, and for ... the others."

We ended it there and called it a night. I drove him back to headquarters and pulled to a stop next to his car. "You heading home?"

He sighed. "Think I'll stop by Nat's club and see how she's doing."

"Better shower first."

"What do you mean?"

I said matter-of-factly, "You've had sex."

Levi jumped a little. "Is it that obvious?"

I gripped the wheel and said to the windshield, "You were supposed to be looking for the bad guy."

Levi frowned and gave me a hard look. "It's like this. Jen left a voice message. All apologetic. So I stopped by while making the rounds."

I exhaled loudly but said softly, "You did it, didn't you?"

Levi pinched the end of his nose and looked away. "I felt so fucking lonely, bro." He turned to me and said simply, "I had to. Don't you see? It'll make us friends again."

"It'll make her pregnant! Hey, only yesterday you were explaining why you didn't wanna get Jen …"

Levi cut in harshly. "That was then! Now I … aw, the hell with it." His mouth turned down and he flicked his eyes toward the floor as the air conditioner whined noisily. "Jen might not be in love with me, but she feels *some* love for me. Two facts: I do care about her, and she wants a baby! If *I* don't give her one she'll go to a sperm bank. So why not mine?" He grunted. "Damn, what'd I just do? Bet my boys are already doing their thing. Now I *will* have two kids." He finished wearily, "God I wish I smoked."

I made a face. "They wouldn't be doing their thing if you'd stayed on the job."

He frowned. "I *am* off-duty." He looked away while fidgeting with his seat belt. "We only fucked for thirty, forty minutes tops, and then I hit the streets again, so get off my goddamned back!"

"You're turning into a caustic son of a bitch, you know that?"

"Kiss my ass."

"The prosecution rests." After the silence dragged out I reached over and squeezed his shoulder. "Listen, I had no right to jump you like that. Tell you what. I'm supposed to go to Anna's in another hour …"

"Then you fucking should …"

"No. Hey, lighten up. This night's been rough on you. Wait up for me and we'll drink a couple of cold ones."

He exhaled noisily and nodded. "Thanks. Another time. I'm just gonna crash."

"You sure?"

"Yeah … and thanks." He tapped my arm. "Hey, you think Nat's gonna be pissed at me?"

"Definitely. Rec sex with others is one thing, but she's got this weird competition thing going with Jen." I coughed lightly. "She's also pissed at her for being mean to you. But she'll forgive you. Not right away, but …"

He nodded vigorously. "But she will forgive me."

A silent moment passed until I formed a perplexed look and mumbled, "Ibba da?"

Levi smiled, play-punched my arm and opened the door. Then he stopped and faced me and said, "Thank you, you know, for this Kodak moment."

I shot him the bird.

He said more deliberately, "Hey ... Michael? Thanks for being my friend."

"Sure," I said, feeling too overwhelmed to respond more fully to this natural man whose child-like instincts infused him with a zest for life and a loving appreciation of all it offered. I think he understood my silence when he whispered, "It's okay, Michael," as he got out.

At a quarter to three I parked my cruiser, dashed inside headquarters and showered and changed. As I hurried toward an exit door afterward I nearly ran into Joe Santoro. He had a folder tucked under one arm and he gave me a hard look. I stared back, figuring that Burke must have told him about today's roll call. Well, fuck *it* and fuck *him*. I pushed down hard on the exit door panic bar, got in my car, and drove to Anna's without passing 'go' and without collecting my two hundred big ones.

I knocked a second time, then a third. I pushed the buzzer. Twice. Three times. I double-checked the car parked in front; it was definitely hers. I walked around the building and checked her windows. There were lights on. I rang the buzzer again and then drove two blocks to a pay phone. I fed a quarter in the slot and dialed her number. I let it ring ten times, waited five minutes in case she was in the shower and called again. No answer.

My concern grew as I acknowledged that I was about to do what many civilians consider doing—calling local hospitals and police departments in search of that special someone who failed to show up as expected. So I called police dispatch. "Michael Brennan here. Any calls tonight involving a Ms. Anna Stewart? Wait a sec ... try Anna Bell, too."

"Hold one," the call taker said. Five minutes later she said, "I'm switching you."

Joe Santoro came on the phone. "Brennan. You're asking about Anna Stewart. Is that correct? Ms. *Anna* Stewart?"

"Yeah. That's right. Anna Stewart. What's goin' on?"

"She's here," he said impatiently, "and she's busy."

"How the hell can she be busy? We've got a date tonight."

"She's involved in an interview and can't be disturbed. She's a reporter for the *Post*, you know."

"*Travel* reporter. What's so important that she has to do a story at three in the morning?"

"We asked for her help. Ed Bell—her brother? Bell suggested she might be of assistance. We've got a reluctant witness to a crime and Ed thought she might talk to a reporter. Satisfied?"

"No. How did Ed get involved in this?"

Joe said impatiently, "That's really none of your business."

I scowled into the phone. "I'm making it my business. When will she be done? Put her on the line. I wanna talk to her."

"You're not going to," he snapped. "We're running an investigation and she'll be done when I say she's done. Go home, Brennan. I'll have her call you there."

I stared at the handset as the dial tone filled the air. Pitching a fit wouldn't alter the fact that Anna had somehow gotten involved in a case. I called it a night and went home and found Levi's car in the driveway. Natasha's car was nowhere to be seen.

His bedroom door was partly open and he lay naked atop his bedcovers, drawn into a fetal position and fast asleep. There was still some beach sand clinging tenaciously to his feet and he smelled of Jennifer. An immense candle on the nightstand flickered near his head, slave to the draft from the humming air conditioner. I stepped inside and touched his arm and he felt cold and dead to the world. I picked up his blanket and draped it over him, unable to get over how vulnerable he appeared; no wonder he'd gone to Jennifer's arms. Levi was a tough hombre, but now I hovered over him, struck by a sudden need to protect him.

I made a decision and then walked through the house turning off lights and checking doors. George whimpered fitfully in his sleep as I swept past him, victim of some canine nightmare. Then I got the pillow and blanket from my bed and took them to Levi's room. I blew out the candle, dropped the pillow to the floor, stretched out on the carpet and pulled the blanket over me. I was offering a silent prayer for him as George waddled in, got down with a groan and put his head on my leg. Afterward I stared at the dark ceiling, wondering about Anna's absence and thinking about Natasha. Sleep didn't come until much later.

CHAPTER 7

A LOUD truck rumbled past the house and hit its airbrakes, and the sudden burst jerked me from sleep like a dog that's run the length of its tether. It took a few seconds to figure out why I was asleep on Levi's floor until I sat up and checked on him. He was still out cold. His clock read 9:00am, so that meant that I'd had a grand total of three hours sleep—well hell; there'd be no more for me now. I grabbed my blanket and pillow and dumped them on my bed, and although I needed a shower in the worst way, other stuff took priority. I grabbed a pair of jeans from the floor and sniffed them. They were just this side of south but I pulled them on anyway. Then I stepped into the hallway, where George greeted me with a soft *whoof* as I stared at Natasha's open door.

I fed George, grabbed the phone, and called Anna. I got no response, no answering machine. I tried her D.C. number; zip. I called the *Washington Post*, but got only as far as her voice mail. I left a message and called Joe Santoro, but he either wasn't in or he wasn't taking my call. In desperation I called Fire Headquarters and got Ed Bell's home number.

Ed picked up on the first ring. He sounded distraught when I asked if he knew where I might find Anna. "She's on her way to see our parents."

"Okay. Will you give me that number so I can call her?"

"No. Umm ... I'll have her phone you."

"Ed."

After a pause, "Yes, Michael."

"What's going on?"

He cleared his throat as something—a newspaper perhaps—rustled near the phone. I had the distinct feeling that she was there. Ed cleared his throat a second time. Finally he said, "She's with someone, Michael."

"What do you mean, she's *with* someone? Who? Jesus Christ, don't tell me she's seeing another cop."

Ed coughed and said, "An old boyfriend showed up this morning. She …
well, she's with him right now. I'm sorry."

I stared at the wall. *Deep, cleansing breath.* "Okay. Thanks, Ed. Please tell
her," I began, "tell her I'm sorry things didn't work out."

I hung-up and went outside and got busy washing and detailing the
Mustang.

An hour later I was drenched in sweat, and as I gave the polishing cloth
one last swipe I wondered where Natasha had been all night. After deciding
I probably didn't want to know, I gathered everything and trudged across the
gravel driveway, feeling every sharp stone. With nothing else to do yet still full
of nervous energy, I slumped down at the breakfast table and picked up the
newspaper. I was scanning the "A" section when Levi's door opened. I looked
up as he trudged down the hallway wearing nothing but faded blue sweatpants.
He sat down at the table, picked up the sports section, and wrinkled his nose.
"Damn. You're freakin' ripe!"

"You don't exactly smell like a daisy. And when's the last time you washed
those grungy-ass sweats?"

He shrugged. "Dunno. Couple weeks." Then he cleared his throat and said
quietly, "Woke up 'round six and found you on the floor." He turned a page.
"Guess I felt kinda down after I got home. Crashed hard. Hey—that was a
classy thing you did."

I kept my eyes glued to the newspaper, "Don't know what you're talking
about."

He whispered, "I know. Anyway, you and Nat are the best." Levi went back
to his sports pages. "Hey," he began a few minutes later, his old self totally
restored. "O's are playing a home game next week. You've always been keen on
them. Wanna go? Come on," he pleaded. "Camden Yards? It's the best."

I said distractedly, "I don't know."

Levi's basketball lay on the floor beneath the table. He put his sand-
encrusted foot on it and idly rolled it back and forth. He was still reading the
paper when he said off-handedly, "Feel like getting your ass kicked?"

"Think you're man enough?"

He snorted. "I fucking know I am. What do you say? Hoops are just down
the street."

I turned a page and thought about it. "Another time."

"Ah, come on," he said impatiently. He picked up the ball and spun it expertly atop his index finger.

"You're awfully calm for a guy who's going from zero kids to a pair of 'em."

Levi put another spin on the ball and watched it twirl with great intensity as he replied, "What do you want me to do—have kittens? This is how I deal with stuff."

I said with great control, "Any idea what happened to Nat last night?"

"Yeah. She got pissed when I told her about Jen, and spent the night with some guy."

My stomach clenched but then I chided myself. Hell, I'd certainly been having sex. Then I calmly dropped a hammer. "Anna gave me the heave-ho."

Levi stopped spinning the ball and arched his eyebrows. "Did she say why?"

"Didn't tell me anything. Ed Bell broke the news."

Levi nodded understandingly but said, "Good. I'm glad."

I looked sharply at him. "What's that supposed to mean?"

He let the ball slip from his fingers to the floor. Then he looked at me through hooded eyes before replying. "Face it, Michael. She wasn't your type. You weren't hers, either." He grinned sheepishly. "Now you're free to give it another chance with Natasha."

After a brief staring contest I said, "You see right through me, don't you?"

Levi cracked a smile. "I just know you."

I said to the table's clean white surface. "I was gonna tell Anna last night."

He nodded. "Why am I not surprised?"

"But she didn't have to dump me this way!" I pounded my fist against the table and growled, "She could've told me to my face!"

Levi said soberly, "Woulda, coulda, shoulda. Thing is, she didn't. Besides," he said as he made an expansive gesture with his hands, "plenty of guys do the same to *their* girlfriends." He quickly added, "I'm not suggesting that turn-about is fair play. It's not. I'm only saying let it go. Don't take it personally."

Still frowning I said, "Yeah. You're right." Then I stood up and flicked my eyes toward the street outside. "Think I'll hit the gym and vent. Wanna go?"

"Don't think so. Nat'll come home eventually. I want some heart-to-heart time with her."

"Oh?"

"I really needed her friendship the other night. After you left for your date with Anna we watched some tube, shot the shit. But then some unfinished business surfaced."

"Such as?"

Levi put his foot atop the basketball and absently rolled it back and forth. "Such as, you're all she talked about." He stopped rolling the ball. "She's more in love with you than even I suspected. Damn," he said, and after a pause he said in a near-whisper, "I figured we'd make this baby and maybe ... maybe *this* time she'd marry me. Then we could have another, and another, and ... and who was I kidding? She wants you, not me!" He drew a deep breath and said, "Michael, look—I know you love her, even if you don't know it." His eyes turned sad. "And I know she's always loved you in ways she never has me." He fell silent until he seemed to reach a decision. Then his face turned fierce and he said, "I love her, and—and I love you too, and I don't wanna see you losing this gift that's there for you and Nat. So I'm gonna spend some time with her; gonna tell her she makes me feel first-rate, that it's great she wanted another go at having a kid with me. But I'll also tell her that there's no way I'll stand between the two of you—and that it's time to stop this baby business."

I felt thunderstruck—the news was that welcome—but I still said, "Don't you think you should ask Nat how she feels? She *wants* that baby."

Levi turned to me in anguish and let out a raspy, "I know." But after a few seconds he scowled and said, "Damn it! You'd better fucking tell her how you feel, or I'm gonna drop kick the shit out of you!" Then Levi looked at me with his large blue eyes and said quietly, "Okay?"

I looked sidelong at him and said, "I've been afraid to admit to myself how I feel about her, and how I want her to feel about me. Maybe I thought it would never happen. That's why I all but gave you guys my official blessing to try again for a kid." I stood and went to the door and hesitated while I stared anew at this unselfish friend of mine. "Umm, Levi? Come hit the gym with me so we can talk some more. It'll do you good."

He shook his head doggedly. "I want that time with Nat. We can talk later." But as I opened the door to leave he said, "Hey. One thing, Smegma Breath. You are my friend so I've gotta tell you this—you really could use a shower!"

"I'll take one at Johnny's."

"Michael?" His eyes took in my appearance. "No shirt? No shoes? This isn't like you, brother."

I looked down at my bare torso, past the malodorous jeans, and then wiggled my liberated toes. I shrugged and said, "Ah, what the hell," and turned to leave.

Levi's laughter filled the air. "You're finally letting go!"

I took a back road into town. Route 90 would be clogged this time of morning and the longer drive through the rolling wooded farmland would give me room to think. Levi sure had nailed it—Natasha and I were friends, best buddies who could lay naked together without shame or expectations to be met, or jealousies to nurse. Anna was a different matter. I was ticked off. I had no idea why she'd ditched me, unless this former boyfriend of hers had reawakened something. If so, then good luck, Anna. But she could have told me—and I should have seen it coming. I needed that workout more than ever.

When I reached the northern edge of town where Maryland and Delaware meet, I cruised past a strip of smart boutiques, drawing stares with my Mustang. Long-limbed girls with sun-bronzed skin and bright eyes and teeth marched like soldier ants in and out of the shops, and when one of them caught my eye I pulled over. She was a big girl with a few pounds on her, and my pulse picked up as she smiled and walked majestically toward me.

"Hey there," she began with teasing eyes. "Nice car. Nice eyes, too. Soft an' friendly. Love your hair—so blonde!" She moved closer and her nose crinkled. "But oh my God, you sure do smell!"

I leaned my head out the window. "Turns you on, doesn't it?"

Her large hips swayed back and forth as she looked straight into my eyes. "Yeah, matter a fact."

"What's your name?"

"Bethany."

"You're very beautiful, Bethany. How 'bout we go somewhere an' have a little car sex?"

She moved closer and brushed her fingertips along my forearm, sending a shiver through me. "Car sex?"

"Yeah. We park, we fuck. Hop in."

Her big softy butt wiggled beneath her shorts as she rested her arms on the door. Then she poked her head through the window until her face was just inches from mine. Her soft violet irises danced as she said saucily, "You look nice an' *raw* in them jeans." Then she gave me a sly smile and said, "You'll look even better out of them." Her nostrils flared, then she went around to the passenger door and got in. "So where're we going'?"

"Place I know. It's near the Greater Ocean City Tri-Rail Commuter Station and Salt Water Taffy Emporium," I explained as I stepped on the clutch and shifted into first. "Maybe you've seen the signs? It's called the Park & Fuck."

She held herself as her body shook. "Oh, but that is so freakin' funny!" Then she stopped laughing, and as her warm moist breath fluttered against my face she said, "God, you really do smell." She dropped her eyes to my lap and her soft red tongue darted from between her white teeth as she reached down, unzipped me, and reached inside. A streak of vermilion flashed across her high cheekbones as she said, "You do stink—and I am so fucking turned on by it!"

I drove to a secluded woods nearby that only a few locals knew of. I'd patrolled the area often, and it was nearly impossible to find even in the daytime. As soon as we arrived we tumbled into the back seat. Then we were all over each other, laughing, pawing and grinning. I said tauntingly, "Look out, girl! You're gettin' it now!" Then I yanked her panties away and scrambled for a condom as she pulled me on top of her. She giggled uncontrollably as she fumbled with my jeans, and as soon as she had me bare-assed we went at it.

As she rested in my arms afterward she said, "God, Michael. What's it been—two weeks since we done this?"

"Yeah. Two weeks, too long." I shifted against the seat; my long frame wasn't made for the back of a Mustang. "How about I take you home?"

Bethany nodded. "Mmm. That'd be nice. You'll stay with me a bit?"

I nuzzled her ear. "Don't I always?"

"Yeah, an' that's why I like you, 'cause ya know how to treat a girl—an' ya know how to fuck a girl." She chuckled against my chest. "How about we do it in the shower, 'cause you really do stink." Bethany sighed, and then her forehead wrinkled. "We've always been such good fuck buddies—but why do you think car sex turn us on so much?"

I kissed her. "Because it's naughty. Juvenile, but naughty." I paused. "Sometimes naughty is healthy."

She smiled deliciously. "Sometimes naughty means a good fuck!"

I wagged my eyebrows and said, "As long as it's a friendly fuck."

"Yeahhh." She got quiet for a minute, then she scrunched her face and asked, "Why do you like me? I ain't exactly slim an' trim."

"Come on, that's a no-brainer. You're beautiful, you're happy, and when we're together we laugh a lot."

She kissed my chest. "An' I like you 'cause you can be so child-like an' kooky."

I replied in a near-whisper, "And you like me for me, and nothing else." Then I started the car, but as I stepped on the clutch the hairs at the back of my neck stood on end. Puzzled, I looked around. I couldn't see anything, but I had the distinct feeling that someone had us under observation. I shrugged it off finally and shifted into first.

We parked in front of her duplex a few minutes later. It wasn't a bad place as far as O.C. rentals go, and only two blocks from the strip of stores where we ran into each other. Bethany had a roomie whom I'd once dated, but I didn't see her car.

Instead of getting it on in the shower we went straight to her bed and experimented with a new position. Afterward we lay in each other's arms and made pillow talk. When it was time to leave I kissed her with great feeling. "Thanks for being my friend."

"Come spend a night with me? It's been a couple a weeks since you stayed over."

"I'd like that. We'll have dinner and then go dancing." I got up from bed, found my jeans and pulled them on, then leaned down and hugged her. "Call you tomorrow," I said.

As I approached my car I was deliberating whether to call Anna now, or wait another day when I did a double take—the good fairy had left another calling card—a beautiful red rose was securely nestled beneath the wiper blade.

I tossed it aside and drove to the gym, determined to have that workout. I wondered if I'd get into a confrontation with Johnny over Levi, but Johnny's assistant was manning the front desk, instead. I asked, "He sick or something?"

The assistant shrugged. "Nope. Had some errands to run."

I got changed, lifted weights for an hour, took a leisurely steam bath and went home. During the drive I thought about Natasha. With Levi's encouragement and Natasha's guidance I was beginning to shake the funk that had plagued me all my life. Damn it—I'm *entitled* to love someone, and to feel loved in return.

I also concluded that it was time to ease off the party clutch, to cutback on sex with Bethany and the others and steer instead toward this fantastic woman who loved me for myself. There was only one problem—a big one. I'd pushed Natasha away so often that she would be justified if she'd already given up on me. That possibility hit me as I drove past the Isle of Wight on the way home, the estuary blurred by my sudden tears.

I pulled into our driveway just as Natasha stepped from the porch wearing a sleeveless T that revealed her lush nipples. She also had on Levi's grungy sweatpants, an old pair of off-white sneakers, and his braided cord on her wrist. "My, look at you," she said as I got out. "No shirt? No shoes? Levi rubbing off on you, is he? Well, whatever—I like it!"

I glanced at the sweats and replied, "Looks like he's rubbing off on you, too."

"Huh?" She looked down and said, "Oh, yeah. Snatched 'em off the floor. The stud won't miss 'em. He's sprawled across my bed, fast asleep." She ran a hand along the sweats and smiled. "They *are* comfortable." Natasha took my hand and drew closer. She smelled earthy, of recently spent energy. "Umm, how about we go for a walk?"

We ambled along hand-in-hand down a quiet lane for several minutes. Torpid heat seemed to dull all sounds but for a few songbirds. After we came under the protection of some shade trees she said, "Levi and I just had a long talk. Did you know he fucked Jen for real last night?" She laughed bitterly. "Of course you know."

I nodded and said cautiously, "Levi did what he did. He's human; he was lonely. So many friends have abandoned him."

"Don't you think I know?" Her mouth worked silently until she said, "It's not that he had sex—it's that he didn't practice birth control. Hey, he can knock Jen up all he wants, *after* I'm pregnant."

"Told him the same thing."

Natasha sighed. "God, he still reeks of *her*... but I've forgiven him." Then she gave my hand a tug and said, "About the other evening—when you had your date with Anna. I'm *glad* I stayed with Levi. Not just to make a baby. He needed a friend, and I needed him."

I gently squeezed her hand. "He's been riding a roller-coaster the past few days."

"He was hurt and angry—especially about the party. Talked some about the baby, too. The first one; still a lot of sadness there." A few seconds passed until she perked up and said, "It wasn't all maudlin—we shared some spiritual moments, watched some TV; fooled around a lot." Then she looked sideways at me and asked, "It really doesn't bother you that I'm sleeping with your best friend?"

"*You're* my best friend. Levi's different. He's family. He's my bro." I scowled. "Why, do you want it to?"

Natasha examined the ground as we walked along. "I have a sudden need to be reassured, that's all. You don't think the three of us are in a tawdry love triangle?"

"It would be—if you and I were having sex. But we're not." I felt a sudden lump and then I blurted, "Hey, Nat? I didn't used to get jealous, but now it does affect me. I care about you and I …"

"You do?" She studied me carefully and said, "Thank you for telling me. I was beginning to think maybe you didn't." She said hesitantly, "But procreation aside, it is different with Levi, don't you agree? He's so much like you—affectionate and gentle, lusty and silly, *and* charming. Know what he did? We were dozing after a really good roll." Her eyes looked up and to the left. "Must've been around midnight. Anyway, he got up and drove all the way into town just to get me some ice cream."

"Pistachio?"

Natasha let out a little laugh. "What else?" She smiled deliciously and added, "Ice cream from my prince."

I took a deep breath; everything so far seemed to indicate that Levi hadn't broken it off with her as he promised he would. Still I said, "He is a prince and he's lucky to have you in his life right now." I put my arm around her shoulder and added, "And I like the fact that he makes you happy. That's what really matters."

Natasha pecked my cheek and said, "Ah, that's sweet of you. By the way, so there're no secrets? Last night? Normally I'd have come home and availed myself of Mister Hart's reproductive capacities." She tossed her head regally and sent her hair flying. "But the little stud needed a handle on where he sows his seed. So I stayed with a friend. Paul. Lovely time, but no sex."

"Hmm, who is this Paul guy, so I can kill him if he does touch you?"

She smiled knowingly. "Oh, you should talk. *You* got laid this afternoon." Before I could reply she laughed and said, "Come on. You've got F.F.L. all over you."

"Huh?"

Natasha smirked. "Freshly Fucked Look?"

I put on a brave face, bumped her hip with mine and chuckled. "Yeah, guess I do." I slid my hand inside the sweats and grazed her bare bottom with my fingertips, then gave the waistband a playful snap. "I'm not the only one with F.F.L."

Natasha placed her hand against her belly and smiled delightedly. "Well, we *were* naked, and he *did* pop a big old woody, and God knows I needed a good fucking." She sighed and looked dreamy for a few seconds, but then she turned serious and watched me carefully as she added, "But we only wanted some skin-on-skin time. He didn't want to fool around and neither did I. We cuddled. It was enough."

Relieved, I pulled her close and grazed her forehead with my lips. "Glad you're enjoying life, Nat. Wish I was more a part of it."

Large creases appeared in her forehead as she said softly, "Everything's been turned upside down these past few days."

All at once I said, "I'm putting the brakes on seeing other women. But listen, the girl I was just with? She's a friend. I needed one, okay?"

Natasha nodded thoughtfully as we walked along. "Don't sweat it, kiddo. It's what you sometimes do when you need to feel something other than pain."

I looked questioningly at her. "How'd you know?"

"Intimacy, you ding-dong. I've seen you pee. I've heard you fart—*smelled* your farts. And I've seen you cry inside so often that I just …" She glanced at me. "Just loved you even more."

"Nat …"

Her fingers flew to the corners of her eyes. "I know you, Michael Brennan. I know all about you! I see through you and I accept everything about you!"

I gripped her arms and pulled her to me. "*Nat.*"

We began walking again, aimlessly I thought. I finally asked, "Where're we going, Nat? You and I?"

"We're going dancing. Tonight. You and me, if—if that's what you want."

"Yeah," I replied in a soft tone. "I'd like that. You and me. Together."

She put her long fingers to my cheek and said, "Especially tonight, I think. Might be just what you need."

I examined her from the corners of my eyes. "Oh, I see. He told you about Anna."

Natasha took my hand and without looking at me said, "Yes, and I'm so sorry. I had hoped that …" She stopped abruptly and shook her head doggedly. "No. I'm not sorry. Forgive me, Michael darling, but I never thought she was right for you. It seemed an inappropriate relationship from its inception."

"I already came to that conclusion—before last night."

She brought my hand to her lips and brushed it with her full, sensual lips. "So what do you say? Do we go dancing tonight?"

"Sure. I'd like that. Take off early. Meet me at headquarters. Eleven sharp." I was about to tug her hand to start walking when I blurted, "I do love you, Natasha."

Her body sagged as she stared at me with soft eyes. "I know, Michael."

"Hey, Nat? I'm fighting for you! I *don't* want you sleeping with Levi. It was okay before, but not now. I want you to be a part of *my* life … okay?"

Her eyes brightened instantly. All at once she grabbed me and kissed me as if in a frenzy. Then she reared back and whispered, "You have no idea how long I've waited to hear you say those words. And it makes me love you more than I already do, because I know how hard it is for you." She looked away as a hint of sadness veiled her face and whispered, "Why didn't you tell me this before? I mean sure—sometimes the three of us push this egalitarian crap to the max; our private utopia of free love and all that—but I haven't been sleeping with Levi to make you jealous. I do—*did*—want his child. Always have. But I might not have gone ahead if I'd been, you know … sure."

"I'm telling you now, Nat. I want to be a part of your life."

She cleared her throat and said softly, "I'd love to have you in my life." Then she arched her eyebrows and asked, "So what're you thinking?"

"I'm thinking that I want us to be together again."

Natasha linked her arm with mine and said in a near whisper, "Good." A few minutes later she said quietly, "Remember a few nights ago? When you told me Levi still wanted to give me his baby? And you put yourself next in the line-up?"

I nodded.

"You were sincere, Michael. You were so willing to put my happiness before your own."

"I meant it, too—and I figured on helping you raise it."

She smiled sadly. "I know you did; I know you would. One more reason why I love you totally." Then she looked at me and said emphatically, "And I do love Levi. But I'm not going to have any more sex with him. We decided today—no more trying to make a baby. Can't wipe away what's already done, so—that's in the past?"

"Nat, I … sure. Yeah. I'm good with it. And … thanks."

We walked in silence for a long time before turning for home. Once, when we turned a corner, I spotted a car in the distance. It appeared vaguely familiar but I couldn't quite place it, and for some reason I felt spooked. Then I shook it off; there was much to do. I had to get ready for work; had to go. Had to do those things that were essential for me—and for her. Now only *one* thing nagged as I mentally prepared myself for the evening shift—my arch-nemesis, the rapist.

* * *

He stood and watched indifferently as everyone filed past. He had something else on his mind; he wanted to fuck again; tonight—again and again. He'd go on the prowl later—maybe catch the girl alone. If not, then so what? He had another on his list. He smiled as an old acquaintance trooped by.

* * *

Levi flashed a smile and wagged his eyebrows at me as we sat down for roll call. The talk died down instantly. Hacksaw made a point of greeting us in a clear voice, and then some desultory talk picked back up. The tension vaporized when Burke burst into the room, followed by Joe Santoro.

Joe appeared grim-faced. Dark bags dogged his youthful eyes, and his thick salt and pepper was disheveled. He stared off into space before opening his mouth to announce, "Another *rape*! North end. Happened about midnight. Victim never saw him coming. He bound her wrists behind her back with a bungee cord. She was alone, same as the others." All at once he roared, "But *yeah*! Our brave boy's turning into a mean son of a bitch! He roughed her *up*! Sodomized her with a broomstick. " He stopped, surveyed the room, worked some of the fury from his eyes, took a deep breath, clenched and unclenched his hands. "Here's what we've got," he began in a weary voice while holding a large manila envelope in the air for everyone to see.

Burke took it from him and distributed the law-enforcement-sensitive bulletins that it held. Several officers began reading. "Goddamn bastard," a voice said. "This'll fuckin' *kill* the season!"

Another voice in the back said, "As if we don't got enough to do with the Bugs. Now *this* asshole's creating more fuckin' work."

Joe cut through the chatter with a fierce voice. "Let's identify and capture the rapist, ladies and gentlemen." He turned to go, but not before giving me a hard look.

Burke dismissed everyone later without as much as a glance toward Levi or me. But Jarl caught up to me in the parking lot as I prepared my cruiser for the shift. "When're you gonna wise-up Brennan?"

I finished checking the rear seat—a favorite dumping place for contraband missed during pat downs—and turned to face him. "Eat me."

He uttered a course laugh. "Yeah, bet you'd like that, wouldn't you? Guess livin' with a fag's runnin' off on ya."

I leveled my eyes at him and said, "Keep your comments to yourself. Got that? Now fuck off."

His lips curled back. "Fuck off? Why don't you go fuck that reporter bitch of yours?"

I got in his face. "Keep out of my business!"

He frowned, then shook his head and walked away. I got in the cruiser and drove off, so pissed that I barely missed a news cameraman setting up for a pending press conference. Out of the way, people—I've got a rapist to catch.

Levi called out with an F.I. around nine. He routinely conducted four or five field interviews per shift, so the fact that he was calling out with one didn't strike me as odd. But something he asked for sure as hell got my attention.

"*Seventy-two-oh-four to Communications,*" he began.

"*Go ahead, seventy-two-oh-four,*" the dispatcher replied.

"*I'll be out with an F.I., to the rear of the house under construction at 408 144th Street. White male adult, mid-thirties, six feet, one eighty, brown and brown. Jeans and biker boots. No shirt. Upper torso's covered in tatts. Copy for a ten-twenty nine.*"

"*Go ahead with it,*" the dispatcher replied.

"*Mark Lee Barukowitz,*" Levi began. He offered a phonetic spelling of the last name and provided a birth date for the warrant check. There was a short pause, and all at once Levi said with a touch of urgency in his voice, "*Okay Communications … better start me a back up.*"

Levi almost never called for assistance. Something was up. A possible rape suspect?

"*Communications to seventy-two-twelve.*"

"*Seventy-two-twelve,*" Perry Ryan answered in a bored drawl.

"*Seventy-two-twelve, at the rear of 408 144th Street, back up seventy-two-oh-four with a suspicious subject.*"

"*Uh, negative Communications. I'm ten-six with a loud party.*"

"Bullshit," I shouted as I worked my way through dense traffic. Ryan's never been busy with anything in his life, especially loud parties. "Come on, guys," I prayed aloud. "We've got a rapist running around up there. *Somebody go.*"

Two more units developed abrupt, non-specific reasons why they couldn't respond.

"Scum suckers!" I stomped down on my accelerator. I didn't call out, but ran 'pink,' hitting my overheads only when I needed to get through red lights and slow-moving traffic. Otherwise I drove with some measure of sanity, reaching Levi five minutes later. But five minutes is an unbelievably long time when you're rolling on the ground and trading punches with some punk.

I doused my headlights while still half a block away and coasted to a silent stop, using my parking brake to avoid giving myself away with a flash of brake lights. I plugged my earphone into the radio and nestled the earpiece securely. The interior lights on police cars are routinely blocked from turning on when the door is opened, so no light betrayed me as I got out.

Dark clouds blotted the waning moon, and a west wind snapped at my back. I cat-walked past the northeast corner of the house and found Levi.

He faced the road, a canal gurgled softly behind him, and a suspect sat cuffed before him on the ground. Levi's flashlight lit the bad guy's face. He looked like a black-leather-jacket type even without his shirt. He squinted and tried to turn his head away. I wrapped my hand around the grip of my Beretta 92F 9mm pistol and watched silently.

"Come on, man. I ain't gonna hurt you. Take that light outta my eyes."

"I will when I'm ready," Levi replied in a firm but fair manner. "Now tell me where your friend went."

"I told you," the guy insisted, "she took off. Come on," he pleaded in a man-to-man voice. "We was just gonna have a little fun. I just didn't have no money for no motel, that's all. You know how it is."

"I'll let you go when she tells me she came here willingly. Until then ..."

"Until then, *what?*" the guy demanded.

Levi spat back in a take-charge voice. "Until then you stay where you are."

I wanted to measure this guy's mood some more before alerting Levi to my presence, and also to look around for the girl—if it was a girl—and anyone *else* who might be around. Serial rapists are lone wolves. Exceptions are rare, but cops must consider the unexpected if they hope to survive. As the Israelis say: 'prepare for the worst, hope for the best.'

"Okay, man," he whined after Levi put him in his place. "You ain't gotta bite my head off. I *just* wanted to get it on with my girl."

"*Communications to seventy-two-oh-four.*"

Levi toggled the mike at his shoulder. "Go ahead."

"*No wants, no record, but he's known to Parole and Probation.*"

"Ten-four. I'll be ten-six a while longer."

I toggled my own mike and whispered, "Twelve o'clock."

Levi acted as if nothing happened, but he flicked his eyes in my direction and nodded imperceptively. Then he tucked his flashlight beneath his left armpit and approached the suspect. "Lean forward," he commanded. As soon as he complied Levi placed his free hand against the back of the suspect's neck and searched him carefully. He swept his fingers through the shirtless suspect's waistband, actively clenched all four pockets, unflinchingly searched his crotch, and then ran his hands along both legs. Levi then pulled his boots off, shined his light inside, upended each one and shook them until he was satisfied that they contained no weapons or drug paraphernalia. Nothing. More meaningfully, Levi found no bungee cords.

"Call your girl," Levi told him. "If she says everything's okay you can hit the bricks."

The guy turned toward the house and sang out, "Sue! *Suzie*. It's okay. Come on out."

I heard a rustling from inside the house and then a board fell against another with a loud *clunk*. A minute later a short, plump woman with a red sweater wrapped around her waist lurched drunkenly into Levi's flashlight beam.

She cleared her throat of rumbling phlegm and said, "It's okay, Officer. We're friends. He ain't been doin' nothin' to hurt me."

"What's his name?" Levi asked.

"Why, that's Mark. Me and Mark been friends for years, Officer … *years*."

Levi nodded as he flashed his light on her and asked in his most-curious tone, "What's with the sweater? Isn't it a little warm for that?"

She nodded vigorously. "Yes sir. It is at that. Warm. Yes sir."

Levi grinned as the tension evaporated. "You're not hiding anything beneath it, are you?"

She seemed taken aback and blinked dull, uncomprehending eyes at him. "Oh! No sir. I ain't hidin' nothin'. I just don't got no tampon, thas' all. It's my time," she explained. Then she added, "Got the sweater wrapped 'round to keep the stains from showin'."

Levi nodded gravely. "Good idea. Damned good idea."

"Yes sir," she said a bit uncertainly.

Levi stifled a smile as he turned to the guy. "Stand up."

"Yes sir," he said as he got to his feet.

"All right. You two can go after Suzie provides some identification for my report. That okay with the two of you?"

When they nodded Levi released the cuffs and got Suzie's state I.D. card. While he copied the information, Mister Romeo embraced his fair Juliet. When Levi was finished he handed the card to her and said, "Okay, guys. No more trespassing. Okay?" He arched his eyebrows formidably to make sure they understood.

"Okay," the guy said. "Don't worry. You won't be seein' no more a us. I promise, Officer." He grabbed his boots, raised his right hand in solemn testament and said, "I swear to God," and then they turned and disappeared. Levi had made a good call. He had no reason to hold either of them any longer, and although the guy had ex-con written all over him, that didn't make him a serial rapist. Levi let him go. I'd have done the same.

I stayed hidden until they were gone. It's best to let the bad guys think a solitary officer can handle situations by himself. It was also good OPSEC— operational security—not to reveal tactics.

"Thanks, brother," Levi offered by way of greeting. He flashed a tired smile beneath sad eyes. "I knew you wouldn't let me down."

"When Levi Hart calls for help, something must be up."

"Hey, we've got a serial rapist running loose," he began, and then his face turned somber as he murmured, "and I'd like to catch the mother." He swept his arm toward the dark, unfinished house. "Caught 'em creeping around. Something didn't look right. When they took off in separate directions I got that hinky feeling. Figured I'd better make the call." He shuffled a shoe against the loose soil and abused its laboriously applied gloss. "Listen, just between you and me?" he asked with raised eyebrows.

"Sure. What's up?"

"This sounds worse than it is, but I wasn't all *that* concerned. Not with these two. I guess …" he looked away and fidgeted with the soil some more, then looked me in the eye. "I guess I wanted to see if anyone would come if I called. I had to find out."

I nodded solemnly. "I'm glad you did."

"Say, can we meet somewhere? I need to talk and this isn't the best place to shoot the shit."

"Sure. 77th Street fire station?"

Levi smiled and said, "Let's go."

We went past Seaweed Lane en route to 77th Street. It was near the spot where the first rape had occurred. As I sped up to keep pace with him, I noticed Demmings' cruiser as it glided ghostlike along the street we'd just left. I saw that as a good omen: it meant that Demmings had discreetly responded to back-up Levi. Either that or he'd done a turn-around from his slacker mentality, and was now actually *looking* for the rapist. Or maybe he was doing a little of both.

We pulled abreast of each other in the fire station parking lot. The station was a concrete and glass affair, with half a dozen cars and pick-ups from the evening crew parked haphazardly in the lot. The place felt desolate despite the clamor of a nearby nightclub. I turned down my radio and the police chatter faded to a dull roar. "That was good police work, catching those two."

Levi nodded slowly. "I aim to get that bastard." He worried the knuckles of his hand against his long jawbone. After a bit he said, "Look, Michael. I wanna thank you again. You know—for backing me up."

"I'm with you like stink on shit."

He nodded, stared through his windshield and said, "Got a phone call from Customs today. I might be out of here sooner than expected."

"Hey! Congratulations, bro. I don't wanna see ya go, but this is great news!" Then as realization dawned I said, "Jesus! You're leaving! God, I'm gonna miss you."

"We'll always be linked, amigo." He looked evenly at me again. "Here's some more news. Nat and I had our long talk, and I know she's talked to you since. She's in love with you. You're in love with her." He turned his head and looked through me, as though his eyes had taken an X-ray of my brain. "Make me an uncle, okay?"

"I will, brother."

"I'll love it totally." Then he looked at me with the eyes of a child and said evenly, "You and Nat are all I've got, Michael." He shrugged. "Sure, I've got my folks and I love 'em to death, but you guys are my authentic family." He stared through his windshield and mumbled something that I didn't quite get.

"Huh?" I asked, realizing my mistake after it was too late.

"Gotcha," he crowed. "Ibba fucking da, but I got you good. Woo hoo, no fuckin' way I'm gonna end this on a sappy note, my friend. Woo hoo," he trumpeted again, and then he dropped his car in gear and roared off, leaving me to deal with a swirl of dust.

I shook my head, smiled and murmured, "You bastard—you got me good! Never saw it coming." As I put my car in gear I thought I saw something in my rearview mirror, and I had an unexplainable sensation that someone had been watching us. I shook away the feeling and drove off as a sudden cloudburst drenched the town.

*   *   *

After the large storm cell blew away he drifted slowly past the house, nosing his way through the unfamiliar territory. He'd strayed from his normal feeding ground, but that had been an ultimate requirement from the outset. He watched; he listened; he even lifted his nose for any scent that she might be home.

She was not. He doubted she would be, but one never knew. One fact he knew with certainty—she did not reside alone, and that was the whole point of his meticulous plan. Otherwise, everything up to now had been wasted effort. He would return.

*   *   *

I got back to my patrol area just as dispatch assigned me to an auto accident, courtesy of the storm. It involved some not-so-serious injuries, but from the way the two drivers bickered I smelled Lawsuit City, and therefore I took great pains to cover my ass with a thoroughly documented account.

My reports were finished and on Burke's desk by 10:30pm. I called Natasha and told her that I'd be ready when she arrived. When I went to the locker room to change, I found Demmings and some others huddled together. "What's up?" I asked as I spun the dial on my locker.

"Pictures," Demmings cackled with a strange energy. "Come take a look."

"I'll take a rain check," I replied. I wanted no part of his sour relationship with Donna, *or* his Peeping Tom activities, and I couldn't believe that the internal complaints that I *knew* had been made to Burke had gone unchecked. But my prudishness evidently hadn't rubbed off on some of the others. "Whoa," a newbie cop exclaimed. "Check the bodacious ta ta's on *this* one."

Perry Ryan stood behind the newbie and peered over his shoulder. He let out a long, low whistle. "Damn, Demmings! You know how to pick 'em. Hey, ever wonder what'd happen if any of them was to see you?"

Demmings chuckled low and deep in his throat. "I'm too slick for that. Slick an' sassy, that's me. Elastic as a rubber band."

"Yeah," Ryan persisted, "but what about the flash?"

I listened attentively. Twisted or not, I always made an effort to pick up on trade secrets. Never knew when something might come in handy.

Demmings replied, "Don't need one. I use super fast film. Hold down the shutter an' keep a steady hand, an' nothin' gets blurred."

Their chatter faded into background noise as I grabbed a towel and headed toward the showers. The steaming water felt good. I thought briefly of Anna and wondered again why she dumped me as I reached out and turned off the water.

Levi walked in as I pulled on a T and tucked it into the waistband of my jeans. He pointedly ignored the others, smiled quickly at me, and wriggled out of his uniform. Then he headed toward the showers and seconds later I heard the water running. I was grooming myself at the mirror when he walked back out. I asked casually, "What've you got planned for tonight?"

"Think I'll head north."

I laughed a little. "Good for you. Me, I'm taking Nat out dancing. Say," I said as an afterthought, "why don't we meet somewhere?"

"*Numbers?*"

"That'll work."

He grabbed the comb from my hand and ran it through his heavy hair. "Sure it's okay?"

"Let's plan on it."

Levi finished with his hair and plopped the comb back into my hand. "See ya there." He flashed a grin, grabbed a pair of Converse high tops from his locker and announced, "I'm outta here."

I slammed my locker shut a few minutes later and hurried out to the parking lot.

Natasha hadn't arrived yet—but someone else had. Tiny droplets on the rose petals sparkled from the rays of a nearby streetlight. I muttered an oath and picked it up. The droplets were too small to be from the rainstorm; they'd been sprayed on—and recently—to keep them fresh. My stalker had gotten bolder.

A spurt of exhaust sliced the air as Natasha arrived. "Michael, it's absolutely stunning! I've never seen such a rose," she remarked as I held it up for her to see.

"Same as the others," I said, and then I balled it up and tossed it beneath my car, just as Demmings walked out of the building. He made a beeline for us and came to an abrupt halt in front of Natasha. "My roommate," I replied to his unasked question.

He nodded slowly and gave her the once-over, then he flicked his eyes at my car. "M B.," he began as he read my license plate. "Michael Brennan. *Mister* Michael Brennan." A loopy, lop-sided grin appeared on his face as he looked at me and said, "Cool car. Nice touch, those plates." Demmings stared at Natasha once more before he turned and walked off.

I didn't blame him for his interest in her—she looked great. She also appeared less diffident in her appearance—no Doc Martens or Salvation Army throwaways tonight, but a more conservative outfit. She also had a serene look that I'd never seen before. "You seem at peace," I said.

She smiled. "A lot of issues have been resolving themselves as of late," she said mysteriously.

"Such as?"

Her nostrils flared as she breathed deeply. "Just ... I don't know. Everything."

I took the hint and dropped it. I knew her well enough to know she'd reveal more later on. Then I told her that Levi might meet us, and turned to another topic at hand as we got in the car and drove off. "You think," I began as I merged into the fast lane, "his wife's been leaving these roses?"

Natasha's attention seemed focused elsewhere. "What's that, Michael? Oh, Demmings? Umm, doubt it," she concluded with cool confidence. "It's someone else."

"You're sure?"

"Positive. But who? That's the question on all the network news stations."

I smiled and softly jabbed her ribs. "I had that coming."

She laughed as she took my hand. "You've got that right, kiddo."

"So," I began in a hearty voice a few seconds later, "what is truth?"

Natasha chuckled softly and began. "Imagine that you are dreaming, and the act of opening your eyes is merely an illusion ..."

"Hey, girl—I'm definitely not dreaming—not with you sitting beside me." Then I said softly, "If it is a dream, I don't ever wanna wake up."

Natasha smiled, and a moment later she wiped away a single tear.

We crossed the border into Fenwick, Delaware, crawled through dense traffic, then finally sped up to sixty as we entered a barren stretch of highway. High sand dunes bordered the road on the right, while the inland waterway hugged the road to the left. A few houses dotted both sides of the highway at odd intervals, and traffic was sparse. I switched on the radio and fiddled with the tuner until I found Earl Klugh's jaunty, *Slippin' In The Back Door*. A short time later I suddenly touched the rearview mirror and asked, "Ever get the feeling you're being followed?"

We turned into Rehoboth Beach twenty minutes later. Throngs of well-dressed people roamed the sidewalks, in sharp contrast to the indifferent attire of Ocean City's tourists. A mix of straight and gay couples greeted us as we began walking, and we answered them all.

Many of the gay men were young, dressed to impress, and in good shape. There were older gay men too, and some walked hand-in-hand with partners. Natasha peered inside various storefronts until we came to *Flicks*, a brightly lit gay bar. There was no dancing here but we paused anyway. The customers inside talked easily among themselves, hurling banter and contrived insults without regard for sender or receiver, their quick and honest laughter overcoming the techno beat that thumped in the background. Like so many gay bars, *Flicks* seemed livelier than its conventional counterparts, and we could have blended in without a ripple.

We walked off and reached *Numbers* after a casual stroll. The noise inside was overwhelming. At least fifty men and more than a few women crowded the polished dance floor. Spotlights and strobes flashed and pulsed and streamed *everywhere,* and the music *rocked*—African and Samba drums spiced with electric piano, accompanied by an urgent female voice imploring everyone to, "*dance a little harder!*"

I caught the beat instantly. "Come on." I tugged Natasha's arm and we dove into the crowd. As a dancer, I easily picked out the really great hoofers, and anyone who thinks white guys can't dance has never been to a gay bar. We found a spot and started dancing when Natasha smiled and pointed to the far side of the room. I followed her finger to a wooden platform that dominated that portion of the dance floor.

There were six guys atop the platform dancing in unison. They had the beat *nailed*, and they moved magnificently as the crowd cheered them on. Two of them were shirtless, and one of the shirtless ones, the guy at the far end, put the other good dancers to shame as he sprang and spun and leaped from one spot to another. But then I wasn't surprised—Levi always had been a great dancer. "Go, Levi," we yelled.

We stopped when the music segued into another number and went to him.

Levi chose that precise moment to step down and greet an admirer. A film of perspiration covered his upper body, beads of water flew everywhere when he ran his fingers through the dark strands of his hair, and his chest heaved from the exertion as he accepted a beer from a passing waiter.

"You're killin' 'em," I said as I slapped his sweat-streaked back.

He smiled triumphantly, and his eyes were alive for the first time in days. "Guys," he began, "it feels so fucking good to be out like this. Glad you're here!"

Natasha kissed him tenderly and opened her mouth to say something when she stopped, stared, and gasped. She looked as if bad news might break at any minute, and nobody wanted to open *that* telegram yet. Then she pointed to a dark corner at the far end of the bar. "Can that be who I think it is?"

Levi and I turned as one to look. Two men were busy making out beneath the dark shadow cast by an overhanging bank of speakers. The larger of the two had his back turned to us, seemingly indifferent to everyone as he passionately kissed the other and groped his crotch.

Levi said somberly, "So now you know."

I did a double take. "You *knew* he was gay? And you said nothing?"

He shrugged. "It's like with the Jews in Europe. Their own neighbors turned them over to the Gestapo. Hey," he said bitterly, "he might be an asshole, but I'm not gonna set the dogs on him."

Natasha said, "Even though he …?"

Levi said quietly, "Jarl can't handle being gay. I won't add to his misery."

CHAPTER 8

LEVI stared through us until he reached a decision. Then he placed a hand on each of our backs and said, "Over here." After he guided us to a distant corner of the dance floor, he looked over his shoulder at Jarl's shadowy form and said firmly, "Let it go."

I shook my head. "I'm not so sure we should—at least not entirely. Look, here's how we'll play it." I worried the end of my nose and pulled them closer. "We say nothing. Not to him, especially not to anyone else. Now it's no secret that he likes me. Let me draw him out a bit, see if I can swing him over to our side. Jarl has access to a lot of inside information. I want in."

Levi frowned. "You're not gonna blackmail him, are you?"

I said crossly, "Of course not. But it might not hurt to let him know that he's not alone in the world." I said in a softer voice, "Surely you know that."

He nodded. "It's worth a shot."

Natasha said to Levi, "How long have you known?"

"Since forever. Plotted him on my GAYDAR the day I met him. Didn't take him long to start coming on to me. Always kept it subtle. Plausible deniability." He chewed at his lower lip and added, "Guess he doesn't like being turned down."

I nodded slowly. "That night at Assateague, when you got pissed at him?"

Levi half-smiled. "You don't miss much. The fucker gets drunk, he gets stupid."

Natasha looked at us and said, "Then that is how we shall play it. Michael, you might even ask him out for a beer to put him at ease."

"Makes sense," Levi said.

"Okay," I agreed. "We'll treat him decently—to a point—and who knows? He just might break free with some odd detail or another on these rapes, and that would turn him into my best friend."

We left *Numbers* for Jarl's sake. Nobody wanted to drive him into a suicidal corner. Nat and I decided to walk awhile and look for dancing elsewhere before going home. Levi said, "Think I'll hit another club and see what kind of trouble I can get into."

After Natasha bussed his cheek I punched his shoulder and said, "It's good to see you enjoying yourself, bro."

I took Natasha by the hand and we strolled through town. At one point she stopped to check the display in a store window, and when I thought I saw a reflection in the glass I turned around abruptly. But there were only one or two tourists casually walking along the opposite sidewalk. By then the mood for dancing had gone south, and by unspoken acclimation we decided to go home.

*   *   *

After a while he decided he still had more to do. He'd make another pass and nose around some more. He got in his car and drove off. It took some time, but he reached the neighborhood without attracting attention. The street was dark, the house darker still. Satisfied—yet disappointed—that she was not inside, he drove past the house and wondered where he could go instead. After a few moments deliberation he knew where he would go. *She* was high on his list, and she might be there by herself.

*   *   *

When we got home I grabbed the bottle of Green Label and held it aloft. "Nightcap?"

Natasha pursed her lips and shook her head. "Tempt me with something else."

"I know." I put the Green Label back and got the *other* good stuff—a bottle of thirty-year old Taylor Fladgate Tawny Port. "Drink this," I said as I handed her a glass. "It warms the heart; gives you a pleasant glow. You'll sleep much better." We clinked glasses. "*Salute.*"

Natasha looked coy and asked, "Who said anything about sleeping?"

I smiled inwardly, held my glass to the light and eyed the deep ruby port inside. Then I held it to my nose and inhaled deeply before taking a sip. "It's the small rituals that give meaning to our lives."

As we sipped the port I found I couldn't shake the evening's revelation. "That's something about Jarl. Careless of him to act out so close to home."

"Virulent homophobes often have the most to hide, especially from themselves," she said matter-of-factly. "That's what compels them to take the greatest risks."

"Levi impressed me. He could've confronted Jarl. Says a lot about the man." I turned the glass and stared at the port. "Levi confronted me, though. Kicked my ass good." When she raised an eyebrow I said, "He made me see that I'm allowed to feel, and that I *do* have emotions." Then I turned and looked lovingly at her. "On the other hand, you've started me on the path to finally feeling *free* to feel; you've gotten me to the point where I now recognize my *right* to feel."

In the silence that followed I began to think I'd said something terribly wrong, but Natasha took my head in her hands and kissed me lovingly. "Oh God, Michael. Thank you for finally saying it." Then Natasha got up from the couch, and with a little tug at my fingers she smiled shyly and whispered, "I love you, Michael Brennan."

She led me to her bedroom and blended into my arms. We kissed, touched and undressed each other. My heart skipped as my hands spanned her waist. I kissed her gently at first, then with greater passion. We explored each other's mouths until I urged her to the crisp white sheets, where I nuzzled her ear and whispered, "I love you, Nat. I love you, and I'm so lucky to have you in my life." Natasha's response was shameless, instant and total as her body surged in physical excitement against mine. Nothing else mattered, nothing at all. I molded myself to her, wanting more, taking all that she offered and giving back more as our familiar rhythms returned. Afterward we lay in silence until just before we drifted into sleep, when she crawled into my arms and snuggled there. I held her through the night, satisfied and feeling so much in love for the first time.

My internal clock told me it was mid-morning. I cracked an eyelid. 9:15. I moved closer to Natasha and sniffed her hair and gloried in the feel of her skin. Half an hour passed before she stirred, her smile radiant when I touched my lips to her forehead. I took her into my arms, and choking with emotion, I said, "I love you very, very much."

The sleep seemed to vanish completely from her soft brown eyes. "I know, Michael. I've always known." She paused, and her mind seemed momentarily transported to some distant place. "What I've never known," she began as she gazed steadily into my eyes, "was whether you would ever admit it to yourself."

Nodding slightly I said, "I've gotten there, Nat."

She smiled—a lovely smile—rare and intimate, and then she began touching me with familiar patterns as we merged into tender lovemaking.

We lay together afterward. As I caressed her beautiful cheeks with the backs of my fingers, I picked up our game. "Tell me again about Occam's razor."

Natasha playfully traced her finger along the top of my thigh. "Occam's guideline," she began, "asserts that assumptions should be kept to a minimum, and explanations should be as simple as possible. In other words, the simplest explanation is often the best one."

"I see," I said with a thoughtful nod. "Does that mean that I simply love you, or that our love is simple, like a paramecium's?"

Nat smiled and dashed her hand between my legs. "I've got your paramecium."

I laughed, kissed her and asked, "Gonna sleep a while longer?"

She stirred, put a hand to her mouth and yawned. "Think I'll veg a bit." She made a shooing motion and said, "Put on some coffee?"

"Sure. Be right back."

"Know what? Think I'll soak in the tub, instead."

"Want me to join you?"

Natasha smiled deliciously but said, "Umm, I need some time to myself."

I slipped out of bed and grabbed my shorts. "Understood. I'll get the coffee going, then see about a shower."

"Good idea. You could use one."

I threw my hands up in despair. "Why is everyone saying that?"

The porch door slammed shut just as I walked out of her room, and Levi entered the kitchen minus shirt, shoes and the shorts he'd had on last night. He looked ragged but smiled happily.

I pointed at the oversized, sweat-stained shorts he did have on and asked, "Where'd you get those loopy lookin' things?"

He looked down, appraised them as if he'd seen them for the first time, and shrugged. "Must've grabbed the wrong ones," he said absently. But then he smiled and fished inside a pocket and produced his wallet and badge holder. "Liked the looks of 'em so I made a swap."

I nodded approvingly. "They suit you."

"Yeah." Then he dug into another pocket, and when he pulled out his hand he held a small knife and several condoms. "Huh! A pocketful of Jim Hats." He seemed surprised. Then he said, "Oh well," smiled good-naturedly, and put everything back.

"Good time last night?"

He grinned, his exhaustion diminished. "Met someone. Kevin."

"Bring him over so we can meet him."

Levi looked shyly at me but finally he nodded. He took a step toward me, then stopped and eyed me carefully. All at once his eyes crinkled, and he threw back his head and laughed. "Slept with Nat last night, huh?"

"Yes," I said, and then I urged him onto the porch. We grabbed chairs and sat hunched together, shoulder-to-shoulder. A cloud passed overhead, providing relief from the harsh sun. Then I leaned forward, rested my forearms on my thighs, and tapped his knee with the back of my hand. "Levi? I'm in love with her. I'm in love with Natasha."

His face lit up. "Hey, I'm happy for both of you." He chuckled. "See? I've always known she was in love with you." Then he looked away and said in a low murmur, "Always you, but never me." Levi looked at me, a wistful expression painted broad across his face, "It's not going to be easy to leave you guys, but I have to do it."

"We all grow."

He tapped his foot against mine and said, "You've changed a lot."

"I have, haven't I?" I patted his knee and left my hand there as I added, "I have you and Nat to thank for that."

Levi opened his mouth to reply but instead he looked away. After a few seconds he said in an undertone, "You know the score. Guys don't say stuff like this to other guys, but thanks for holding onto my knee just now. It means a lot."

I said quietly, "You're still adjusting, aren't you?"

Levi sighed and looked away again, and when he did try to speak he couldn't. Finally he said, "I guess I am. Hey, listen ... thanks for not finding me repulsive."

I ruffled my hand through his hair and said, "Hey. Never in a million years, so stop that right now."

He nodded and whispered, "Okay."

At that I reached over and pulled him to me and kissed the top of his head. Then I slid my fingers to the back of his neck, and as I massaged the coiled muscles I said with conviction, "Look, Natasha is the love of my life. I know that now. But I also know that I'll love you for the rest of my life. Okay? Are we done with this now?"

Levi stared at the distant trees for a long time. Finally he nodded and said, "Sure. We're done with it."

I slapped him on the back and said, "Good. So, how about those Bears?"

The door opened behind us and Natasha stepped outside. She had on splotched painter's coveralls and a freshly laundered T-shirt. She smiled and kissed Levi before pulling over a chair and sitting next to him. "Love those shorts," she remarked.

He smiled sheepishly. "Yeah, an' they came equipped. Look." He pulled out the knife and showed her. "Got some Jim Hats, too." He fished through the pocket again and produced the condoms.

"Everything you need for a great time," she said dryly. "Speaking of great times, whatever became of the guy who outed you after you showed *him* such a great time."

"Dan?" He fiddled with the knife for a bit until he leaned forward and said, "Guys, there's something I never told you about Dan." He turned to me, "Remember when you asked why I wanted a piece of this rapist?"

I shrugged. "You told me why."

Levi wet his lips and stared at the trees again. "That part was true. But there's something else. The first girl who was raped? I know her. She's Dan's sister."

Levi and I glanced at one another when Burke stormed into roll call. "Everybody prepare to stand the fuck by. Chief's comin' in." He put his hands on his hips and glared at us. "What the fuck are you people doin' out there, huh? You fuckers are supposed to be out lookin', but I don't see nobody findin' no motherfuckin' rapist." His eyes darted about the room until he thundered, "It's Saturday fucking night, people! What do I gotta do to light a fire under your miserable asses?"

Chief must've reamed Burke a new one.

The door opened and the chief marched in wearing his dress uniform. He stood indifferently as he addressed us. "Men, hotel listings are down. Way down. Lotta businessmen are up in arms." He rubbed the end of his nose. "I don't even wanna *begin* to get into CNN, an' what they're saying about us." He stopped and stared pointedly at Burke. "There's also been a significant reduction in the number of day-trippers coming to town." He put a hand in his pocket and began jangling his keys. "Lot of lost revenue. Lost revenue, lost pay raises."

Someone from the back said, "How they know there's less day-trippers comin' in?"

Another voice replied, "Raw sewage figures."

"That don't mean nothin'," someone added in a bored drawl. "Just means most of them daytime folks are too fuckin' stupid to flush. No turd count, no tourist count."

A roar of laughter erupted despite the chief's deep frown. When it finally subsided Hacksaw Jones stood up, looked around the room and asked, "Know why them tourists don't flush? It's 'cause they too dumb for bubble gum." As the second wave of snickers died down, Hacksaw added in good grammar, "Of course, regardless of all other variables, that still puts them far ahead of us in the food chain." When the room turned dead silent he snorted and said, "You guys are fucked up."

When we broke from roll call I went to a phone and called Anna. There was no response and after I hung up Jarl sauntered over with his hands in his pockets. "How's your homo buddy doing?"

I stared at him and replied, "Which of my colleagues would you be referring to?"

He snorted. "Nice safe answer. So, you an' Levi been getting' it on? Bet he likes sucking that big dick a yours. Or is he your little bitch-boy? He like it when you hump him?"

I said woodenly, "You tell me. Which do you prefer, Jarl?"

"Yeah, I fuckin' knew it. Listen, Brennan … change of patrol assignments, per the Sarge. You're working the south end tonight, where we can keep an eye on you."

I pointed to my crotch and said, "Keep an eye on this," then walked away and went to work. I didn't mind his bullshit so much—I even felt sorry for the cheap-shot bastard; but I resented not being able to work the north end, where the rapist lurked.

*   *   *

He watched her leave the club. The girl was alone and he knew from previous observation that she would remain alone when she got to her summer place. He knew what her roommate looked like, where she worked and what time she got off. He had all the time he needed.

He encountered a modicum of difficulty in getting past her door, and that pissed him off. He'd learned his trade well, and he took no small measure of pride in his ability to let the shadows absorb him—consume him even in his white shirt—as he worked whatever barriers barred his way to his victims. But he didn't see them as victims; they were tributes—battle prizes that spoke of his prowess, his skill and his daring.

Why not say it? They were his source of power.

"That's right," he boasted. "Bitch had it coming. She shouldn't have done what she did with …well, you already know with *who*."

Once inside he kept to the walls; fewer shadows that way. He spotted her and saw that she had on a Walkman. Good—that helps. He waited until she reached the kitchen. It had to be the kitchen. That's where the food is kept; that's where she'd get the *meat*.

She turned around.

Fuck! No … wait. Her eyes are closed. Her eyes are closed as she gets into the music! Now she's gyrating her hips, and now—now she's spinning around and putting her back to him.

He pounced. Like a panther, he was.

"I'm tellin' you boys … I was a *panther!*"

He got her neck inside his bicep and he let his arm become his fangs as he squeezed his muscle.

"An' then I dropped her like a *gazelle!*"

Yes, he knew what he was doing. He did her from behind, and if she woke up he could tweak her again before she could see his face. As always, he finished quickly. "Get it in and shoot it in; give her my seed! That way she knows who her boss is. She knows who owns her. She fucking knows who controls her." Yes, it's true that he'd used a condom, "But listen here—I had to. Couldn't risk leaving evidence behind." No, he was too smart for that; he knew not to leave anything behind that was traceable to him. He was as careful this night as always—sticking to the shadows to conceal his presence.

Besides, wasn't *he* the one who dealt with presence? Sure. He also *left* presents! "Presents ... ah, yes! Gifts, my friends. Gifts from their new God!"

He left her sprawled face down on the floor as he stepped calmly to the kitchen counter. He'd seen something there earlier that he could use. Yep. There it is. He picked up the long-necked wine bottle and leisurely shoved it up her vagina as far as he could.

He started to leave but then an idea occurred to him. He smiled as it formed in his mind, and without another thought he whipped out his new slender knife and carved a little something on her buttocks. Call it a remembrance. Only one more item remained on his list of things-to-do-today, and a feral grin took control of his lips and spread to his eyes as he pulled the plastic bag from beneath his white shirt. He opened it and carefully removed the object inside. After he laid it next to her head he lifted his eyes to the ceiling and gave himself a high-five. "Yes!"

"Boys ... she should have thanked me. I mean, Jesus fucking Christ—it's not as if I kicked her 'round. No, nothing like that."

*　　*　　*

"Communications to seventy-two-oh-four, seventy-two-oh-four."

Levi answered.

"Seventy-two-oh-four, proceed ..."

When the dispatcher finished the call I said aloud, "Oh fucking *wow*." I easily pictured Levi heading to the newly reported rape in his north end patrol area. "Jesus fucking *Christ*," I yelled as a rage took me almost over the top.

Of course, he couldn't have made the connection once he arrived on-scene. How could he know who she was? I would have known *if* he'd been dispatched to her actual residence. But Levi was sent to a location two blocks away, where the elderly couple found the naked, bleeding girl trudging slowly up their street.

I might have known if I could have gotten there even half an hour later. But Jarl made sure I was held over to cover the south end until 3:00am, while other units were deployed north to hunt down her attacker. By the time I was cut loose it was too late—all the units had cleared. I went home to be with Natasha. I'd get the details from Levi in the morning.

CHAPTER 9

LEVI was nowhere to be found the next morning and since I couldn't pick his brain about last night's rape, I got busy and moved some clothes into Natasha's room. She shook her head in dismay when I slipped my off-duty snub nose revolver beneath the mattress, but I told her that I didn't want to leave it in my room unattended. That done, I jumped into my 'stang and drove to the gym beneath overcast skies. The estuary smelled ripe as I sped past, and when I saw that the road ahead was clear I floored it until the pipes roared. I backed-off at ninety-five and checked my six for troopers—and saw not a trooper, but a beat-up white Chevy that had kept pace with me. I goosed it again to see what would happen, but this time the car only got smaller in my mirror.

Johnny appraised me with a long silent stare as he handed over a towel. I knew he couldn't keep it buttoned for long, so I wasn't surprised when he opened his mouth and started in. "The boys are all talking up a storm about Levi, you know." He smiled smugly and added, "They plan on giving him the treatment, or so I'm told."

"Johnny," I began, "stay the hell out of it."

"The Dickens, you say," he leaned against the counter and said, "Queers like that Levi ought to be given their notice, and if they fail to pay heed they should be run right out of town. That's what I say." He took off his Braves cap, wiped his hand across his bald pate, and settled the cap back into place.

I took the towel from him. "I told you before—don't call him names. Are we done with this conversation now?"

Johnny's body grew taut. He stood up straight, spread his legs and put his hands on his hips. Finally he said, "As you wish." He fiddled with some loose papers on the counter and said conversationally, "How are you boys proceeding with these abominable attacks? You've made progress, I take it?"

Another fishing expedition; it merited a non-answer. "There are some damned fine people working the case."

"Yes, I'm sure of it. But what have they found? Or have you boys not found anything?"

I sidestepped his inquisitiveness with a stock response. "There'll be a press release in an hour."

He looked at me shrewdly from his potato sack face and said, "Aye, that's all well an' good for these tourists, but I'm a local. Now surely you can tell *me* what none of these twits what visit don't deserve to know. Have you boys gotten any clues? That's the part what fascinates me. Have you anything to work on? Have you now?"

I shook my head. "Afraid I'm out of the loop. Those investigators, you know them," and then I smiled for his benefit. "They play their cards close."

Johnny nodded. "Aye, an' it's a damned sad thing. Just a nugget here and there, and those of us what lives here might be of assistance. That's why I bought that scanner, so I could dash out and give you boys a hand if I'm able. That's what I'm about, you know—safeguarding our community." He touched his fingers to the bill of his ball cap in a little salute and said, "Well, good on you men of the force for all you do. Now be sure to let me know if I can be of any help. Have a good workout, now there's a good fellow." He turned his back and began restocking the nutritional supplements in the glass display case.

Jarl said as I entered the free-weight room, "Your little Levi's not here."

There were five other people working out but they didn't seem to be paying any attention to him. That included me. I ignored him, went to the bench press and put two forty-five pounders on the bar. Then I got on the bench and found my marks, and I was about to lift when Jarl settled his hands on the bar.

He said ominously, "You'd be wise to stop hanging 'round him."

"You'd be wise to get your hands off my fucking bar!"

"Fuck you, Brennan." He snapped his hands away and moved back.

I did ten reps and settled the bar down with a *clang*. Getting up, I felt his eyes on me. I ignored him and added another seventy pounds and cranked out ten more reps. When I got up and saw him staring again, I said reasonably, "Why don't you and I call a truce. We've always gotten along. As for Levi, he's his own man. He goes his own way and he'll be goin' far away once the Feds hire him. What do you say?"

Jarl drove his clenched fist into his palm. "Yeah! That's what I was hopin' to hear ya say. So he's *out* of here!"

I nodded slowly. "In time, sure. Now about that truce?"

He squared his shoulders and took his time answering. "What's in it for me?"

"What do you want?"

He stepped closer. "How 'bout we do that tag-team action with Donna? Just you an' me."

"How about we sit down over a couple of beers and act like normal folks?"

Jarl's lips lifted in a fake smile, "How 'bout we drink beer an' talk shit an' see where things go from there?"

Before I could answer a female voice sang out from the doorway. "What a pleasant surprise. My two favorite men." Donna Demmings came forward with a graceful toss of her head. "Jarl Jackson and Michael Brennan. How're you two doing?"

Jarl walked forward in a loose-boned, easy gait and met her. She took his proffered hand, but her smile went beyond him toward me.

"How are you, Michael?"

I grabbed two more forty-fives and put them on the bar. "I'm fine, Donna."

She pouted in a mocking, poor-me way. "You don't seem particularly happy to see me," she teased.

"What do you want me to say? Alright, I'm ecstatic."

Donna moved toward me with the sure grace of a lioness. "I haven't seen you in quite some time. Where've you been?"

"Safeguarding freedom and democracy." I went back to the bench and punched out five reps.

"Hmm. Nice form."

I said pleasantly as I pulled off my workout gloves. "Donna? You're married and I'm not available. Let it go, okay? Save your compliments for some other stud."

She looked over her shoulder at Jarl and then back at me as a droll smile crept across her lips. "Don't flatter yourself. I simply meant to compliment you on your strength, stamina and poise."

"Then, thanks." I turned and walked off toward the water fountain.

"Of course," she called after me. "If you should find yourself available, I might be predisposed to accept a dinner date from you."

I got my drink, waved at her in response, and went to the Nautilus room in search of solitude. I found it gloriously deserted and got to work on the pec deck, knocking out three sets of eight reps apiece before proceeding to the parallel bars. I'd done only two reps on the bars when I sensed her presence. I turned and found her leaning against the doorway, her arms folded across her breasts and her eyes on me.

"Surprised to see me?"

"No," I said wearily. "Sad to say, but I've got your act nailed." I frowned. "How many times do I have to tell you? I'm not interested."

She uncrossed her arms and walked slowly toward me with enough hip-sway to attract my eyes. "But I'm interested in you. Mmm, yes. Nice eyes you've got there. Very lovely. Nice ass, too. How about you?" she teased. "See anything you like? It can be all yours. I'd never tell a soul. My dear husband certainly won't be the wiser."

I replied in a nice but firm manner. "You're a beautiful woman. I doubt many men could deny you. But it's not going to work. You're married. I'm in a relationship. Please let it go."

"May I suggest a brief assignation? Just once, and I promise not to pester you ever again. Just one night in bed with that big cock of yours." When I raised my eyebrows she said, "Don't pretend you don't know what I'm talking about." She paused and wet her rouged lips with her tongue. "Remember the boat? Anyway, I know some of the many women you've bedded down, and they're all in agreement—you've got a big dick and you know how to use it."

"They shouldn't have run their yaps. Besides, they exaggerated."

She smiled indulgently. "Why, I thought you'd feel flattered. But I won't let you off that easily. Even Jarl says you're well equipped. Offered a surprisingly detailed description." Her eyes sparkled. "So you're intacto, huh? Bet I could coax that head from its turtleneck."

"What're we, in high school? Jughead tells you something in homeroom, you tell Veronica, and she passes it on to Archie during detention?"

She laughed wickedly. "He might be a Jughead, but Jarl painted a lovely picture of what you've got hanging."

I should have left it alone but anger had taken hold. "What is it with you and my package? Jesus, don't you get it? It's not the size of the ship but the motion of the ocean that counts."

Donna pursed her full lips. "Granted, but why cruise in a runabout when you can ride the *Queen Mary*? Anyway, I'm told your hip action generates those desirable ocean motions you've alluded to. Now how about it—do I get to ride the swells on your luxury liner?"

I looked at her in sudden disgust. "Is that all I am to you? A big cock?"

She ditzed past the Nautilus machines and ran her hands up and down her flanks. "Something wrong with that? Come now. Playing hard to get?"

"Playing impossible to get."

Donna stepped toward me and stopped just inches away. "Oh my, that sounds like a challenge." Then she lunged forward and went for my crotch.

I stepped back. "Keep your hands to yourself and listen to me. That day skiing was a mistake. I gave you the wrong impression. I am not interested in you, got it?"

She threw back her head and laughed. "Oh, now I've got it. You can't get it up! That's it, isn't it? I'll bet that darling Levi doesn't have any problems."

I threw up my hands. "I can get it up and I can do things to your clitoris that you never imagined. But it's not gonna happen. Know why? Because there's no friendship involved!"

Donna's face dissolved in anguish as she leaped forward and wrapped her arms around my neck. "That's what I'm asking for," she cried as she tried to kiss me. "I want to be your friend." She ground her hips against mine and clutched me with a terrible need. "I'm never going to leave you alone. You're the best thing I've seen in this town." Her eyes got wide as she searched the room like a trapped animal. "I want a lover, don't you see? I want a lover, and I'm not getting any younger."

"Get off!"

Tears rolled down her proud face as she clutched harder and whispered, "I just want to be loved."

Something turned inside me. Maybe it was the simple recognition of someone in pain, of someone invisible her entire life. All at once I did a one eighty. I embraced her and said softly, "I'm sure you deserve to be loved. We all do. But we need to be loved by someone who can offer it."

Donna hitched a couple of times and looked into my eyes. "Do you mean that, Michael? *Do* I deserve love? Do you *really* mean that?"

I held her trembling arms in my hands and whispered, "Yes. But I'm not the person who can give you that love. You need more than I can provide." I held a vision of Natasha, and wondered what it was that I'd been unable to give *her* when we first met.

Donna touched a finger to her eyes and sniffed. Then she smiled bravely and said, "You're a true gentleman. Here I am throwing myself at you, offering all the sex you could ever desire."

I replied in a quiet voice, "You don't need to throw yourself at anyone, Donna. You're a fine woman."

She swiped at her eyes again. "You're just saying that to be kind."

"I'm not. You're intelligent, you're lively and you have great beauty."

Donna smiled weakly and examined the floor. "You're a true gentleman, all right. Man enough to push me in a direction you think best for me." She looked up and now her eyes were red and slightly swollen. "What a sad little slut I've been." Her voice waned as she added, "All I've done is throw myself away."

I rubbed my fingertips lightly up and down her slender arms. "You've done nothing of the kind. Maybe something happened to you along the line. So what? Things happen to all of us. You made some decisions. Bad or good, they've led you to this point. Now do something about it!"

Donna stepped back and folded her arms across her breasts. "Maybe it is time to make some changes." She stared at something distant and whispered, "Will you help me?"

I promised to do what I could and then I showered and changed and went in search of Johnny. I felt we'd gotten past his issues with Levi and I wanted to be sure that we'd made solid amends. But he was nowhere to be found. His assistant shrugged and mouthed, "*Who knows?*" so I turned and walked out the door. The gravel in the parking lot crunched noisily, but with so much on my mind I didn't see the rose until I'd gotten behind the wheel. "Goddamn," I said. I snatched it from beneath the wiper and marched back inside. When I found Donna I held the rose at arm's length. "Why do you keep leaving these on my car? Stop following me!"

Donna's jaw dropped, and she stared like an animal looking out from the brush.

A chill traveled up my spine. "You recognize this, don't you? What do you know?"

She shook her head and turned her back to me.

I gently touched her shoulder. "*Donna.* For the love of God, if you know something then tell me."

Donna whipped around like cornered prey, her face a mask as new tears streamed down her cheeks. "Leave me alone!" she cried, and then she ran off.

I got home and found Natasha sitting calmly on the porch as I pulled into the driveway. She watched with a set expression as I approached her. When I held up the rose for her to see, deep lines etched her forehead.

"Wonderful," she said in a strange, neutral voice. "Looks just like this one." She reached down and picked up an identical rose. "Found it stuck to our door."

I left early for work to seek expert advice. "May I be of some help?" the graying woman in a pale green smock asked as I entered the floral shop. She stood behind a counter with an unfinished arrangement before her.

Dozens of flowers filled the room, roses and lilacs and even some small citrus trees, the fragrances commingled but also competing for dominance. I set my police briefcase down on the counter and opened it. "Yes, ma'am," I began. "What can you tell me about roses?" I handed her the long-stemmed one from Johnny's.

She held it to the light and peered through old-lady bifocals. "This is quite lovely," she said with great interest. "Where did you get this? I don't believe I've ever seen another quite like it."

I leaned against the counter and shifted my weight to one leg. "Someone left it on my car."

She smiled as she examined it from different angles. "Oh, a secret admirer. How romantic."

"Do all the local florists carry it?"

She wrinkled her nose and shook her head with short, jerky movements. "Around here? Absolutely not. This little beauty is the product of patience and attention. I doubt it's even for retail. Someone cultivated this at home."

"A supplier couldn't provide one of this quality?"

Her eyes pored over the flower. "Whoever grew this lavished time and loving care upon it. See these delicate petals? This is prize-winning caliber. No supplier would waste time growing these. There'd never be enough return on the investment. Not in this market area."

"So it's unique?"

"Yes. Quite." She smiled. "You're fortunate to have someone who cares this much about you."

"Yes, ma'am." I dipped my hand in the briefcase and got the rose Natasha had plucked from our door. "Twin sister to the first?"

She had only to glance at it before she nodded. "Absolutely."

I stuffed them in the briefcase. "Thanks. You've been a very big help."

The woman returned to her arrangement. "Please come by anytime," she said hopefully.

"I will," I said as I snapped the briefcase shut.

I left the store, took note of a beat-up white Chevy parked unobtrusively at the far end of the parking lot, and reported to roll call. Levi was already there, and as I sat down I said, "What happened to you last night? I wanted 'the word' on that rape."

"Spent the night with Jen."

I barely had time to nod when Burke began his preliminaries. When he finished he called for Joe Santoro. Everyone seemed to sit up as he entered with a sheaf of papers, his reserved demeanor absent. In its place he'd adopted an edgy, gum-popping, eye gouging attitude that said, *Look the fuck out, 'cause I'm gonna rip out someone's guts if I don't nail this guy.*

He balled his right hand into a fist and punched it repeatedly against his open left palm while he looked at each of us in turn. "We've got another rape. A mother fucking, getting-as-bad-as-they-can-get, rape." He stopped and his face turned brutal as he thundered, "Another fucking *rape!*"

A ripple moved through the room as he took half a step back and composed himself. His jaws worked rapidly against his chewing gum. Finally he stepped forward and cleared his throat. "Hart got on-scene quickly. Summoned the medics, got the investigators moving …" He paused and looked thoughtfully at Levi. "Damned good job, by the way." Joe continued. "Same M.O. as before. Knocks her out. Blindfolds her. Binds her hands with—you guessed it—a purple bungee cord. Rapes her, shoves a wine bottle up her vagina, then uses a knife to carve a design in her buttocks. But he's not finished *yet.* No fucking way! Not *this* cocksucker. Leaves behind a tenderhearted remembrance while she's sprawled unconscious on the floor, and then—*poof!* He's outta there—and gents, I do mean he was fuckin' *out of there*. Vanished! Nobody sees him enter, nobody sees him *leave*... ." He paced back and forth with nervous energy and suddenly said, "I've had my guys scouring every fucking hardware store, every department store, even the yellow pages for hardware supply *outlets*, trying to get a handle on these fucking bungee cords. We've sent samples to the Feds to identify the manufacturer—still no fucking *dice*! We're no closer now than we were the first time!" He ran his hand across his face, pinched the end of his nose, and then startled everyone as he screamed, "What are we gonna *do*, ladies and gentlemen? When're we gonna *find* him?"

Burke watched silently from the side of the room, and while Joe calmed down, he filled the gap by robotically handing out new information fliers. When one reached me I gave it a casual once over—until I read the victim's name and address. It was as if someone's fist had clamped down on my chest. I gasped and bolted upright in my seat and flicked my eyes toward Joe. He nodded slightly and wordlessly pointed a finger in the general direction of his office. "I'll take Brennan with me if it's okay with you, Sarge. Just remembered—he's got some info for me."

Joe leaned back in his chair and propped his hand-tooled leather shoes on top of his desk. "Talk to me."

I plunked my briefcase down, took a seat and gestured at the flyer. "I know her. Bethany."

That got his attention, but in a way I hadn't expected.

Lt. Joe Santoro nodded and regarded me through hooded eyes. Then he snapped his gum, dropped his feet to the floor, leaned forward and fished a small laminated card from his shirt pocket. "Officer Brennan," he intoned as he began reading, "You have the right to remain silent... ."

"Do you understand your rights as I've explained them?" Before I could recover he added, "Because you are now a suspect in the rapes of at least two women." He picked up a case file from his desk and tossed it at me. I opened the file and stared dumbfounded at the name of the *other* victim whom I now stood accused of attacking.

Anna Stewart.

It felt as though a powerful, malevolent vacuum hose had suddenly sucked all the oxygen from the room. Everything spun as I stammered, "I—I ... I don't understand."

He said flatly, "Before we continue, do you voluntarily waive your rights and consent to speak to me?"

I couldn't breathe. Anna's typed-in name dissolved in a blur. When I could see again, the cop in me took over and I said, "Within reason, but ... Joe! I know *both* these women! I ... I would never harm them!"

Joe gestured toward the file in my lap. "She's the victim from a couple of nights ago. We found a photo of the two of you on the nightstand. Care to explain?"

"I met her at Johnny's Fitness Center. We spent some time together. She was a guest at Levi's party. I ... I cared about her, Joe. We were—well, we'd become close."

His eyes narrowed. "How close?"

I drew a deep breath, held it and exhaled slowly. Then I whispered, "Intimate."

"How intimate," he demanded as he leaned toward me.

Something turned inside me. I shot back, "Do I have to draw a picture?"

Joe nodded slowly. "Examining physicians didn't find any semen in her, but that doesn't rule out ..."

I replied through clenched teeth, "I use protection."

He rubbed the end of his nose and said, "Yeah, you would." He arched his eyebrows and added; "She's been in a catatonic state ever since. You claim she's had consensual sex with you. That doesn't rule out the possibility of forcing non-consensual sex upon her." Joe sat back abruptly and draped an arm over the back of the chair, as if he'd suddenly reached a conclusion. Then he casually examined the nails of his hand and said, "I purposely said nothing to you about her." He leaned forward and propped his elbows on the desk. "I played hardball with you. Don't like it? Tough titty. I have a job to do. I gave you a bullshit story and asked her brother to help in case you asked too many questions—in case you *are* guilty." Joe leaned back as he seemed to consider something. "I was going to snoop around a bit more, maybe cop a DNA sample from you without your knowledge." He put his stern face on again and said in a sudden loud voice, "And now you come here, and you fucking tell me that you *also* know *last* night's victim, and I gotta wonder—hoo yah! What the fuck do we have here?"

I nodded to show that he had my undivided attention.

Joe turned shrewd eyes toward me and asked, "This Bethany girl ... you were intimate with her, too?"

I swallowed while considering my legal standing, and decided not to hedge any bets. Finally I nodded and said, "Yes. Many times." I wet my lips and added, "Her roommate, too. But that was a while back, before they were roomies."

All Joe said was, "I am not unaware of your reputation with the ladies."

I pointed at Anna's case file and asked, "How's she doing? I ... we were supposed to have dinner that night. I tried several times to reach her. Then Ed told me she'd found another guy. I still leave messages on her machine, but she ..." I stopped, suddenly overcome by a picture in my mind of the attack she had endured. I shuffled my shoes against the linoleum floor and my voice threatened to break as I asked, "Will she be okay? Is she ... recovering?" I stopped and tried to keep everything in focus. Images popped up as I tried to imagine the agony she'd suffered. "What about Bethany?" I asked in a defeated voice. "How's *she* handling this?"

Joe nodded almost imperceptibly and cleared his throat. "Bethany's doing as well as can be expected. Anna's recovering physically. Emotionally? The docs are still out on that."

Now it was my turn. I glared at him and asked, "Why the fuck didn't you just come right out and tell me? We might've learned something! We might've stopped him in his goddamned tracks!"

It was a fair question and from the expression on his face Joe seemed to think so, too. "I already explained," he began in a not unfriendly voice. "I wanted to gather evidence in case you *were* guilty." He screwed his eyes tighter as he jabbed a forefinger at me. "I also wanted to keep things looking normal for appearance sake; to keep you on the streets where I could keep an eye on you. You ... *and* Levi, *and* Hack."

I looked sharply at him.

He nodded as he slouched against the back of his chair. "Yeah, that's right. While my guys were looking for a suspect, *I* was watching the three of you."

I drew a deep, audible breath and waited.

He said, "I wanted to know why *you* guys were out there."

In a quiet voice I said, "We were out there to do our job. And if you knew who was where the night Anna was attacked, then you knew I had an alibi, because Levi was with me."

He shook his head, and with large eyes pinned on me he said, "No he was *not*. Except for a brief visit to the home of a certain female attorney, Officer Hart was traipsing around by his lonesome, while you cruised the side roads and byroads by *your* lonesome."

That sure as hell brought me up short; I *had* no alibi.

Joe continued. "So I've got you, with previous intimate knowledge of the victim. She's expecting you, ergo you have knowledge of her whereabouts and her lone status, *and* there's a break in time during which you have no alibi. You've got opportunity, you've got capability. But do you have a motive? I don't fucking know." He pursed his lips and added, "Perhaps you've got some grudge to bear; a score to settle. Maybe you decided to rough her up, teach her a lesson."

I sat in stunned silence. I knew I was innocent of course, but the cop in me had to acknowledge the possibilities he'd outlined. I had no alibi—nothing to go on, except the truth—and a deep resentment. All at once I leaned forward and slammed a fist down on his desk. "You should have fucking told me! We might have been able to do *more!*"

Joe scrutinized me for several long seconds. Finally he dropped his eyes and said in a conversational tone, "I'll call Anna's brother. Tell him to expect to hear from you. Maybe you'll want to visit her when the doctors allow." When I looked questioningly at him he explained. "Her brother doesn't know that you were a suspect. I wanted it that way. You understand." That last part wasn't a question. It was a statement—one cop to another.

I swallowed several times. My throat felt parched. "Water," I whispered.

"Tell me more about Bethany," I asked Joe as he handed me a soda.

He leaned back and folded his hands across his lean stomach. His Mediterranean eyes were softer now, more deeply set against his olive complexion. "Two things I haven't revealed to the rank and file. The suspect carved a little remembrance into Bethany's right buttock."

"Yeah, you told us."

Joe propped his feet back on top of his desk and leaned back precariously as he closed his eyes. His fingers worked the bridge of his nose as he said, "But I didn't reveal *what* he carved." He sighed; this professional cop was exhausted. Finally he said quietly, "He carved a rose on her butt, and he left another rose—a real one, a very *unusual* one—on the floor next to her."

I stopped breathing. "Jesus H., Joe! Someone's been leaving roses on my car! Levi's, too. And we found *these* today." I reached down and flipped my briefcase open. "I just got a florist's expert opinion on these." I took the roses out and placed them on his desk. "She told me they're unique." I pointed to the first. "Found that one on my car when I left Johnny's today. That one," I said with a flick of my wrist, "was stuck to the door of my house. My roommate Natasha found it while I was at Johnny's." I screeched to a halt as I made the connection, and in a doom-filled voice I uttered, "Aw, *shit*. Natasha!"

I grabbed Joe's phone and called the house, then remembered that Natasha had gone to work early. I punched the number for her club. "I need to speak to Natasha Panova," I said when someone answered. "It's an emergency."

When she came on I looked at Joe with raised eyebrows. Sharp man that he is, he understood and slowly nodded his head. I said, "Nat, I can't explain now. It's the roses. You've got to watch your back at all times. Don't go anywhere alone. Wait for me or Levi to take you home. I'll fill you in later. Got that?"

Her voice sounded far away when she replied. "Don't leave me hanging like this. What's it all about?"

I looked at Joe, shrugged helplessly and said, "Don't ask me why I know— and don't breathe a fucking word of this to anyone, but you might be on the rapist's hit list."

Joe nodded as he carefully appraised me with his dark eyes. "Back to business. I'll need samples of your pubic hairs, Officer Brennan."

"What the hell for?"

"To isolate yours from the suspect's."

"Oh. Okay. I understand."

"I knew you would." Then he picked up the phone and punched an internal extension. "Santoro here. Come to my office. Bring Jim and Stan with you." He and I sat in silence until three of his undercover guys marched in and stood quietly against a wall. Joe inclined his head toward me and said, "Officer Brennan is forthwith free and clear. Thus sanctioned, I want the three of you to drop everything you're doing—and I do mean *everything*." He stared at each one before continuing. "The three of you are hereby directed to provide 24/7 protection to Officer Brennan's girlfriend, whom we've just identified as a most-probable entry on our scum-sucker's hit list."

"Better include Jennifer," I said. "She and Levi now have a special relationship."

Joe nodded and said to his men, "I'll give you the straight skinny upon Officer Brennan's departure from this office." Then Joe looked at me and released a pent-up sigh. "Officer Brennan," he began, "You've been under partial surveillance since Anna Stewart's attack. Would've been total, but my resources were limited."

I frowned and said, "The other night in Rehoboth Beach—an old white Chevy? And today—bridge coming into town?"

One of Joe's men coughed. "Yeah. Had a feeling you made us."

Joe leaned forward. "Michael, I can only wish that our department had more dedicated officers like these three men against that wall, and Officers Hart, Jones and yourself. Keep up the good work. And Michael," he began, and he looked kindly at me. "I'm sorry for what I've put you through."

I nodded, overcome by a mixture of relief, clarity concerning Anna, and inner turmoil at the mere thought of what she and Bethany and the other victims had suffered. And then there was the great fear that I now felt for Natasha.

Joe said, "Now that we're all here, let's discuss these roses."

"Jesus, I'm losing it!" I'd been pummeled by so many revelations that I hadn't told Joe of another relevant detail. "I fucking forgot to mention this, but Levi has a close relationship with the brother of the first victim."

That got Joe's attention. His eyebrows shot up formidably. "Speak to us, Officer Brennan."

"Here's how I see it," I began. "Night of the first rape? I find a rose stuck to my cruiser. It was just after that melee at Ragnar's. Know the one I'm talking about?"

He nodded and I continued. "Okay. Seems Levi has a six degrees of separation connection to the first victim, and that night *he* finds a rose pinned to *his* car. Now then—I spent an evening with *Anna*. When I left the following morning, there's a rose on my Mustang. After that, Anna's raped. I leave *Bethany's*, find *another* rose on my car, then *Bethany* is raped. *Today* ... I find one on my car, and Natasha finds one stuck to the door of our house."

One of Joe's guys cleared his throat. "I don't get it."

Joe explained in a weary voice. "Seems whatever women Brennan and Hart are associated with are being systematically attacked."

I frowned, looked at each of the detectives in turn and asked, "So what does that make Levi and me—the hunters—or the hunted?"

"It might make you and Hart the common denominator," Joe said. He leaned forward and seemed to pull me into him. "There are some obvious patterns. The bungee cords ..."

"*Purple* bungee cords," I corrected. "In the Lüscher Personality Profile, violet is often associated with repressed homosexuality. It also speaks of a magical environment of subject and object. In other words, master and slave."

Joe nodded rapidly. "Hmm, that's good! I'll make a note of that." He penciled something on a notepad and continued. "Other patterns—there are the north end crime scenes. Here's something else—a card we've kept close to our vests: he likes to do them from behind. It indicates ..."

"Someone who lacks self-confidence ..."

"Or someone who wants us to think he does, or who hates women." He leaned back and laced his fingers behind his head. "Got a call in to a friend. Works homicide for Baltimore. He's also a profiling genius. See, there's an anomaly in this guy's M.O. that troubles me. The girls are all pretty, but ..."

"None of them have similar bodies." Then I frowned and said, "Assuming you've told me about *all* the victims."

Joe nodded.

I continued. "Attractive? Sure. But Bethany isn't exactly petite, while Anna is. Different heights, hair colors, skin tones—there's no similarity."

Joe half-smiled. "You're a good cop, Brennan." He flicked his fingers at me and said, "Okay, how about this? Each case has revealed an increasingly ritualistic behavior."

I nodded and said, "He's also become more violent; even sadistic. Means he could be leading up to ..."

"Homicide," Joe whispered. "I'll have my staff review every arrest you and Hart have made. Might luck out and find our connection."

"Wait! There's something else with the roses. Sorry. It slipped my mind with all the shit that's just happened ... but it could be another link."

His jaw worked as he chewed another stick of gum. He appeared distracted and even more exhausted than he had less than an hour ago. "Give me what you've got."

I described Donna's reaction when I showed her the rose. I sketched her previous sexual advances without getting graphic, and mentioned my offer to help her through her difficulties. Then I said, "I don't know if she really knows anything, or if she only *thinks* she does. Look, let me work with her. I think she trusts me and I might get more out of her than if she's pulled in for questioning." I looked at Joe man-to-man. "She's no dummy. Pressure her and she'll clam up. Let me give it a shot."

He rubbed his eyes and asked, "You know what you're getting yourself into? You'll have reports out the ass to write. You'll spend more time in courtrooms than bedrooms if you develop something—and I don't mean the clap. Are you ready for that?" He stared pointedly at me.

"Think you're man enough to hold me back?"

He offered a curt nod and said, "Good! See what you can do, but work with me every step of the way." Then he returned to his old self and said brusquely, "Everything we've discussed stays in this room. Most particularly you are to say nothing about the roses. That remains privileged information. I mean, I don't even want you yappin' to Levi." *Capiche?*"

"Capiche."

Joe reaffirmed his pledge to arrange for additional protection for Natasha and Jennifer, and then he dismissed me while he spoke privately with his guys. I hot footed it out to my cruiser and dashed north to see Nat for a confab. She *had* to know the danger she was in. I *had* to convince her not to take this lightly. Natasha took me to a quiet back room and we worked through it. She convinced me that she clearly grasped the threat and would take no chances. We returned to the customer area and I waited until one of Joe's men walked in. He caught my eye and swiped a finger along the bridge of his nose to indicate that he was taking the handoff from me.

It was dark when I hit the streets again. I worked my way north and made a pass by Natasha's club. By the time I reached 96th Street I'd worked out a way to contact Donna discreetly. The more I pictured her reaction to the rose, the more convinced I'd become that she could help identify the North End Rapist.

*   *   *

He turned down the volume and drove slowly down the dead-end lane. Subdued light shone past her closed drapes and someone's car was parked curbside. A visitor? He'd wait and find out; this one was high on his list.

An elderly couple soon emerged from a house on the other side of the street and got into the car. He nodded with satisfaction. She *was* alone. He waited another fifteen minutes after the couple drove off, then drove to another street before getting out of his car; wouldn't do to get boxed-in on a one-way street. He stuck to the shadows as always and crept to the rear yard. The thin-curtained French doors were closed and he knelt and tested them. A barrel bolt secured it from inside. No problem—it would take a little effort, but he would get it open.

He glanced over his shoulder four or five times as he worked the specialized tools between the doorframes, until finally he held his breath and pushed steadily. The doors began to yield under his pressure. Then they bulged slightly. Only a tiny fraction of pressure more would be needed ...

Crack! They burst open with a vengeance and a girl screamed from inside. Then she screamed again.

$$*\quad*\quad*$$

It takes time to process a request for police service. The call-taker must calm the often-distressed victim, ascertain the address and callback number, obtain possible suspect descriptions and prioritize the call before relaying the data via computer to the dispatcher. If the call is classified urgent, a light flashes on the dispatcher's screen. But first the dispatcher must read the information, digest it, determine the closest available units, and only then can he or she put the information out over the air. Even when everything works as advertised, a minimum of forty-five seconds will pass from the time the victim's shaking fingers press 911, to the time when the dispatcher's finger touches the transmit key. Suspects can reach surprising places in those forty-five seconds.

"*Seventy-two-oh-four and all units in the vicinity, 219 Tidelands Court, report of an intruder.*"

Levi acknowledged breathlessly, "*I'm just down the street! Put me on-scene!*"

I called out as backup. "Seventy-three-oh-nine's en route." I floored it.

"*And units responding, report of a white male adult. White shirt. Attempted entry from the rear of the house. Direction of travel unknown.*"

"*Clear the air!*" Levi shouted. "*I'm in foot pursuit. Headed north from the back yard; white shirt. All I got.*"

I punched my lights and hit the siren. "Two minutes," I said into the mike, as three more units called out.

A minute passed as I wove through the congested traffic, then Levi yelled, "*I'm down! Lost him. Last seen northbound from Seaweed.*"

I screeched to a halt next to Levi's cruiser half a minute later. A beautiful girl ran out of the house as I burst out of my cruiser.

"Michael!" she yelled. "Oh Michael, thank God you're here!"

I stared dumbfounded. Then it all made sense. "Crystal!"

Hack and Perry Ryan arrived seconds later. I passed Crystal off to Hack as two plainclothes units screeched to a halt. I grabbed Ryan before they could even get out of their cars and we took off through the back yard. We found Levi with little difficulty; we only had to home in on his curses.

His uniform was tattered and filthy, and small scratches covered his arms. "Fucking chicken wire," he said disgustedly. "Look at this shit."

He'd been one street away from his old girlfriend's residence when the call went out. Levi followed Crystal's pointing finger to the back yard, where he caught a distant glimpse of a white shirt bob-tailing through the neighboring yards. He'd taken off in pursuit, only to encounter a tangle of chicken wire surrounding a small vegetable garden.

"What the fuck," Ryan began. "You couldn't see that shit?"

Levi looked sourly at him. "Mighta seen it, but I was too busy looking at what the fucker dropped." He held up his hand and revealed a purple bungee cord.

I heard labored breathing, and then footsteps crunched noisily through the underbrush. All at once Demmings appeared from the dark yard just north of us. He gasped for breath as he wiped a dirty white sleeve across his sweaty face. "Nothing. I went north. Thought I'd cut him off. No sign of him." He drew a deep breath. "Nothing, boys."

Ryan growled at Levi, "You got here awfully damned quick."

Levi glared at him. "What's that supposed to mean?"

"Just seems odd."

Levi regarded him with half-lidded eyes and muttered, "Maybe you'd have gotten here too if you hadn't been driving 'round all night with your dick in your hand. Come on. I'll give you a driving lesson." He put his hand in his pocket and pulled out his car keys. When he did, something fell to the ground.

Ryan stooped down and retrieved it. "*Trojans.*"

Levi glanced at the package of condoms and nodded. "Yeah? So?"

"So why are you walkin' around with Jim Hats?"

Levi stared him down and said, "In case I decide to bend you over, dip shit."

Ryan said, "You haven't answered my question! Bungee cord, Jim Hats; what else you got in your pockets?" He made a move toward Levi.

Levi clenched his fists and stepped toward Ryan. I jumped between them. "Cool your heels," I said to Ryan. "I carry condoms, too. See?" I got out my wallet and produced one.

Demmings snorted, "Yeah, pretty boys like you two would."

I regarded him with a cold eye. "Would you prefer we act irresponsibly?"

He said in a sudden, bitter whisper, "I prefer you two stop *fuckin'* every beautiful woman in sight."

*   *   *

He cursed his bad luck an hour later as he cleaned-up. If that damned door hadn't crashed open—if she hadn't screamed—he would have gotten her. At least she hadn't seen his face, although he was confident that he would have explained his presence to her satisfaction if she had.

He'd dropped a bungee cord, too—but he doubted it could ever be traced to *him.* At least he still had his surgical gloves and the slip-ons for his shoes. He dug his hand into his other pocket and smiled. Still had his condoms.

CHAPTER 10

BURKE shocked everyone the next day when he opened roll call and grudgingly praised Levi for his quick if somewhat abortive action in chasing the intruder. Levi's trophy—the bungee cord—highlighted the urgency that drove us anew to identify and capture the suspect before he struck again.

Jarl was a different matter. After we broke he strolled over and said to Levi, "A real man woulda caught the fucker."

I met Levi's eye and said to Jarl, "Hey, about that beer. What's a good time to hook-up and grab a couple?"

Jarl turned his back to Levi and said, "Don't know. Tonight, maybe?"

I stroked my chin thoughtfully. "Possible. I'll let you know later." After he walked off I turned to Levi. "Time to get to work, Hoss."

* * *

He returned as darkness descended. The neighborhood seemed lifeless for some reason, but *he* felt energized, alive as he'd never been. He adjusted the volume on his radio and cruised up one street and down another.

* * *

During patrol I found a phone booth and called Nat at the club. I knew Joe's guys were on her but I wanted no margin for error. When she came to the phone I told her that I might meet Jarl after work. He might be twisted, but he might have the straight dope.

I resumed patrol and worked out how to reach Donna without risking a run-in with her husband. I settled on one possibility when three alert tones shattered the relative calm.

The dispatcher said in a quick, strained voice, "*Communications to all units in the vicinity of 45th and the beach, all units in the vicinity of 45th and the beach, for a report of a rape in progress.*" She paused, drew an audible breath and continued. "*Caller confirms man with a gun chased female subject to the beach … caller is on the line, advises suspect is now raping the victim. All units use caution, 10-32 man with a gun, no further description.*"

I was northbound at Coastal and 70th. I stomped down on the parking brake and spun the wheel violently to the left. The cruiser shuddered; the rear end whipped around; classic bootlegger turn. I reached down, pulled the brake release and pushed the accelerator through the floor. The cruiser sprinted forward. I toggled the lights and siren. I zipped past 65th and announced, "Seventy-three-oh-nine's en route."

"*And Communications to all units, caller now states suspect has shot at two civilians, repeat, suspect has shot at two civilians attempting to aid victim, stand by for description.*"

A pedestrian stepped defiantly in front of me at 60th. I jammed on the brakes. The tires groaned in protest. The cruiser screeched to a stop. A cloud of blue smoke drifted past me. "Mother *fucker*," I screamed through the closed windows. I took off again.

Burke got on-air and growled, "*All units, slow it down until we get some manpower on-scene.*"

I said aloud, "Fuck *that.*"

"*Seventy-two-oh-four's on location,*" Levi declared.

I whipped past 55th street and tried to escape the Earth's gravitational pull.

"*I'm in foot pursuit,*" Levi yelled into his mike, "*northbound on the beach.*" A second later he added, "*Suspect's a white male adult. Six foot. Hundred eighty. Mid-thirties. No shirt. Lots of tatts.*"

I *knew* that guy. The tires screamed against the pavement as I executed a hard left. I whipped the wheel again. Up 50th. To the beach. Intercept course. Almost there.

Burke got on the air. "*Slow it down! Consolidate.*"

"*Clear the air,*" Levi shouted over him. "*Victim's on the beach. Civilian's helping her. Pursuit's still on … north on the beach.*"

I stood on the brakes. Ground to a halt. Flew out the door. "On the beach at 50th," I roared into my mike. I ran to the soft sand and stopped. Nothing. I looked north. A bobbing white blur caught my eye. Levi's uniform shirt. I took off in pursuit. The sand clawed at me.

I saw the muzzle flash first.

Then I heard it.

CRAAACK!

Another flash, and ...

CRAAACK!

The second shot echoed off the condos lining the beach.

"*I'm hit,*" Levi screamed over the radio.

Then, POWPOWPOW!

I yanked my Beretta from its holster. My hand shook. I nearly dropped it. My knees turned to mush. Sweat popped across my forehead. I ran forward.

CRACK!

POWPOW. *POW.*

"Levi!" I hollered into the night.

"*I'm hit I'm hit I'm hit,*" he bellowed over the air.

Chaos filled the radio. I couldn't get on the air. I could only run. My chest ached with the effort; my shirt clung to me. My knees were rubber.

Then the night erupted as sirens ripped the sky apart.

I ran blindly on—and nearly stumbled over Levi. His legs had collapsed beneath him. His knees were buried in the sand and he sat on the backs of his shoes. His left hand was clasped against his hip; his right hand clutched his 9mm. A fine wisp of blue smoke drifted upward from the muzzle. The cordite stank.

I yelled to him, "Where're you hit?"

He panted in reply, "Don't worry about me. Check *him* out. Cuff him," he ordered, and he jutted his jaw toward the beach where the surf broke.

I looked carefully and breathed, "Holy Christ." The limp, twisted form of the suspect lay at the water's edge. I held my 9mm in front of me with both hands and walked toward him, all the while keeping his head centered in my sights.

"He's not going anywhere," Levi said in great pain.

"How do you know?" I asked without taking my eyes off the suspect.

He said quietly, "I know."

I got on my radio. "Seventy-three-oh-nine's got an officer down. Repeat, officer down. Suspect's down too. On the beach at 51st. Get me two ambulances … now!"

"Watch him anyway," Levi rebuked from behind me. "Hit him three times," he panted. "Bastard kept coming … so I double-tapped him. In the chest." Levi coughed and added, "Still kept coming." He stopped and wheezed. Then he said very quietly, "The head shot stopped him."

A crowd was gathered along the street side of the beach by the time I reached the suspect. Lights from the condos lit the blood that blossomed from his head and formed a small puddle. The surf rolled in and threatened to dilute it as his dull, open eyes stared lifelessly beneath the neat round hole at the center of his forehead. I stepped back in shock—it was the guy Levi had confronted behind the house, the guy whose girlfriend couldn't afford tampons. Then I saw it, a tattoo that neither of us had noticed previously—a rose, inked in black and red on his right shoulder. It was our man; Levi had nailed the North End Rapist.

My knees shook from unspent adrenaline as I holstered my 9mm. I grabbed the suspect's hands, twisted them behind his back, cuffed him and checked the back of his trousers for hidden weapons. Then I turned him over onto his back. That's when I saw the five holes drilled in a neat symmetrical pattern in the middle of his bare chest.

"That must've been one bad-ass bastard," Hacksaw said.

I whipped around, startled. "Huh?"

"Levi's okay," he said. "Just checked on him. He told me to check an' see how *you* was doing. Don't worry—I left Ryan with him." A film of sweat shone on Hack's dark face as he shifted gears. He whistled softly, holstered his pistol and said, "Look at that, will you? Must've been fifty feet away. In the dark, too. Levi sure plugged him good." Sometimes even cops can't resist being impressed.

I heard running footsteps from behind. "Everyone okay?" Demmings asked.

"This one's not," Hack assured him as he thrust a forefinger at the body. Then with a satisfied *harrumph* he said, "So much for our North End Rapist."

Demmings nodded as a gleeful smile appeared on his soft face. "Good."

"It's a righteous shooting," I added. "I heard the shots. Gotta find his weapon. Must be here somewhere." Then I raced back to Levi.

I knelt at his side. He'd gotten very pale but otherwise seemed okay. It was only when I looked at his hip that I saw the growing stain of dark blood.

"You're hit," I exclaimed, still not quite believing it as I reached out to support him.

He jerked slightly and said, "It's not so bad." Then he gritted his teeth and blurted, "God, it *burns!*"

"Hang on. Medics will be here soon."

Grimacing, he said, "Find that weapon." His eyes glazed over as he stared in the direction of the body. Then he tried to focus on me as he said, "Didja know that no matter where you are in London, you're never more than thirty feet from …" All at once he slumped forward. I grabbed him as his hand slipped away, revealing the angry welt above his hip.

"Tell Nat not to worry," he murmured just before he passed out.

We found the suspect's .380 caliber pistol half-buried in the surf a few feet from his body. The crime lab guys got on the scene and broke out the metal detectors, and they eventually found three freshly spent .380 shell casings in the sand between 49th and 51st, and five of Levi's six 9mm casings.

Joe Santoro arrived and examined the body. He didn't appear so tired now. Jarl Jackson brought the fourteen-year old victim to the scene: a runaway. Her nose had been busted, her eyes were blackened and bruises marred her arms and thighs—large purplish blobs that stood out even in the dim light. She wasn't nearly as pretty as the other victims were reported to be and certainly not someone whom Levi or I could have known. Pretty or plain, she shook like a jaybird sitting atop an iceberg—but she held it together long enough to make a positive ID. Jarl had the paramedics load her into the ambulance, and then he followed them to the hospital.

The state police helicopter whisked Levi to the regional trauma center. I approached Joe in a panic. "Hey, umm, how's it going?"

"As you'd expect."

Shifting from one foot to the other I said, "Do me a favor. Go on the air and order me to the trauma center. I don't have time to explain. Just do it. Okay?"

He nodded slowly as he fished his portable radio from a pocket. He reached Burke on the tactical channel and said, "I'm sending Brennan to the trauma center with an evidence kit. That okay with you?" When Burke grumbled his assent Joe looked at me and said, "Levi's a tough mother—now get going." I thanked him and took off.

I arrived thirty minutes later and luck was on my side when I encountered a familiar doctor. He clamped a reassuring hand on my shoulder and said, "Your friend will be fine. Bullet grazed his hip. Tore away some meat. He's sedated. We'll keep him that way until morning."

"Thank God," I replied. "What can I do for him? Anything at all."

He squeezed my shoulder again and smiled. "Nothing you can do right now. But be here in the morning when he comes around. I'm sure he'd like to see a friendly face." He stopped and added, "He'll be in a lot of pain."

I commandeered a phone from the nurse's station and called Natasha at the club. "Listen," I began. "Levi's okay. I'm with him. We umm—we're at the trauma center."

Her voice trembled as she asked, "What do you mean, trauma center? How can he be okay if he's been taken to a fucking trauma center?"

"He's been slightly injured." I felt my way cautiously. "There's been a shooting. A bullet nicked him in the hip, but he'll be fine, Natasha. *Fine.*" I paused and gave her the good news. "Listen, Nat … he nailed our man. You're out of danger. Now stay where you are. Nothing I can do here now—Levi's been sedated. I'll come get you and we'll return together." We talked for a few more minutes and then I hung up the phone. A wave of euphoria washed over me as I acknowledged the end of the rapist, the end of the danger he had posed to Natasha, and to other potential victims. I walked down an antiseptic hospital corridor as the tension drained from my shoulders—that bastard was *history*.

Yes. He liked this girl at first sight; liked her the instant he spotted her walking out of the north end 7/11. It had gotten quiet now and she would do—would *have* to do after the commotion at 51st Street disrupted his *earlier* plans.

Yes. Nice girl. Younger than the others—maybe sixteen—but that was fine. Always did have a hankering for young meat. Black, too. Nice, young black bitch that he'd make bleed red *after* he fucked her cunt.

"Don't know why I wasted my time with the white bitches. Black women always were more my style."

He followed her home at a discreet distance. After she went inside he sat low in his car and waited. But then he broke a cardinal rule: he didn't wait after all—couldn't wait. "Yes, yes, yes, boys. I wanted some of that black pussy—*my* kind of pussy."

As his heart beat faster he decided what the hell—why wait to confirm that she was alone? One must sometimes run wild. He opened his door silently and blended with the shadows as he knew he would—as he knew he had a right to do—and got around to the back of her house. Now he had her in view. He smiled and whispered, "Fuckin' aye," as he studied her long, slender back.

After a quick look-around he put on the surgical gloves and slipped the covers over his shoes. His preparations complete, he crept silently to the patio door. He looked at the lock and smirked—it posed no challenge. Not to him. He reached into his trouser pocket and grabbed the picks. He selected a slender shim, bent down, and worked that lock like a pro. *Click!*

Carefully—oh so carefully, he slid the glass door open. He did another quick-peep when all at once a flash of light from an upstairs window broke the dark night. Fuck! Someone else *was* home! He got out of there in a hurry.

*   *   *

The local newspaper opened its morning coverage of the incident with, "LOCAL COP RUNS ASSAULT SUSPECT INTO OCEAN AND GUNS HIM DOWN." The suspect's criminal history ran to fifteen pages. He'd done hard time at The Cut—Maryland's State Pen—for two assault convictions that could have been precursors to rape. The autopsy showed that he'd been so amped-up on PCP that probably nothing less than that headshot could have stopped him.

I tossed the paper aside in disgust and got busy with the coffee I'd gotten from the hospital cafeteria. Natasha smiled gratefully as I set a steaming cup on the waiting room table. It was hot stuff—cop stuff—and she took only two sips before she glanced at the wall-mounted clock and announced, "It's time." I picked up a small bag containing some clothes and we wandered down one antiseptic-smelling corridor after another toward his room.

We found him sitting up in bed in a green hospital gown. His face was pale and his eyes seemed dulled by painkillers. He greeted Natasha but dropped his eyes when I edged closer. I put my hand on his knee. "*Mi amigo!* How're you feeling?"

He fidgeted and mumbled, "I let you down."

I grabbed his big toe and twisted it. When he cried out in pain I twisted it again. "Knock it off! Jesus, I'd dive in front of a bus for you. You could never let me down."

"I shouldn't have let the bastard get me," he whispered.

"Darling Levi," Natasha interjected, "You've got survivor's guilt. It'll pass."

I laid out his clothes on the bed. "By the way, Horse Breath, you're to meet with some guys from the Critical Incident Response Unit. They'll help put it in perspective."

He whispered in a lifeless tone, "Oh, great. So now I'm a candidate for Post Traumatic Stress Disorder."

"Relax, bro. One step, then another. You're the man of the hour. "

Levi remained solemn as he stared at the foot of the bed. "You're not just saying that?"

My heart sank as I groaned. "*Levi.* Am I gonna have to kick your ass?"

He winced in pain as he tried to cross his ankles. "Sorry." Then he looked at me as he fought to focus his eyes. "Jen make it here?"

Natasha glanced sideways at me as I coughed nervously and said, "She was here earlier, but she's got court. Major felony. Had to leave, said to tell you how worried she is." When his eyes glazed over I added truthfully, "Jen was sincere, bro."

Levi nodded and then he got quiet and looked away. But when Natasha kissed him tenderly he began to smile. He eventually looked at me and seemed about to say something when he covered his mouth and coughed. Somewhere in that cough I failed to pick up his *ibba da.*

"Huh?"

Levi's eyes sparked as he shot his fist against my shoulder. "Gotcha!"

Okay. Good cleansing laugh. Then we talked for a while. Levi became more animated, his face less pale. Natasha stepped forward, pulled the gown from his hip and examined the wound. He grimaced when she tugged a corner of the compress pad, revealing an ugly welt held together by two metal sutures. She replaced the compress and hugged him. "I'm so relieved." She kissed his cheek as I reached out and squeezed his shoulder. That was a guy thing, of course.

Natasha scooted Levi to one side and lay next to him. When she put her head against his chest he closed his eyes and sighed. We talked in low murmurs for almost an hour, and as he came out of his stupor I said, "Hey, Toecheese. You are very brave. Damn—chasing that guy when he was shooting at you! I'm proud of you."

He looked shy and said, "Thanks. And umm, come on. It's time for me to clear outta here."

"That's more like it! Want us to wait outside?"

Levi said quietly, "I ... think I'm gonna need some help getting outta bed. I'm freaking stiff as a board."

As we helped him down he touched his feet gingerly to the floor. He experimented, then put the rest of his weight on his legs and took a cautious step forward. "Damn," he whispered, wincing while taking another step. But then Levi laughed out loud. "Hey, gotta tell you guys. It feels so great to be alive, ya know?" He looked at us with animated eyes as he undid his gown and shrugged it from his shoulders. As it fell to the floor he said to Natasha, "Hand me my boxers, will you?"

Joe Santoro was just turning the corner toward Levi's room when we emerged. He excused himself to Nat and Levi and pulled me to one side. "Listen," Joe began, "and keep this to yourself. I'm not closing this case. Not yet. Not until I see the results of some lab tests we ran. I want to place him inside one of the crime scenes, first. I also want to get a match on the pubic combings." He stared down the hallway and added, "Soon as we determine his last known domicile I pull a search warrant." He pursed his lips and added, "I find purple bungee cords, I get a match on some solid physical evidence—I put this case behind me."

After we got home Levi opined that we could plan an evening out now that the rapist had been eliminated.

I approved the plan but held back on something that gnawed at me, a topic that Joe had sworn me to secrecy on—the roses. Donna had been scared witless; she might even have been a rape victim herself, and never reported it. So I thought it best *not* to contact her and open *those* wounds. But if that *was* the reason, it still didn't reconcile the big *why* that lingered: *why* were Levi and I so closely connected to the victims?

Maybe the guy he'd killed had a grudge; maybe Joe would eventually trace our dead rapist to a long-ago police case that Levi and I were once involved in. But in the end I pushed the attacks aside; I had other concerns. With Natasha's safety resolved and Levi back home, I still had Anna and Bethany to think about, and despite all rationalizing to the contrary, I somehow felt responsible for their suffering.

Later that day Natasha and I left Levi in George's good care while we went to the beach. The sun shone over an ocean of glass, the sky was high and clear, and a breeze puffed across the water. We sunbathed, and later on we got up and walked along the water's edge. The sun felt warm on my shoulders and the moist sand was cool against my feet. Someone's radio had an oldies station tuned, and it was playing Three Dog Night: '*One is the loneliest number that you'll ever do. Two can be as bad as one, it's the loneliest number since the number one ...*'" And *one* is a number that's divided by two. Yeah, that about said it.

We walked in silence until I decided it was time for the intimacy of private love talk. Turning to Natasha I asked, "So ... how should criminals be punished?"

She smiled indulgently as she picked up the challenge. "Societal laws vary, as do their punishments. Administer the death penalty for burglary, and burglars will continue to break in and steal from people's homes. Solutions are polarized, from the abolishment of private property altogether in an effort to establish equality, to truly draconian measures. Vigilante squads are often seen as a ..."

I squeezed her hand sharply and she stopped. The sun's glare cut through my sunglasses, forcing me to squint as I looked out over the water. I cleared my throat and addressed the ocean. "He used to fondle me."

"Your father," she stated emphatically.

"Of course." I walked on and she fell in step. "As I got older he grew bored with the whole fondling thing and tried to make me suck his dick. When I said I'd bite it off he beat the shit out of me. Literally. Beatings then became the nightly ritual; he'd try to make me suck his dick, I bared my teeth. One night he got so pissed that he pushed my head down the toilet. He took a liking to *that* for a while. Then he decided to get creative; busted down my door one night and tried to stick his finger up my ass. Bad move, 'cause by then I was big enough to fight back."

Natasha tugged my hand until I stopped walking. She pulled me close and kissed me fully on my lips.

"What's that for?"

She took off her sunglasses and gazed at me with her soft brown eyes. "For opening up to me. I've dreamed of this day, sordid though it may be."

"You don't seem surprised."

She put her nose against the base of my throat, inhaled and let out a sustained sigh. "No. I'm not." Natasha tugged and we began walking. "I suspected as much shortly after I met you. Levi and I have discussed it from time to time. He's always understood your pain, your history."

The sea smells were fresh and strong, and as the breeze picked up I peeled away layer upon layer from my past. Natasha absorbed everything, nodded encouragement, and stroked her fingers along my back during those moments when I turned suddenly pensive. At some point during our walk I turned around and looked at the footprints we were leaving in the sand, and a steel spring loosened inside of me. I said hesitantly, "Thanks for being part of my life, Nat."

"You know," she began, as if I hadn't said anything, "what's truly remarkable is how you've dealt with all of it." She looked at the ocean and said, "Most abused children take one wrong turn after another. Their lives become shambles. They often end up in prison and …"

"They often abuse other children—especially their own."

She touched her fingers to my cheek and asked, "Why do you suppose that didn't occur in your case?"

I squeezed her hand. "I made a conscious decision not to let it happen."

"Was your father gay?"

I shook my head adamantly. "Not even a little bit. Ninety-nine percent of all child molesters are heterosexual, even when it's man-on-boy. Pedophiles don't seek sexual gratification. They're all about power and control."

Natasha nodded and said softly, "I didn't know that."

I grunted. "What's lust when there's dominance to be had?" I paused and looked out to sea. "There's a bit more I need to say," I began in a clear voice, "and then it's time to move on." I told her how I'd run away as a youngster. I described my life on the streets, sleeping in abandoned buildings, cadging quarters and dollars for food, fighting off the predators—everything. Then the authorities caught up to me and I described how it felt to be shunted from one foster home to another—secretly grateful for the marginal safety of even the most uncaring foster parents. "The last ones were total assholes. I finally convinced them *and* the state to sign-off on me the day I turned seventeen. I enlisted. Army. Best move ever. The military gave me three gifts: teamwork, discipline, and a chance to say goodbye to poverty. And what did I do with my newfound wealth? I'll tell ya what I did. I did what the sergeants said to do. I put money aside for college." I stopped and examined a strangely convoluted seashell and added, "Anyway. Yeah. School. In school ..."

She wrapped her arm around my waist and smiled. "In school, you met Mister Levi Hart."

I laughed and proclaimed, "Yes. I met Mister Levi Hart. And I became a better person for it. Now," I said as I embraced her and kissed her and rested my chin atop her head, "this is hard for me to ask—I want you to finish what he started. I got rode hard and put away wet. But ya know what? I'm through being the hurt child. Make me better, Natasha. Help me, okay? No," I said before she could reply. "Make me better*er*."

She pushed lightly against my chest and studied my face with arched eyebrows. "Better*er*?"

I smiled and pulled her back into my arms. "That's right. Make me much more betterer. Sounds less maudlin, don't you think? It'll be something for us to share. Betterer. Yeah, I like that." I bussed her cheek and we walked on. "Hey," I said as I ran my fingers along her arm. "Always been meaning to ask, got any photos from when you were a kid? I'd love to see them."

"Ohhh," she said delightedly, "that's so *sweet*."

A visitor awaited our return home. "Guys," Levi announced as we entered the house, "this is Kevin. We met in Rehoboth a couple of nights ago." Levi caught my eye and said glibly, "I told him all about your cock."

I stared at him. "You did not!"

He raised an eyebrow and nodded. "Did. It's all over Rehoboth. I expect suitors will be clamoring at the door any time now."

"Bullshit."

"Kevin dissented, however; doesn't believe it's that big." Levi smiled. "Told him you'd demonstrate."

Kevin got up from the couch and said, "Get fucked, Levi." He was tall and lanky with soft brown hair and blue eyes, and he wore a tan polo over loose-fitting blue jeans. "Hi, Michael, and *hello*, Natasha." He kissed her cheek and then offered his hand to me. As we shook he winked and said, "Wish *mine* was fourteen inches," and then with perfect timing he rolled his eyes and added, "'Cause it's closer to sixteen. Helluva burden sometimes."

I liked him instantly. I said over my shoulder, "This one's a keeper!"

Kevin seemed nice, someone I'd have wanted my sister to date, if that could have been a reality. In a twist, it seemed he might now be dating my surrogate brother. Kevin had a summer rental place facing a canal on the north end of town, Levi explained, and he aspired toward a career in law enforcement. The introductions complete, we shot the breeze for a while. So okay, I stole an occasional glance at his crotch, one swordsman appraising another. He caught me looking one time and winked. Then he shook his head and said with a wry smile, "Okay. I lied. Eight inches—and that's a stretch."

I liked his honesty even more.

A week passed without further incident. No more roses were planted to taunt us, Donna seemed to have gone into retreat, and Joe mumbled good-naturedly as he awaited test results that would show a match on the suspect's pubic hairs against those combed from the victims.

Levi lounged around the house for the most part and watched with a touch of amused wonder as the angry welt on his hip turned into a gleaming red spot. Jennifer stayed over one or two nights, Kevin the others. He helped Levi with his morning exercises, and drove him to see a psychologist who worked with the Critical Incident Response Unit. Levi reported back to us that while he regretted being forced to take a life, he understood that he'd acted in good faith. He experienced a few dark moments, but those quickly passed and he seemed not to have manifested any of the symptoms of post-traumatic stress.

I dropped in at Johnny's a couple of times and fielded questions concerning the dead rapist, the evidence that tied him to the attacks, and our certainty that we'd nabbed the right guy. Then Johnny voiced his opinion that those tourists driven away by fear didn't deserve to return to *Johnny's* town.

With Joe's consent I dropped in on Bethany. She totally absolved me of any sin. "Oh, Michael! Don't even sweat it, baby. Shit happens."

Anna remained in another world.

Natasha experienced some mood swings. One day she noticed my inquisitive look as she grabbed her car keys. She said curtly, "Got some shopping to do."

I sensed something out of the ordinary and asked, "Where're you going?"

She busied herself with the keys. "Does it matter?"

"No. Just thought I'd tag along."

Natasha averted her eyes. "I'll be in and out of some stores. I don't know." She turned and pecked my cheek. "You'd get bored. Some other time."

Levi returned to work on the eighth day after the shooting. He was reassigned to communications until a review board formally cleared him. The department issued him a pistol to replace the one he killed the rapist with, while routine ballistics tests were made.

I entered the locker room slightly ahead of Levi that day. Jarl grunted and smiled as I brushed past toward my locker, and I felt his eyes on me when I stopped dead. A person or persons unknown had taped a poster board across Levi's locker, and scrawled across it in bold black letters: **GOD HATES FAGS. THAT'S WHY HE GAVE THEM AIDS.**

I'd been staring dumbfounded at it for so long that Levi's voice startled me. "If God truly hates fags He must have a real hard-on for straights."

I whirled around. "Huh?"

Levi stood barefooted in a dark blue T and yellow shorts as he pointed calmly at the sign. His somber blue eyes were hooded, his mouth pursed as he said in a tired voice. "God must *really* hate straights. After all, he gave them *two* killer diseases."

"Two?"

"Sure," he said reasonably. "God gave straight people syphilis and gonorrhea. Ergo, He must really hate straight people." He ripped down the poster, shook his head sadly, and added somberly, "God also hates rapists. That's why he gave them 9mm hollow-points in the centers of their foreheads." He glanced at Jarl and said, "Tell them I said that. Tell them everything I said."

Jarl snickered. "Tell 'em yourself, you AIDS-spreadin' mother fucker!"

I glared at him and said, "Shut the fuck up!"

Levi put a restraining hand on my arm and whispered in my ear, "Let me handle this." Then he turned to Jarl with clenched fists and said in a deadly voice, "Shut your mouth or I'll shut it for you."

"Yeah? A cunt like you? Hey, what were you just doin', whispering sweet nothings in your lover's ear?"

I stepped toward him. "Suck my dick, Jarl."

He opened his mouth, shut it, and regarded me with a pinched-face as he nodded.

Levi and I entered roll call in time to hear Demmings moan aloud, "Fuckin' bitch just dropped separation papers on me! *Me*. Goddamn bitch! What's she think she's gonna do on her own? Nothing! That's what. Nothing!"

Jarl glowered at Levi and said loud enough for the room to hear, "Glad you finally fucking decided to join us, Hart ..."

Levi cut him off and did an Eddie Haskell. "Couldn't help it, *Jarl*. We've got serious problems. Why, did you know there are rats in the locker room? Imagine, and fewer than thirty feet from where we sit." He shook his head in wonder.

All eyes turned and nobody else said a word, the impasse finally broken by a burst of clapping. "Officer Hart," Hack began in a loud voice, "Let me congratulate you in front of everyone for your magnificent job in apprehending the rapist. You were wounded in the line of duty and for that alone you deserve everyone's respect. I don't care if I only speak for myself when I say, 'you're the man!'"

Levi turned and opened his mouth when a booming voice interrupted. "You *don't* speak for yourself!"

Sgt. Billie Burke stood front and center. When all eyes were on him he thundered, "You're a helluva cop, *Officer* Hart." He lowered his voice. "And I'm a horse's ass." He locked eyes with Levi. "What can I say? I did you wrong. Wish I could take it back but that milk's done been spilt. Levi, I'm sorry."

Two hours later Jarl made it a point to proclaim to the seven officers at the scene of a disturbance call that despite Burke's act of contrition, Levi Hart was still a fag. Of those seven officers, two nodded in apparent agreement. In the wake of that dark cloud a small cadre of Levi's peers confronted him in the locker room at end-of-shift, and spirited him away to a raucous Irish pub at 4th and the Boardwalk. A trio played Celtic music every night, the owners didn't care that neither he nor I wore shoes, didn't seem to give a shit that none of us drank more than three beers, and they didn't object in the least when Levi climbed atop a table to dance a jig in time to a lively tune. It was his dance of life, of wild abandon and unbridled joy, of life as it was meant to be for him—uninhibited, non-judgmental, and permeated with nonsensical laughter. I was haunted by this vision of Levi—enthralled as he transcended the barriers thrown at him and reached instead for a life to be lived on his own terms. As I watched his droll dance, his jaunty jig and composed countenance, I couldn't help but be thankful that he'd pulled me along with him. He stood in testament to all that I was thankful for—him, and one other. Natasha.

When he finished; after he stepped down from the table and accepted a burst of spontaneous applause; as the hour approached 1:00am, I hugged him and buddy-punched him and urged him—finally, while he was still able to do so soberly—to follow me home. I didn't want to take a chance on driving foolishly; I didn't want to risk anything now that Natasha was a part of my life again—Natasha, the only person on the planet for whom I felt a greater love.

I woke up alone the next morning and found Natasha at the breakfast table drinking coffee with one hand, grasping the telephone receiver with the other, and leaning forward with an intensity I'd seen only once before—when she and I waited to see Levi after he'd been shot. Intense or not, she appeared beautiful in her shapeless pink robe, her hair unkempt and her body exuding a faint aroma of womanhood. I kissed the top of her head, grabbed a coffee cup, filled it and sat down across from her.

Natasha quietly finished her end of the conversation and hung up. She appeared pensive and seemed to look through me. She worried her lower lip with her fine white teeth until she smiled and gazed lovingly at me. "Midnight tonight," she began. "Late supper. You. Levi. Me. A celebration, while there's still time."

I raised my eyebrows and smiled cagily. "Surprise going-away party?"

Natasha offered a shy half-smile. She took her time, sipped coffee, put down the cup, became more animated and exhilarated, and then asked, "Why does it have to be a special occasion? Can't I treat two men whom I adore to a late-night repast?"

Laughing, I replied, "You most certainly can. We'll be here right after work."

That evening after work I changed into civvies and secured my service pistol in my locker as I always did. Levi entered the locker room as I slipped into my flip-flops, and as soon as he was changed we headed home.

One of my college friends joined the Secret Service. He told me over a beer one evening that when agents are in training they use a code phrase to signify that the person under their protection—the principal—is under attack. When the bad-guy role-players make their hit, the agents yell out, "Attack On Principal!" That code leaped to mind as I pulled into our driveway.

The porch door was wide open. Something—a jumble of clothes perhaps— lay on the kitchen floor a few feet inside. I looked questioningly in my rear-view mirror at Levi as he coasted to a stop behind me. He nodded to indicate that he'd also seen it. I stepped quietly out of the Mustang and silently cursed the fact that my pistol sat inside my locker.

Levi got out of his car just as stealthily, but with pistol in hand. He might be careless with his clothes, leaving shoes and other bits and pieces unaccounted for—but he never went anywhere without his weapon, whether tucked inside his waistband or secreted in his car. I fell in behind him as he padded up the wooden steps to the porch, his weapon at the high ready.

He stopped abruptly. "Next to my foot," he whispered.

I looked down. Blood drops—their patterns indisputable—led *from* the house. My pulse shot to one sixty as I whispered, "Stop!" He kept his eyes glued to the door as I touched the back of his elbow, leaned forward and whispered in his ear, "Let me check our six." He acknowledged with a nod. I backed away a few feet, checked to make sure an adversary hadn't gotten behind us, and tapped his elbow. He planted one foot at a time as he edged forward, both of us doing our best to avoid the evidentiary bloodstains. He got to the edge of the door, did a quick-peep, and nodded once to signal his intention to move inside.

Kitchen, first. A rapid glance. I gasped. Total denial of the body sprawled across the floor. I whispered, "Oh my God," and my shoulders sagged at the sight, at the teeth drenched in blood after apparently ripping into an attacker. Even worse, George's head lay at an obscene angle to the rest of his body, broken by powerful hands.

Then I saw it: the purple bungee cord wrapped around his neck—and a delicate rose protruding from his jaws. I opened my mouth and half-whispered, half-yelled, "*Natasha!*"

We rushed forward using a dynamic entry technique. Levi cleared the living room, the kitchen, then the hallway. His arms and head swept the rooms as one, his weapon at the ready. Then we began the longest journey ever, down the hallway toward Natasha's room—while I steeled myself for what I *knew* we would find within.

We reached her door. Took positions. Both sides. This time my voice had a dead quality as I said in a low tone, "Na-ta-sha."

I heard a whimper on the other side of the door, then a small, quavering voice: "Michael?"

In my hushed, deathly voice I said, "We-are-coming-in-Na-ta-sha. Both of us. Levi, and me."

A short pause, then, "O-okay. Come in. *Please* come in!"

Levi pushed the door open; held his weapon at the ready, executed a quick-peep.

He nodded.

I pushed past.

Rushed inside.

Natasha lay huddled in a corner of the far wall, her face ashen, her eyes huge, her hands trembling as they pointed my off-duty revolver directly at my chest.

I extended both palms and gestured *down*, and said in a calming voice, "It's okay. It's me. I'm right here."

Levi guarded the doorway while I took the revolver from her. I put a finger to my lips and whispered, "Stay here while we clear the rest of the house." Then I rejoined him and we checked the remaining rooms, and then the attic. When we were satisfied that nobody was hiding, Levi ran to the kitchen to phone it in as I returned to Natasha and cradled her in my arms. "Jesus H.," I wailed, and then I broke down completely and bawled. "Oh my God—*Natasha!* I—I don't know what I'd do if you'd been hurt ... oh, *Jesus* fucking *Christ!*"

I cried uncontrollably, hugging her so hard that she let out a little cry. I whispered "Natasha" in her ear again and again and again. I was reduced to a quivering blob, kissing her face repeatedly. I buried my nose in her hair—literally inhaled the jasmine-scented shampoo from the roots. Then I wrapped my hands and my arms and my legs around Natasha and held her in a death grip.

She trembled non-stop as I cried against her shoulder. But when tires screeched to a stop on the street, she began to describe what happened in a near-whisper. "I was in the kitchen, preparing dessert. The ... the door opened. I hadn't seen your cars pull in, so I turned. George was on him in a second; I've never seen him move so fast! I ran. Oh, Michael! I ran for it. Then I heard him scream ... I—I got inside ... got your gun, and I ... I waited." She looked at me with terrorized eyes. "I ... what else could I do? No phone here ... so I waited." Her voice trailed away. "I waited."

I swiped angrily at my tear-stained cheeks. "It's okay," I said as I cuddled her. "I'm right here. I won't let anything happen to you." Footsteps bounded up the steps outside and someone pounded against the door. Levi opened it, said something and then shouted a warning to the officers to watch out for the blood drops.

I kissed the top of her head. Now the cop in me began to take over and I asked, "What'd he look like?"

Natasha shook her head violently. "Dunno. Sorry. Just a—just some guy. Dressed in black. Wore a mask. Not a kid. Don't think so, anyway. Too stocky for a teen. I don't know. Not too big. Not too small." She tore a tissue from a bedside dispenser and dabbed at her eyes. "I'm sorry. I'm no help at all."

"Shhh. Don't even think that. You're doing okay, babe."

She got very quiet in marked contrast to the growing number of voices outside her room. "Is George ... is he ... okay?"

I hugged her and whispered, "He's our hero, Sweetness. Poor old George. He gave his life for you."

She caved and cried uncontrollably.

A special police force protected Ocean Pines. Directly commissioned by the State of Maryland, they held full police powers and they would take the lead in this small part of what had just become a multi-jurisdictional investigation. After I spoke privately with their supervisor he put in a call to Giuseppe "Joe" Santoro. As soon as Joe came on the line the supervisor made an official request for assistance, and at Joe's prompting the supervisor also asked for Ocean City's crime scene unit.

Joe arrived half an hour later with the crime scene van. The technician gathered some equipment and he and Joe assessed the kitchen. Joe pointed out the blood drops, the bungee cord, the rose, and especially the congealed blood on George's fangs. "Tag all blood samples for DNA," he ordered in a deadly voice. "Never mind the cost. Anybody argues," he said as he thumped his chest, "*I* authorized it."

Natasha emerged and provided a more in-depth account to the local officers, then Levi and I walked her back to her bedroom. I held her arms and said, "I'll be busy for another half hour." I nodded toward Levi and said to her, "Get in bed. Levi will stay with you until I'm back. Nothing more will happen to you. We'll both make sure of that." She nodded dumbly, and her eyes were vacant as she stretched out atop the bed. Levi cradled her in his arms as she planted her head on his shoulder and shivered violently. I took the blanket and draped it over them.

Joe and I stepped outside, where the muggy night air played host to swarms of mosquitoes. He said, "I'm putting my men back on Natasha. 'Round the clock protection. That goes for Jennifer, too. Now speak to me, Michael."

I filled him in, adding that I'd said nothing about the rose's significance. Joe nodded and moved until he stood inches from me. Then he said in an urgent undertone, "Find Donna Demmings, Brennan. Doubt you'll find her at her home, though. Guess you heard."

I nodded. "Filed against her old man."

"Yeah." He gave me a look that said, *no surprise there.* "Find out what she knows about these goddamn roses." He rubbed the end of his nose vigorously. His eyes peered into mine. "Get me that information. Are we clear?"

I nodded as a long-suppressed anger awakened inside me. "I'm one fucking step ahead of you."

After Joe shoved off with the crime scene tech, I got one of the locals to help me carry George outside. I covered him with a blanket and thanked all the officers, and as the last one departed I went inside and cleaned the kitchen floor. When I was finished I went to Natasha's room.

She lay with her head against Levi's chest, and she clutched him with a desperate need.

A single tear trickled down his cheek as he whispered, "I love you, Natasha."

"That's good," she murmured, "because I'm going to have your baby."

CHAPTER 11

ARE you sure? Levi asked.

Natasha nodded slowly. "Positive. That was the reason for tonight's dinner."

Levi stared at me but said to her, "But we haven't had sex in more than ..."

"Ten or twelve days," she said listlessly. "I know. But I had an egg in the chute, and one of your boys fertilized it."

He looked away from me and said quietly, "Maybe we shouldn't have ..."

I clamped my hand on his shoulder and said, "Come on, we discussed this! You guys wanted a baby. Hell, I wanted it for you! So it's okay ... okay?"

Natasha nodded and looked at me with grateful eyes. "You're not hurt?"

I bent down and kissed her. "Sweetheart! No way! This is great news." And it was. It had happened before we were together again, and anyway it would make her happy. I added with genuine conviction, "I'll help you raise it, Nat."

"You and me both, bro," Levi said softly. "I'm calling Customs today. I'm not leaving you guys. No fucking way."

Natasha looked at him with fierce eyes and said, "Like hell! You're going onto a new life, my love! You'll just ... be away from home a lot."

Levi's face finally shone. "Nat ..."

We remained together throughout the night, dozing at times, talking at others. Levi investigated each strange noise, while I guarded Nat. In the morning we held a brief ceremony, and buried George in the back yard among some poinsettias that she'd planted the year before.

$$* \quad * \quad *$$

He pulled up the trouser leg and winced as he peeled away the compress. The area around the six puncture marks was red and swollen. "Set her dog on me, did she? That bitch will pay for this!"

He'd already taken a healthy dose of bourbon to soothe the pain; now another dose would diminish his anger. He hobbled to the pantry and poured himself a double, then he sat down and closed his eyes and sipped and sipped. "All women are bitches."

After two more drinks he had a new strategy, a new plan, and he went to the closet and carefully examined the uniform. He could alter it readily enough into an Ocean Pines uniform. Yes, it might work. No man's fool, he played devil's advocate and developed a back-up plan over another bourbon.

*   *   *

Around noon Natasha's legs folded beneath her and she collapsed on the kitchen floor in the exact spot where George died. Levi sat with her in the back seat as I rushed her to the hospital. Her face was pale and she trembled non-stop. "Hurry," she cried at one point.

The doctor explained later that a stress-induced reaction had caused her to lose the baby. Nobody needed to spell it out; we knew what caused it. I called Joe and told him. "Can't go for homicide," he said tiredly. "A fetus in the first trimester doesn't qualify. But let me look into another possibility."

After she took the prescribed tranquilizer we left her hospital room and went to a deserted cafeteria, where Levi cried against my shoulder for nearly an hour. When he could be consoled no longer, we went back to her room and lay on either side of her.

The next day we moved an ashen-faced Natasha into Kevin's north-end rental for safety's sake. Levi and I banked against the possibility that while our nemesis might attempt a return visit to Ocean Pines, he would be unlikely to trace Natasha's whereabouts to her newfound sanctuary. We also counted on the ironic reality that center stage often serves as the ideal hiding place. As further hedge against the oft-mistaken assumption that criminals are morons, Kevin graciously offered us the use of his two-car garage, since we had to assume that the rapist knew our cars by now. Levi, Kevin and I established overlapping schedules to ensure that one of us would be home with her at all times. I did trust Joe's guys to watch over her, but I wanted a buffer zone.

After we were settled in, I gathered Levi and Nat on the rear deck. The sun was high and hot, but the canal lent a calming balance as it gurgled on its path to the bay. Mindful of my promise to Joe, I opened the discussion by telling them, "Don't ask for details, but I might have a lead." I cleared my throat. "I can tell you that it involves a woman, and ..."

"Michael," Natasha cut in. "Listen carefully." Her face turned to stone as she placed her hand on mine. "We've got to stop this bastard. He's a vicious woman-hater. This ... woman you're going to see—she could be next! Another baby could be lost. What I'm telling you is this—you have my unqualified permission to have sex with her. Fuck her brains out, if that's what it takes to get her to talk!"

Levi regarded me thoughtfully. "If it's who I think it is, you'll have to."

I said to them, "No. She's not like that anymore." Then I went inside and made the phone call.

We reported for duty later that day. I checked my secure voice mail but Donna still hadn't responded to my request to see her. Burke glanced at Levi and nodded as we took our seats, then he grumbled about Demmings for banging in sick at the last moment. At 3:00pm sharp he called everyone to order, and then the side door opened and Joe walked in. He discussed last night's attack in detail and ended his briefing with an announcement. "Today I finally got the lab reports on the guy Officer Hart nailed. Get this: there's absolutely nothing to tie him to any of the rapes. On the other hand, last night's perp left a trail of evidence that conclusively ties him to all the other attacks. The North End Rapist lives."

We broke from roll call. Levi went to communications. I checked-out my cruiser and worked my way north. When I stopped for a red light at 94th Street, Hacksaw pulled abreast of me, lowered his window and said, "Meet me at 139th Street."

It was only a short drive. Hacksaw parked and got into my passenger seat, and then he peered at me and asked, "What kinda evidence they find at your place?"

Joe wanted nothing said about the trail of roses. They were the key to solving the case, in conjunction with the blood George drew. I rubbed the end of my nose and said, "I believe he already mentioned the purple bungee cord."

"Uh huh," he said with great irony. "An' the Easter fuckin' bunny's givin' away free bottles a Scotch at that 7/11 over yonder."

I looked meaningfully at him and replied, "I've been ordered not to disclose any details."

Hack regarded me thoughtfully. "Fair enough. I can respect that. Just thought, you know, there was stuff you could pass on."

To change the subject I told him that Levi had recovered better than expected. "Jesus, Hack. I don't know if *I* could've gone to guns the way *he* did."

He gave me a direct look as he touched a finger to his temple and asked, "He doin' okay up here?"

"Doing fine."

Hack's forehead wrinkled. "You know, it's good he got the guy. Someone woulda cancelled his ticket sooner or later. But umm, what got me was, 'fore Levi shot that mutha, I was beginnin' to think that maybe the rapist was a cop. Now that's a possibility again."

"The choke holds? Hell, I guess that's crossed many minds."

He cleared his throat. "Just that nobody wants to admit their suspicions."

I smiled. "Just as nobody wants to admit they take that occasional whiff when they pick their feet."

He nodded vigorously. "There you go! But yeah—suspect uses choke holds. Ever hear a anybody 'sides a cop who knows how to do that?"

"Nobody outside of martial arts instructors."

Hack stroked his chin with his short fingers. "Makes sense. Yeah! An' it makes even better sense when ya consider this: most a the cops 'round here couldn't sneak up on a dead flounder. But a Ninja wannabe?" He slumped down in his seat. "Sure. Some wimp wantin' to test his skills in the real world." Then he bolted upright and said, "Or maybe it's the other way 'round. Maybe it *ain't* some wimp, but someone just the opposite. Someone who also hates women. Maybe," he said with a sudden excitement, "maybe someone like Jarl fuckin' Jackson."

"Then why not Perry Ryan? Or Demmings?"

Hack frowned and shook his head vigorously. 'Nah. Couldn't be Perry. Him an' Joe was working a case the night one a the rapes was takin' place. Joe's his rock-solid alibi. Demmings? Doubtful. He hate's women, but Peepin' Toms are too fuckin' passive. That's why they peep 'stead a pounce, 'cause they is too flaccid to do much a anything else."

I tended to disagree; ritualistic behavior escalates a perpetrator's confidence level—a Demmings-like suspect could not be ruled-out. But I couldn't say anything without revealing the information that Joe had given me in confidence. So I replied, "Hack, why can't the rapist be me, or *you?*"

"Well we know it ain't you, 'cause you an' Levi was together when Natasha got assaulted." His brows arched and he pawed at his face with the backs of his knuckles while he thought it over. Finally he replied, "Jesus Christ! Yeah. Of course. We been assumin' it's a white dude. No reason to rule out a brother."

"Nope. No reason to." I watched him carefully as I said, "Listen, I'm tired of all this. Let's get off the topic. How's life treating you these days?"

Three alert tones pierced the silence before he could reply. An ambulance and a rescue unit zipped past us with lights flashing and sirens blaring as the dispatcher called out, "*Seventy-three-oh-nine. At Sable Towers, One Hundred and Nineteenth Street, assist the fire department poolside with a 10-56 F. Medics and rescue en route. Respond Code Three.*"

Hacksaw raced to his car and called out to back me up as I hit the lights and turned north onto Coastal. The ten-code for intoxicated pedestrian confused me until I matched it with the "F" for fatal, and the instruction to respond to the pool. Then I understood the call and stepped down harder on the gas.

Sable Towers was built in the late sixties as a condo community. The twenty-floor monolith of dull concrete and uninspired design—what many called Ocean City Modern Mundane—loomed tall along the oceanfront. It boasted a huge ground level pool built on a raised concrete deck that sat thirty feet away from the building. But from a fifteenth floor perspective, thirty feet shrinks to three, especially when visual receptors are distorted by alcohol and testosterone. Each summer at least four adolescent males felt the need to impress their girlfriends by doing cannonballs into various high-rise condo pools from one hundred sixty feet up. Maybe they figured to get a little something on the side after the big splash.

This particular Bug got something on the side all right—two hundred and ten pounds of ivory colored flab, pink viscera, portions of his skeletal support system, and several pints of scarlet-tinged blood. He splattered himself against the concrete while still twenty-five feet shy of his mark, successfully transforming himself into a strawberry parfait. I think it was the two eyes staring sightlessly from the remnants of his shattered skull that sent the last of the bystanders fleeing.

In their hasty departure they left the area littered with overturned chairs, discarded drinks, items of clothing and other detritus. I sent Hack to the top floor to get a statement from the hysterical girlfriend while I conducted poolside crisis management. The medics could do nothing for this kid and neither could I, so I made a conscious decision to put some distance between the dead Bug and myself. I'd learned long ago that first responders have to put a filter on some of the reality if they want to keep from turning into a basket case. So when I spotted Ed Bell among the medics I decided to attain a sense of normalcy by having a quiet talk about Anna. I walked over and greeted him. "Hi, Ed. Listen, has Joe Santoro had a chance to talk to you?"

He eyed me cautiously. "Yes," he said in a low tone.

I held out my hand. "How's Anna doing?"

He fidgeted as he removed his surgical gloves, then he shook my hand. "Better. Not much, but she's improving. Thanks for asking."

"Ed, I'm sorry things didn't work out between us. Anna's a wonderful woman. I enjoyed her companionship."

His eyes softened and something seemed to turn inside of him. "I'm sorry too, Michael. You're a good man and a good friend. Wish something more could've developed between you two. She's the best," he said with great feeling. "The best." Ed flicked his eyes toward the ground before he looked me in the eye. "Umm, listen. Heard some stuff about Levi." He shuffled his feet and pinched the tip of his nose. "Michael? Tell Levi … tell him I understand what he's going through. Tell him to call if he needs to talk with someone who can empathize. Will you do that for me?"

I shook his hand again. "I'll tell him, Ed. And thanks for trusting me."

He nodded and turned to help cordon off the area with yellow DO NOT CROSS tape. As I watched his retreating back I made a mental note to send another basket of flowers to Anna, a fruit basket to Bethany and a bottle of Johnny Walker Blue to Ed, and screw the cost of the good stuff. Then I stared silently at the remains of the high-dive victim and awaited the investigator.

"*Seventy-two-twenty to seventy-three-oh-nine. 10-20?*"

I pulled the mike close to my mouth and gave Jarl my location.

"*10-4. Meet you there in two.*"

Jarl arrived precisely two minutes later and ambled past scattered pool chairs and chaise lounges as he calmly smoked a cigarette. "Let's go over here," he said with barely a glance at the PSA—the Person Scattered About. He led the way to a low seawall at the far end of the pool. His smug expression revealed an air of conquest. "Word has it that your AIDS-spreadin' homo buddy's outta here soon."

I planted both feet and got ready to square off. "Jarl?"

He dragged at his cigarette and blew a long plume of smoke through his nose. Then he said, "Yeah?"

"Would you like to suck my cock?"

He nearly choked on smoke. "What'd you fuckin' say?"

I looked steadily at him. "I'll let you suck my cock, but only if you'll let up on Levi. Is it a deal?"

He grinned crazily and said, "I knew it! I fuckin' knew you was fruit for me!"

"I'll take that as a 'no,' then." I turned my back on him and sauntered away.

Fewer than twenty seconds passed before Jarl approached. He regarded me shrewdly until he stubbed his cigarette against the seawall and said, "Let's have a couple of beers tonight. Just you and me."

I realized too late that I shouldn't have taunted him, but I was tired of his shit and wanted to set his ass straight. "Let's."

"Good. Maybe we can be friends or … something."

"I'll call my girl and see what she's up to. If not tonight then some other time; let's see, okay?"

His breathing picked up. "Linda and the girls are still outta town. We can go to my place. You can umm, sleep over if you want."

"I can barely contain myself," I deadpanned.

The investigator arrived and Hack and I assisted him. I cleared around nine and hit the streets with two hours left in the shift. Now I had to make a decision—go home to the woman I loved, or set Jarl straight enough to keep him off Levi's back. Another variable—Donna. I found a pay phone and dropped coins in and listened to the voice message. By the end of the message I knew what I would be doing after work.

*   *   *

He eschewed his north-end feeding grounds for the more promising Ocean Pines supply. Although he'd caused a minor ripple when he stayed home today, he made sure that his absence wouldn't be too great an issue; his cover story would absolve him of any suspicion—of that he felt certain. Better a cover story of his own, than to risk inquiries into his limp.

Now he cruised slowly through the dark lanes, sniffing this way and that as he zeroed in on the scene of his aborted feeding. It *would* have been a feeding frenzy if that fucking dog hadn't been there. He'd planned specifically for her; he'd saved her for the last, so that he would be the last man to ever touch her, fondle her and fuck her. He meant for her to be his for a while, and then he meant to take her from *him* permanently.

Now he turned down the lane. With one glance he checked to see that his white uniform shirt was close at hand, in case he had to don it quickly. The French blue uniform pants were another matter, but if pressed he could explain why he had them on. He smiled as he glided slowly toward the empty house. He hadn't expected to find anyone home, so he only scanned it to survey his ultimate conquest. He turned down another lane and settled in for the short trip to Ocean City's police headquarters. A certain car was sure to be parked in the employee lot, the one with *M.B.* on its plate. Michael Brennan. *Mister* Michael Brennan.

*   *   *

I changed out of my uniform into a dark aloha shirt and baggy shorts. I also strapped on a fanny pack to conceal my pistol, having vowed to remain armed at all times now. Levi came in and changed, and then he walked me outside to my Mustang. "I've got that business to take care of," I told him as we stood next to the car. "How about stopping by Nat's club and keeping an eye on her. Tell her I'll be home later."

"I'm on her." Then he said quietly, "So was George." He briefly looked away before saying, "Let's buy a German Shepard. I know a guy who trains K-9s."

I watched him closely and said, "Maybe."

Levi studied me. "Be careful tonight. You don't wanna take any bullets from her old man. Remember—he banged in."

"We're meeting in a safe place. Take care of Nat 'til I get home. Make sure she gets some rest."

Levi said grim-faced, "As if you have to ask." In a lower voice he said, "Do what you've gotta do tonight. Nat's good with it."

"I'm not. I love her too much. I don't wanna be with another woman." I sighed and said, "Maybe we can put it all to rest after tonight."

I turned off Route 90 onto the Isle of Wight's rutted dirt road just before midnight. Donna said she would park at the end of a long dirt lane. There was no moon and the darkness was complete, a veritable no-man's land isolated from passersby. More importantly, the area made it too difficult for a tail to remain undetected. I parked next to her car and got out, but where was she? There was only a single path leading to a spot where the estuary merged with the bay, so I started down the path. My flip-flops began trapping soft sand and flinging it everywhere, so I took them off and went looking for Donna.

In no time I was in heavy undergrowth that completely blocked the breeze. The mugginess became unbearable, so I unbuttoned my shirt. When I finally reached a clear area the breeze from the bay swept against me, flapping my shirttails with sharp *snaps*. The welcome breeze also carried the sounds of Ocean City's nightlife across the narrow bay, bringing laughter and reggae from the clubs that lined the far shore. The tide was out, and the exposed mudflats released a pungent stench. The odor was seasoned by condiments of reeds and cattails and countless dead creatures mingled amongst the shallow root systems. I thought that smell anything but repulsive. It signified endless cycles of rebirth and growth, of regeneration and maturation. The odor carried strength and conviction in its God-given right to exist. It wasn't stench; it was perfume, an intoxicating, liberating aroma that could anoint small veins close to the skin, in direct defiance of the finest Parisian perfumes.

Donna stood near the water's edge with her back to the path. She had on a red blouse tied loosely around her midriff, solid black shorts, and white sneakers. Her loose hair fell against her shoulders like reeds bending before a summer breeze.

"Why didn't you stay with your car?" I asked as I stopped next to her.

Donna smiled and looked me over. "I thought I'd find a more secluded place." She flicked her eyes at a folded blanket where the ground yielded to sand. "It'll be more comfortable this way, don't you think?"

I frowned. "We're here to talk, not have sex."

She raised an eyebrow and angrily demanded, "Why can't we do both?"

I edged closer. "Let's talk about the rose."

Donna took a step toward me as she caressed her forearm with long tapering fingers. "I'm no longer bound by marriage, Michael. I separated from my husband for *you*. Sleep with me. Here! Now! Or else I leave."

"Who're you kidding? You filed because you were in an abusive relationship. You're here now because you want to help. The rose, Donna. Why did it rile you?"

She took a tentative step toward me. I opened my arms prepared for anything, but when Donna entered my embrace she only put her head against my chest. When she looked up again, her eyes searched mine while she asked in a quiet voice, "Did you mean what you said at the gym? Did you mean it when you said I deserve to be loved?"

I brushed my fingers through her hair and said, "Yes, I did. Look, I know you're confused and scared. But it'll be okay. I'm right here. You're not alone."

Donna said nothing for a moment as she looked at me with soft eyes. Then she said, "I thought of castrating you."

"Ca ...? You can't be serious!"

"Fantasized."

"Jesus, Donna!"

"I wanted to take your manhood from you. Emasculate you. Take away your balls and your cock. Did you know I was once a surgical nurse? I've seen it done. It's a remarkably simple procedure. I devised an equally simple plan: we have sex, and after you're spent and exposed I inject you with a sedative. You remain conscious, yet you're incapable of lifting so much as a finger to stop me. You plead with me not to of course, but I only laugh as I spread your legs apart and take scalpel in hand. You're begging by now, but I hack your balls off anyway, and hold them up for you to see.

"Then I grab your penis and slice it off at the base. When I'm done you're left with a gaping hole where your scrotum hung, and a stub to pee from. But don't think me all evil—I do administer morphine, and I do tie the severed vessels with ligatures. After all, it does me no good if you bleed to death. As for your genitalia, I put them in formaldehyde and lock them in a safe deposit box. I go to jail, but eventually I'm released, and you come begging to me every time you want to see your manhood." A sob escaped her. "How twisted is that?"

This woman who knew nothing of my history could not realize that I understood the nature of the suffering that had driven her to this level of depravity. I looked at her and whispered, "How long has he been beating you?"

Her body trembled. She looked away. "Too long," she said in a dead voice. Then she looked up and regarded me anew. "You certainly know women."

"I know pain." I pulled her close and kissed the top of her head.

When her trembling stopped she took a deep breath. "You made me realize more than you think that day at the gym." Then her face dissolved in anguish. "I wanted your sex, I wanted to take from you, to emasculate you, and yet you still give me compassion." She stared at some distant vision.

"Why didn't you go for help? There's a women's crisis center in Salisbury. Have you discussed this with a friend? Sometimes that makes all the difference."

"I wanted to tell *you*! I almost did—the other day. But I—I couldn't."

"I'm sorry you felt that way about me. Maybe I need to do some soul-searching."

"Don't blame yourself. I—I don't know that I really wanted to regard you as a friend. I just wanted sex—I wanted something to kill what I was feeling inside, if just for a short time." She held her hands up beseechingly. "It's just that you're so damned gorgeous—and so fucking principled. The more you held to your standards, the more diminished I felt. And the sadder I felt, the more I had to have you." She put her hands to her head and cried out, "Don't you see? I don't want just flesh anymore. I want feelings! I want *love*!"

I held her closer and brushed her forehead with my lips. "You deserve all that and more. I just can't give you that love—not from the heart anyway."

Donna wept silently as I held her and soothed her, kissed the top of her head, stroked her hair and massaged her neck. When she finally brought her face away she gazed into my eyes and said, "That's the irony. Now that I understand and accept that fact, I no longer want to sleep with you." Then she laid a Mrs. Robinson on me and said, "Well, maybe I would." She laughed mirthlessly. "What a killer, because I suddenly care about you, Michael. About what's here," she said with a tap against my chest, "not what's down there," and she pressed her hand against my genitals.

"Thank you for that, Donna. You have no idea what that means to me."

She sighed heavily. "It took a series of rapes to teach me that another side does exist." Then Donna looked sideways at me and whispered, "I suppose I should take comfort in knowing that he hasn't killed anyone."

My pulse bounded against my temples. "Who is it, Donna?"

She looked away, hesitated, and then said, "I wasn't sure. Not at first. I couldn't—*didn't*—want to believe it." Donna looked at me. "I mean, all those poor girls. Who could be that vicious, that sick? I simply could not accept it. But when you showed me that rose I knew. I *knew*." In a haunted whisper she added, "But at least he hasn't killed anyone. At least my husband is *not* a killer."

I touched my finger to her chin and said, "But he is the North End Rapist. Isn't he?"

"Of course."

I turned light-headed for a few brief seconds as I considered killing him with my bare hands. "What can you tell me?"

Her voice seemed to come from the other end of a long tunnel, and she had difficulty meeting my eyes. "My marriage has been a sham. It's been mutually beneficial to us on the surface, but that's all. He—my husband—he's impotent, except when he's been angered by something." Donna inhaled deeply. "I'm afraid I made him angry. You see, I mocked him one evening. You've no idea what it's like to go without sex for years—*years!*" She looked away and stifled a sob. "This is still a small town, especially in the winter. People talk. Nothing's sacred. I've heard plenty of women speak of you and Levi, about how they love going to your beds. And then there was Jarl, vulgar Jarl, offering to service me." Donna moved closer to the water's edge. "Jarl gave me sex. No passion, just sex—and not even good sex. One evening I returned home after seeing Jarl. I took one look at my husband and I suddenly felt contemptuous. That's when I screwed up. I mocked him. I contrasted his failures against the triumphs of Levi Hart and Michael Brennan, as trumpeted throughout this town by so many well-loved women."

I touched her forearm to interrupt her. "That doesn't explain the rapes. Or the roses."

She looked at me pathetically, the teacher regarding the slow student incapable of mastering even the simplest arithmetic. "I believe he's been trailing you. Levi, too. I just don't know."

I squinted sideways at her, "I still don't follow."

Donna's chest heaved as she drew a deep breath. "My husband might be impotent, but he is quite the photographer—and quite the horticulturist. He grew that rose you showed me, Michael. It's one of a kind."

A light went off in my head. The tumblers clicked. The connection had just been made. Donna unwittingly gave her husband a grudge to bear. One night he followed Levi to Dan's house. He assumed Dan's sister was Levi's girlfriend. He raped her and left a rose on Levi's car to proclaim his victory and mark his territory.

But the next victim? I didn't see a connection. Not yet, anyway. Sadly, she might have been mistaken for someone whom Levi or I had known. She might also have been a wild card—a random target for an attacker with a sudden, uncontrollable urge to renounce society—to punish *someone*. But then he begins following me after he hears I'm seeing Anna. He rapes *her*, and all along he's leaving roses as a message—or as warnings. I see Bethany—Demmings rapes her. He meets Natasha in the police parking lot, then he … I pinned Donna with my eyes and demanded, "What else can you tell me?"

"What else do you need to know?"

"When did you last see him? How's his leg? Has he been limping?"

She frowned. "I haven't seen him in days. I've been staying with a girlfriend."

I put my hands on her shoulders as a sense of urgency took hold. "I need evidence, Donna. Physical evidence. Have you seen any bungee cords lying around the house? *Purple* bungee cords?"

"I don't know. I can go look. Why? What do they mean?"

I shook my head. "I can't say anything more. But umm, photographs! He might have taken photos of the crime scenes. And statements—I'll need statements from you."

Donna opened her mouth to speak, then shut it and avoided my eyes. After a long moment she said, "I'm not so sure I can go any further with this."

"But why?" I asked plaintively. I took a step forward but she backed away. "Come on, Donna. You've already gone this far!"

She shook her head doggedly. "No! I'm beginning to understand where this will lead. I *don't* want my home disrupted when they arrive with their search warrants. I don't want media vans camped outside. I don't want my life exposed! Not ... not yet." She stared into my eyes and asked, "Do you think I'm as selfish as I sound?"

I touched her cheek and said neutrally, "I think you are very, very frightened."

She turned her face away. A moment passed until she said, "I—I'm sorry. You're right."

"Let me talk to my supervisor. Let's see if we can protect you as a C.I."

She slowly nodded. "Yes. Well. Let me think about it."

That was sufficient. I had enough for Joe to seek search warrants. Demmings could be compelled to submit to a doctor's examination for George's bite marks, and provide blood samples for a DNA match. That might be enough to connect him to the aborted attack on Natasha, but pubic combings could tie him to the rapes. I said, "Let's get you out of here."

Donna nodded, but instead of moving to pick up her blanket she edged closer until I took her into my arms. Her body seemed to relax in degrees. A moment passed. Another. Finally Donna looked at me and said, "Kiss me, Michael. Kiss me like you mean it. Kiss me with some feeling. That's all I ask."

I embraced her and let my lips drift to her cheek. When she turned her face to meet mine I kissed her mouth. I kissed with sentiment and raw emotion; I kissed with humanity. Donna responded in kind.

Finally she buried her nose against my chest and drew a deep breath. When she pulled her face away she said, "You kiss exquisitely. I like your smell, too. Earth. Vitality." Then Donna's eyes glazed over and she said in a child's voice, "Make sweet love to me?"

"I can't," I whispered. "I'm in love with another woman." I pulled her head against my chest and stroked her hair. "Look," I began. "You'll meet someone. You're quite beautiful and you're certainly young enough to have children."

A single tear ran down her lovely face. Then from some wounded place she wailed, "I'm *barren.*"

"Oh, Donna." I closed my eyes and rocked her back and forth in my arms as I came to a decision. Finally I stepped back and looked at her. In a near-whisper I said, "I want to show you something." Then I took her hands and placed them inside my unbuttoned shirt. She looked at me, and when I nodded she slowly moved her hands across my torso and slid my shirt from my shoulders, letting it fall with a muted rustling behind me. Then she undid the fanny pack. It hit the ground with a thud as she moved her fingers to my waist. Quickly, deftly, she undid my shorts and slipped them from my hips. As they fell to my ankles she reached her fingers inside the waistband of my boxers and, gazing steadily into my eyes, she slipped them off.

Donna took off her shoes as I stepped out of my clothes and loosened her shorts. They fell with a sigh to the sandy soil, exposing her lean muscled buttocks and legs. She kicked them away with a desperate sense of urgency. I undid her blouse and let the fine fabric slide through my fingers until it fell away, then I unsnapped her bra and removed her panties. When we were both naked I embraced her again. Donna's breasts felt firm and fine against my chest; her hips flush and warm against mine.

She kissed me hungrily, stopping only to say, "The blanket. Let me get the blanket."

"No," I said softly. "You're going to feel my skin against yours and we're both going to feel the earth beneath us." I eased her to the soft, cool sand and began kissing her, softly at first, then with greater passion as I moved from her head to her neck and then to her shoulders.

Donna moaned, and something deep in her throat rattled as she kissed my ears, my neck and my throat. Every curve of her body molded against mine while she ran her fingers like soft butterflies along my arms and back and then across my buttocks. Yet when she moved her hand between my legs I stopped her.

"No sex," I whispered. "This is a different form of intimacy, Donna—one that I want you to know. This is friendship, and *this* is from my heart." We held each other for nearly an hour and kissed amid the brine-scented air and gentle surf sounds, while water creatures skimmed along the surface. We charted for ourselves a singular island of sanity and respite from the tortured, unvarnished world around us. Our bodies, though not physically connected, merged into a union of honey and milk, of raw textures and ancient harmony. I whispered endearments to her—said those things to her that she needed to hear, but had always been denied. As far as I was concerned this was all about Donna the woman—none of this had anything to do with Demmings or my anger toward him.

When we reached the summit of our world's Mount Everest, I initiated a new phase in the evolution of our private world. We explored each other's bodies thoroughly, completely and intimately, always hovering just shy of intercourse while bringing ourselves to indescribable levels of ecstasy, until she closed her eyes and went to some serene place. When she opened them again, I smiled and nodded; now she understood. Now Donna recognized the combination of trust and passion as the sublime synthesis of intimacy. As we descended our Everest's far slope, I lifted her from the soil and carried her into the calm waters of the river, and there we bathed and touched and caressed, and in the end we convulsed in each other's arms until finally laughter rose in a vapor to form soft all-encompassing clouds—clouds that would shield us from all the hostilities that were, and those that were yet to come.

It was almost midnight when we got dressed, our souls purged as we walked hand-in-hand to the cars. After she drove off I stood and whispered to the water, "The invisible, wanting to be visible." Then I climbed inside the Mustang; I had a duty to perform, and only then could I be with my Natasha.

*   *   *

Where was Natasha? Where had she gone? The anger surfaced unbidden as he swung up one road and down another in search of his elusive prey. Had she left work early? Had someone borrowed her car? Had she gone into hiding? Then he had an epiphany—he remembered seeing Hart's black Firebird parked along a north-end street. He adjusted the volume until the police chatter faded, turned north, and stepped on the gas. He'd find her—and he had his pistol. No dog would stand in his way this time.

*   *   *

I raced to headquarters and called Joe. He arrived fifteen minutes later and we went to his upstairs office. After I briefed him, he nodded and said, "Fantastic job, Michael. I'm putting Demmings under immediate surveillance while I call the judge. Maybe we'll get lucky and get a verbal warrant. If Demmings moves before then, so help me God I'll clip his wings and neuter him myself." He gave me a hard look. "All this stays between us. Is that understood?"

"Thumbs up on that one, Joe."

I went to the locker room and showered, then drove to Kevin's. I looked for Joe's men as I pulled into the garage but they were damned good, because I couldn't spot anyone. I closed the garage door, opened the interior door leading to the kitchen, walked quietly toward Nat's closed door—and came to a screeching halt.

Something was wrong.

I squinted in the ambient light. There, in front of the door—a shadow; something, or someone.

A crumpled form.

My hand went instantly to the pistol in my fanny pack until I heard, "It's me, Horse Breath."

Levi was curled up on the carpet in front of her door, his head on a pillow, a light blanket draped over him. His pistol was inches from his gun hand. I reached down and helped him to his feet. "I see George's spirit lives on in you. Thanks, *mi amigo*."

He nodded slightly as he bent down and retrieved his pistol, and then his unwavering gaze asked the question.

I shook my head and whispered, "No. She volunteered the information. It's going to be okay now." Then I gripped his shoulder and said, "Thanks again for watching over Nat."

Levi stared woodenly and said, "I love her, too."

I flicked my eyes at the closed door. "You could've slept next to …"

He shook his head. "No. I could not have." Then he grabbed his pillow and blanket and went to Kevin's room. When the door clicked behind him I went to Natasha and found her in a deep sleep. But when I touched her ankle her eyes snapped open. She bolted upright, looked around the room in alarm, and sighed as the fear drained. Finally, she settled wearily against her pillow. I slid into bed and held her as she studied my face. I smiled. "Everything's fine, Sweetness. I think it's over." She looked steadily into me and then nodded. After a short time she fell asleep in my arms. I lay quietly and stared at the ceiling for hours.

A persistent knocking woke me up. When I answered, Kevin pushed open the door and said, "Phone call. Sounds urgent."

I picked up the kitchen extension and heard Joe say, "Get down here right away," and then all I heard was a buzzing after he hung up. I dressed hurriedly, told Natasha that I had to leave, debated whether to bring Levi along, but decided not to. Something in Joe's voice alarmed me, and I didn't want to peel away any of the layers of protection that surrounded Natasha. Not yet.

As I went out the door she said guardedly, "I might keep an appointment with a hair dresser before you return."

I stopped. "Really? You've always done your own ..." I checked myself and said, "I know, I know—it's a girl's prerogative." I reminded her to bring Levi along, and then I urged her to stay within sight of Joe's men. Just in case.

"What's up?"

Joe indicated a chair in front of his desk. "Have a seat." Then he leaned back and closed his eyes. "Demmings has disappeared."

I gripped the chair and leaned forward. "Disa ...?"

"Gone. He's either off with a bottle sulking, or he got wind of what's coming down and hit the bug-out trail." He rubbed his eyes wearily. "We searched his residence. No bungee cords, no bloodstained clothing, no nothing to link him to the crimes."

I frowned. "What about the roses?"

"We did find them, and yes—they all match. Also," he began as he stifled a yawn, "also, we went through his laundry. Zip. Everything's been washed. Lab's checking his skivvies for pubic hairs, but I'm not optimistic."

"Anything else?"

He studied me carefully. "Photos. Tons of photos. Shit's gonna splatter when it hits the proverbial fan." He pinched the bridge of his nose and closed his eyes. "We're sorting through them as we speak."

I ticked off a few points on my fingers. "He's disappeared. Is he on the run because he's got a chunk of meat missing from his leg? He's cleaned all his laundry. Why now? No bungee cords or other evidence. Did he dump everything in a hurry? If not, then what motivated him to hightail it outta town?"

Joe nodded. "I'll make a cop out of you yet."

I sat back in the chair. "We've got all the essentials—motivation, opportunity, even capability. All we lack is solid proof beyond a reasonable doubt. Until then he's an innocent man."

Joe said, "Admirable outlook. But?"

I frowned. "But then there are those damn roses. Gotta tell you, doesn't look good for him. Time for a 'come to Jesus' meeting." I looked at him. "Should I ask Donna if she knows where he might've gone?"

He nodded. "Absolutely."

"Then I'll call her now."

"Please do," Joe said as I got up. "And please close the door behind you."

I found a phone and called the number she'd given me. There was no answer so I left a message. Then I called the house, hoping to catch Nat and Levi before they left, but there was no answer there, either. At least Levi was with her, and Joe would have alerted his men to the continuing menace. I went to Johnny's.

"Aye lad, and where might you have been of late?"

I took a towel and locker key from him and replied, "Working extra."

He nodded knowingly. "The rapes? I suppose they're running you ragged, shuttling back and forth from The Pines."

I blurted before I could think, "Not staying there anymore. I …"

He screwed his eyes tight. "Oh, that's right. I heard. Your female room-mate was attacked, and in the sanctity of your very home. So where have you taken refuge?"

"Rather not say, Johnny. You understand."

He nodded rapidly. "Right, right. There you are now. Cheers. I only thought it would help—an extra set of eyes looking out for her well-being. That's all."

"Thanks. I'll tell her you said that."

He got busy with some towels. "I hear," he began cautiously, "that young Levi's not long for this town."

Frowning, I asked, "Who told you *that*?"

He shrugged. "Oh, one of the lads. Jarl, I suppose."

Me and my big mouth; I'd let that slip, too.

Johnny peered at me and said, "By the by, whatever happened to that young lass you met here nearly a fortnight ago? Anna, I believe you said her name was."

"She's gone home, Johnny. Lot of work to do; you understand." I clutched my towel and said, "Speaking of work, time to hit those weights."

"Have a good workout. There's a good lad, then." He stood behind his counter and watched as I turned toward the locker room.

I was still running the case through my head an hour later while I parked in Kevin's garage and walked inside the house. All of a sudden an elegant woman leaped up from the living room couch. I jumped back and said, "Holy cow! I'm so sorry. I'm in the wrong house!" I began backing away, "Don't worry ... I'm on my way out."

"*Michael*," Natasha cried out.

Natasha hurried toward me. I could not have been more shocked. The hairdresser had rinsed her hair to a soft, natural brown and cut it short. She had on a clean white blouse, a charcoal gray skirt, and black, low-cut shoes. Tiny gold earrings adorned each ear, and a thin strand of gold hung from her neck.

I stood against the door and said in a deadpan, "You've changed your hair."

She touched her fingers to her head. "Do you like it?"

I gazed admiringly at her lovely face, the high cheekbones of her Slavic features, her long limbs and the bulge of her breasts against her white blouse. "Love it."

She smiled prettily. "So did Levi."

"Where is he, by the way?"

She pointed toward Kevin's closed bedroom door. "They're in there."

"I *like* Kevin—good match for Levi, and ... I'm so sorry about the baby, Nat." A few minutes later I was pouring coffee for the two of us when I decided it was time to resume our old game. "So ... what is truth?"

Natasha faced me and beamed. "No good. You've asked that one."

I nodded, and turning serious I said, "I know. So ... what *is* truth? *The* truth," I began, "of what you've been up to these past couple of months. Natasha, I didn't recognize you when I walked in. I thought I was in the wrong house."

She nodded as if awaiting that inevitable question and cleared her throat. "People follow interesting paths after they've acquired a Yale M.B.A." She paused and added, "Class of 1988. *Summa cum laude*."

"But why? *Why* have you been wasting your time *here*?"

Natasha touched her palm to my cheek. "I was being groomed by a top Wall Street firm when my father died. I thought someone had reached inside my chest and yanked my heart out. That was five years ago." Natasha looked briefly away. "A year after his death I handed in my resignation and told everyone I was moving to Phoenix. Then off I went. My colleagues were dumbfounded, of course."

"As well they should be," I exclaimed. "Didn't anyone try to stop you?"

Natasha offered a wan smile as we moved outside to the deck and sat down. "I think they were in too great a state of shock. Anyway, I disappeared before anyone *could* intervene. Now I wish to hell someone had."

"Why?"

"Because I might have gotten the professional counseling I so desperately needed."

"What was the problem?"

Natasha smiled. "Silly old me; too smart to think that something as frivolous as grief could topple me." She sighed. "But it did. Caught me good." She shifted gears and made a point of studying her nails before announcing, "I went into therapy half a year ago. It's made all the difference."

Bingo. That explained her mysterious absences. "So how's it been?"

Natasha's eyes grew softer. "It's answered my questions." She crossed her legs and let her foot jangle as she talked. "I entered therapy with every classic symptom of deep grief. Everything—the abrupt change from cutting-edge financial whiz to *cockatiel* waitress, my move to the opposite end of the country, and—well, everything fit a nice, convenient pattern." She stopped and drew an audible breath. "But patterns I can live with, because patterns I can break. You can too."

"That explains the recent changes," I said, staring at the canal that swept past the house. "I never said this before, but I am a cop. I *do* notice things. I never really bought into that 'happy-happy, joy-joy' face you wore."

"No, I don't suppose you *were* fooled. Nor am I surprised that you had the good manners to keep your suspicions to yourself." She sniffed and touched a finger to each of her eyes. "I'm returning to the person I was meant to be." She stopped and choked back a sob. "A moment ago I said I wished my colleagues had stopped me." She gazed at some distant object, her mouth sad, her face lined. Then in a quiet voice she said, "That's not entirely true, because if they *had* intervened, I would have missed knowing some of the people I've met along the way." She touched my hand. "What I'm really trying to say, Michael," and now a tear trickled from her eye, "is that I never would have met *you*, would never have known your compassion, and knowing you has made all the difference in the world."

I got up and led her to the bedroom. We lay in silence, caressing and kissing each other. After a while she whispered, "Oscar Wilde once said that it's not the perfect, but the *imperfect* who are in need of love." She leaned forward and put her palm on my forearm. "We're both imperfect, Michael."

I put a finger to her lips. "That's why we love one another so deeply."

Later, we entered the kitchen at the same time as Levi and Kevin. We sat and joshed a bit, and later I pulled Kevin aside and we went outside to the deck. I turned to this tall and lanky guy who smiled a lot, and said, "Thanks for being a good friend to Levi."

He looked at me and said, "He's a bastard."

"Huh?"

"Yeah. Swept me off my feet. I'm falling in love with him."

I put my hand on his shoulder. "But that's great!"

He shook his head stubbornly. "Not so great when he leaves."

I shrugged. "So go with him."

A long silence until he said, "He hasn't asked."

"Give it time, Kev. He's got a lot going on in his head right now."

We shot the breeze some more and then we rejoined Nat and Levi. "Jarl's still being an ass," I said to Levi as an aside, not expecting Kevin to know who he was.

But Kevin perked up. "I know a Jarl. Works for you guys."

Levi said casually, "Did you have a run-in with him?"

Kevin shook his head and settled his long legs atop a stool. "I don't want to give away something I shouldn't, but … do you guys know that he hangs around Rehoboth?"

Natasha said, "We stumbled upon him at *Numbers*."

"They know he's gay," Levi added.

Kevin nodded, deep in thought. "Gay, and kinky. Likes to be photographed."

I made the connection and said, "And you just happen to have those photos?"

"It was an after-hours party. Jarl hooked-up with some frumpy dude I'd never seen before. He wanted pictures taken. Someone volunteered. They went to another room. I happened to be nearby when they came out. The guy taking the photos popped the film out and handed it to me."

"Why you?" Natasha asked.

"I do free-lance photography on the side. I developed them, but nobody ever claimed them. Jarl was smashed when they were taken; doubt he even remembers. He'd shit if he knew." He looked at each of us in turn and said, "Guess you guys have figured him for what he is."

Nat nodded. "Bottom boy."

"He was shit-faced, that's for sure."

I coughed and said, "Look, let's not go there. We don't want to threaten him with compromising photos."

"Just thought you should know."

Levi said, "Yeah, but keep it to yourself, okay?"

We dropped it, put on some tunes, and played a few rounds of gin rummy while Natasha prepared lunch. When she called everyone to the table, she startled us with a casual announcement. "I've decided to open a restaurant."

I stared dumbly at her. "You can do that?"

She laughed. "It's quite legal in this day and age. I'm even allowed to vote *and* smoke. Or is it that you doubt my capabilities?"

"Not one bit, but why a restaurant?"

She shrugged. "It's something I've always wanted to do."

"You'll need start-up money."

"Money I can get," she said simply. Then a small smile crept across her face. "I went to Yale, remember? What, you think I paid the tuition by myself? Come on, guys—I'm a trust-fund kid!"

I nodded. "Okay, but aren't you still afraid of losing everything?"

She laughed. "No guts, no glory. I don't care about the risk, and I'll have no problem raising capital." She paused. "You've got to spend money to make money. I'll succeed."

As we ate I stole occasional glances at this tremendous woman whom I loved so much. Her trust-fund status surprised me, but it filled in the many gaps. It especially explained how she figured on raising a baby—Levi's baby—by herself. The tumblers had been steadily clicking into place for her—she gotten counseling and come full cycle to the professional person she'd always been.

I checked my voice mail afterward but found nothing. I fell into a funk, gathered the others, and warned them of the danger.

* * *

He knew he would find her. It was a matter of time. Wise-ass bitch was probably hiding in plain sight.

* * *

Levi and I reported for the evening shift. The chief entered as roll call was about to begin, and stunned everyone else with the announcement: "It grieves me to announce that a warrant has been issued for the arrest of Officer Dennis Demmings. He is the primary suspect in the serial rapes. This information is about to be disseminated to the media. I wanted you to hear it from me first. I repeat—he is a suspect. If anyone has information regarding his whereabouts, I am ordering you to come forward. You may direct any further questions to your supervisor, Sgt. Burke." The chief gave Burke a nasty look and left the room.

As soon as we broke I went to see Joe. "Guess the word's out. Okay if I discuss everything with Levi?"

He leaned back in his chair and loosened his tie. "Yeah, it's a go."

"Thanks. Nothing from Donna yet; I'll try again."

Joe looked carefully at me and said, "I've always respected you, Michael. I knew you were a gutsy mother the day you came to work for me." He wet his lips. "If Sharon and I had been blessed with a son, we would have wanted him to be like ..." He paused and his eyes bored into mine. "You're a *cop*, Michael. A mother loving, no-holds-barred, fucking *street* cop. Now let's nail the mother fucker who tried to harm your girl."

I left his office and called Donna. She picked up on the first ring.

"Michael! I was just sitting down to call you."

"Listen, I ..."

"No. Wait." She paused, and in a soft voice said, "Michael, I want to thank you for the other evening. You gave me back my dignity, and you—gave of yourself. I will always love you for that."

I said gently, "You'll always have my love, Donna." I cleared my throat. "Hate to cut this short, but I've gotta know—do you have *any* idea where he is?"

"No. None. I called his parents and they don't know, either. I would know if they were lying."

"Any idea why he cut and ran?"

A protracted silence followed. Then, "I think he's running from himself."

"Explain, please."

"He could not have known that I spoke to you. But he's been terribly upset by the separation. I think he's gone off to be by himself. I know him. He'll show up. But when he does ..."

I gripped the phone. "Listen, stay away from your house and call me immediately if he contacts you. Okay?"

"I will," she whispered. "And Michael?"

"Yes, Donna."

"I love you. Very much."

I nodded slowly. "Thank you, Donna. Thank you for loving me."

"Michael? When this blows over I want to go away for a while."

Without hesitating I said, "San Diego."

"You know it?"

"Intimately."

She laughed delightedly. "Intimately. How I love that word now. You were so right; I've never known such wonderful intimacy. It was delicious."

I sidestepped the image. "Give yourself a couple of weeks. See La Jolla and Hillcrest. Visit Ocean Beach and Coronado." I closed my eyes and recalled the sights, the sounds, and the aromas of San Diego. "Bring a friend. Share some intimacy."

Donna let out a little cough. "I wish it could be you."

Now I smiled. "I do, too. I can't, but I will always feel love for you."

*   *   *

Why hadn't he thought of it previously? He knew where she *worked*. Stupid! Why did he let that slip? He parked across the street from her nightclub and waited.

There *he* comes to pick her up. Now she's in the car with him. Excellent. He blended with the traffic, fell in behind the Mustang, and followed from a discreet distance. Even if discovered, he knew his cover story would hold.

He fell back a bit more when the Mustang turned into the north-end street. Then it slowed, stopped, and got swallowed up whole by the garage. He drove past.

He knew where to find her.

CHAPTER 12

I did another double take at Natasha's new appearance when I picked her up from the club. It seemed such a drastic departure from the Natasha I'd known, but I loved this Natasha as much, if not more. Her willingness to take a risk—to challenge herself and to grow—I loved those qualities of hers.

Maybe it was my nerves, but I couldn't shake the feeling that we were being followed as we drove to Kevin's. I let it go once we were safely inside the garage and the four of us had gathered in the living room over drinks—martini straight up with olives for me, thank you. During the second round I mentioned Jarl and suggested that it was time to have a talk with him. Natasha said, "Know how I would go about it?" Levi, Kevin, and I put down our drinks. "Now then ..."

Afterward I caught Levi's eye and we went out onto the deck to talk. We leaned against the rail and watched as the receding tide moved the normally sluggish canal with a new urgency. I asked, "How're you doing these days, bro?"

"Aw, I'm fine. It's Nat I'm worried about. You know, the baby."

I tapped my hand against his forearm and said, "You did nothing wrong. Look, I encouraged her to have that baby with you. You both agreed, and big boy rules applied, now get over it." I paused. "There's something you've got to know. I umm, I was ordered not to say anything until now." When I told him that Anna was among the rape victims he hung his head. "Bro, I was on the beach—I walked right past her place. If Jen and I hadn't been fucking I might have been there! Jesus, I might've caught him red-handed! I'm so sorry, Michael. What a selfish bastard I've been!"

I cuffed the back of his head rudely with my open hand. "What the hell's wrong with you? Christ, you weren't being selfish. You—you did what you did to keep from going crazy." Then I told him about the roses, and how Donna helped make the connections.

The next day I drove down noticeably deserted streets on my way to work.

The tourists were avoiding the town in greater numbers, courtesy of the media feeding-frenzy over the identity of the real North End Rapist, especially now that the commentaries concerning his subsequent disappearance had gone ballistic. As one CNN pundit observed, "There are Keysian economic theories and there are Keystonian Kop Theories. These Keystone Kops have done little else but fall all over themselves in pursuit of what has turned out to be one of the very officers whom they've been, well, falling over. Right under their noses all the time, Bob—and then he managed to slip from under said noses. In *my* opinion …"

The hot topic at headquarters also swirled around Demmings. Endless debates flew from all corners of the locker room while I changed into my uniform. The talk droned on as I hitched my gun belt around my waist. Then I loitered in the hallway like a hunter seeking his prey. Jarl finally appeared at the far end of the central corridor. His dark eyes darted throughout, and he moved with an effort.

"What's up?" he mumbled.

I greeted him jovially. "Hey, how're you doing?"

He stopped, smiled, and loosened up. "Ahh, hell. Same old shit. Linda and the fuckin' kids are back, so she's got me busy with honey-do's."

"Aw, that's bad news. Hmm. Say, how about that beer?"

His eyes lit up. "Really? Yeah! Why not?"

"Tonight. After work. *O'Toole's?*"

At end of shift, I changed quickly and rushed over to *O'Toole's*. I had to get there before Jarl did, because seating was key to our plan. *O'Toole's* had a solid reputation as a north-end pub with a down-to-earth quality. It offered subdued lighting and dark wooden booths where customers didn't need to shout to be heard—while their conversations were muffled from unauthorized ears by the ever-present ambient noise.

I took a booth near the rear and sat facing the entrance. The waitress appeared and I greeted her warmly. We'd gone out a couple of times, and as a favor she reserved the adjacent booth for me, effectively providing a buffer between my booth and the entrance. Hidden speakers provided Celtic music, and the air began to buzz as patrons arrived and moved about. A slight odor of stale beer and spent tobacco filled the place, but I thought it anything but bad.

Jarl sauntered in ten minutes later. We ordered beers and delved into meaningless but safe chitchat. I brought up the topic of Demmings but Jarl glossed over it; he seemed eager to get down to business. But first he wanted to drink. He drained his beer and signaled the waitress for another. He tossed it down, and as the waitress brought him a third round, I followed the progress of two new patrons as they entered the pub. They went directly to the reserved booth, and I raised no objection when they unobtrusively seated themselves.

"Jarl," I began robustly. "Levi will be gone soon. I want you to let up on him."

He frowned. "Why are we wastin' time talkin' about him?"

I raised my beer glass and studied his distorted features through the amber liquid as I drank. When I put it down I asked, "Suppose he is gay? I'm not saying he is, but people don't choose their orientation. The only choice is to live a lie or to be honest about it."

Jarl drained half his beer, put down his glass and said, "Okay, you've got the denial shit outta the way. So ... when're we gonna do it?"

"What are you talking ..."

"I'm talkin' about you an' me gettin' it on."

"Whoa! Slow down there, sailor."

A burst of nervous laughter escaped him. "Still playin' the denial thing? Okay. Listen up. I brought some leather straps. Someone ties you up, you can always claim you had no choice; lots of sex without the guilt trip."

"Jarl," I said in a louder voice.

He coughed into his fist and said in an undertone, "Let's get a room. We'll have a few drinks, get undressed, hop in bed. Then I break out the straps and we'll..."

"Jarl, wait!"

His chest heaved as he said hurriedly, "I—I'll do whatever you want—anything at all, okay?" All at once he thrust his hands to his lap and crossed his legs.

I said quietly, "Jarl, I ..."

He seemed not to hear me as his eyes glazed over. "Come on. Let's do it!"

"Jarl!"

He frowned and said impatiently, "Jesus! What the fuck is with you?"

"I'm trying to tell you something. I'm not gay, and I'm sure as hell not going to have sex with you."

Jarl looked as if he'd been slapped. "Wh—*what?*"

I leaned forward. "That's what I'm trying to tell you. I know I led you on. I had to. It was the only way to get you here. But I'm not gay. Not even a little bit. And—it doesn't matter to me that *you* are."

Jarl's face flushed red. He put both hands up as if stopping onrushing traffic. "Hey—you've got it wrong. I thought *you* was comin' on to *me*. I just wanted to see how fruity you really are." His hand shook as he grabbed his beer and gulped down the last half. He dropped it to the table and said, "Wait'll the boys hear this! You're fuckin' history, Brennan."

I looked coldly at him and said, "No, I'm not. But you will be if you don't cut the shit."

The whites of his eyes showed and his lips trembled. "Fuck you, Brennan."

I said reasonably, "We saw you at *Numbers,* Jarl."

He worked his jaw. "Don't know what you're talkin' about."

I leaned toward him. "It's okay, Jarl. Your secret's safe with us. But we did see you."

He regarded me shrewdly. "Yeah? What's this *Numbers*—some fag joint? An' if it is, then what the fuck was *you* doin' there—assumin' it was me you saw, of course."

I said patiently, "Jarl, straight couples do go to gay clubs. They dance. They accompany their gay friends. It's nothing to be afraid of," I continued in a calming tone. "We saw you, Jarl. It's okay with us, but we did see you and it's time for you to leave Levi alone."

He glared. "You threatening me, Brennan? Cause if you are …"

I looked hard at him and said, "Shut your yap, Jarl. I'm offering an olive branch. Take it."

His upper lip curled. "You got nothin' on me. You …"

"Yes he does," a voice from the adjoining booth said. Levi and Kevin leaned out and Levi said, "I was there, Jarl. I saw you groping another guy. Seen you there other times. And my friend here," Levi paused and swept a hand toward Kevin, "my friend has some photos that you don't want others to see. So cut the sanctimonious crap and lighten up."

I said in a low tone, "We're not a threat to you, Jarl."

The blood drained from his face. "Then what do you call it?"

Kevin answered, "We call it bringing you face to face with your reality."

Jarl blustered. "Only reality 'round here is that I'm surrounded by a bunch a fags."

"*That's* it!" Levi leaped up and squared off. His bare feet were spread and braced on the rough wooden floor, his fists clenched as he stared through half-lidded eyes. "Enough of this bullshit. Listen up, Jarl. Sexuality doesn't dictate masculinity. We're not here to box you in. We're …"

"Giving you an honorable out," I said. But my mood wavered. I wanted to remain the peacemaker, but now I teetered on the cusp of all-out belligerence.

Jarl glowered at Levi even as his hands remained flat atop the table. Like most bullies, Jarl didn't care to fight when the odds were against him—and the odds definitely would not favor him in a physical confrontation with Levi. Jarl finally broke the impasse by saying in a low, threatening voice, "I ain't gay, an' you fuckers better not say nothin' to nobody."

Levi unclenched his fist and replied in measured tones, "Be whatever you wanna be, Jarl. But don't fuck with me or anyone else. Not ever again. If you develop an issue with what somebody does in bed, then keep it to yourself. Are we clear?"

"Cocksucker!" Jarl snapped.

Levi could barely suppress the amused look that spread across his face as he pointed a finger at his own chest and said sardonically, "*Moi?*"

Jarl grumbled and looked over his shoulder toward the exit. Then he said, "Let's just say that I'm letting up 'cause you ain't worth the effort."

Levi started to say something when I put up my hand. "Not good enough. We'll agree that you're gonna zip it—permanently. You're not going to say anything about Levi, about me, or about people who are gay or Jewish or bald or whatever."

Jarl worked up some courage and his eyes turned suddenly cruel. "Fuck you guys. I'll say whatever I want. I …"

Kevin glared menacingly and said, "Shut the fuck up, punk! You fucking asshole! These guys are trying to give you a chance. But *I'm* done with you. So keep on fucking around. Call it blackmail, but I'll send my photos to everyone you work with. Now are we finished here?"

We weren't finished. Not really. One problem remained—where was Demmings?

*   *   *

He parked across the street from her club. Maybe she'd leave by herself this time. He wouldn't let her get to the house if she did. He'd make the grab on one of the darker streets. Then he'd make her grab for her life; he'd make her do that for a couple of weeks, and then he'd take everything from her. He patted the large lump against his waist; it comforted him to feel the pistol with its hard barrel and its load of slugs.

*   *   *

After we left *O'Toole's* we drove to the club, picked up Natasha, and went to Kevin's. I put a *B-Tribe* CD on and we took our drinks to the rear deck. I felt that we'd found an island of sanctuary here; the canal gurgled softly as it moved with the tides, a whip-poor-will sang from one of the many trees along the far side, and fluffy clouds, their bottoms illuminated by city lights, passed silently overhead. The music embraced us, the Scotch warmed us, and our world felt right. Natasha beamed happily, and we stole private glances while Levi and Kevin carried on with the small talk.

She and I went to bed afterward and made love until near dawn, and then I lay entwined with this woman whom I loved so much.

*   *   *

He watched the house from afar. At one point he drove to the street parallel to the other side of the canal. He could see them plainly, but realized he could never get off a shot. Too many trees; too much distance. He'd have to close ranks.

Meanwhile, he sat and watched and waited, until the rising sun threatened to betray him. Then he drove off. Another time, another place.

CHAPTER 13

THE kitchen phone rang persistently. Someone finally picked up and then Levi's muffled voice carried into our bedroom. A few minutes later he knocked, cracked the door open, and walked in, wearing only the paint-stained shorts he'd acquired the night before Jarl's ski party. They hung loosely, revealing the gleaming red wound where the bullet grazed him.

Levi came to the side of the bed, tapped my arm and commanded, "Move over." He plopped down atop the covers and sat with his back against the headboard, his triangular face relaxed, but his blue eyes somber beneath his heavy, red-glinting hair. "Last night," he began with no apparent aim, "you handled Jarl like a pro. But be careful. He's got friends and they're a spiteful bunch. They'll come after you. Jesus, they're so *bain dramaged*," he said, slipping into our old private joke.

"Let 'em."

Natasha tugged the bed sheet a bit and moved against me as she studied Levi's face. "What's really wrong," she finally asked.

Levi said nothing as he looked at us in the dreadful way cops do when they're about to tell parents that their child's been killed. Then in a quiet voice he said, "Customs just called. I've accepted their offer. I'm to report in two weeks."

I reached out and squeezed his shoulder. "Hey, that's great news!"

Natasha burst into applause. "Yay, Levi!"

He shook his head. "No yay. I don't want to leave. Not anymore. But I've got to." He paused and then said quietly, "I'm giving my notice today. I've got some leave to burn but I want to spend time with my folks. So—guess I'm outta here in two days." He turned to Natasha and smiled ruefully. "I'll call every day and bug you." To me he said, "You always look out for everyone else. Time you looked after Michael."

Levi was right, but looking after myself would mean selfishly encouraging him to follow his gut, turn down the job offer, and stay here. I felt miserable at the prospect of his departure, but it was in his best interests. At least he'd finished what he'd set out to accomplish—he'd given me a gift of friendship that had made all the difference in the world to me—and he'd made Natasha infinitely happy by being her lover, but mostly her friend. That above all else made him more remarkable. I glanced at the sheet that covered Natasha and me and said to him, "Stretch out and stay awhile." He seemed pensive but then he smiled and joined us. Natasha reached across me and rested her hand on his hip. We lay quietly for an hour, sometimes discussing our futures, other times lapsing into silence. It was our most intimate moment ever, when the three of us combined our energies and our dreams and made for ourselves a world that turned with the seasons, obeyed the concordance of tides, and moved with quiet determination toward the culmination of all that we believed in. As so often happened in *our* world, a bed became the level playing field where each of us could be whatever we wanted—gay, straight or in-between; sometimes in pain, often in love, but always in friendship. This final time together became our *raison d'être*, our dictum—our dance of life amid the swirl of all that was, and all that would be.

Speculation ran rampant at that day's roll call that Demmings had eaten his gun, "Else he'd a surfaced by now," Perry Ryan asserted. "Or been caught," another suggested. The troops tossed around two or three theories until they grew tired and dropped the topic. But the buzz about Burke *wouldn't* quit; he had punched in sick among speculation that he'd been caught-up in the aftermath of Demmings' Peeping Tom activities. Word had it that he faced demotion as a consequence for failing to take forceful action. Burke's closest ally also failed to show; Jarl too had fallen victim to the blue flu.

Roll call ended and we hit the streets. Levi made several drive-by checks of Natasha's club, then he and Hack and I got together for our meal break. "Gonna miss you," Hack said to Levi after we placed our orders. "I always been proud to have you as my friend." Levi thanked him graciously, while I felt bad that I'd briefly suspected Hacksaw of the attacks. It was our shift's Friday, and it ended uneventfully. Natasha's apprehension by now had dimmed sufficiently to consider moving back to The Pines, and with only a short time remaining, we decided that tomorrow we'd celebrate Levi's career change with a night out.

The timing couldn't have been worse; Jennifer begged-off, citing daylong bouts of nausea. Kevin had to work, and Hack called to report that he'd become ill. "Love to come, but I'm laid up with some kinda bug. Better not leave the house. Not tonight, anyway." Then he broke into correct grammar. "You guys go ahead. Give Levi my regrets. Tell him I'll stop by tomorrow if I can to see him off."

Levi suggested a fine dining restaurant in Rehoboth Beach. Natasha put on a black evening dress and low-heel shoes, tiny gold earrings, and a delicate gold necklace. Levi and I accessorized ourselves by packing guns; Demmings still hadn't been accounted for, and we refused to take any risks. Levi slid his 9mm automatic into the waistband of his trousers, and his Tommy Bahama shirt concealed it nicely; I slipped my snub-nose revolver into an ankle holster. We weren't supposed to carry guns into Delaware except on official business, but cops on both sides of the state line always looked the other way.

As we headed out the door the phone rang. "Forget it," I said. "Let someone else take care of the world tonight."

Levi snorted. "Speak for yourself, Toecheese. Could be my ma, telling me to dress warm." He picked up the phone and I watched his face as it changed from pleased, to somber, and finally to grim. "Good," he said quietly. "Yes. I will. Yeah, it's something, alright. Okay—and thanks." He turned to us. "Joe Santoro. They've got Demmings."

I watched him for any clues. "Yeah, but what's the problem?"

His lips were pressed tight as he shook his head absently. "They nailed him less than a block away. Said he was headed this way."

Natasha said forcefully, "Fuck him! Let's not ruin Levi's night out." She turned to me. "Michael? Drop it. We're out of here."

I nodded. "Agreed. This is the one night that we're not gonna be civic-minded do-gooders. Tonight's for Levi."

He grinned broadly and shot a raised fist toward the ceiling. "To us!"

"To Levi!" Natasha cheered.

"To freedom," Levi crowed. Then he tapped the pistol beneath his shirt and arched his eyebrows at me. "Ditch 'em?"

I opened my mouth but then slammed it shut. Instinctively I said, "No!"

Levi nodded. As we went out the door, the phone began ringing again. Natasha looked at us and said ominously, "Don't even think about it." Then she flashed a sparkling smile when I slammed the door shut. We piled into the

Mustang and left for Rehoboth Beach, with Levi complaining loudly about all the books scattered across the rear seat. I wisecracked, "Yeah, and there'll be more if you ever get around to returning the ones you borrowed." We reached Rehoboth forty-five minutes later. Parking was at a premium and we were forced to look for space in the older part of town. We finally parked near a dark alley that separated two antique stores. It seemed an ironic match; the bright red Mustang with its personalized license plates actually complimented the foreboding storefronts. We set off on foot for a restaurant that claimed the best seafood on the East Coast.

River Walk was located on a quiet side street near the downtown district. The austere restaurant boasted a grand view of the stately river that coursed through Rehoboth, but the best seats had already been reserved. Luckily the night was pleasant, and Natasha chose a table along the clean, wide sidewalk.

Classical music greeted us from hidden speakers as we sat down to a table set with linen and fine cutlery. Natasha cocked an ear. "Rachmaninoff. *Rhapsody on a Theme from Paganini …*"

"*Opus Forty Three,*" Levi said.

"*Variation Eighteen,*" I added.

I scanned the leather-bound menu and ordered a meat dish out of habit, until Natasha prodded me into letting go and choosing seafood. We ordered clams casino as an appetizer, and I had a lobster tail and crabmeat entrée. As someone who loved to cook and cooked well, I appreciated the subtle flavors, seasonings, and aromas that our chef created. We shared a bottle of wine—a superb Northern Rhône viognier, especially suited to the strong flavors of our seafood dishes. Natasha sipped hers reluctantly, until finally she looked at Levi and me with tired eyes. "I feel guilty, as if drinking might harm the baby that's no longer inside of me."

Levi placed one hand on my forearm and the other on hers. He brought my hand to Natasha's and offered a brave smile. "Michael will give you plenty of children, Nat. You—you'll have more than you can handle."

She thanked him with her eyes and then the three of us offered a silent prayer for the lost child. Natasha smiled finally, drank heartily of the wine, and then we discussed old times, recent events and our philosophical takes on life in general. After the main course we sat quietly over coffee and mulled over the topic that we'd avoided all evening—Levi's pending departure from our daily lives.

"Say, aren't you Officer Hart? Sure, I'd recognize you anywhere."

I looked up as a middle-aged beat cop approached the table. He carried a wooden nightstick in his left hand, secured to his wrist by a long leather thong. While still a few feet away he let the nightstick fly from his body in a practiced motion. When it reached the end of the thong the veteran cop jerked it smartly, and the end of the nightstick struck the sidewalk with a sharp *tonk!* before bouncing back into his waiting hand. The old cop stopped next to our table. He carried a few too many pounds, and experience had etched his face deeply, but he struck me as a professional.

He said, "Sure. Levi Hart, in the flesh."

Levi put down his napkin and stood. "Good evening, sir. Yes, that's me." He narrowed his eyes as he studied the beat cop's face. "Have we met?"

"No," he said good-naturedly, "but everyone in this department knows *you*. Why, you're no less a hero to us than you must be in Ocean City." Then he looked at Natasha and me and said, "Hank Arnold, by the way. Sorry to disturb you folks."

I stood and looked for an empty chair. "You're not disturbing us. Please join us. May I present Natasha Panova, and I am Michael Brennan."

Hank shook my hand and then touched his finger respectfully to the bill of his hat, as he smiled at Natasha. "Pleased to meet ya. Can't sit, unfortunately." Then he looked at me and asked, "You with Ocean City, too?"

"Sure am."

Hank shook his head back and forth as a grand grin spread across his face. "Levi Hart. Yes sir. When we heard about your gunfight every one of us said, 'Yes! Good guys, one—bad guy, zip!' And here you are. Doggone. That was some shootin'. Wish I was that good." He sighed and placed a hand against his soft belly. "Gettin' too old, though. Can't trust these eyes so much—'specially at night. Well, I'm old school," he said as he hefted the nightstick close to his face. He let it fly and it hit the sidewalk again with another *tonk*, before bouncing back up. Then Hank stopped abruptly as deep furrows stood out on his forehead. He studied Levi and asked, "How're you doing, son? Heard you took a bullet. Healing up alright, is it?"

Levi's shoulders dropped as he loosened-up for the first time in days. "It's healing fine, thank you." He shook his head and appraised the old cop again. "Gotta tell you, I'm still surprised you recognized me."

Hank Arnold smiled. "Well, I know or see most everyone comes to town. Seen *you* around."

Levi said, "*Flicks*, maybe—possibly *Numbers*. It's okay," he said. "My friends know."

Hank's eyes remained steady as he replied, "Yep. *Flicks* once or twice, an' *Numbers* quite a few times. Go to both places myself—and you're a damned fine dancer!"

I swept a hand at the street. "It's good to see how people here accept gays. Jesus, this would never make it in Ocean City."

Hank smiled and danced the end of his baton off the sidewalk. "Rehoboth Beach is old money, son. With old money a fella can do as he damn well pleases. What most of 'em do is, they get an education. Education wipes away the ignorance. Ocean City? Well, no disrespect—you've a mighty large police force down there. But for my money well, hmm—maybe on second thought I'll just keep my trap shut." An awkward silence followed until Officer Hank Arnold cleared his throat. "Can I tell you all something?"

"Certainly," Natasha said.

"I'm proud that I'm gay," he said quietly.

I looked at Levi and said, "I hope Ocean City gets the message, and soon."

"Sad," Hank said as he gave two passersby a cop's once-over. "Ocean City's only twenty miles away, but twenty years behind." He looked at Levi. "Nobody 'round here cares. It's as if I introduced myself as Henry, 'stead of Hank."

Levi asked, "What about the guys you work with?"

He shrugged. "All of 'em know the score when they come here." Then Hank looked shrewdly at me, and declared, "You're not gay. You're straight."

I nodded.

"Wish there were more like you around." He touched the brim of his hat again and said, "Thank you for the pleasure of your company. I wish you the best, Officer Hart." Just before he turned and walked off he added, "Wait'll I tell the boys I ran into *you*. They'll be so jealous. Le-vi *Hart*." He sent the nightstick spinning. *Tonk*.

The streets were nearly deserted when we left *River Walk* and strolled back to the car, a walk made slower by full bellies and Natasha's reluctance to pass any of the darkened display windows without stopping to peer inside.

"I'll miss you guys," Levi announced.

"You think?" Natasha kidded.

"Hey, it's not like we won't see each other again," I said. "Come on. Don't get syrupy."

He looked at me from the corner of his eyes. "I see you're wearing the St. Michael's."

I punched his arm and said, "Always and forever." Then I threw an arm around his shoulders and eased him toward the curb. The Mustang was just across the street, flanked by the narrow alley and two darkened stores. A tall, older gentleman had his back to us as he peered into one of the storefronts. He wore a long-sleeve shirt and baggy khaki trousers, and a floppy sunhat was settled so low over his head that it covered his ears. He looked vaguely familiar, and I decided he reminded me of Officer Hank Arnold.

Natasha reached the sidewalk first and waited patiently at the passenger door for me to unlock it. I began to go around the front, while Levi hurried past the trunk in an unspoken contest to see who could open her door first.

Then I heard a thud.

Levi yelled, "Christ," and doubled over in pain.

From the front bumper I cried out, "Jesus! What's wrong?"

"Aw," he said in a peevish voice, "Took a misstep. Twisted my damn ankle."

Natasha shrieked.

I whirled around.

The old man had Natasha.

He was pulling her into the dimly lit alley, one arm wrapped around her neck, a pistol to her temple.

Natasha struggled in vain.

"Keep back!" the old man warned in a strident, nether-worldly voice as he pulled her further into the alley's dark recesses.

I freeze. Disbelief. Incredible. My jaw drops. I yell, "*Johnny*! What the *hell* are you *doing?*"

Then …

A blur to my right as Levi goes for his gun.

I drop to my knee; go for my ankle holster; grab my snub-nose; stand back up.

Levi in my peripheral vision. He advances toward the yawning mouth of the alley in lock-step fashion, his pistol at the high ready.

I take aim at Johnny.

No good. It wasn't going to happen.

Johnny might have gone beyond some lunatic fringe, but he knew his tradecraft. He was pressed so close to the back of Natasha's head that only a mere few inches of his face was exposed. Natasha squirmed in vain, and I could tell from the way her eyes were patiently fixed on mine that she looked to us for a solution.

Johnny stopped midway down the alley. A faint light revealed the escape route behind him. Natasha's breathing came in loud spurts; otherwise she held it together.

Levi took up a position against the brick corner of the storefront; his eyes, his face—both were fierce and deadly. I went to the other corner and took deliberate aim. I didn't kid myself, though—a two-inch snub nose at night just wasn't gonna cut it, and I wasn't half the marksman that Levi was. On the other hand, his 9mm had a four-inch barrel, and Levi had proven his deadly nighttime accuracy.

"Levi," I whispered. "Got him?"

He said in a deathly quiet voice, "No good. She's in the way."

I said to Johnny, "You can't get away! Let Natasha go. She's done nothing to you. Look, we can resolve this." Give him the facts, put a name to his hostage and remind him that she's never done him wrong—and then offer a way out.

"Ooo, la la la la la *laaaa*," he jabbered. Then he said in a conversational voice as though we were best buds again, "Maybe this cunt didn't hurt me, but I will sure as shit hurt her." His already strange demeanor changed yet again as he thundered, "You fuckers don't know how to handle women! *I'm* the king!"

Nothing made sense. Johnny had lost his brogue as completely as he'd lost his sanity; he might do anything to her at this point. I whispered frantically at Levi, "Take him. *Nail* him!"

"No go. Can't get a sight picture," he replied.

Johnny lowed like a steer, then abruptly changed gears and said in a normal tone, "I'm gonna fuck her *up*, Brennan … *after* I'm done fucking her!"

"Leave her alone, Johnny," I said reasonably. "Take me, instead. Do whatever you want to me, but leave her out of it." Then I stuck my revolver in my waistband, stepped into the middle of the alley, and raised my hands. "Here I am, Johnny. Let her go. Take me."

A glint of steel as Johnny points his pistol at me.

A blur to my right as Levi springs forward.

A thud as he tackles me to the rough pavement, and ...

Zing—a bullet zips past, followed by a smart *crack* as the sound catches up.

Johnny laughed hysterically and said, "Don't fucking worry, Brennan. I *will* do whatever I want. I'm in control now. Not you. Not Hart."

I scrambled for cover as Levi ducked back to his corner. I said desperately, "You can't run!"

His eye gleamed from behind her head as he replied, "No, but I can splatter her brains against these walls. You wanna try me again? Come on. See how quickly I put a bullet through this girlie's head." He took another step back.

Natasha's eyes never wavered, despite her heavy breathing.

I saw Levi from the corner of my eye as he edged forward. Johnny turned slightly and said in a cold, furious voice, "Don't even think about it, you fucking faggot."

"Mother*fucker*," Levi said from someplace deep in his chest.

I grabbed my snub-nose and trained it on Johnny again, keeping the slight bulge of his head in my sights while I formed a plan. Then I noticed a flicker of—something.

There. Again—and I understood. I said to Levi in a low voice, "Let him go."

"Whaaat?"

I whispered, "Do what I say. Lower your weapon."

"Are you *crazy*?" Then in a half-sob he said, "It's Nat!"

"I know what I'm doing. This is me talking, okay? Ibba da, buddy."

A long pause followed until he replied with a subdued and almost defeated, "Ibba da."

I lowered my snub-nose slightly and said to Natasha, "There's nothing more I can do, Nat. Don't resist. He'll only hurt you. Go along with him." Then I shouted, "You've got to stay alive, Nat! Do what I say. It'll be much more better*er* this way."

Natasha's breathing slowed instantly. She nodded; she understood.

Now that Johnny had put some distance between us he looked ready to chance it. He slid his face past hers just far enough to reveal the feral grin that had taken hold of his face. An instant—no longer—and then he ducked behind her again.

To Johnny I said, "Come on. Give up now. I'll see that nobody harms you."

"Do la la la la *laaa*," he said as he dragged Natasha rapidly toward the end of the alley.

Levi said, "Michael! For God's sake—what're we gonna do?"

"Shut up! We're gonna wait."

Johnny began moving faster, Natasha's neck still in the crook of his arm. Then it was done; he reached the end of the alley and no matter what Levi or I did, his escape was now a sure thing. He hooted triumphantly. "See ya," he yelled, and turned away. Then ...

Tonk!

Johnny crumpled to the ground as a blossom of bright red blood burst from the top of his rubbery scalp. From behind the building's corner Officer Hank Arnold proclaimed, "Guess that settled *his* hash!" He appeared at Natasha's side, and as his bloodstained nightstick dangled from his wrist he asked softly, "You okay, miss?"

Joe Santoro called the next morning. "Step outside of the house and wait for me. We're going for a ride."

Joe pulled to a stop in a black unmarked car ten minutes later. I jumped in and he turned the car north, toward Delaware. "Can't start extradition proceedings until tomorrow. Might be moot. I'm told he'll waive and return voluntarily." Then Joe filled in the details. "It was never Demmings."

I interrupted him. "Know what? I'm relieved that it wasn't."

Joe nodded. "He's not out of the woods yet. We found *so* many photographs. One especially caught our interest."

"Yeah?"

"Shows a large, older man slipping a rose beneath your cruiser's wiper blade."

I slapped my leg. "Ragnar's!" Demmings had shot three or four photos after the fight.

"The same. Came across it not one hour ago."

I shook my head. "Jesus. Who'd have guessed?"

Who *would* have guessed that Johnny was the North-End Rapist? But as Joe talked, it all fell into place. Johnny knew our tactics, he'd gathered uniform parts to masquerade as a local officer, and he'd developed a grudge against Levi and me. He'd nurtured the grudge for three years; at issue was his interpretation of our easy-going approach toward relationships in general and sex in particular. Johnny believed that nobody should have sex unless they were married—and only then to a woman, and more specifically, to one who would obey her master's every command. He thought he'd found such a woman long ago. He'd fallen hard for her, but she never returned the feeling. In fact, she barely knew he existed—such was Johnny's failure to approach any woman other than those he could pay money to.

Demmings had known Johnny from *O'Toole's*, and each week provided Johnny with the pick of his prized roses so Johnny could place them against the urn of his sainted wife. Demmings' intentions were honorable but he'd been duped—Johnny had never *been* married, a truth that Joe revealed as we crossed the Delaware line. However, Johnny did have a history of violent attacks against women, stretching from Seattle to Miami, *and*—he'd been born and raised in Chicago to parents of Polish ancestry. His accent and his deceased wife—in fact, nearly everything about him outside of his career training wrestlers— were complete fabrications.

When Demmings heard from his parents that an arrest warrant had been issued, he abruptly ceased commiserating Donna's decision to leave him, sobered up, and fled the fleabag hotel where he'd been holed up with a bottle. When he arrived in Ocean City he sought a degree of balance by driving aimlessly through the north-end streets he knew so well. It was mere coincidence that his fellow officers stopped him near Kevin's. He had no bite marks on his leg, no incriminating evidence in his car, nor any motives that could be readily established. Then he did the best thing possible by throwing himself at Joe's mercy and cooperating completely. Unfortunately, Levi and Natasha and I had already left for Rehoboth Beach before Joe could tell us any of this.

"I never would have guessed," I said when Joe finished. "Fucking Johnny."

Joe guffawed. "Yeah. Fucking Johnny, accent and all. Only deviation from the serial profile is his age—past the prime meridian for serial attackers. Otherwise …"

We arrived at the Rehoboth Beach Police Department half an hour later. An investigator met us in the lobby and led the way to an interview room, where a uniformed officer stood guard over the closed door. The investigator pushed it open and ushered us inside. I put on my cop face and regarded Johnny with emotional detachment. No matter his crimes, I would keep my cool; Johnny would suffer punishments a thousand-fold greater than anything I could mete out, now that prison or a mental facility surely awaited him.

A medium-sized bandage covered the top of his head where Officer Hank Arnold brained him with his nightstick. When the old beat cop heard the commotion he swept past the littered rear lots of his turf and positioned himself at Johnny's back. Old Hank held to his plan even after Johnny took a shot at me; all he had to do was bide his time and handle Johnny the old school way.

Johnny appeared calm, aware of his surroundings, and oriented as to time and place. Both his hands were securely cuffed to a heavy chain cinched around his waist, and leg irons were fastened to his ankles.

Joe whispered into my ear. "Investigators still haven't Mirandized him. They can't. Dumb fuck won't shut up long enough for them to ask anything. Doesn't matter. He's already spilled his guts."

I nodded. I'd arrested my share of suspects, cuffed them, brought them to headquarters and charged them with misdemeanors and felonies, only to have them laugh in my face as soon as I was finished. They invariably said, "I'm gonna sue your ass for false arrest." They always got this loopy grin as they added, "Ha ha ha. Know why? 'Cause you handcuffed me and forgot to read me my rights. Ha ha."

They stopped laughing after an attorney—usually a public defender—got them *edge-ma-cated*, as Joe used to say. The requirement to advise a suspect of their right to remain silent under the Supreme Court decision in Miranda vs. Arizona is liberally seasoned with exceptions. However, these exceptions don't work for Hollywood, so they're rarely publicized. But they do exist—and Joe had informed me in cop-talk that Johnny's braggadocio was admissible under the 'spontaneous utterance' exception to Miranda.

Johnny glared with savage hatred as I stood silently against a wall. His wrinkled face and large, veined hands seemed the only remnants of the man I'd known. I did nothing to show him what I felt, thought, or wished about him, and when he could stand my silence no longer he broke. "Almost had her," he taunted. "Was gonna fuck her good and proper. Was gonna show her what it's like when a real man's doin' it."

Joe and the investigator took seats across the table from Johnny. Joe opened with a friendly question. "How's it going today? Feeling better? They treating you okay? Can I get you anything? A soda?"

Johnny looked mildly at Joe, then wet his lips and shook his head. "Nah. I'm fine. Lemme finish what I was sayin' earlier, though. See, none of this is my fault. They fucking asked for it. Shouldn't a made it so easy for me." He paused to make sure Joe acknowledged this truth that Johnny had just revealed. Joe nodded and Johnny continued. "Where was I? Oh yeah. Best thing about it? Everyone was looking in the wrong places. I was doin' it under your noses all that time. Same with the fuckin' tourists. They saw me in my uniform in the shadows an' they figured, 'good, I'm safe.' Safe from who, though? That's what I wanted to show 'em. Somethin' else: them tourists—none a them belonged. It was *my* town they was coming to. My town, my terms. That's what I say." He sniggered and shuffled his long legs as he waited for Joe to join in the laughter.

Joe chuckled to ingratiate himself but said nothing. Johnny continued. "Yeah, an' everyone was so fucking hot to fuck over Hart; couldn't be bothered with comin' after a *real* man, like me. I couldn't a planned it better. Let 'em chase the fag, that's what I figured." He quipped, "Besides, it was more fun that way. You know, goin' after Hart's harlots an' Brennan's bitches." He stopped and glared malevolently at me. "Yeah, that's right. Admit it. I got 'em, one way or the other. Almost fucked your little *Natasha's* cunt, too."

He might have. But the bite marks on his leg showed that George certainly put a stop to *that* attack, and the DNA match would show conclusively that it was Johnny's blood on George's teeth. Sometimes you get the bear, and sometimes the bear—in this case a bear of an old dog named George—gets you.

Johnny bragged on about the ease with which he committed his crimes. He described years of horse-trading with the police who patronized his fitness center, inveigling them for odd uniform patches and even a white shirt that Demmings had given him. Johnny reminded me that he'd been monitoring our activities on his police scanner for years—he knew our tactics, our rhythms and our predispositions.

Then he looked at me and said, "Saw you fucking that fat-assed bitch in your car, Brennan. What, you think you're the only one 'round here who knows about that lover's lane? Made it real easy for me to find out where she lived."

Later on he mentioned a young black girl he'd been about to lunge for until he realized she wasn't alone. He gave an account of the measures he took to avoid detection: surgical gloves to avoid prints, surgical slip-ons to cover his shoes, and purple bungee cords because he thought, "Hell, I figured it'd make everyone suspect a shop mechanic. Somebody like that."

He forgot about the evidence he took *with* him from the crime scenes—pubic combings from Bethany, and trace amounts of DNA from George's teeth. A search of Johnny's car at the far end of the alley revealed something far more disturbing. He had handcuffs, manacles and a soldering iron. There were also large plastic bags, butchering implements and shovels. Johnny himself revealed a gruesome plan to torture Natasha with the soldering iron before killing her, and disposing of her remains in a nearby landfill. Unrepentant to the end, he crowed, "I nailed them bitches right under everyone's noses," and then he smirked and said, "It was there in the details, but you guys were too lazy an' too occupied with goin' after Hart." Johnny fell silent, and just when I thought he was finished he smirked and offered one more tidbit. "Hart almost nailed me. Just got inside your bitch's beachside condo when Hart turned the corner." He nodded in self-satisfaction and grunted. "Yep! Missed me by that much." I decided never to tell Levi; he'd have felt terrible knowing he missed that chance because he had made love to Jennifer—and all for nothing, since she apparently failed to conceive.

We walked out of the room an hour later. Joe nodded at the uniformed officer and we moved a few feet away as he locked the door behind us. Joe said, "I hope you didn't let him get to you. Male serial attackers justify abhorrent behavior by blaming others. It's 'everybody else's fault.' Females focus the faults inward. It's always themselves who are to blame. Let it go, Michael."

"Thanks, Joe. I already feel better now that I've seen him in chains. I know it'll make a difference with Natasha, too."

Joe squeezed my shoulder and asked, "How *is* she doing?"

I smiled. "She's a trooper. Told me this morning she's not gonna let any of this get to her. Johnny's already a non-person for her."

Joe smiled. "Better not tell *him* that. 'Real men' don't take to that sort of talk."

I laughed. "No. They certainly do not." When I noticed the uniformed cop watching, I paused for the dramatic effect and laughingly asked, "Joe, just what is a real man, anyway?"

He turned deadly serious and stared at me. Then he hugged me, kissed my cheek and said loudly, "You'll see a real man every time you look in the mirror—and whenever you look at Officer Levi Hart."

CHAPTER 14

LEVI took off the next day. He would see his folks and then attend the Criminal Investigator Training Program at the Federal Law Enforcement Training Center, near Brunswick, Georgia. On graduation he would report for advanced training before he could take some leave.

ONE MONTH LATER

I bumped into Donna as she was leaving Joe's office. She had on a soft yellow blouse, a dark skirt and shoes, and a simple gold necklace. "Hello," I began, and when I opened my arms she stepped into them.

She beamed and said with great feeling, "What a surprise! I was about to call you. I've just returned from San Diego and I wanted to thank you again for all that you've done for me. That night will always be special." She paused and smiled somewhat sadly. "I'll always love you for that, Michael Brennan."

"Thank you for your friendship." Then I asked, "Where will you go now?"

Donna chuckled. "It's true what they say—things do happen for a reason. I might never have discovered San Diego if you hadn't suggested it."

I did the math and nodded. "You'll do well there."

"Great place to start over, or so I'm told." She stopped and regarded me with clear eyes. "I've been hired as a surgical nurse. Leading-edge hospital. Fantastic bennies. Oh, and they have a most wonderful new intern. He was quite lovely."

"Found a friend, huh?"

"I've never known such passionate sex. I felt so relaxed with him."

"You felt loved," I corrected.

A look of amazement flashed across her face. "Yes, I do believe you're right. It wasn't just sex. Someone was actually making love to me." Donna looked obliquely at me. "You laid the groundwork, you know. For feeling loved." Her gaze lingered, then she said, "Thank you for giving me your heart, Michael."

I took her in my arms again and kissed her fondly. "Good luck," I said, and as we parted company I added, "Call when you get settled in. I like to keep in touch with my friends."

SIX MONTHS LATER

Johnny went to trial, evidently not quite as insane as originally thought. The jury wasted little time and convicted him of four counts of first-degree rape, as well as a variety of burglary, assault, maiming, and cruelty to animal charges. The state's attorney did not move on Natasha's lost baby—he explained that he would never be able to prove that Johnny's attack caused it. But Johnny would never leave prison. The judge sentenced him to four consecutive life terms plus fifty years in The Cut—Maryland's notorious state pen. I had no sympathy for him, despite The Cut's well-earned reputation for harsh treatment of serial rapists at the hands of the other inmates.

Burke was busted to police officer within days of the Peeping Tom exposé. He took it well and he publicly congratulated his newly promoted replacement.

Jarl never did return to work. He exhausted his sick leave, wangled a stress-related retirement, and moved away. In time, stories of his non-hetero activities emerged from Rehoboth Beach and filtered down to Ocean City. There were even rumors, sworn to by those claiming to have seen them, of photos too riveting to turn away from.

While leaving court during a downpour one day, I spotted Jennifer as she ducked into a side door reserved for attorneys. She was unmistakably with child.

I checked on Bethany many times. She healed quickly, lost almost thirty pounds, and she hinted that several sessions of car sex would accelerate her on the road to total recovery. But she understood when I informed her that I'd fallen in love, and she graciously wished us well. I saw her for the last time after she testified at Johnny's trial. She shrugged off the ordeal by saying, "I don't hold nothin' against him. He's sick. Besides, he'll suffer lots in jail. And the scars? From where he carved my ass up? I'm goin' to Brazil next month. There's this plastic surgeon my doctor told me about. Then Brenda and me are gonna spend some time in Rio." Her violet eyes got wide as she exclaimed, "I hear those crazy Brazilian boys are really something in bed."

When I asked how she would be able to afford all that she chirped happily, "Oh! Well. The settlement I'm getting from the sale of Johnny's Gym? From when I sued him?" She rolled her eyes mischievously and said, "Well, let's just say I ain't gotta work too hard no more." Bethany looked deeply into my eyes and brushed her fingers across my cheek. "I had a great time with you. You sure do love women. Wonderful skin, too." She shifted her weight to one foot, scrunched her facial features, and asked, "How do you get your skin to be so pretty?"

Anna recovered sufficiently to testify at the trial. We spoke during court recesses, and once more after the verdict was read, but the Anna I'd known had retreated. She seemed incapable of reconciling the savagery of the attack with the civilized world she'd known. I never heard from her again. I prayed for her and made a wish that time would restore the purity of her soul. Sometimes I'd stop what I was doing, think of her and whisper, "Follow the middle path, Anna."

EIGHTEEN MONTHS LATER

Levi phoned one day to say that he'd accepted a position with another federal agency. He remained vague, and toward the end of the conversation he informed us that we might not hear from him for a year, "or maybe two." He paused and then casually added that he'd call when he could, but not to expect much more. Then he hung up.

How alone he must feel. I thought back on the agony he endured as too many so-called friends drove him into an isolation so profound, that it spurred him into a procreative frenzy. In the end he was left with not even one child to provide him a sense of community; instead he had only his free-spirited nature to give him peace.

THREE YEARS LATER

As I looked over the contents of a jewelry store display case one day I sensed someone behind me. I turned and found Jennifer smiling at me. She held a little boy by the hand. He had auburn hair, large blue eyes, and a distinctly triangular face. Jennifer greeted me quietly. "Hello, Michael. Long time, huh?" She licked her lips and glanced down at the boy. "I'd like you to meet Cameron. I—I named him after my brother."

I got down on one knee, opened my arms wide and whispered, "Hello Cameron. My name is Michael. Come here—there's nothing to be afraid of."

When he stepped unflinchingly into my arms and laid his cheek against mine, Jennifer touched her fingers to her lips and cried out, "Oh my God! He never does that with strangers."

I smiled and kissed the boy's forehead, and looking at her I said, "I'm *not* surprised. Something in him recognizes me."

Jennifer nodded, and what she told me next came as no surprise. "Levi doesn't know. I learned I was pregnant before he left but I panicked. After Nat lost her baby I became paranoid. I convinced myself that he might want custody, that he—that he would take my baby from me! Now I'm so ashamed of myself."

I smiled at the boy, and he watched me with solemn eyes that grew animated as I spoke soothingly. "Levi would never have done that. But demons attack us all. Hey … Jen? It's okay."

Jennifer looked at me gratefully. "I want Cam to have a sib. I—I want so much to ask him."

"Cam *should* have a sibling, and you *should* go to the best possible daddy. Jen," I said as she opened her mouth. "You and he were friends. That's more than many other parents can claim." I paused before asking the inevitable. "When will you tell him?"

She looked away and shook her head with tiny, jerky movements. "I felt so guilty at first—now I'm afraid I've waited too long. My letters always come back marked, 'no forwarding address.' But you know how he is. He'll show."

I smiled and brushed my fingers through the boy's hair and then stroked his cheek with the backs of my knuckles. "He'll show." I glanced up at her and added, "Don't take it personally—we get the odd letter from him, but that's all. He's doing some sensitive work." I turned back to Cameron, who had yet to say a word. Then I wagged my eyebrows at him as his father would have done, and said gently, "*Ibba da?*"

He studied me through half-lidded eyes that I knew so well and said, "Huh?"

I threw back my head and laughed. "Gotcha," I said as I reached out and tickled him beneath his ribs, thus reducing him to a wriggling heap of laughter. Then I kissed the top of the boy's head, stood, and drew Jennifer into my arms. "I'll call you. I know I speak for Natasha—we'd love to see more of you and Cam."

Jennifer wiped a sudden tear from her cheek. Reaching out, she took my hand in hers and squeezed it softly. "Give him my best if you hear from him, and … tell him I'd love to see him." She looked back down at the boy and said, "So would he."

As I turned to go a tiny voice behind me called out, "*Ibba da?*" I whirled around, paused for effect and said, "Huh?" Cameron shrieked with laughter and I smiled back, but when he triumphantly crowed, "Gotcha," my hand shot involuntarily to my eyes, and I could only stare at him until finally Jen took his hand and led him away.

EPILOGUE

I still fight occasional phantoms of my deeper synapses, but those child-hood memories have been fading. One day as I sped toward the Isle of Wight I slowed and stopped at the estuary. The two rivers, individual in their salinity, their currents and their temperatures lapped at the island's shores from diverging sides. They flowed past the leading end and intermingled at the opposite end where they joined their personalities to become one. The rivers celebrated their own character, even as they sought to unite. Merge on, rivers—merge on. I believed in the rivers; I understood their message.

Not long after Natasha announced that she was pregnant with our second child, she took some time off from running her stunningly successful restaurant, *Rainwater*. We spent an afternoon preparing a garden behind our home next to where George was buried, while our son slept in his crib on the porch; I thought she looked wonderful in my flannel shirt and old sweat pants.

"Planning a garden helps us think about the future," she said simply. "It's therapeutic."

She had me pegged all right, but because I felt I'd already shed my childhood traumas I resisted the idea of seeing a shrink; something deep within shouted with all its might that it was something to be ashamed of. But as I thrust my spade into the rich black earth I thought to myself, maybe one day.

In the meantime we had our garden to work on, and as I helped Natasha prepare the soil, something uncontrollable surfaced, and turning to her I asked, "You really do love me, don't you?"

Natasha had her back to me as she dug with a small trowel. "Yes," she answered, "very much."

"And you love me for *me*, right? Not for anything else?"

She stopped and turned around with a warming smile. "I love you for your heart, Michael, and I'm not the only one. Someone else loves you too." She flicked her eyes toward the crib where our son dozed contentedly. "And someone else," she added, and her smile grew as her eyes focused on something behind me.

Gazing intently at her, I asked, "Who?"

"You're about to find out," she said, and then she gestured with her gloved hand that I should look over my shoulder.

I turned and stared, unbelieving.

He called out so very quietly. "Hello, Michael. How've you been?"

I dropped the spade and stepped forward. "Levi! It's so good to see you! I ..."

"Hello, Natasha," he interrupted as he swept past me. "How are *you* doing, Sweetness?"

She rushed into his arms and embraced him. "I'm wonderful, just wonderful." They kissed and stared at each other with loopy grins. Finally she turned to me and said, "Sorry, but I promised to keep this a surprise for you."

Levi put his hand to her already-swollen belly. A fleeting sadness veiled his eyes before he dropped his hand and came over and embraced me. He kissed my cheek and then held me at arms' length as his eyes searched my face. He whispered, "Good to see you, Michael." His eyes searched further until he offered a droll half-smile. "That's a cool medal you're wearing. St. Michael, Patron Saint of Police, if I'm not mistaken."

"My brother gave it to me."

He stifled a smile. "Sounds like a great guy."

I shook my head sadly. "He's a schmuck, but what're you gonna do?"

"Nothing you can do. You're stuck with him for life." He winked and started to shoot me the bird, but then he reeled it in and patted my shoulder, instead. Then he turned to Natasha and pulled a small velvet-covered box from his pocket. "Nat, I've never given you anything, and God knows I love you."

She took the box from him and opened it. Her eyes lit up as she let out a little gasp. "Oh, Levi! They're absolutely marvelous! Wherever did you find these?"

"Paris," he said cheerfully, and his eyes sparkled as he took the strand of pearls from the box and fastened them around her neck. "Now you have something to remember me by."

Natasha said softly, "I don't know what to say. Look, Michael. Aren't they fabulous?" Then to Levi she said, "Come. *Come,*" she insisted, and taking him by the hand she led him to the porch. "Come see our son."

A wide, warm smile erupted across his face as he bent over and whispered his greeting. "Hello there, little one. We haven't been formally introduced, but I'm your Uncle Levi." He brushed his fingertips along our sleeping son's face and smiled again. "He's gorgeous," he said in a low voice.

I said guardedly, "You must've been surprised to hear from Jennifer."

He looked at both of us and said, "I was. Strangest thing, how that old letter caught up to me." Then he choked-up and looked away. "God, the boy is so ..."

Natasha said with great feeling, "He's adorable, Levi. Michael and I love him very, very much."

His eyes sparkled as he said quietly, "Jen and I spent a week in Hawaii a while back." Then he offered a shy half-smile and added, "And now Cam will have a sister to love. Jen's due in four months." Levi studied the ground before looking up and adding, "But I'm sure the two of you already knew that."

Natasha nodded and said, "Still no marriage plans?"

Levi shook his head. "I wanted to, but Jen doesn't want a husband so much as a companion." He shrugged. "We feel affection for one another—at least that's something. Cameron I love completely." He licked his lips and said, "We'll raise the children with love and I'll run myself ragged between my West Coast job and my East Coast family. And *this* family." He beamed and said, "I'm so lucky!"

Physically he appeared no different, not even diminished by time, despite fine lines that etched the corners of his eyes. But he had changed as I had, and now here he was after all. He smelled of pure soap and fresh water. His speech had become articulate and he even had on shoes—Johnston & Murphy lace-ups. His shirt and trousers were tailor-made and impeccably pressed, and an elegant Patek Phillipe adorned his left wrist.

Natasha rested her head against his shoulder and sighed. "I was dreadfully afraid you wouldn't make it. That telephone connection was horrid."

Levi looked at me and explained. "I caught a red-eye out of Honolulu. Took two days to get here from Kuala Lumpur."

I whistled in surprise. "Kuala Lumpur? Holy cow! That's in Malaysia, isn't it?"

He nodded.

"What the hell were you doing there?"

"Job-related."

I frowned. "You ever gonna tell us who you work for?"

He coughed politely and looked at the baby as he replied. "Let it go, okay?" But then he worried the end of his nose. Finally he looked at me through hooded eyes and said, "We travel to hot spots. K.L. just hosted the Asian Free Trade Summit. We—did some work there."

I nodded. "How do you like it? The job, I mean."

Levi's eyes sparked. "I *love* it. It was a small outfit when I came aboard but we grew after Oke City. I'm in management now. GS-14."

"Is that good?"

He looked down at the ground and shuffled his feet. "Well, I've got a six figure income, and when I deal with military counterparts I carry the weight of a lieutenant colonel. I suppose that's good."

I whistled again. "I should say so. Beats what I'm doing as a sergeant."

"You and Hack are investigators now."

"And working for *Captain* Joe Santoro. Say, how'd you know?"

Levi looked sideways at Natasha and chuckled. "Heard it in a bar in Casablanca."

I snorted. "Well, you haven't missed anything here. This town can still be petty, but someone has to fight for change. Besides, I've always wanted to settle down. This place will do."

Levi turned pensive. "It's so ironic. The majority of my associates are former SEALs or other SF types. *Genuinely* masculine hombres, not macho wannabe's."

Natasha said, "Regular guys. Not muscle-bound creeps."

Levi suppressed a smile but then turned serious. "The thing is, none of them freaking care about what puts the whiz in another guy's wick. Their only concern is whether or not you're a team player." He laughed. "They know Kevin and they like him, and they go to the bars with us when we're Stateside. It's not their game and they don't necessarily understand, but this different side of life fascinates them. Isn't that something?"

I nodded. "That's something, all right." I jabbed his shoulder. "Are you planning on sticking around for a bit? Because I'm thinking we could call Jen. We'll hire babysitters, have dinner at *Rainwater* and then go dancing in Rehoboth."

He beamed. "I'd love that."

There didn't seem to be anything else that needed to be said, so after an awkward silence the three of us gathered again at the crib and gazed down at our sleeping son.

"You still haven't told me his name," he remarked.

Natasha nodded. "On purpose. We wanted to surprise you."

I put my arm around his shoulder and pulled him close. "His name is Levi. Levi Hart Brennan."

THE END

Printed in the United States
212293BV00006B/5/A